學友社簡介

學友社致力於青年學生培育工作，以培育青年探求真知、建立良好品德為宗旨。成立七十年來，社務不斷擴展及改革，現以全港青年學生為服務對象，協助青年學生構建人生，並為未來社會培養具廣闊視野及多元思考力的人才。

專注三大範疇　多元培育青年

憑著多年培育青年的經驗，學友社近年專注學生輔導、生涯規劃及全人發展三大工作範疇。

* 學生輔導服務——助學生抉擇出路。有見青年學生面對課業及出路抉擇的壓力，學友社自 1980 年代起，創辦多種涵蓋應試及放榜出路的學生輔導服務。

* 生涯規劃教育——助青年規劃人生。憑藉三十多年的學生輔導經驗，學友社以「知己」、「知彼」、「抉擇與部署」及「行動與反思」為介入點開展中學生生涯規劃教育。

* 全人發展培育——培育明日社會領袖。透過舉辦潛能發展、領袖培訓及考察交流等活動，引領青年學生立足香港、認識國家、走進世界。

學界稱譽

學友社在學界廣受稱譽，深受學生、家長及教師的信任，每年服務人次逾一百五十萬。此外，本社常年獲政府當局及教育機構委託承辦各項青年及教育工作，並就學生輔導及青年發展等事務發表建議。

力求變革　始終如一

求變只為育才，學友社不止是切合社會現實所需，更是先於社會所需而行，適時調整服務計劃，一如社徽上的火炬，為青年學生領航，亦由青年學生照亮未來社會的路向。

學友社將繼續與學界保持良好的伙伴關係，並擴展與商界企業的合作，共同開展各項培育青年的工作，適時回應青年學生及社會所需。

目錄

序言

學友社與學生同行，關顧學生福祉。除了提供為大眾所熟悉的高中學生應試及放榜出路的輔導服務外，本社更連續二十七載舉辦「全港中學生十大新聞選舉」，以增強中學生閱讀新聞的廣度與深度，提高對香港社會、國家事務及國際局勢的認知，培養反思能力，作出批判。這與通識教育課程目標一致。

隨著社會急劇變化，我們越益關心影響學生學習的課程、考評實踐與及品格培養。本社理事、「學友智庫」召集人梁麗嬋博士，過去多年於本港通識教育科考評、學與教及課程目的關係作了深入研究，並完成博士論文。梁博士研究發現香港跟國際教育的評估、學習目的、學習方法的趨勢一致，那有別於傳統常規，影響深遠。為此，梁博士將有關發現與現行課程及考評發展進行表述及進一步探討，先後寫成數篇論文，其中一篇已於中大國際教育論壇上發表；另有十多篇相關短篇文章於星島日報「學友智庫」專欄刊登。由於研究內容豐富，具一定的參考價值，因此，本社邀請梁博士合作，將其已發表的相關文章，及其研究成果結集成書，以讓本港及其他地區關心教育最新動態、學生學習、課程與考評發展的教育界、學術界及各方朋友閱讀參考。此外，本社也藉此新書發布，擴大與學術界與學校的連繫，就課程與考評進行交流討論，希望共同為學生未來優質的學習，提供可行的建議方案。

學友社主席序言

學友社成立七十年來，一直關注包括課程設計在內的學生成長議題。自去年開始，更專門成立了學友社智庫。這除了是作為七十周年慶祝的新嘗試之外，更希望以此鼓勵成員從嚴謹的學術態度，探討所關心的學生相關題目。

梁麗嬋博士這本探討通識教育的著作，便是智庫成立後支持出版的第一次努力。梁博士本身更為智庫負責人，數十年來投身在學生成長問題的研究當中，一直是學友社思考工作的重要人物。學友社智庫的運作原則，秉承關心學生成長的廣泛議題、相容並包的學術自由，以及堅持高水準的研究成果，希望為學界、政府和社會作出專門的貢獻。

我十分高興有幸為本書作序，不只是因為我的學友社主席身份，更重要是這書的本質。麗嬋博士長時間研究有關問題，這本書便是出自她博士論文成果，加以深化而成。書中有多個審視當下課程的視角，例如對未來世界學生能力的思考，無疑為讀者帶來更多有意思的反思，為香港學生的通識課程優化提供有用的參考。同時，作者除了靜態分析之外，還結合了本身參與學友社學生工作的經歷，對學生的學習情況進行動態分析。在這方面，學友社的深入和長期學生工作，例如已經進行了數十載、香港社會的第一個「中學生十大新聞」選舉活動等等，也為研究人員提供了大量一手和獨特的材料；而這也是本書的特別價值所在。

希望所有有興趣於相關問題的朋友，都能夠閱讀本書，認真思考其中觀點。

李浩然博士，MH

通識教育　回歸初心

梁麗嬋老師早前曾多次跟我分享有關通識教育評估與課程的關係，她的研究結果與我在一些公開場合上對通識科的評論不謀而合，更重要的是她提供了具備學術的理論及實證的論據。當她的心血之作即將出版，邀請我提供序言時，我非常樂意接受。

在過去的幾年中，梁老師大量走訪老師同學及不同的持份者，並輔以同班師生的問卷數據及質性的示例，在她有關學術論文的分析當中，她對通識科教育理論做出了系統而全面性的深入探討，成果豐碩。除了在學術上的辛勤耕耘，梁老師更費心將其研究內容寫成報刊文章，不遺餘力的革新大家對通識教育文憑試評估、學與教及目標關係的認知。梁老師的工作成果對當下香港通識教育的研究意義重大。

作為一個因應 2000 年香港教育改革而推出的嶄新教育科目，通識科對孩子們的學習具有很大的影響。學科推行以來，社會上對通識教育有很大的關注及討論，甚至存在各種「爭議」，那是好事，也是必然的。教育的目的是為了孩子的將來。作為教育工作者，我們有責任對現行的通識教育進行反思和回顧。

我想在此首先回顧一下構建香港通識教育的歷史背景。當在 1999-2000 年通識教育被首次提及時，我們正面臨著香港學生過早分流的困境。當時的香港中學生，自中學三年級起就要選擇分流，就讀文科或理科。學生對文理科的知識尚未產生全面的認識，這會影響學生見識的開拓與日後能力的培養。為應對此種情況，我們當時提出構建一個新的「綜合學科」，希望在高中時期教育學生能獲得「文理兼備，文中有理，理中有文」的學習目標。

我們當時的想法是希望學生回歸基礎知識的拓展，同時具備兩類學科的學習機會，因為社會的趨勢需要同學兩類思維均兼備。一個文科管理者在當下科技發達的時代，不能缺少對科學的認知。同理，未來的科學家和工程師也不能缺乏相應的人文素養、人文的情懷與思維。但後來不知怎樣，這個為了達至「文中有理，理中有文」的「綜合學科」都變了 "Liberal Studies"，成為了一科開放性的學科，且命名為「通識教育」科。

到了今天，梁老師的研究發現，當下的「通識科」教育已經脫離了原先設計學科的目的——忽略了對科學與人文素質的涉獵，不重視學習內容及基本知識的拓展，反而變成了一個側重於時事議題討論的學科。加之這個學科沒有指定教科書，所以各種各樣的學習材料都紛紛在社會上出現，這進一步丟掉了立科之初我們希望對文理知識平衡的考量，甚至有些背道而馳。因此，我們應該現在對當下的通識教育做出一些適當的改變。

在我看來，開展通識教育，應該注重三個教育目的。其一，幫助學生建立正確的社會責任感與人生價值觀。其二，要有知識的開拓，並注重跨學科扎實的內涵。其三，要提升學生多元學習的能力，包括溝通能力、明辨事非的能力和創意解難的能力。現在的通識教育過度注重對「批判思維」的考量而忽視了對更重要的第一及第二個目的的培養，這是我們應當反思的關鍵。梁老師提出通識教育中加入 STEM 教育的元素，我很贊同她的觀點，因為這可以加強學生對科學知識的學習及掌握。

現在的通識科實踐，或無心或著意，已被異化為「偏向時事議題討論」的學科，這是教育的不幸。對於年輕的高中學生而言，討論複 雜的政治議題實為時過早。在他們對複雜時事議題缺乏認識及親身體驗之前，對當前時事事件缺乏真相的認知之前，強求他們對相關時事討論及表態，實是不負責任的行為。作為教育工作者，我們應當從根本上杜絕這種情況的發生。

通識科改革的方向，就是要回到我們原來的「初心」。即建設「文中有理，理中有文」、知識性較強的學科學習，加強知識的構建及開拓。這些年來，選拔性的紙筆考卷及批判性思維能力考評，已對通識科產生一種異化的作用，使通識教育已經偏離了我們原先的目的。

無論課程如何，教育的目的始終都是為了學生的成長與福祉著想。通識教育對香港的影響很大，對於教育工作者而言，在當下為通識科作出正確的改變是我們義不容辭的責任。

黃玉山教授
香港公開大學校長
前課程發展議會主席及前教育統籌委員會委員 (2001-2007)

Evidence speaks volumes: A journey to identify the extent of alignment of assessment, pedagogy and curriculum aims of "Liberal Studies"

In November 2012, I first met Simy (Lai-sim Leung) in the Educational Assessment and Evaluation unit that I teach at our Doctor of Education programme in Hong Kong. At the unit tutorials, Simy expressed her interest in developing a case study on teachers' perception of whether the exam-oriented teaching modes are compatible with the learning of higher-order thinking skills as anticipated in Liberal Studies in Hong Kong such as "learning to think", "learning to live" and "learning to respect". The overall design of the research project started to take shape. Simy submitted her assignment in January 2013, clearly spelt out her detailed plan for data collection. As part of the feedback to her assignment, I wrote:

Simy, this is an excellent assignment, clearly demonstrating your research ability and your understanding about the various issues in teaching and assessing LS in secondary education. It is clear that the research is well informed by your experience and knowledge about LS and development of higher-order thinking skills. You've done very well in linking the assessment and teaching of LS with the development and assessment of higher order thinking skills. The assessment of 21st century skills is an interesting research area. I wish you good luck with your doctoral research on the same topic, using much more developed and sophisticated data collection methods. In this assignment, the interview data was not fully explored, due to the limited space; however, in your doctoral dissertation, I believe your interview data will play a more prominent role in addressing your research questions.

When Simy successfully completed all the required courses at the "taught-stage" of her EdD study, I agreed to supervise her doctoral research project. It was through a number of regular supervision tutorials on skype or face-to-face in Hong Kong that the design of the doctoral project was revised progressively. In this iterative process, it was evident that Simy's dedication to her dissertation project and her belief in forging a strong alignment between teaching, learning and assessment played a vital role in ensuring the success of her dissertation project, which I am immensely proud of as her supervisor. I was very pleased to witness her growing confidence in conducting the research project involving large-scale survey with over 500 students and teachers, classroom observations and in-depth interviews with key stakeholders.

The viva voçê took place on 7th November 2016; the examiners recommended that the degree sought be awarded subject to minor revision of her dissertation. We have been in regular contact after her viva voçê, to discuss the plan for disseminating her findings through various channels. Her strong sense of responsibility as an educator to contribute, with solid empirical research evidence in hand, to the debate on Liberal Studies as a compulsory subject in HKDSE has motivated her to publish the findings of her doctoral research in local newspapers in Hong Kong, several of which are included in this volume. I admire her persistent efforts in engaging the public to better understand Liberal Studies and relevant topics in educational assessment. I believe the publication of this volume is timely when Liberal Studies as a subject in HKDSE is under further scrutiny by academic researchers, policy makers, teachers, students, parents and the public, perhaps from different perspectives. It is empirical research evidence that should speak volumes.

Well done, Simy!

Guoxing Yu, PhD
Director of Centre for Educational Assessment and Evaluation
University of Bristol

作者自序

此書謹獻給關心香港通識教育科、跨學科課程發展和香港現行教育評估政策的朋友們——在當前本港乃至國際教育變革的背景下，希望本書的實證研究與分析能夠帶給大家對相關領域的新思考。

筆者視這本書的出版是時代人才培育轉折「必然」大勢下的一個「偶然」！「必然」是指筆者的研究處身於國際教育變化的大背景，為回應社會、經濟與科技急劇的變化，對人才培育的要求正不斷更新轉變，產生與過去傳統不一樣的教學模型與評價。在此背景下，香港創設的通識科為了達到國際認可的水平，確保考評的信度和效度的同時，又能體現教育改革的新思維，因而產生過程的異化。由於新課程為回應時局而變，卻缺少相關實證及學理支撐，因此，筆者認為在此國際教育動態變化的過程中，或早或晚「必然」為創新實踐與試驗付出代價，我們當吸取教訓與認知所得。之於「偶然」者，乃因緣際會，筆者接觸到相關研究，梳把文獻其中，萌發種種困惑，惘然若失，矢志求學理之源頭，遂捨棄全職工作，埋首鑽研，終於有本書的發現與所得。

通識科的目標是培養具有獨立思考和明辨性思維、勇於承擔社會責任的新一代，但實踐上，卻把態度、知識與能力分割，狹隘的追求「能力為本」的教學成果。雖然大部份教師認同評估、學與教及目標能夠結合一致，但是，根據研究數據及面對面採訪的結果，真正能付出時間與心力，建構高階思維能力學習的教師卻不多。相反，應試的答題模型與操練卻非常普遍。實踐效果事與願違，未能培育真正獨立思考、自主創新的能力，更沒有培育學生的家國情懷、國際視野，以及承擔精神。

然而，倘若沒有近十年來教育工作者的奮力拼搏，難望有今天學校師生對通識科的普遍認同；沒有創新性地設立兼具信度及效度的考評系統與制度，也難望獲得國際二百多所高校的學術認可。值得香港自豪的是，從教育改革推行開始，便有不少敢於帶領創新的前行者，踏出能「通」且「識」的跨學科課程推展與設計，並致力促進評估、學與教及廿一世紀能力學習的一致性，創設具備信度及效度的評估體系與實踐。這引發師生更多地參與到自評與互評中去，教師專業的討論增加，教學範式產生明顯的轉變，幫助學生拓闊了自主學習的空間。改變，源於國際評估與學習模式的引入，香港自身的評估與學習模式亦有別於過去，更著重能力學習。

作為一名獨立研究員，經歷五載全情投入的研究，處理應付大量數據及質性資料，慶幸過程獲得不少有心人協助，終於梳理出主體內容的清晰邏輯。綜合國際及香港歷年有關跨學科及評估的文獻研究，筆者結合自身教學的經驗，成功設計了一個能縱橫貫通的評估、學與教及目標一致的模型，並以此作為研究框架，設計師生問卷，進行數據搜集和資料分析（設計與模型的應用見於書中兩篇論文）。透過高中通識跨學科實踐的示例研究，捕捉明顯的數據落差，研究結果折射出一個更廣闊、不為人知的能力學習效果。限於促進能力學習的評估政策和廿一世紀能力學習的倡議實行不足 20 年，仍留於理念及實踐摸索階段，實證研究不足。筆者個人的研究也有局限，雖然數據很能說明問題，卻不容易為習慣思維與經驗所理解。為此，筆者完成博士論文之後，仍然堅持每天走進大學圖書館，進行後續整理與研究工作。筆者的目標只有一個，就是希望以更具體的理據分析及清晰的闡述，讓學界及教師理解問題的源頭，掌握課程與考評發展的關係，反映通識科推行的原旨本意——即尋求個人和社會、人文學科以及科學與科技跨學科之間的平衡。最終能重整通識教育，讓學生全面成長。

本書內容分為三個部份，以下作簡單介紹。第一部份是中文短文，由筆者過去幾個月來，於《星島日報》學與教學友智庫專欄刊登的十六篇短文組成。內容圍繞筆者的論文研究發現，分析並破解本港教育改革下必修必考的香港通識科的實踐成效與影響。從本科設科的原旨與目標、學與教的推行過程重點，到最終文憑試考評對學生的影響作分析，論述通識科處身於國際評估大潮流以及「問責」承擔的大氣候之下，把追求廿一世紀能力的學習作為重點的意想不到的效果。例如從分析本港中學生十大新聞選舉候選新聞的數據，也能發現通識科考評影響學先閱讀新聞的向度與思維習慣。基於對通識教育的功能及設科原意，筆者提出一些跟進的建議，並進一步分析通識科就是跨學科。作為廣義的通識教育，跨學科學習，需要打穩知識基礎，讓學生學會「舉一反三」；掌握跨學科概念，在日常生活中轉移與運用相關知識。

第二部份是筆者投稿於香港中文大學香港教育研究學會 2018 國際研討會，發表的一篇論文。內容引用自第三部份的教育博士論文數據、訪談及課堂教學分析，說明促進能力學習的過程反饋可以同考評的標準參照工具結合一致。同時，突出學與教的課堂設計如何能有效提供建構學習，真正做到目標、學與教過程與學生學習的表現結果一致。由於科學與科技快速變革，除了推動 STEM 教育為未來經濟與職種轉型作準備，更重要是過程讓學生學會手腦並用，發揮創造力及解決問題的自主學習能力，讓學習的內容與廿一世紀能力學習的目標結合一致。筆者的研究，正好啟迪 STEM 教育當吸取通識科推行的經驗與教訓，系統地將 STEM 教育與通識教育作有機結合。

第三部份原文載錄筆者整篇的英文教育博士論文。這是筆者修讀英國布理斯托大學的教育博士課程期間，完成探究有關香港通識教育科文憑試與課程的學習能否一致，以推動廿一世紀能力學習的論文，供有興趣於教育評估、教學法、廿一世紀能力、課程及評估政策等研究的讀者參考。

本書的出版，要多謝為本書寫序言的我的論文導師 Dr. Guoxing Yu、前課程發展議會主席、公開大學校長黃玉山教授，以及學友社主席李浩然博士。也要感謝不少國際及香港學術與教育界的朋友：Professor Patricia Broadfoot、Professor Leon Tikly、馮俊樂副教授、蘇詠梅教授、謝伯康博士、林建教授等，於研究過程給予啟發、評審或提供鼓勵與協助，特別是參與研究的師生和接受訪問的來自不同領域的受訪者以及協助筆者將研究發現進一步提煉、優化與整理出版的工作人員。當中學友社及友好出資此書的出版是對筆者研究的肯定，沒有大家的支持及鼓勵，本書出版未必能於短短幾個月內完成。

筆者研究的動力來自對教育專業的追求，以及對青年學生有效學習的關注。那是源於過去學生時期及過去十二年在學友社的義工生活參與，啟發筆者終身樂於追求學問、探求真知，感受「從服務中學習、從參與中成長」的精神內涵。這些生活經歷驅使我堅信教師需「搭建鷹架」，推行建構式跨學科專題研習和體驗式學習。這對於基礎教育時期的學生成長，具有非常重大的影響與意義。透過教育專業的設計，提供情境任務，系統地將跨學科課程融入到正規與非正規課堂去，以培養青年學生擁有良好品質與靈魂，終身追求學會生活、學會思考與學會尊重，健康快樂地成長。

最後，期望本書從評估的新角度、縱橫建構學習的新視野，為未來新一代的教育發展提供具跨學科通識的學理支撐與實證研究的啟示。

梁麗嬋博士
學友社理事
學友智庫召集人

第一部份：

評估、課程與廿一世紀能力學習的啟示

1. 通識之釋

「通識」一詞概念多元，不同人各有演繹，卻總離不開主軸的軌迹：人類追求認知生活，對所處社會及自然界的現象作思考，尋求當中的經驗整理，化成故事哲理以傳承，用以指導生活，於不同處境中作出明智的抉擇。當中「識」要能博大，要能「通」。博大指的是能「通通都識」；認識的過程要「識通」，即能「一理通，百理明」。

人類有別於其他動物的特徵，在於擁有決策行動的意志力。意志力源於個體生活的經歷，結合他人的經驗學習，構成自身價值的判斷，並外顯於行動。因此，人類生存依靠的是不斷學習，從生活中建構知識與概念，掌握前人累積與傳承下來的成果與經驗，從「識」與「通」中求變。人類的大腦，學習過程既能將生活中相同的概念同化，也能將不同的訊息跟自身已有的概念作調適。同時，也能記憶與理解別人的故事與教訓，站在歷史巨人的肩膀上，進一步發展。

理想的通識，在認知與經歷局部生活的過程，能連結貫通他人相關的經驗。例如，我既認識自己學校的校規，也明白不同地域年代學校因文化各異而設立不同的校規，以保障同學的學習環境安全與有序，傳承價值觀。推而廣之，處身的地方有法律，不同處境的地方也有不同的法律，用以保障居民生活的素質。「識」與「通」之間是多向度循環互動，以深化與提升不同思考的層次。

動態發展中的生活處境多元，個體不能「通通都識」，但須培養廣泛涉獵的興趣。當我們認知多元學校的特色，將能謙虛對待，尊重自身學校校規傳承的文化價值觀之餘，也懂得尊重其他學校的文化。

通識既追求廣泛知識的認識，掌握思考生活的規律，更重要是謙虛求學的態度。把握思考的方法，客觀認知世界運行的規律，最終能通過經驗或知識的建構與累積過程，上通古今與下達未來，橫貫中西、跨越領域與範疇，以能通過現象看本質。通過示例，舉一反三，以有效類推及預測未來，趨吉避凶，作出較準確與明智的選擇。

2. 通「天眼」

新高中通識教育科自成立以來，實踐效果備受質疑，對科目評價爭論不休，其主因在於大家對本科的學理弄不清，教學的目的弄不明。

筆者曾於前教育學院任教跨學科概念與思考、常識科及通識科教學法，綜合常識、生活與社會和通識教育科，此等科目的學習目的在於培養學生的「識通」能力。「通」在於人如何客觀地掌握自然、社會和人文學科之間的規律，懂得以謙虛及開放的態度進行探究，善用思考方法預測未來，作出明智的抉擇。

筆者剛到貴州一遊，實地近距離參觀貴州省平塘縣天坑群，欣然發覺「天眼」的科技及平塘國際天文體驗館，能具體地展示天文發展的歷史與規律。「天眼」是設在天坑群中的一台 500 米口徑球面望遠鏡，英文簡稱「FAST」，其觀象功能較美國 Arecibo 300 米望遠鏡高約 2.5 倍，據聞能直觀宇宙盡頭。中華民族由古至今，有系統地觀察天象，發現天體運行的規律；設計精密而獨創性的儀器如規矩、圭表與日晷，用以作觀察與測量；利用所得數據創設系統的工程。我國農業的生產及建築物的座向，便受天文知識所影響。

中華大地對天象運行的規律掌握，開創了數千年的農業文明。過去五百年西方文明開啟天文研究的高峰，透過天文規律的發現、儀器的發明，哥白尼的日心說替代了地心說。近年中國承接前人於天文和數字科技的掌握，創新太空科技和超級電腦。從長征一號到嫦娥登月計劃、神舟、天宮與「天眼」工程，擴展了對宇宙及人類社會活動的探索。「貨車幫」企業參觀，便見證大數據科技與貨車業發展的關係。

貴州之行，從「天眼」通向天文發展的探索與應用，讓人們明白科學、科技、工程及數學如何能結合人文及社會科學。啟迪廿一世紀的通識教育，當能善用舉一反三的示例，類推學習事物的規律。理想的通識教育應從小開始作有序的規律知識探究，從而深入掌握跨學科的概念與思考竅門，貫通中外古今及各學科知識，開闊胸襟與視野。

3. 走向胡同的通識教育科

英國一位頗負盛名的教育評估專家 Patricia Broadfoot 曾指出：高風險的教育考評，容易導致學生走向黑暗的胡同和盲目的幽徑（Dark alleys & blind bends）。

二零一五年教育局通識科中期檢討報告，87％的教師認同「通識科的公開考試與課程宗旨和設計一致」。然而，筆者的研究發現：68% 學生及 61% 教師認為文憑試考卷設計未能有效反映學生的多元學習能力；只有 48% 教師及 66% 學生認同，文憑試有助培養學生成為對社會有責任與承擔的公民。近日香港青年協會有關通識科的研究報告發現，與筆者早前的研究大同小異。

早於二零一六年，筆者就本港通識教育課程與考評關係，完成教育博士論文研究，並於一七年獲得英國布里斯托大學授予學位。實證研究結果證明，新高中通識教育科能夠引發學生對社會的關注（Awareness of the society），擴闊他們的視野（Broadening students' minds），卻無意識地導引他們走向自利性而非獨立的明辨性思維（Critical thinking）胡同。

研究於二零一四年向全港中學發出問卷，最終以四十二所學校中，四百八十九位剛考畢文憑試的學生及其五十位通識科任教師的問卷作量化對比，找出十多項具明顯差異的數據，並結合三十五個持份者(包括政策與考評高官)的個別訪談及十次課堂教學觀課作引證及分析。

研究發現，起動通識科的上列 ABC 三項目標初步達成，卻對學生的學習造成下列影響：一、求學的態度、能力與知識分崩割離。能力為本、知識為副，態度備受忽視。二、評估、學與教及目標未能如政策主張，作無縫銜接。三、考題模式要求作立場論證，無意識地催使學生傾向非黑即白，版模化的兩極思維，有違真正獨立的思考。四、跨學科本意將文理學科融合，然學理不清，以爭議性的時事作考題，聚焦了今日香港單元，弱化了自然科學和人文學科。五、紙筆為主的考核，狹義化了學科起動的學習目標，過程並未能真正培育學生全人發展及多元能力的學習。作為以廿一世紀學習模式設計的跨學科，通識科實踐未足十年，已有不少創新性的嘗試與意料之外的發現，筆者將逐一拆解。

4. 通識科與廿一世紀能力的學習

進入廿一世紀，人類社會競爭白熱化、資訊數字化與認知碎片化。國際社會期望學生能全人發展，跨學科學習，成為具責任承擔、獨立思考的公民。「廿一世紀能力」（21st century skills）學習目標應運而生，而通識科六項課程目標與之大同小異，可歸納為培養學生學會生活、學會尊重與學會思考。

分析通識科課程及評估指引的學習成果和評估目標，可見本科重視培養態度（Attitude）優先，其次為能力（Skills），然後是知識（Knowledge），更重要是課程主張三者融合，而不分割。學會生活和學會尊重重視跨學科公民素質與社會文化的培養，協作、溝通、自主學習，容忍多角度的觀點，掌握綜合資訊媒體的能力，以應對生活所需；學會思考重視高階思維和量度能力，包括明辨性思維（critical thinking）、創造力與解難能力，以提升獨立思考的素養。廿一世紀能力學習需從鷹架建構的歷程中，有效運用思維工具，掌握自然與社會規律，善用當代或前人實踐的示例與經驗。

可惜筆者早前研究發現，教師雖然高度認同本科目標，卻認為文憑試（DSE）無助學會尊重，少於半數教師認為 DSE 有助培養社會有責任與承擔的公民。教師對 DSE 有助促進通識科目標的達成觀感明顯較學生低，學生只重分數，對學習的目標概念模糊。受訪的不同持份者均不約而同表示，通識科設科原意在提供「文中有理、理中有文」的學習，實踐卻偏重於「今日香港」社會科學。考評局本科負責人更指 DSE 不具考核學生態度與價值觀的功能，考評不搞立場，只在區分思維能力的高低，知識錯誤也不扣分。研究觀察的十節教學均環繞議題學習，短小分割的時事議題多以兩節課處理，強求立場清晰的答題技巧，學生表層關心社會、視野拓闊，卻傾向將角色版模化與思維兩極化，日漸走向自利與自以為是的「獨立批判」思考。

通識科之本在培育學生情理兼備、觸類旁通、全人發展，學科起動的實踐卻弱化了學會生活與尊重，聚焦於明辨性思維而欠創意與解難訓練則狹義與扭曲了學會思考。結果由原先目標的「ASK 融合」變成了割裂的：能力＞知識＞態度。

5. 考評、學與教及目標一致的迷思

廿一世紀，國際社會以評估促進學習，推動考評、學與教及目標的無縫銜接。學習的重點從知識轉移到能力（或稱技能與素養）。建構學習的歷程才是教育的主體，以提升學生的競爭力、培養企業家精神及成為具責任承擔的公民。香港的通識教育科正是這股潮流背景下的新學科。

歷史上考評、學與教及目標三者的實踐模式與重點，隨社會需要時有變化。今年 9 月 28 日，正值孔子誕辰 2569 年，筆者適逢到訪山東曲阜，聽了一場講座。專家指經學是完整的系統，是尋找人生的指南。儒家的經典學習就是教育，也是科舉考試的題材。考試、學習與追求完美的人格目標相一致。歐洲工業化前期，手作坊採用師徒培育的制度，工匠選拔的指標與指導內容也一致。到了大規模工業生產時代，學校體制出現，課程首先訂立目標、然後施教，最後才考評學生掌握知識的多寡。

時代巨輪推動考評從知識為本轉變為能力為本。成效為本（Outcome-based）的評估與課程目標一致，能力的學習廣受追捧。通識科應用布魯姆思維層階（Bloom's Taxonomy）作為標準參照的評量標尺，用以評核開放性時事議題的論述水平。教師面對有別於過去知識為本的教與學，只能緊隨考評局提供的練習卷及文憑試試題作為教學藍本，為年度考試「貼」題，導引學生掌握評核試卷的規律與答題模型。

經歷九載，通識科公開考試的思維能力評核標準已廣泛應用於學與教，學生的自評與互評，教師的回饋，皆以統一的標尺作準繩。筆者研究發現，雖然大部份師生認同本科考評、學與教及目標三者一致，但卻少於半數師生認同考卷能全面反映學生的多元學習能力。考題偏重於明辨性思維，卻缺少手腦並用、創意解難的經歷和情意價值觀的反思啟迪；考評將態度、技能與知識的學習分割，聚焦於具備立場、機械程序性的思維論説操練。未能全面地驅動真正建構學習的參與，學生對通識學習缺乏興趣，只為考試而讀書。

通識科考評、學與教及目標一致的政策，用以追求廿一世紀能力的學習，可惜實踐趨向狹隘，未能有效達成。

6. 通識考評養成偽批判性思考

新高中通識教育科，以培養學生批判性思考（教育局現改稱「明辨性思考」Critical thinking）能力為學科起動的重點目標，以助培養正確價值觀、具責任承擔的獨立思考者，學習過程卻產生始料不及的異化，事與願違。

筆者的通識科研究發現，師生均認同文憑試（DSE）主導了議題模式的教學，過程側重於考試為本多於學習為本。不設教科書而採用大量議題，師生只能付出有限的時間進行徒具形式的小組討論或角色代入。數據顯示，全部教師表示經常或間中在教學中「導引學生清晰表達立場，對議題提出具理據的意見」；值得注意的是，數據分析亦指出，教師認為「靈活運用議題探究論證、訓練邏輯思維」和「建構宏觀或微觀、推理或舉證的學習歷程」等教學方法，與學生在 DSE 取得較佳成績之間並沒有關聯，可見學習傾向淺層思考。

筆者亦發現，教師較學生更認同學生愈能掌握 DSE 標準參照及考核模式，愈有助獲取佳績，並以大量的兩正一反、正反立論等論說模型作操練。有老師每天早上觀看網站熱點議題，跟學生討論；也有於考試前，將百多份新聞或議題分類給學生，讓他們上網查證觀點與立場。為獲取高分，學生功利地追求自利性的「批判」思維論證，有的更認為考試未必要依據個人立場作答；亦有些走「捷徑」的學生只看一份報章，因為立場更清晰。爭議性議題立場論證，強化了自我與他人的分別，有同學便批評 DSE 試題把黑白分得很清楚，讓複雜的問題簡單化。這種欠缺創意及解難配合的偽「批判性」思維，容易讓學生走向事事懷疑和否定。

須知真正的獨立批判思考者，持守以事實為根據及對所有人公平的態度。他們關心不同立場人士的觀點，尊重不同持份者的價值觀，照顧大眾的福祉；在理據未充份時，寧願保持懸念而不妄下判斷。他們重視邏輯的規律、歷史文化的背景，從而辨析對錯、矯正錯誤，及驗證前設與結論。

可惜在通識科的起動實踐中，為回應問責與學術認受性，DSE 在無意間強化了兩極思維，間接驅使學生確立自視為「真理」的立場，縱然辯說能力了得，卻跟成為真正獨立的批判思考者的目標相違背。

7. 追求文理兼備的通識教育科

筆者在 2014 年進行通識科研究時，教育局政策高官及曾負責推行通識科的官員在訪問中不約而同地表示，設科目標之一是提供「文中有理、理中有文」的學習。可惜，通識科推行九載，筆者認為實踐效果與設科原意相去甚遠。

「文中有理、理中有文」的原意概念模糊，未有清晰的定義和指引。筆者曾為常識科與通識科準教師提供「跨學科概念與思考」課程教學，其中重點在於掌握事物之間的連結關係，學習系統思維。例如視單車為一個系統，由兩輪、腳踏、把手及齒鏈組合，發揮力學原理來運動；消化系統由口腔、牙齒、大小腸及胃部組成，發揮消化食物、吸收養份的作用；學校、社區與政府則分別由不同人員組成部門，發揮獨特系統的功能。示例説明自然科學系統概念，能夠類推到社會科學系統，一理通，百理明。

STEM 是科學（Science）、科技（Technology）、工程（Engineering）和數學（Mathematics）綜合而成的一個跨學科，可視為一個獨特的系統。由四個原來是獨立的學科系統作有機的綜合，構建而成。人工智能、3D 打印、「魚菜共生」等創新項目，便需結合物理、化學、生物、工程、數學編程等理論與技術。STEM 教育是讓學生掌握科學原理，配合相關的技術及工具，通過情境應用與達成任務，來讓學生發揮群組協作、手腦並用，從而達至創新思考及解決難題。STEM 教育可與文藝（Art）結合為 STEAM，加入環保 3R（減廢 Reduce，重用 Re-use 及回收 Recycle）便成為 STREAM。

筆者認為，通識教育要能導引學生掌握能「識」且「通」的跨學科概念，便需從建構參與中，全面提升學生的「廿一世紀能力」，提供文理學科兼備、具創意解難及系統思維的跨學科主題學習，好讓自然科學的生活概念能靈活轉移與運用於社會科學上。

作為教育改革必修必考的通識科，學校課程檢討專責小組宜深入反思課程的本源與學理，修正學科起動的偏差；從教育專業出發，研究如何能從小學開展文理兼備、易於舉一反三的跨學科主題學習；刪減現行偏重於社會科學的議題教學，加入 STEM 教育示例，以取得建構學習的平衡，達成設科的目標與理想。

8. 重整通識教育
讓學生全面成長

培育新一代全人發展，讓學生掌握多元能力的學習，筆者認為應從個人、社會及人文學科（如常識、生活與社會）、STEM 教育、專題研習等跨學科（筆者歸類為廣義的通識教育）課程開展。有關學科乃一脈相承，透過生活示例、情境任務、難點議題等提供建構學習的歷程，以學會生活、學會思考與學會尊重。

「天生我才必有用」、「若要人似我，除非兩個我」，每個人都是獨一無二的。人之所以為人在於其擁有獨立的思考與意志，為自身的志趣目標，作出適切的行為和抉擇。然而，人可以自由地犯錯，但不可盲目自由地達至成功，必須從經驗中體會客觀的規律與教訓。因此，除了語文、數學及術科的學習之外，人還需要綜合跨學科的知識來應用，在過程中發揮潛能、靈活變通、學懂抉擇。通識教育正正能配合新一代的人才培育需要，透過探索，建構跨學科知識；提供情境，讓學生手腦並用；賦予任務，實踐創意解難；在追夢的過程，磨練意志與提升執行力；導引反思和回饋，以能尊重規律，開懷面對逆境與挫折，育養品格與正向人生。

當下影響升學選校的通識科文憑試（DSE），導引基礎教育階段的跨學科課程學習方向。由於紙筆考卷佔整體 80% 的評分，內容多環繞社會爭議性的議題，聚焦明辨性思考文字的論述，欠缺自然科學的探索以培養創造力及解決問題能力；而獨立專題探究（IES）僅佔總分的 20%，備受忽略，結果，實踐中窄化了通識教育的學習目標，未能導引學生作全人發展及多元能力的學習。

除非改變大學收生的標尺，重視建構學習的歷程及 IES 的佔分比重，改革通識科紙筆考題，否則，全人發展與多元能力的學習難於在課堂上推展。客觀而言，通識科實踐證明成效為本的能力學習，能有效透過必修必考的制度，產生教學範式的轉變。筆者認為，只要加強跨學科學理研究，提供能舉一反三的專業教材，改善紙筆考評，重視 IES 實踐與評核，善用評估促進學習，將能有效貫通通識教育的功能。

9. 縱橫貫通的通識教育

通識教育之本在培育學習者的思維及態度能「通」且「識」。竅門是橫向把持形成性（又稱進展性）與總結性評估（即測考）的一致性，縱向提供能貫通目標、學與教及成效表現一致的建構式學習。

Black & Wiliam 於 1998 年對形成性評估作出具權威性的論證，倡議促進學習的評估。總結性和形成性評估被視為學習的一個連貫互通的過程，教師善用能力達標的層級描述，對照學習過程的成效表現作即時的回饋，好讓學習者能夠掌握了解自身的學習狀態、達至甚麼水平、還有什麼可改善的空間，以及需要付出怎麼樣的努力來改善。教師切實到位的學與教回饋，有助學生提高學習效能，最終顯示於總結性評核的評級上。

杜威的建構主義學習理論、維高斯基的鷹架理論、近代研究腦神經系統學習的理論等，皆指向教師的專業需導引學生自主有效地參與到建構學習的歷程。教師提供具成效指標的手腦並用探究、情境任務、道德兩難討論等，學生便能從過程中作創意解難、價值反思，深化情理兼備的學習。通識教育是讓學生透過態度、能力與知識（ASK，Attitude，Skill & Knowledge）的有機統一主題來靈活學習。知識能從前人及個人的經驗中獲得，能力可從實踐中磨練，態度和價值觀則從人際互動中得以啟悟，學生從而有興趣及動力，終身追求「廿一世紀能力」學習，達成設科的目標。

過去教育局和筆者等的研究均發現，師生多認同通識科的評估、學與教及目標的實踐能夠達成一致。然而，筆者認為這種一致性的表象，只因考什麼、學什麼都被窄化於爭議性的時事議題作為思維訓練，偏重於以批判性思維的能力為本，而不重視知識對錯、學習態度、價值觀、創意、解難等難於量化的軟性元素學習。影響升學選校的紙筆考評與問責制，助長短視式的操練，考題未能結合日常能舉一反三的生活示例，以考核學生對關鍵性跨學科概念的理解與運用能力。

教學當回歸專業，是時候成立專家小組，研究能縱橫貫通的常識、通識、STEM 教育及專題研習等跨學科課程學理，從小開始塑造既「通」且「識」的學習歷程。

10. 塑造既「通」且「識」的通識教育

通識科要能既「通」且「識」，其竅門在讓學生經歷自主學習的過程，背後是教師的鷹架設計，因應學生的生活興趣及能力水平，提供學習活動及配套。學科首要是具備整全學理，教師能提供學生適切的建構學習內容及活動設計。評估、課程學習與短中長期的目標一致，才能有效促進學習。

須知知識（Knowledge）有如人的軀體肌膚、能力（Skills）有如骨骼筋腱、態度（Attitude）價值觀有如主管行動抉擇的大腦，再強健的骨骼軀幹但若失去靈魂和執行的意志力，人只是空有軀體的動物。因此，通識科的智慧在於把 ASK 融合於課程活動之中，並優先關注態度與價值觀的培養。教師的角色有如編劇與導演，因材施教，確立以學生為本、自主探究，從參與中學習，從實踐中成長。利用學生的已有知識及熟悉的生活情境作為學習的示例，以能於過程中掌握跨學科概念，並能反思與轉移運用。導師的即時及具成效指標的回饋，有助掌握事物（或視為大小系統）的連結、成長與演變的規律與關係。有效的通識科有助客觀認知世界，將自然科學的規律類推於社會與人文生活，培養有靈魂、家國情懷與國際視野的公民，讓他們具自信地面向未來。

筆者研究過程中發現，專業的通識科教師經常規劃及部署構建學習的歷程。假設是「多大程度」類型的考題，教師便組織學生四人小組或正反立論兩大組，分工進行資料搜集，透過小組討論或辯論過程，掌握能反擊論點及論證立場，最終能作綜合評析，導引微觀與宏觀的跨學科思考。有學校便透過集體備課，教師分工負責議題資料整理和建構模式的教學設計，出卷、改卷及向全級分析答題的優劣，以驗證學生的思維技巧。較高能力的學生，教師導引自主式的探究，尋根究底找論點。為了培育價值觀，更有教師利用情境建構，讓學生模擬打架，引伸討論國與國之間的矛盾，如何能和平解決。

通識科奠基於整個基礎教育的不同學科及跨學科課程學習，同時其文憑試反過來塑造基礎教育的學習。因此，本科既「通」且「識」的關鍵，在於對廿一世紀能力學習的學理掌握及檢視。

11. 課程檢討先要定義問題

愛因斯坦曾說：假如他只有一小時拯救世界，他將花 59 分鐘定義問題，再以 1 分鐘提出解決問題的方案。教育局早前成立的學校課程檢討專責小組，負責整體檢討中小學課程，就以下四點提出方向性的建議：其一是學生的品格素質如何透過有效學習來提升；其二是如何照顧學生的獨特性，發展他們多元的能力、興趣和抱負。其三，如何優化課程，創造空間，促進學生全人發展。其四，如何促進中小學階段的銜接。筆者認為當前香港課程檢討的關鍵，在於找到課程存在甚麼問題。

筆者早前多篇通識與考評關係的研究評論，以實證發現為基礎，剖析通識科的設科學理不清、評估素養不足，以及目標窄化的學習實踐。以通識實踐異化為例，可說明香港整體課程現存的主要問題。

從閱讀大量相關國際論文及自身研究發現所得，筆者推斷現行課程問題的根源在於香港與國際社會正處身人才培育的大轉折：從教師為中心轉向以學生為中心、知識為本走向能力為本、課程目標為本走向成效為本。可惜大家對轉變的學理掌握不足，而實證的研究示例亦不多。

筆者從通識科的示例研究，發覺先進國家正追求評估、學與教及目標一致的理念，並以標準參照的評量來推動廿一世紀能力的學習。國際性 PISA 測試的評價量規及數據比較，便成為指導各國教育政策制定的考量。與此同時，國際間盛行行政管理與教學「問責」的機制，將學生的學業成績用作評價機構與教師教學成效的標準，因而強化了評估的重要性與影響。

基於香港處身於高度開放的國際大環境，新學制下各學科為了達到國際認可的水平，偏重思維技能的考核。考試及評核局為確保考評的信度和效度，採用可量化的測考試題，而難於以紙筆評價的多元智能、價值素養、創意解難等能力則被受忽略。由於學理不清，課程只加不減，因而難於騰出空間照顧個別差異及鼓勵全人發展。期望小組以實證研究作啟示，宏觀檢視整體課程，專業尋求解決問題的方向。

12. 為課程發展尋路

在通識科課程與考評關係的研究過程中，啟發了筆者對現行課程發展的一些看法：寄望基礎教育能確立既「通」且「識」的跨學科課程學理與規劃。

香港學校除了中英語文、數學和術科的核心課程學習之外，便是廣義的通識教育，包括常識科、綜合科學與人文學科，以及高中通識科，其餘為中國歷史、世界歷史、地理、經濟、生物、化學、物理等專科的學習。由於知識爆炸，人類急需擁有符合生活所需的基礎知識與概念作類推，以及可供轉移運用的技能訓練，因此，現代社會日趨重視跨學科課程的學習。香港正受自身發達地區及中國新興發展地區的兩大系統所影響，亦是國際金融及貿易中心之一，市民面對多元法治、經濟、文化、價值觀等的爭議及挑戰。新一代如何有效掌握思考方法，以開放的態度面對多元的變化，自小掌握能舉一反三、手腦並用、靈活變通的跨學科示例學習非常關鍵。

本港推行小學的常識科已 22 年，中學的通識科亦有 9 年。筆者曾擔任小學常識科主任及進行高中通識科研究各 7 年，推行跨學科課程設計與支援更愈 20 載。近年曾為準教師教授常識科和通識科教學法，與及「跨學科概念與思考」，發覺甚少學者或決策者於常識科與通識科進行學理的分析與研究，對評估政策的施行更是一知半解。常識科至今仍是健康教育、科學科和社會科的單元拼湊，幸好教學法活潑多元，故此較有效提供多元智能的學習。相反通識科偏重於社會學科的時事評論，較多採用小組或角色代入作探究或辯論，教學法單一，無助學生的全人發展。

筆者認為跨學科課程的設計需解決如何從具體到抽象、從自然科學到社會科學、從舉一反三示例到自由探索、從概念基礎到轉移概念的運用、從具學理的教科書學習到校本的主題探索，最終學生能自信地完成獨立專題探究。教學宜提供多元能力的學習，從認識理解知識的基礎開展，到參與探索發現、想像創造的活動，配以反思、評價與實踐應用的歷程學習。

當前整體課程的未來去向需從小學到中學的跨學科課程根源學理梳通開展，並分析如何才較有效學習、善用評估的工具推動時代所需的學習。

13. 未來人才培育工程

筆者近日聽黃錦輝教授有關工程科學與 STEM 教育的介紹，並拜讀他的一篇文章。文中介紹去年瑞士洛桑管理學院《二零一八年世界人才報告》，全球六十三個經濟體中香港排名十八，新加坡十三。排名落後的主因是「準備度」不足，於「現有人才能否滿足市場需要」一項，香港位居第九，而新加坡則第二。當中「學校內科學」一項，新加坡排名第一而香港第二十位。黃教授認為與政府缺乏清晰的 STEM 教育指引有關。

追溯歷史，任何科學與科技創新變化，都帶來生產力的提升與產業變化。美國陸軍《2016-2045年新興科技趨勢報告》，確立二十項最值得關注的科技發展趨勢。當中包括機器人和自動化系統於 2045 年將無處不在、全新合成材料和生物 3D 打印、大數據智慧平台、人類增強技術、醫學、能源、智能城市、物聯網、糧食與食水、混合現實消費與社交媒體平台等將有重大突破，那需人才培育創新以應對。

筆者從通識科課程與考評關係研究發現，以及了解學友社十大新聞選舉的候選三十條初選運作，是由學生整合各新聞媒體的資料和論調得出，推論通識科及新聞媒體對中學生評選時事項目的影響。分析過去十二年中學生十大新聞選舉候選新聞三百六十條，涉及科學與科技內容的選項不到百分之五，而涉及政治議題的則達百分之三十五。剛公布排第六位的「港珠澳大橋正式通車，超支和安全問題惹關注」的焦點便放到社會的爭議點而非建橋工程的突破上。筆者推論通識科評分講求清晰立場，較重視爭論二元對立的新聞，以突顯考生的獨立明辨性思維能力，而忽略排難解困的科學與科技學習。因此學生思維意識或多或少受切身的考評標準所影響。

倘若重視通識科設科原旨，培養學生多元能力，便需更新課程與考評標尺，加入文理共融和手腦並用的 STEM 教育，將 STEM 加入 ART（人文元素）變成「STEAM」。當前教育先要掌握處境、打通學理，實行跨界別與跨地域協作，試行整理能舉一反三的示例，構建評估、學與教及目標一致的學習歷程，才能有效推展人才培育的工程。

14. 從十大新聞看中學生時事取向

學友社「全港中學生十大新聞選舉」已踏入第二十七個年頭，歷屆都不少於全港四分之一的中學參與。其運作原則是從初選的設題，到總選投票的過程，皆讓學生自主參與，以便能貼近中學生的思維意識與及其認知作判斷。而最終選出的十大新聞，更反映年度中學生的價值意識及關注的新聞事件。筆者重溫過去十二年選舉的結果，試行梳理當中的特色，過程中發現中學生對時事的關注與重視，受新聞價值要素以及通識科設科所影響。

新聞價值要素包括受眾傾向對切身、震撼、簡易、懸疑的時事感興趣。他們選取新聞時，多考慮新聞的時宜性、影響性、衝突性、顯要性、接近性及人情味。對與自身相關的或引發共鳴的新媒體分享及片段，中學生更常作回應或轉發，互動參與過程加強事件的感染力，因而影響他們對有關新聞事件的排名。去年超強颱風「山竹」襲港便獲得遠多於第二位的得票率，一五年台灣樂園粉塵爆炸、一六年馬航事件等便屬此類特質的新聞。

通識科強調以爭議性時事議題作為學習與考評要點，那與學生切身利益相關，對學生的時事觸覺及取向，或許構成不可預測的影響。二零零九年本港開始推行必修必考的通識科，考題模式與內容一定程度上改變了學生對時事議題的關注。追溯過去十大新聞選舉結果，零七年前政治新聞甚少，當年特首選舉及港島區補選不入十大，一二年特首選舉，三十則候選新聞當中，便有二十二則屬於政治新聞；一四年政改討論，接近一半候選新聞屬政治內容，其中三則有關政改的新聞更躋身十大；一六年特首選舉，十大新聞中共有五則涉及政治表態的新聞。

筆者認為存在的媒體報導決定學生對時事的認知與思維意識，而公開試考評要求跟學生相關，更影響他們關注時事的優次。倘若通識科學習被傳媒熱炒的議題牽著走，中學生十大新聞選舉結果，反照的將不獨是社會氛圍的變化，更是傳媒處理時事議題報導的手法與及影響學生切身利益的相關考評與課程施行。

15. 教育還是百年不變

「AI（人工智能）年代已經到臨，社會巨變已經開始，我們準備好了嗎？」那是筆者參加一個有關《AI 時代：職場、人才、教育》論壇上，大會提出的一個疑問。當中一位專家展示兩幀 1910 和 2010 年學校課堂面貌的圖像作對照，質疑「一百年過去了，為什麼教育還是老樣子？」

二零一六年 AlphaGo 智能機械人戰勝了人類棋手冠軍李世石，一七年便被定義為「AI 元年」，開啟智能發展新篇章。智能醫療、機械人、家居與安防，無人駕駛、物聯網等一一走上人類生活的舞臺。專家們分別介紹了各自領域 AI 科技的發展，更有以中國五千年歷史與 AI 發展史、趨勢與變局作對照，用意展示 AI 瞬間經歷起伏挑戰，變化峰迴路轉，影響深遠。然而人才培育卻跟不上。

筆者經歷了通識與考評關係的研究，發現公開考試的模型與制度，以及日趨重視的問責制是影響課堂教學不變的主因。因此好奇地問：作為影響學習的指揮棒—公開考試，AI 能作出怎樣的改變？一位專家樂觀的表示正有專家進行相關研究，未來將不用考試。另一講者說教育是複雜的科學，包含心理學與大腦神經學，教師也當如中醫師，懂得對症下藥，認知學生學習的歷程，懂得「患病」的學理與治療的「藥理」。更有專家形容今天教師為「囊中」，只有部份擁有妙手回春的醫術。

筆者不希冀 AI 專家們真能解答教育百年不變的因由，以對症下藥，反珍視探討問題的過程。當前教育仍採用能操作、較省錢的紙筆模型考試，以確保評估的信度、效度，用以公開、公平、公正的分配學位。教師只是體制內的一員，能否善用評估的魔術棒，讓考評、學與教與所需人才培育的目標一致變革，才是「對焦」問題的關鍵。期望 AI 專家與教育專家們合力，利用大腦神經的發展以及數字科技的進步，有效推行考評與建構學習一致的課程與評估政策，好讓學生能扎扎實實進行自主學習，以成為比 AI 機械人更具思考、靈魂、決策與執行力時代的主人。

破解教育百年不變，當從教育評估與課程更新開展。

16. 教育之變與不變

人類文明進步，需要自強不息的意志力與成長智慧。當中人的堅毅不屈和抉擇素質，帶領文明進步是不變的，卻需隨時代變遷變更學習的範式。

人類學習的範式隨著時、地、人於社會中的生產模式與關係組合而變化。農業社會處境緩變，人們發展的機會不多，識見局限，家族聚居互助以確保生存。年長者經驗與智慧累積、富裕家族聘請「家教」培育後人，以便成為族群帶領者。中國農業社會歷經數千年，自秦始皇一統天下，便「車同軌、書同文、行同倫」，建立相對穩定的典章制度。漢武帝更接納董仲舒建議，獨尊儒術，以四書五經作為人才培育的典籍，採用相對公開、公平的科舉制度，選拔貧富不拒的人才。考試的題材與典籍導人修身、齊家、治國、平天下；具備「天將降大任於斯人也，必先苦其心志，勞其筋骨…」等心志，視艱困苦難為磨練。科舉制度塑建中國農業文明，開創人才選拔、培育範式與價值評估的一致性，成就農業社會高度的文明。

現代化工業文明起源於歐洲。十五世紀末地理大發現、文藝復興、宗教改革促使個性解放；航海時期廣建殖民地，啟動重商主義；其後科學革命推動工業革命成功，開展現代機器生產的文明。隨著圈地運動開展，大量人力轉移到工廠生產，城市化管理與技術勞工需求急增，驅使現代學校及學科的設立。體育、工藝、宗教著意鍛煉學生的體格、技術與精神意志，卻與主導人才選拔而知識分割的學科評估不統一。二次世界大戰後，隨著全球化，已發展地區的人民生活走向繁榮安逸，不少體重超高，缺乏自理磨練的意志力。

今天工業走向 4.0，進行人工智能、大數據等科技與產業創新，人們追求個性化與自我實現，而社會則需求敢於冒險與堅毅創新的專才及企業家。現階段教育重視能力考評，卻欠磨勵意志的經歷。當務之急可利用新科技、新媒體、新策略培訓所需的專才，更需研究如何選拔與育養具備堅毅承擔精神與成長型思維潛質的通才，帶領社會前行。

第二部份：

中文研究論文

香港通識科評估政策的成效對推行 STEM 教育的啟示

梁麗嬋，獨立研究員，香港

（本文於香港中文大學香港教育研究學會 2018 國際研討會上發表）

1. 摘要

基於對香港通識教育科文憑試、教學法及課程目標是否配合一致的研究，本文分析了學生學習的得與失。該研究對於如何推行 STEM 教育，以培養「廿一世紀能力」（21st century Skills）學習的目標，具有參考價值。

本研究採用 42 所 50 班本港學校師生問卷調查，35 位不同持份者獨立訪談，以 10 節課堂教學觀察的混合式數據比較，得出結論。

結果發現，標準參照的考評和評估的監測機制，能有效推動批判性思維，開闊學生的視野，激發學生對社會問題的關心。成效為本的政策更能有效引導議題教學、反轉教室、群組互動。但是，由於評估和課程指引目標與教學並不一致，導致教學法於務實的短期目標和理想的長期目標之間失去平衡。機制與政策推行有利於學生學會思考，不利於學會生活，更輕視學習尊重他人。跨學科本意將文理學科融合，在實踐當中卻僅僅聚焦了社會科學，而弱化了對自然科學和人文學科的關注。

STEM 教育在科技領域積極餞行廿一世紀能力的學習，重視於生活中辨難、解難、自學、溝通與協作，在教學實踐方面與通識科一脈相承。隨著 STEM 教育的推行，成效為本（Outcome-based）的考評必不可少，而參考香港通識科推動課程目標、學與教及評估一致的經驗，將有助避免資源的浪費。

關鍵詞：
評估政策、通識教育、STEM 教育、廿一世紀能力

2. 前言

回應廿一世紀人類處身於全球化下，高競爭、高科技、高連結、高變速的年代，培育具解難能力的人才，是國際社會共同關注與重視的課題。根據麥肯錫全球研究所發表的調查報告（MGI，2017），預計 2030 年全球最少有 8 億個職位被人工智能（AI）所替代。美國教育界帶動全球開展跨學科 STEM 教育（范斯淳、游光昭，2016），香港政府也於 2016 年底提出具體 STEM 教育方案，以培養學生創造力、協作和解決問題能力，發揮開拓與創新精神。2017 年在港每所中學更獲發放 20 萬港元作為 STEM 教育津貼。

過去 20 年，國際教育創新推動「評估促進學習」（Assessment for learning）的理論與政策，積極梳理及實踐廿一世紀能力的培育框架。採用成效為本的中央評核標準作為指導課程、學與教及目標的規劃，更以其成效達標的水平作為學校、教師及相關機構問責的依據。評估系統如 Programme for International Student Assessment（簡稱 PISA）的表現及排名已成為國際各國推動學校改革、問責、規劃及政策發展的關鍵槓桿（OECD, 2013）。必修必考的香港高中通識教育科（下簡稱通識科），已成為廿一世紀能力學習的首推跨學科課程。在儒家文化影響下，公平與具效能的公開試，是東亞地區如香港，個體得以作社會上流的依傍。因此，對通識科文憑試成效優劣的研究，將對時下國際關注的跨學科教育（如 STEM 教育）的推行，具備非常切合的參考作用。

3. 文獻閱讀

新時代課程目標、學與教及評估之關係

通識科一方面主張建構學習的過程，啟發思考，讓學生從情境生活中了解事物的動態發展與關聯（Tse, 2010），另一方面，通識科運用恆常性議題，梳理與運用前人累積的經驗概念，用以轉移應用於新情境與議題方面。評估被視為提高標準和賦予終身學習者權力的最有力的工具（ARG, 2002）。「*評估與課程、學和教的協調，是改善所有學習機會和結果的關鍵*」（Wyatt-Smith, Klenowski & Colbert, 2014, p.3）。為實現課程目標，本港跟隨國際，實行「*課程、教學法和評估*」協調一致的政策（CDC / HKEAA, 2014；Looney, 2011; UNESCO, 2014）。傳統的課程，通常先行確立教學目標（Aims），並用目標指導學與教（Pedagogies）的進行，評估（Evaluation）則視作學習成效的檢視。但跟據筆者之前的研究（Leung, 2013, 2017），卻發現通識科及廿一世紀能力的學習，採用成效為本的逆向評量，評估的層級標準描述，導引學

與教的表現回饋，用以達致設科的目標。圖一展示了課程目的、學與教及評估系統的關聯圖（引自 Leung, 2017, p.24），然而，「*創新性的評估挑戰教師已有的評估概念。在轉向以成效為本的課程時，形成性與總結性評估創新性地結合起來，那是一項挑戰*」（Gulikers, Biemans, Wesselink & Wel, 2013, p.116）。

圖一：課程目標、學與教及評估關聯系統

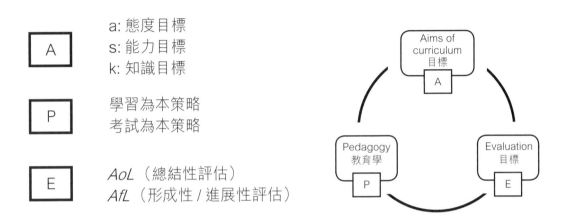

A
a: 態度目標
s: 能力目標
k: 知識目標

P
學習為本策略
考試為本策略

E
AoL（總結性評估）
AfL（形成性／進展性評估）

廿一世紀能力為本替代知識為本的學習

根據通識科指引的學習成果和評估目標（CDC/HKEAA, 2014, 第 97 頁），筆者對態度（Attitude）、能力（Skills）與知識（Knowledge）學習進行了重要性分析，結果顯示，通識科重視 A 優先，其次為 S，然後才是 K，ASK 三者相互關聯，不能割裂開來分別審視。筆者將有關目標跟 Voogt & Roblin（2012, p.299）研究中多個國家，共八個不同「廿一世紀能力綜合框架」作比較，發現內容大同小異，便將廿一世紀能力（素養或技能）學習的目標，歸類為「學會生活和尊重」及「學會思考」兩大類（表一，引自 Leung, 2017, p.48）。前者重視跨學科公民素質與知識，團隊協作、有效溝通及對不同意見的包容，從不同訊息來源綜合證據的能力，以應對生活所需；後者重視高階思維和測量的技能，包括批判性思維、創意、問題解決及獨立思考的能力。廿一世紀能力的涵義廣泛，綜合連結學習者的 A、S 與 K 培育，在引導從建構學習的歷程中，運用有效器物與思維工具，掌握自然與社會規律，善用當代或前人實踐示例與經驗，讓學生學會生活、學會思考與學會尊重，而非只著眼於知識的獲得。

表一：通識科廿一世紀能力學習框架

學習如何生活和尊重

A. 跨學科技能和知識

- 社會和 / 或文化技能，公民素養
- 對核心主題的靈活性和適應性

B. 容忍不同的觀點

- 協作、溝通、自主學習和獨立性

C. 從不同來源和觀點綜合信息或證據的能力

- 信息素養
- ICT 素養
- 媒體素養

學習如何思考

高階思維和測量技能

- 批判性思維
- 創造力
- 解決問題
- 獨立思考

促進廿一世紀能力學習的評估趨勢

隨著數字科技的發達與腦部神經研究成果的逐漸豐碩，鼓學生重視學習的歷程而非結果，才能讓學生有效掌握廿一世紀能力的學習（Looney, 2011）。國際評估浪潮採用促進能力的「學習為本」策略，相信以標準參照及其水平指標的評估跟學與教過程結合，能有效引導廿一世紀能力的學習（ibid, UNESCO, 2014；Wyatt-Smith, et al., 2014）。為實現目標，不少學者均提出「課程、學與教和評估協調一致」的主張，目標從成效為本的評核標準（E）出發，用以指導學與教（P），從而提升學生習得廿一世紀能力的效果（A）（見圖一）。政策驅動學與教及評估設計與施行的範式轉變：從教師為中心轉為以學生為中心；知識為基礎轉為能力為基礎等。歐洲各國的基礎教育便已採用學習成果為標準（Cort, 2014）。

通識科評估政策與系統

作為廿一世紀重設的高中新學科，通識科學術水平需獲得本地及國際院校的認可。香港創新性地將「*課程目標、學與教和評估協調一致*」的理念，寫入通識科指引（CDC/HKEAA, 2014, p.130），「*通識科的公開考試與課程目標和設計保持一致*」（EDB, 2015），便成為中期檢討檢視的重要事項。新課程起始，便以標準參照為本的評估示例與樣本，撬動跨學科與跨單元的課程學習，以培養高階思維（Leung, 2013）。進展性（又稱形成性）評估跟隨著總結性評估指標，且因數字科技的廣泛運用，而有助融合互用。香港考試及評核局（下稱考評局）設立中央評卷機制，透過中央電腦系統進行評卷員培訓及評卷監察制度，確保開放性的考題能達到信度、效度與公平性（Coniam, 2011）。影響高中學生升學選校（屬於高風險，high-risk）的總結性評估考題及評分標準，具有指導日常課堂如何善用「建構式」的功能，設計學習（Adamson & Darling-Hammond, 2015；Griffin, McGaw & Care, 2012）。通識科的文憑試運作，具備下列特點：爭議性的時事議題作為高風險考試的內容，答題運用適切的示例及具邏輯與關聯的概念，顯示考生的論證與思維能力。考試著重思維能力而非知識或觀點的對錯，導引教師於日常課堂教學和回饋過程中，將進展性評估跟總結性評估結合起來，用以實踐設科 ABC（Awareness of the society, Broadening their minds & Connection skills & Critical thinking）學習的目標（EDB, 2010），卻不是包含創新、問題解決等全面廿一世紀能力的學習。

課程與評估模型

時至今日，人類仍無可避免，採用相對公平、公正、具信度與效度的公開考評作為人才選拔的主要方式。普遍可行及廉價的紙筆評核結果，常影響個人升學及出路。建基於國際評估文獻閱讀（Black & Wiliam, 1998；Broadfoot, 2007；Gipps, 1994）與及通識科課程特點的分析，筆者建構一個橫向進展性和總結性評估一致，縱向目標、學與教過程和成效表現一致的課程與評估框架（圖二，引自 Leung, 2017），作為是項研究的設計構思，用以分析及評價廿一世紀跨學科課程與評估能否貫通一致，達至無縫銜接的效果。總結性評估（Summative assessment）（包含高風險的公開試）的標準參照及其水平指標是指導學與教及課程規劃的準繩。進展性評估（Formative assessment）被視為學習過程的不斷的及時回饋，並按總結性評估的考題樣本及評分標準，作為指導學生學習的參照。當中關鍵在於學習過程，能否讓學生真正參與到建構學習過程去，並能透過即時反饋，啟發學生思考與激發進一步探究。總結性評估的標準源於對課程目標（Aims）的學習，即廿一世紀能力的目標，例如明辨性思考需透過一個議題探索、問題回應與判斷過程，才具高階思維運用與成長的歷程。理想的應試策略與學習策略如能結合一致，並能有效促進學習，最終達至成效指標（Evaluation of outcomes），那麼，學生便能於過程真正運用廿一世紀能力。例如提供情境、任務與行動設計過程進行 STEM 教育，過程發揮團隊協作、創意解難，啟發參與學習的興趣，便較能達成表一追求學會生活、學會思考及學會尊重的效果。評估與課程一致的成敗關鍵在於學與教的過程（Black & Wiliam 指稱為黑箱介入 black box intervention, 1998）是否有效，教師能夠提供適切的學習目標方向、鷹架配套及作精準的回饋，引發學生思考學習，樂於參與建構的過程，最終能從學生的自評、行為表現與及評估結果中，反映總體學習的成果。

圖二：評估與課程縱橫一致模型

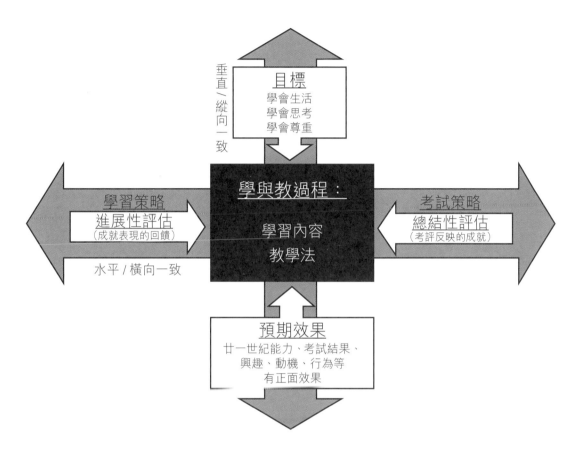

4. 研究目的和問題

文獻整理廿一世紀能力學習的追求，透過「目標、學與教及評估的一致性」政策作為通識跨學科的推行準則。政策看似具備理據與理想構思原則，但在實踐過程能否切實可行？是否能如構思推行？推行過程的成與敗或得與失的經驗與分析，將對本科及其他跨學科的推行，具備參考意義。為此，本文從下列兩道研究問題作分析：

    1.「目標、學與教及評估的一致性」政策多大程度有助廿一世紀能力的學習？

    2. 政策為推行 STEM 教育帶來什麼啟示？

5. 研究設計

研究採用混合方式，解釋性順序（Creswell & Clark, 2011）實證設計。建基於評估與課程縱橫一致研究模型，筆者按通識科文憑試與本科目標、教學法、對學生構成的影響三個方面，設計問卷內容，問題各部份均採用李克特量表的四個選項供選擇。問卷於 2014 年向全港 458 所中學發出，最終獲得來自 42 所中學 50 班的通識科教師及其任教的十位以內 489 位學生的有效數據。問卷取得同班師生對同一問題的觀感意見作比較，好處在排除其他變項因素後，能聚焦師生對同一問題的觀感作回應，從而更客觀地比對當中的數據落差，以作分析及論證。所有問題作正向調整，最高正向獲分為 4，最低為 1，中數為 2.5。數據以 SPSS 工具分析，Shapiro-Wilk 常態測試，證實數據屬非參數的現象，故所有數據輸出使用非參數測試工具整理。

配合問卷填寫的同期，筆者進行半結構性個別獨立訪談。包括當中 6 所學校的 10 位教師及 17 位學生，及其餘 8 位教育局、考評局代表、學科導師專家（表二）等。此外，受訪學校當中的 3 所之 6 位教師，提供 10 課節通識課堂作教學觀察（表三）。質性訪談及觀課數據與示例，用以引證問卷的發現，以作研究問題的分析與闡述。

表二：參與個別獨立訪談持份者

個別獨立訪談者	數目	時間（分鐘）
S= 學生	17	20-40
T= 教師	10	45-90
OS 1= 教育局資深政策制定者	1	60
OS 2= 前教育局通識科資深課程主任	1	120
OS 3= 考評局通識科高級行政人員	1	60
OS 4 & OS 5= 通識科專家	2	60
OS 6= 家長	1	20
OS 7 & OS 8 = 取得通識科文憑試最高級別（五星星）準教師	2	40

表三：參與個別獨立訪談及觀課學校學生和教師資料

學校編號	1	2	3		4		5		6	
教師編號	T1	T2	T3	T4	T5	T6	T7	T8	T9	T10
觀課次數	/	/	2	1	2	2	/	/	1	2
學生編號	S1-3	S4-6	S7-9		S10-11		S12-14		S15-17	
學校組別	1	1	2	2	2	2	3	3	2/3	2/3

1 = 收取最佳成績組別的學生；2 = 收取中等成績組別的學生 ；3 = 收取最弱成績組別的學生

6. 研究發現

i）不同持份者對通識目標與考評關係的觀感差異

表四：教師對通識科課程目標及師生對通識科文憑試是否有助目標的達成觀感比較（節錄及譯寫自 Leung, 2017）

1A. 就你個人的理解，LS 學習的目的是什麼？	認同目的	DSE 有助目標的達成		Mann-Whitney U test	Wilcoxon rank test	Spearman correlation
1B. 公開文憑試（DSE）是否有助目標的達成？	T1A（n=49）	T1B（n=49）	S1B（n=489）	T1B vs S1B	T1A vs T1B	T1A vs T1B
項目	Mean（SD）	Mean（SD）	Mean（SD）	Z(p)	Z(P)	r
學會生活	3.22 (.353)	2.92(.370)	2.94 (.465)	-.691 (.490)	-4.184 (.000**)	.379**
學會思考	3.17 (.482)	2.81 (.49)	2.90 (.547)	-1.045 (2.96)	-4.191 (.000**)	.373*
學會尊重	3.17 (.443)	2.69(.509)	2.93 (.556)	-2.979 (.003**)	-4.563 (.000**)	.174
h. 懂得從多角度思考，分辨不同意見背後的價值觀	3.36 (.525)	3.09(.694)	3.10 (.635)	-.168 (.866)	-2.676 (.007**)	.385**
i. 培養協作與溝通能力，寬容對待不同意見	3.08 (.566)	2.65(.72)	2.91 (.700)	-2.243 (.025*)	-3.257 (.001**)	.392**
j. 培養對社會有責任與承擔的公民	3.08 (.534)	2.44(.659)	2.80 (.767)	-3.288 (.001**)	-4.272 (.000**)	.179
各項平均數	3.19 (.370)	2.83 (.403)	2.91 (.458)	-1.419 (.156)	-5.029(.000**)	.331*

*p <.05, **p<.01
T1A= 教師對 1A 問題的回應； T1B= 教師對 1B 問題的回應； S1B= 學生對 1B 問題的回應
備註：Shapiro-Wilk 常態測試證實數據是非參數的。所有數據輸出使用 SPSS 的非參數測試工具。

教師高度認同通識科學習的目的，十項平均數於四個選項中達 3.19（SD=.370）（表四），然而對照於公開文憑試（下稱 DSE）是否有助目標的達成認同度相對較低 2.83（SD=.403）。當中能否達成學會尊重評分只為 2.69，j. 培養對社會有責任與承擔的公民為 2.44，i. 培養協作與溝通能力，寬容對待不同意見為 2.65。可見教師傾向認為 DSE 無助學會尊重的目標。學生認為 DSE 有助學會生活評分 2.94、學會思考 2.90 與學會尊重 2.93，平均分相若為 2.91（SD=.458）。教師跟學生對能否有助學會尊重觀感有數據上明顯的落差（M_T =2.69，

SD =.509 vs. M_S =2.93，SD =.556；z=2.979，p<.003**）。可見教師與學生評價 DSE 是否有助三組學習目標的達成有不同的認知與觀感。學生對三組學習目標概念模糊不清。

教師質性訪問引證量性發現結果，其他不同的利益相關者均同意學會生活，學會思考和學會尊重的課程目標，但每一個都僅限於目標範圍的某些部分。教育局官員（OS1&2）與學科專家均重視宏觀的目的及態度的培養。考評局 OS3 則表示：「…這個考試（三改四）已經變成了一個大學的入學試，入讀大學的入學試不能修讀很多的科目，因為水平要求相對較高…」，他們一方面重視學生態度培養，但要為大學的入學試水平及認受把關，指 DSE 不具評估學生價值觀的考題與標準。各持份者認同設科目標，但因考題設計，過濾了不可測量的態度與軟技能，選擇性地按照他們隱藏的目的來運作。 在不同利益相關者的心目中，目標和公開考試之間存在著一種理念和實施差距。

ii）實踐中的學習評估和考試評估策略

教學法方面，教師的教學策略採用考試為本的策略（3.57）多於學習為本策略（3.17）（表五）。作為直接操作者，教師和學生都認為考試導向策略更有效地獲得分數。教師大多引入生活與時事（3.69）作議題學習，導引清晰表達立場（3.61），採用與 DSE 要求及模式一致的形成性評估（3.60）。採用合作學習議題的頻率為 3.14，卻於認同有助學生獲取較佳成績明顯偏低 2.83（z=-3.138，p<.002**），可見學習為本的策略被視為次要。 教師採用妥協的策略，通過考評局的支持，縮小對明辨性思維（即批判性思維）學習和評估的差異，以務實的方式鼓勵在課堂上，形成性地使用總結性標準和評量標尺。「…基本上重視能力訓練多一些，而不是知識的灌輸（T10）」。城中各類持份者例如傳媒、政黨、補習社都積極提供議題教學援助，參與了通識科的學習過程。

觀課過程突顯大部份教師均懂得運用建構學習策略，導引學生有效學習。十課節教學內容均採用議題教學，多聚焦分組作正反立論與明辨性思維訓練，採用課前資料搜集、課堂討論或口頭報告及課後作書面報告。觀課 6/10 教師採用建構式教學，3/10 採用傳授式，1 位中五、中六時採建構式，中四則採用傳授式。然而只有 1/10 課堂包含創意解難與創新思維的運用，3/10 課堂師生發揮論證藝術。有教師認為傳授式可行：「合作學習是好事來的。…但是我會覺得他們（學生）自己所做的與我所給的相差不太遠…（T5）」。「…平時基本上我不會分組的，不會有合作學習…在有限時間裏我就會犧牲一些很理想的東西…（T6）」。然而，半數以上學校教師發揮集體備課與分工，預測年度考題形式及內容，分工負責考題及過程為學習準備。教師表示不難預測考題模型及內容，以深入讓學生進行學習。

OS1 表示：「*我們沒有說 assessment 怎樣考就怎樣去教⋯*」，而 OS3 則認為「*我們只能透過考試，尤其是題目、評分標準、要求等去 "inform" 老師。⋯我們會 inform 老師說，題目跟課程的關係是什麼⋯*」。考評局於學科起動過程的介入較積極主動，教育局相對較傳統。

表五：師生對使用通識科教學法頻率及對 DSE 效能影響的觀感比較（節錄及譯寫自 Leung, 2017）

2A. 你個人 / 科任教師採用下列教學方法的頻率為何？	2A: 頻率		2B: 效能	Mann-Whitney U test	Wilcoxon rank test	Spearman correlation
	S2A	T2A	T2B	S2A & T2A	T2A & T2B	T2A & T2B
2B. 就 DSE 的要求，下列教學方法的採用，是否有助學生獲取較佳成績？	Mean (SD)	Mean (SD)	Mean (SD)	z (p)	z (p)	r
學習為本策略	3.19 (.499)	3.17 (.356)	3.07 (.396)	-.645 (.519)	-1.676 (.094)	.545**
a. 提供合作學習，結合生活議題作交流與探究	3.24 (.713)	3.14 (.645)	2.83 (.601)	-1.165 (.244)	-3.138 (.002**)	.418**
b. 運用資訊科技協助學習、思考與交流	3.20 (.719)	3.16 (.657)	2.87 (.575)	-5.80 (.562)	-2.884 (.004**)	.345*
考試為本策略	3.29 (.478)	3.57 (.341)	3.38 (.394)	-4.028 (.000**)	-3.162 (.002**)	.373*
c. 直接講解傳授基礎知識及概念	3.44 (.611)	3.54 (.613)	3.02 (.668)	-1.263 (.206)	-4.642 (.000**)	.522**
e. 導引清晰表達立場，表達或書寫對議題具理據的意見	3.30 (.643)	3.61 (.492)	3.43 (.542)	-3.278 (.001**)	-2.183 (.029*)	.374**
f. 引入生活與時事作提問、討論或論證	3.37 (.653)	3.69 (.508)	3.43 (.580)	-3.44 (.001**)	-2.982 (.003**)	.363*
g. 運用考評局練習卷及 DSE 試題作教學藍本	3.10 (.796)	3.41 (.643)	3.50 (.548)	-2.571 (.010*)	-.894 (.371)	.433**
h. 採用與 DSE 要求及模式一致的形成性評估	3.26 (.734)	3.60 (.610)	3.48 (.623)	-3.249 (.001**)	-1.732 (.083)	.629**
各項平均數	3.24 (.440)	3.37 (.264)	3.23 (.345)	-2.056 (.040*)	-2.891 (.004**)	.488**

*p <.05, **p<.01

T2A= 教師對 2A 問題的回應； T2B= 教師對 2B 問題的回應； S2A= 學生對 2A 問題的回應

iii）師生對學生學習成果觀感的比較

表六展示教師與學生對 *c. 關注不同意見背後的價值觀，並能寬容對待*的評價有數據上的落差（T:2.76< S:2.95*）。師生均對 *h. DSE LS 考卷設計有效反映學生的多元學習能力*的評分非常之低，師生之間更有明顯的觀感差異（T:2.43> S:2.18*）。師生都認為學生對學習通識的興趣偏低（T:2.50 > S:2.48），並只為考試的需要而讀書（T:2.34 > S:2.30）。師生對考試影響學生學會生活的觀感有明顯的落差（T:2.77> S:2.69**），學生較教師更有負面的感受。然而，DSE 有助鼓勵學生 *i. 嘗試用不同的思維策略、角度，來解決問題*（T:3.10 > S:2.99），*l. 改變學習範式*（T:2.94 > S:2.87），*a. 對身邊事物作更深入的思考*（T:3.00 > S:2.98）。學生較善於學會思考（T:2.91，S:2.83），但弱於學會生活（T:2.77> S:2.69），而忽視學會尊重。

表六：師生對學生學習成果觀感的比較（譯自 Leung, 2017, P.102）

你是否認同現行 LS 考評對學生構成下列的影響？	Mann-Whitney U test		
	學生（S） *Mean (SD)*	教師（T） *Mean (SD)*	S vs T *z (p)*
對學會生活的影響	2.69 (.424)	2.77 (.431)	-3.443 (.001**)
a. 對身邊事物作更深入的思考	2.98 (.646)	3.00 (.612)	-.233 (.815)
b. 經常關注時事	3.00 (.800)	3.00 (.639)	-.169 (.866)
c. 關注不同意見背後的價值觀，並能寬容對待	2.95 (.658)	2.76 (.657)	-2.115 (.034*)
d. *對 LS 學習感興趣#*	2.48 (.842)	2.50 (.614)	-.117 (.907)
e. *不單只為考試的需要而讀書#*	2.30 (.838)	2.34 (.658)	-.405 (.685)
f. 個人獨立專題探究有助培養獨立思考及運用各科知識與能力#	2.85 (.713)	2.67 (.747)	-1.550 (.121)
g. *真實情境的考卷設計有助師生重視學習過程，包括建構知識及多作生活體驗#*	2.85 (.713)	2.67 (.747)	-1.550 (.121)
h. *DSE LS 考卷設計有效反映學生的多元學習能力#*	2.18 (.743)	2.43 (.736)	-2.026 (.043*)
對學會思考的影響	2.83 (.560)	2.91 (.469)	-.947 (.344)
i. 嘗試用不同的思維策略、角度，來解決問題	2.99 (.657)	3.10 (.544)	-1.008 (.314)
j. 改變死記硬背的學習方式	2.65 (.842)	2.70 (.647)	-.372 (.710)
k. 注重高階能力的掌握	2.80 (.727)	2.88 (.659)	-.628 (.530)
l. 現行 DSE LS 有助 學生改變學習的範式，例如思維運用	2.87 (.638)	2.94 (.592)	-.752 (.452)

*p <.05, ** p <.01； S= 學生、T= 教師； d, e, g, h 斜體標示 # = 項目文句已編輯（從負向轉為正向）

此外，教師較學生更認同 c. *學生愈能掌握 LS 標準參照及考核模式，愈有助獲取佳績*（T:3.20>
S:2.90**）（見表七），但不太認同 g. *應試策略與學習策略有很大分別，不能相容*（T:2.57>
S:2.31*）。教師也多認同 b. *DSE LS 有助教師改變教學的範式，例如以學生為本*（2.88），並
認同 a. *現行 DSE LS 有助 學生改變學習的範式，例如思維運用*（T:2.94、S:2.87）。

質性訪談發現，「*…通識在命題方面很公式化，只是方便評卷（S1）。*」學生 S3 也表示「*回答
公開試題目時會覺得把複雜問題簡單化。…會把黑白分得很清楚。*」教師 T10 表示：「*…課程
的內容覆蓋面太廣了，亦都焦點不算清晰。*」。OS5 表示考題「*問題來來去去都是差不多，
很容易摸索到答案的方法。*」，出現套用框架、背誦熱點議題與將複雜問題簡單化的兩極化不
良現象（OS2，OS8，S3）。大家基本認同共通能力中的思維能力提升及培養，但難於在紙筆
考題中加入創意及解決問題能力的考核（OS5，T2，T3）。OS4 説：「*他們應該未達到這個階
段的（解決問題或創意貫通跨領域看事物），因為我們見到大學生回來都要到第二或三年才有
見地，但不能抹殺新高中的同學思維是好了的。*」

表七：師生對通識科考評與本科學習目標的關係觀感與意見比較（節錄及譯寫自 Leung, 2017）

你對 LS 考評與本科學習目標的關係有何觀感與意見？	學生 (S) (n= 475)	Mann-Whitney U test	教師 (T) (n= 49)
	Mean SD)	*z(p)*	*Mean (SD)*
a. 現行 DSE LS **有助**學生改變學習的範式，例如思維運用	2.87 (.638)	-.752 (.452)	2.94 (.592)
b. 現行 DSE LS **有助**教師改變教學的範式，例如以學生為本	/	/	2.88 (.666)
c. 學生愈能掌握 LS 標準參照及考核模式，愈有助獲取佳績	2.90 (.723)	-2.762	3.20 (.577)
d. 個人獨立專題探究**有助**培養獨立思考及運用各科知識與能力	2.75 (.771)	-.458 (.647)	2.71 (.764)
e. DSE LS 考評模式、學校教學模式與學習目標相互一致 / DSE LS 的設計模式、內容與組織**能夠**促進優質學與教的實施及達至課程目標的良性環迴效果	2.85 (.713)	-1.550 (.121)	2.67 (.747)
f. 筆試的重點在評估考生的知識概念和思維運用，記憶與背誦**無助**提升考試成績 #	2.42 (.774)	-2.620	2.69 (.719)
g. 應試策略與學習策略有很大分別，**不能**相容	2.31 (.765)	-2.394 (.017*)	2.57 (.736)

*p <.05, **p<.01 斜體標示 # = 項目文句已編輯（從負向轉為正向）

7. 討論

i) 「目標、學與教及評估的一致性」政策多大程度有助廿一世紀能力的學習？

研究發現，開放性的思維能力運用考題，採用標準參照、成效為本的評估模型，可有效驅動，引導考試為本及學習為本的學與教歷程，達至廿一世紀能力（例如通識科設科的最初目標）的培育。新建立的中央評卷監控機制，確保能運用布魯姆分類（Bloom Taxonomy）（柯孫燦，2011）最低的五個層階評卷，及作具信度與效度的設題。然而，未能具備條件機制，為第六個創新層階作思維及價值觀領域評分。

數據與質性訪談反映，廿一世紀能力 ASK 目標獲得高度認同（T：3.19），佔 80% 紙筆模式的 DSE 卻對 ASK 產生篩選與割離作用，將寬廣的通識科課程目標有效地狹義化於較可操作的明辨性思維目標，對難於評分的價值觀、創意、解難與多元智能等排減。因此，直接參與者如教師和學生，將爭議性時事議題作考試和學習的重點是常態。其中約三分之二師生均同意考試模式與學校教學模式和學習目標相一致；應試策略與學習策略能相容。直接問責參與者如考評局更積極宣傳和支持教師，確保新學科可信性、公平性、有效性和獲公眾及院校認受。他們認為總結性評估可供教師發揮形成性功能，以改善學與教。間接參與者如教育局政策官員與學科專家，堅持自己的信念，指導教師的專業改進，卻較少提供總結性評估支援。不同的利益相關者根據其不同的立場、自身利益、信念和實際需要，對評估，教學法和課程週期採取各種不同的影響及參與。為此，OS2 慨歎：「*如果一個課程，讓社會人士自主參與太多，出來的結果就不會專業。*」

師生認同教師使用學習為本策略或考試為本策略的評分，均超越 3.17，說明現行 DSE 有助教師改變教學的範式。教師多採用 DSE 評估的要求和模式作為形成性的目的。考試為導向的策略運用率大於以學習為導向的策略，可預測的議題模型和內容知識，便成為用作論證技能的操練，導引學生掌握具有模型和形式的論證性寫作的程序性知識。

政策的實踐有助使用形成性評估來準備最終的總結性考試，學校更多地進行集體備課，分工為學生展開深度探究學習的歷程。同時教師於學與教過程，形成性地使用總結性評估。問卷數據及課堂觀察所得引證開放性的議題式考題及標準參照，讓學生有更多的參與及思考。也有教師將價值觀納入問題探究，為培育價值觀學習提供反饋。示例反映，只要緊扣 ASK 目標，廿一世紀能力能透過情境建構，得以有效學習。再者，中央雙閱卷員評分制度，通過統一評分會議，就每個問題的評級標準和繁瑣的標準達成共識，加強了教師之間對議題評分的討論及專業對話。

然而，政策推行也帶來意想不到的效果：

A. 外部和內部專業認受縮窄了廿一世紀能力學習的目標：採用紙筆考評的廿一世紀能力學習，於國際評估上缺乏示例。新設的通識跨學科要求嚴謹、具信度與效度的國際學術水平認證，考評局應用國際較成熟的布魯姆評估標尺，過濾了難於測量的學會生活和學會尊重元素，透過時事性議題，集中學習明辨性思維。

B. 評估與課程模型縱橫連結尚欠一致：不設教科書使學與教內容欠專業梳理及監管，教學法受紙筆考題主導而傾向單一。具跨學科建構學習的獨立專題探究（IES），因只佔總體分數 20% 而不受重視。紙筆模式考題只局限於明辨性思維，未成功確立學理模型以導引理想的通識科政策施行。

通識科實踐雖然出現偏差，誤入自利的批判性思維訓練，不少考題塑造了思維二分法的趨勢（Leung, 2017），但是，推行通識科短短數年已被本地及海外高校認同與接受，數據顯示約三分之二師生認同課程追求評估、學與教及課程目標連結一致，跟當局中期檢討 87% 教師認同結果相近。結果發現，成效為本（Outcome-based）及考評推動（Exam-driven）現象明顯，考試倒流效應深刻地影響學與教，那與國際教育例如歐洲（Cort, 2014）的現象一致。總結性評估與形成性評估，在有意識的連結下能相互一致，具推動廿一世紀能力學習的成效。可見以廿一世紀能力學習為目標的成效為本考評機制，有待進一步開發與利用。

ii）通識科評估與課程政策，為推行 STEM 教育帶來什麼啟示？

研究發現廿一世紀能力的考評模型具有強大的驅動學與教功能。儒家社會的文化背景，與及國際評比潮流，賦予高風險的總結性評估帶動形成性評估的橫向一致性目標，同時成效為本的考試成績及問責要求也具備指導學與教的範式變化功能，支持廿一世紀能力目標的學習，使目標、學與教及成效結果追求縱向連結。因此，參考通識科推行經驗，如能以總結性評估層級標準作為規劃與檢視形成性的學習過程，重視建構學習的經歷，最終能達至有效的產出。

至今國際文獻尚欠 STEM 教育的評估實證研究及統一認同的評估機制（Tan & Leong, 2014；Popham, 2003），而相關通識教育實踐中的評估政策及機制，可說具備實證研究的參考作用。由於 STEM 教育與通識科追求廿一世紀能力學習的目標一致（許漢榮，2017），其教育目標有利於提升學生的創造力以及問題解決能力，現行的通識教育，則以批判性思維學習為重點，二者可產生互補作用。

研究發現通識科考評達成設科的狹義目標，同時亦帶來意想不到的不良效果，引入 STEM 教育將有助補足現行跨學科課程手腦並用、科學探究、創意及解難成份的不足，矯正過程走向兩極化思維及程序性思維模型的訓練 (Leung, 2017)。分析通識科成功起動的關鍵，在於聚焦確立設科目標，並採用成效為本的評估策略驅動，評估與課程縱橫連結，導引總結性評估與形成性評估雙結合，成功引入爭議性議題的學習，普及到課堂去。因此，原有的明辨性思維目標與教學可保持下來，重點於優化能舉一反三的教學示例之外，可加入創意及解難學習的內容。筆者整理表八之現行通識科實施狀況，並建議加入 STEM 教育內容。

表八：現行通識科與建議 STEM 教育比較

比較項目	現行通識科	STEM 教育
能力培育	明辨性（批判性）思維	創造力及解難能力
成效產出	爭議性時事論證短文	專題探究成品或完成指定任務
課程	六大單元及課程指引	中央系統課程指引及多元校本課程
內容	熱點時事及恆常性議題；社會科學為重點；不設教科書	研發具學理的 STEM 課程示例與教科書，提供能舉一反三的跨學科概念與教材運用
學習要素	議題探究、爭議性時事議題、論證立場、跨單元、關鍵詞概念等	問題為本、情境任務為基礎。科學探究、手腦並用、真實評量、科技統整、跨學科、科學原理與規律等
考評	紙筆考試 80% 獨立專題探究（IES）20%	紙筆考試 50% 獨立專題探究 (IES) 配以小組成果展現 50%
評估機制	中央雙閱卷員監察紙筆考卷機制	中央評審員制度，監察與評核專題報告及作口語交流過程錄影
評估標尺	布魯姆分類（Bloom Taxonomy）至分析和評鑑	布魯姆分類至創意、通達與解難。理論與實踐結合，構建統一的認可機制與標尺

倘若預測未來 STEM 學習必不可少，當於公開試中，加入 STEM 教育成份。只有讓公開試的標準參照評估，加入 STEM 教育的評價標準，並於學習的過程，運用評價量規，不斷地作適切性的反饋（Belland, Walker & Kim, 2017；Lin, et. al., 2015; Lucas, 2016），才具普及推行 STEM 教育的功能。將 STEM 教育作為必修必考的通識科部份學習內容，採成效為本的評估，將有助與形成性歷程結合，有效促進廿一世紀能力全方位的學習。

8. 總結

通識科創新性地採用國際廿一世紀能力學習評估理念，以目標、學與教及評估一致的政策，確立跨學科學與教模型。評估機制成功建立起學科及達成設立學科之初的 ABC 目標，卻無意識地誤入偽批判性思維學習的死胡同。同時跨學科本意將文理學科融合，實踐卻聚焦了社會科學，弱化了自然科學和人文學科。評估與課程的縱橫模型雖然尚未能有效作無縫銜接，但已有九年實踐經驗的通識科經受考驗後，終能獲得國際與本港高校及教師認可與接受。只要從專業角度，透過實證研究作深入檢視，作出優化、調整及矯正，讓總結性評估及形成性評估能結合一致，目標與建構學習將能連結以達成設科目標。STEM 教育有助學生達成「文中有理、理中有文」的設科目標，能透過優化現行議題探究，加入 STEM 教育，採用成效為本的評估導引建構情境學習，相信可以達成通識科的有效目標。STEM 教育重視在科技領域實行廿一世紀能力的學習，包括在生活中辨析難題，發揮創意解難能力，激發自學精神，科探過程的溝通、協作與互助等，那與通識科一脈相承，分別是 STEM 教育沒有強制成為公開試的一部份。本研究論證國際考評潮流在於評估能與能力學習結合，因此，隨著 STEM 教育的重視，遲早將加入正規課程。正規課堂學習必然加入成效為本的考評，並於課程推行過程中，提供適切及具建設性的反饋。因此，研究與參考通識課程目標、學習與評估適切一致的經驗，將有助防範重蹈覆轍，避免浪費機遇與資源。

參考文獻

柯孫燦（2011）。〈考評拆解〉。香港考試及評核局。（明報於２０１１年９月22日轉載此原文）。擷取自 http://www.hkeaa.edu.hk/DocLibrary/HKDSE/HKDSE_articles/LS_2011/LS_20110922.pdf

范斯淳、游光昭（2016）。〈科技教育融入STEM課程的核心價值與實踐〉。《教育科學研究期刊》第六十一卷第二期，頁 153-183。

許漢榮（2017 年 11 月）。〈STEM 教育的策劃與實踐：以三所本地小學為例〉。論文發表於「世界教育研究學會會議暨香港教育研究學會國際研討會 2017(WERA-HKERA 2017)：當代世界的創新、改革與教育變革」，香港教育大學，香港，中國。

課程發展議會、香港考試及評核局（CDC/HKEAA）。（2007，2014 修訂）。〈通識教育科：課程及評估指引（中四至中六）〉。擷取自 http://334.edb.hkedcity.net/doc/chi/curriculum/LS%20C&A%20Guide_updated_c.pdf

Adamson, F., & Darling-Hammond, L. (2015). Policy pathways for twenty-first century skills. In P. Griffin & E. Care (Eds.), *Assessment and teaching of century skills: Methods and approach* (pp. 293—310). Dordrecht: Springer.

Assessment Reform Group. (ARG). (2002). *Assessment for learning: Ten principles*. London: Nuffield Foundation.

Belland, B. R., Walker, A. E. & Kim, N. J. (2017). A Bayesian Network Meta-Analysis to Synthesize the Influence of Contexts of Scaffolding Use on Cognitive Outcomes in STEM Education. *Review of Educational Research.* December 2017, Vol. 87, No. 6, pp. 1042—1081. DOI: 10.3102/0034654317723009

Black, P., & Wiliam, D. (1998). Inside the black box: raising standards through classroom assessment [electronic version]. *Phi Delta Kappan*, 80, 139—418.

Broadfoot, P. (2007). *An introduction to assessment*. Continuum International Publishing Group.

Coniam, D. (2011). The double marking of Liberal Studies in the Hong Kong public examination system. *New Horizons in Education*, Vol.59, No.2, October 2011.

Cort, P. (2014). Europeanisation of curricula in Europe: policy and practice. *European Educational Research Journal,* Volume 13 Number 5 2014.

Creswell, J.W. and Clark, V.L.P. (2011). *Designing and conducting mixed methods research*. 2nd Edition, London: Sage.

Hong Kong: Education Bureau. (EDB). (2010). *The new senior secondary curriculum Liberal Studies parents' handbook*. Retrieved from http://334.edb.hkedcity.net/doc/eng/ls_parent_handbook_eng.pdf.

Hong Kong Education Bureau (EDB). (2015, June 8) Panel on education discussion on *"The Liberal Studies subject under the new senior secondary curriculum"*. LC paper No. CB (4)1098/14-15(01)

Gipps, C. V. (1994). *Beyond testing: Towards a theory of educational assessment.* London; Washington, D.C.: Falmer Press.

Griffin, P., McGaw, B., & Care, E. (Eds.) (2012). *Assessment and teaching of 21st century skills.* Dordrecht: Springer.

Gulikers, J. T. M., Biemans, H. J.A., Wesselink, R., & Wel, M. (2013). Aligning formative and summative assessments: A collaborative action research challenging teacher conceptions. *Studies in educational evaluation* 39, 116-124.

Leung, L. (2013). An inquiry of teachers' perception on the relationship between higher-order thinking nurturing and LS public assessment in Hong Kong. *Hong Kong Teachers' Centre Journal*, Vol. 12. P.183-215.

Leung, L. (2017). *Aligning summative assessment with curriculum aims of Liberal Studies in Hong Kong.* Dissertation. Doctor of Education, University of Bristol.

Lin, K., Yu, K., Hsiao, H. Chu, Y., Chang, Y. & Chien, Y. (2015). Design of an assessment system for collaborative problem solving in STEM education. *J. Comput. Educ.* 2(3):301-322. doi 10.1007/s40692-015-0038-x

Looney, J. W. (2011). Integrating formative and summative assessment: Progress toward a seamless system? *OECD Education Working Paper No. 58.*

Lucas, B. (2016). A Five-Dimensional Model of Creativity and its Assessment in Schools, *Applied Measurement in Education.* 29:4, 278-290, DOI:10.1080/08957347.2016.1209206

McKinsey Global Institute (MGI) (2017). *Jobs lost, jobs gained: workforce transitions in a time of automation.*

Organization for Economic Co-operation and Development. (OECD). (2013). *Synergies for better learning: An international perspective on evaluation and assessment*. Final synthesis report from the review. Retrieved from http://www.oecd.org/education/school/oecdreviewonevaluationandassessmentframeworksfori mprovingschooloutoomcs.htm

Popham, J. (2003). *Teach better, test better: The instructional role of assessment*. Alexandria VA: Association for Supervision and Curriculum Development.

Tan, A. & Leong, W. F. (2014). Mapping Curriculum Innovation in STEM Schools to Assessment Requirements: Tensions and Dilemmas, *Theory Into Practice,* 53:1, 11-17, DOI: 10.1080/00405841.2014.86211

TSE, P.H.I. (2010). *Order behind disorder in school change: Dynamical systems theory and process structures.* 354 pages. Germany: Lambert Academic Publishing. April. ISBN (978-3-8383-3395-3)

United Nations Educational, Scientific and Cultural Organization (UNESCO). (2014). *Learning to live together Education policies and realities in the Asia-Pacific*. UNESCO Bangkok Office. Retrieved from http://unesdoc.unesco.org/images/0022/002272/227208e.pdf

Voogt, J. & Roblin, N. P. (2012). A comparative analysis of international frameworks for 21st Century competences: Implications for national curriculum policies. *Journal of Curriculum*.

Wyatt-Smith, C. W., Klenowski, V., & Colbert, P. (eds.) (2014). *Designing Assessment for Quality Learning,* Springer Science+Business Media. Dordrecht ISBN: 978-94-007-5901-5 (Print) 978-94-007-5902-2 (Online)

第三部份：

英文研究論文

ALIGNING SUMMATIVE ASSESSMENT WITH CURRICULUM AIMS OF LIBERAL STUDIES IN HONG KONG

Leung Lai Sim

Doctor of Education (EdD)
University of Bristol
A dissertation submitted to the University of Bristol in accordance with
the requirements of the degree of Doctor of Education (EdD) in
the Faculty of Social Science and Law

January 2017

ABSTRACT

This research aims to understand the extent to which the Hong Kong Diploma of Secondary Education Liberal Studies (LS) examination is aligned with the curriculum to develop students' 21st century skills. In particular, it examines different stakeholders' (students, teachers and policy makers) views on the relationship between LS examination, pedagogy and curriculum aims.

I conducted questionnaires survey with 42 schools in Hong Kong, 35 semi-structured individual interviews with different stakeholders including students, teachers and policy-makers, and 10 classroom observations.

It was found that standards-referenced summative assessment and monitoring mechanism can lever critical thinking, broaden students' minds and arouse students'social awareness. However, assessment and curriculum were not aligned. Pedagogy was not appropriately balanced between the pragmatic short-term goals and the ideal long-term aims for nurturing 21st century skills. The realization of the official aims of LS processes bred unpredicted side effect. Direct stakeholders focused on exam-oriented teaching and learning for higher scores. Formative use of summative criteria and rubrics in class encouraged argumentative procedural drilling in a pragmatic manner; much less concern about interdisciplinary mind nurturing. Students are relatively strong in learning to think but weak in learning to live and neglect learning to respect. Indirect stakeholders, policymakers for instance, believed in theory they espoused, yet paid lip service only on 21st century skills practices. As a result, LS did not help nurturing responsible independent thinkers as intended.

Synergy should exist between curriculum and assessment. Aligning summative assessment with holistic curriculum aims through formative functions for learning ought to be the explorations forwards. The underlying guiding principles are the integration of attitude, skills and knowledge, and aligning public examinations with curriculum aims horizontally and vertically. Further research should be done on the theories and practices of assessment literacy and the practical alignment of curriculum and assessment.

ACKNOWLEDGMENTS

It is the love of Hong Kong that strengthens me to accomplish breakthrough step by step towards my mission. Really, it is a miracle to finish the enquiry and the thesis on the complex changing theme of public examination in Liberal Studies under the unique circumstances of 'One country, two systems'In Hong Kong. Contributions from the brilliant teachers in Liberal Studies are to be praised. They hold idealistic espoused vision but struggle for their students, reshaping their theories-in-use to overcome the high-stakes interdisciplinary core subject examination. Without the bold trying, there will not be the bitter fruit. Only that we shall overcome, the sweet fruit is ahead.

I have to take this chance to express my heartfelt thanks to many people who support this research. If not for their support and kind encouragement, it may not be so fruitful. Dr. Guoxing Yu has inspired me on the research methodology, data collection and the final stage in formulating the structure of the research report. I am grateful for his trust on my ability to overcome the stress of tight deadline. As my spiritual supportive supervisor, Professor Broadfoot enlightened me with brilliant ideas in the field of assessments. Her professional critique and analysis on the 'dark alleys and blind bends' illuminate my blind spots. It is important to recognize Dr. Tse. He supported me not only in proofreading my article, but plays the role as a mentor to guide me out of the black box these few months. His academic achievement on the dynamical systems theory matches my ontology. He points my way out and suggests theories to accomplish relational breakthroughs. Professor Lam, Dr. Cheng, Kirt, Ho, Alan, and many others offered me hands to overcome various aspects of technical difficulties. It was beyond my expectation to have over 50 schools' feedback on questionnaires responses. I am lucky to have met teachers and students from six sample schools. They generously shared their teaching and learning experiences in hope to help improve LS curriculum. Other stakeholders' sharing also contributes significantly to my research.

I hope the strengths and pitfalls revealed from the case of Liberal Studies in Hong Kong can be useful for future assessments for learning, of learning, and as learning in this interdisciplinary curriculum improvement. Let us uphold the goodwill to align summative assessment with 21st century skills practices. Hope we can have further research and improvement for the infant baby of Liberal Studies in Hong Kong.

TABLE OF CONTENTS

LIST OF ACRONYMS

AaL	Assessment as learning
A level	Advanced level
AfL	Assessment for learning
AoL	Assessment of learning
ASK	Attitudes, skills and knowledge
ASL LS	Advanced Supplementary Level of Liberal Studies
CDC	Curriculum Development Council
CPS	collaborative problem solving
DSE	Diploma of Secondary Education
EC	Education Commission
EDB	Education Bureau
EU	European Union
GCSE	General Certificate of Secondary Education
HKSAR	Hong Kong Special Administrative Region
HKALE	Hong Kong Advanced Level Examination
HKDSE	Hong Kong Diploma of Secondary Education
HKEAA	Hong Kong Examinations and Assessment Authority
HKedCity	Hong Kong Education City
HKIEd	Hong Kong Institute of Education
ICILS	International Computer and Information Literacy Study
IEA	International Association for the Evaluation of Educational Achievement
ICT	Information and communications technology
LS	Liberal Studies
MOI	Medium of Instruction
OECD	Organization of Economic Cooperation and Development
PIRLS	Progress in International Reading Literacy Study
PISA	Programme for International Student Assessment
PRC	People's Republic of China
SBA	School-based Assessment
SD	Standard Deviation
TIMSS	Trends in International Mathematics and Science Study
UK	The United Kingdom
US	The United States
UNESCO	United Nations Educational, Scientific and Cultural Organization

LIST OF TABLES

LIST OF FIGURES

Chapter 1   INTRODUCTION

1.1 Introduction to the study

We are living in an era of complexity; turbulence and uncertainty are common (Amadio, Opertti, & Tedesco, 2015). Globalization, conflicts, competitions, unemployment, demographic aging trends, balance of power, changes and new mode of decision-making by multi-level governance are the global and local disturbing phenomena. Education, which plays an important role in helping construct social settlements (Robertson, 2012), is the focus of equitable development for all nations. Education reforms have swept through the world in the last two decades; consequentially with emerging 21st century skills frameworks and new forms of assessments appearing. Hong Kong Special Administrative Region (Hong Kong) of The People's Republic of China (PRC) is an international city. It faces keen competition from cities outside and new demands for self-administration inside. Nurturing quality citizens and higher-order skills talents for sustaining development is the crucial aim of the city. Aligned with the education reform blueprint, the New Senior Secondary (NSS) Liberal Studies (LS) has become a compulsory subject in the new curriculum. LS was made one of the key subjects in Hong Kong Diploma of Secondary Education (HKDSE) for all students from 2009 onwards. After six years of implementation, the public LS examination is claimed to have aligned with the curriculum aims. Grounded on the concept of alignment, this thesis inquires on how and the extent to which LS examination enables teaching and learning. Perceptions of stakeholders form the basis of judgment. Stakeholders are the students, teachers, parents, policy-makers and others such as curriculum experts. Data evidences were collected using mixed-methods. The research aims to discover gaps, to propose how gaps should be bridged, and to validate the role of public assessments towards realizing educational goals in 21st century for NSS students.

1.2 Research context in Hong Kong

For historical reasons, Hong Kong remains very different from Mainland China, despite the return of sovereignty of the British colonial Hong Kong to China in 1997. The political situation in Hong Kong experienced great change (Chou, 2012). Under the principle of "One country, two systems" after the return, Hong Kong maintains a capitalist economy while PRC runs a socialist system; wrestling before convergence into mutual understanding, inevitable power struggle for change of usual practices, and reluctance to adapt to a different political, social, cultural and economic development are not difficult to envisage.

Meanwhile, the world is in a stage of multi-polarization, induced by social instability, climate change, and economic globalization (Ball, 1998; 2008). The civic society demands bottom-up influences endorsed with top-down policy-making empowerment. Governments have to face a 'crisis of legitimation' (Usher, 1996). This critical 'moment' (Ball, 1990) calls for nurturing quality, responsible talented citizens. Educational reform becomes a major inclination all over the world. The 21st century skills campaign worldwide seeks ways of equipping a new generation with aptitudes such as independent thinking, effective communication, and flexibility. They are a generation who know to observe mutual respect and capable of higher-order-thinking. If successful, educational reform solves regional problems and drives national development engines.

The top priority of education reform is to enhance educational quality to match with economic goals (Lo, 2010; Tang, 2011). Next is to solve social problems such as inequality, aging issues, and conflicts within groups (Dale, 1997; Fischer, Bol & Pribesh, 2011). Third is to respond to the demand for accountability and responsibility (Y. C. Cheng, 2009). Fourth is to call for mindful learning and teaching for quality citizens (Y. C. Cheng, 2013; Hargreaves & Shirley, 2009). Complementing the reform, education has ushered into a new orthodoxy of testing, accountability, regional and national comparisons, and data-driven decision-making (Yeung, Lam, Leung & Lo, 2012).

Locally, the socio-political underpinning under the 'One country, two systems' principle led Hong Kong to become the meeting place for two conflicting ideologies and powers. The polarized controversy shattered harmony, if any, and tore apart the territory from inside (Lau, 2011), breeding recent youth advocacy for the city's independence, the Umbrella Movement, the confrontations between the Blue-camp and the Yellow-camp, the demands for universal suffrage, forcing the government to withdraw the Moral and National Education curriculum and so on. Political and educational preferences in Hong Kong are being divided. The macro global, national and local political influences constitute the backdrop for the implementation of the NSS LS curriculum.

Education reform shifted public concerns from seeing *"knowledge as product to knowledge as process"* (Yeung, et. al., 2012, p.30). This constitutes legitimacy for NSS LS to nurture higher order skills, positive attitudes and concrete knowledge for discussion, debates and critical thinking. Nine 'generic skills' are emphasized (Curriculum Development Council, 2001). Only with successful cultivation of 21st century skills, that effective thinking can turn new generations into active problem-solvers and responsible citizens. International educational assessment trends may alter local reform outcome; that have to be included in this research and are described in the following section.

1.3 Education assessment issues around the world

Globalization has increased competition and activated greater demand for mutual understanding and collaboration between interacting economies. Education assessment is the practice of collecting evidences of student learning achievements. Educators and scholars agree that the learning power or capacity and the desire-to-learn dispositions structure lifelong learning inclination of students, which sets the precondition for educational success. Without better assessment, there would be no effective education reform. Large-scale examination systems and a criterion-referenced output-based approach have been levering the learning process recently. International examples include collaborative problem solving in the *Programme for International Student Assessment* (PISA), using common core standards for instruction and assessment in the US (Marzano, Yanoski, Hoegh, & Simms, 2013), building up 21st century skills framework with the *Assessment and Teaching of 21st Century Skills* (ATC21S) project in six countries (Griffin & Care, 2015a). There is also a constructing the global post-2015 development agenda on UNESCO's 195 member states (United Nations Educational, Scientific and Cultural Organization, 2014a). They all focus on the role of assessment to improve critical thinking, creativity, problem solving, collaboration, self-directed learning and other lifelong learning competency. Summative assessment of 21st century skills to enhance students learning is regarded as a shared enterprise. Different kinds of stakeholders come together not only to realize educational goals, but also to promote and create new ways for better learning. Nevertheless, the movement may devolve into fads. Fads depict weak fidelity to the original intent and may shortchange for an ephemeral pursuit of skills (Rotherham & Willingham, 2010).

1.4 Curriculum and assessment system of NSS LS in Hong Kong

The 'One country, two systems' (capitalism and socialism) is unique to Hong Kong; no other country has such experience before. Conflicts are predictable over different conceptualizations of key concepts and understandings of diverse culture, ideologies, history, economic development and political situation. Mutual trust, understanding with interdisciplinary mind, and reciprocated empathetic citizenship are in urgent need. The city needs students to become logical, rational, and responsible individuals who have enough basic knowledge to justify and to choose their future based on the contextual situation of the society, the country and the world. The ideal function of NSS LS is to promote good citizenship and interdisciplinary-mind (Fung & Su, 2016).

1.4.1 Overview of the education and assessment reform in Hong Kong

The blueprint of 'Learning to Learn', 'Life-long learning' and 'Whole-person development' education reform in Hong Kong was laid out in 2000 (Education Commission, 2000) starting with basic education. The policies of *'Learning for life – learning through life'* emphasized building a lifelong learning society while the policy paper of *'Learning to learn: The Way Forward in Curriculum Development'* helped students build up their capabilities to study independently (Kennedy, 2011). The Hong Kong assessment-related reform agenda, which favours greater integration of assessment with teaching and learning and more focus on learning processes, was first outlined in the Curriculum Development Council document in 2001 (CDC, 2001). Later, after a multiple-strategy and multiple-stakeholders' consultation, a 3-year senior secondary and 4-year undergraduate academic system ("3+3+4") was announced (Education and Manpower Bureau, 2005, p.1). In 2009, the number of public examinations secondary students need to take was reduced to only one public examination in Form 6. Without screening and other choices, all students have to study four core subjects and at least two elective subjects in the new 3-year senior secondary school. LS is one of the four core NSS subjects. All senior students attempting DSE will be assessed.

Common to the Short-term Review in April 2013, the Medium-term Review in April 2014 and the Medium-term Review and Beyond in 2015, one of the guiding principles for the renewal of New Academic Structure (NAS) in all subjects is to *"Align assessment with curriculum aims, learning objectives, curriculum design and expected learning outcomes"* (Education Bureau, 2015a). The Medium-term Review on LS shows that 87% of teachers agreed or strongly agreed that the public examination of LS is aligned well with the curriculum aims and design (ibid). Nevertheless, as a nascent subject for all senior secondary students in the first five years period, the undesirable occurrence of exam-driven learning and teaching in practice emerged as anticipated and had to be resolved.

1.4.2 How ASL LS inform NSS LS

The British colonial government decided to promote students' social awareness of the 1997 sovereignty transition by introducing the Advanced Supplementary Level of Liberal Studies (ASL LS) (Bray and Koo 2005, p. 169 cited in Fung & Yip, 2010) as an optional subject for Advanced Level students (Grade 12 & Grade 13) in 1992. The Curriculum Development Council announced in 2009 the reintroduction of LS that would become mandatory for all senior secondary school students; the new compulsory subject was intended to develop a sense of citizenship (Fung & Yip, 2010). *"LS aims to liberate students' autocratic thought by providing them with a great variety of studies"* (Curren, 2007, p.12 cited in ibid, p.18). Implementation and impact of the two curricula were different; ASL LS was designated to higher abilities students whereas NSS LS was designed for all. In 1996/97, only about 6.5% of the advanced level students opt to sit for the subject in public examination, and also, the ASL examination allowed students to skip some of the modules. Students selected two modules for deep learning in relation to Independent Enquiry Study (IES). Hui's analysis of ASL LS examination reports (1994-2005) has presented the public-exam-oriented subject experience (Hui, 2007), featured emphasis on contextualized knowledge, and stressed on basic facts; samples were highlighted in the examinations. The textbooks provided baseline knowledge and concepts for teaching and learning, which were aligned with the way students were asked in public examination. The curriculum and assessment systems of NSS LS is not the same as the ASL LS; this is discussed below.

1.4.3 The LS curriculum

LS aims to cultivate students' independent thinking, positive values and attitudes, social awareness and adaptability to change by borrowing knowledge and perspectives from other subjects to study authentic contemporary issues (Curriculum Development Council and the Hong Kong Examinations and Assessment Authority, 2007, updated in 2015, p.3). Factual knowledge of LS is not the focus but the thinking skills are of greater concern. The curriculum aims, teaching and learning and assessment need to be aligned (ibid, p.130). The nature of LS is described as follow:

> *"Liberal Studies plays a unique role in the NSS curriculum by helping students to connect concepts and knowledge across different disciplines, to look at things from more than one single perspective, and to study issues not covered by any single disciplines. It is more than just about developing thinking skills and positive values and attitudes. The nature of Liberal*

Studies is different from that of General Education or Liberal Education in universities. It is a curriculum organization that suits the curriculum contexts of Hong Kong and achieves the learning goals identified for senior secondary education." (EMB, 2005, p.6-7)

LS is considered a modular curriculum, which provides teachers and students with self-reliance and flexibility in teaching and learning (Antony Leung, 2012, p.156). Three areas of study are incorporated in six modules. There are themes and key questions for enquiry (CDC/HKEAA, 2007, updated in 2015). The themes cover different issues that arouse heated discussion and debates in the society, the nation, and the world, and also the knowledge students acquired from different disciplines. With those, students are driven to explore things around them and issues which affect their lives (ibid, EDB, 2015b, June 8). Generic skills are highlighted as *"learn to acquire knowledge; construct knowledge; and apply knowledge to solve new problems"* (CDC, 2001, p.24). The overall curriculum structure in LS is outlined in Table 1.1.

Table 1.1 Overall curriculum structure in LS

Areas of Study	Modules	Independent Enquiry Study (IES)
Self and Personal Development	Module 1: Personal Development and Interpersonal relationships	Students are required to conduct an IES making use of the knowledge and perspectives gained from the three Areas of Study.
Society and Culture	Module 2: Hong Kong Today Module 3: Modern China Module 4 : Globalization	
Science, Technology and the Environment	Module 5: Public Health Module 6: Energy Technology and the Environment	

(CDC/HKEAA, 2007, updated in 2015, p.11)

Attitude and skills are the priority of LS curriculum aims. Curriculum change and innovation is great in Hong Kong (Yeung, 2012). School-based curriculum development is encouraged with diverse learning processes. Bloom's taxonomy (Bloom, Engelhart, Furst and Krathwohl, 1956; Krathwohl, 2002) is widely used for designing classroom questioning or drafting assessment items because the theory is helpful in developing various levels of cognitive abilities in the students (Yeung, 2012, p.42). According to the trio dimensions of attitude, skills and knowledge nurturing, I analyzed the priority of the components in the curriculum aims in Table 1.2. The results show that attitude is the first, skills is second, and knowledge is the third.

Table 1.2 Priority analysis on the three dimensions of the aims in LS

	Aims of LS	Dimension focus		
		1st	2nd	3rd
a)	to enhance students'understanding of themselves, their society, their nation, the human world and the physical environment;	K	A	S
b)	to enable students to develop multiple perspectives on perennial and contemporary issues in different contexts (e.g. cultural, social, economic, political and technological contexts);	A	S	K
c)	to help students become independent thinkers so that they can construct knowledge appropriate to changing personal and social circumstances,	S	A	K
d)	to develop in students a range of skills for life-long learning, including critical thinking skills, creativity, problem-solving skills, communication skills and information technology skills;	S	A	K
e)	to help students appreciate and respect diversity in cultures and views in a pluralistic society and handle conflicting values; and	A	S	K
f)	to help students develop positive values and attitude towards life, so that they can become informed and responsible citizens of society, the country and the world.	A	S	K
Remark: A =Attitude; S=Skills; K=Knowledge Item priorities: 1st : A; 2nd : S; 3rd :K		3 A 2 S 1 K	3 A 3 S /	/ 1 S 5 K

(CDC/HKEAA, 2007, updated in 2015, p.5)

The initial aims of LS were published in a parents' handbook (EDB, 2010). EDB introduced LS as a core subject under the NSS curriculum to let every student have the opportunities:

A. *to enhance their awareness of their society, their nation, the human world and the physical environment, as well as develop positive values (Awareness);*

B. *to broaden their knowledge base and expand their perspectives on things (Broadening);*

C. *to connect knowledge across different disciplines and enhance their critical thinking skills (Connection skills & Critical thinking).*

(ibid, p.24)

The curriculum intends to cultivate new generations to be responsive to the ever-changing world. Students learn how to learn, how to live, how to think, how to respect each other through interdisciplinary mind nurturing, by issue-based enquiry in classroom learning and Independent Enquiry Study (IES).

1.4.4 The LS examination

The LS syllabus was revamped from the Advanced Supplementary Level of Liberal Studies (ASL LS). It plays a unique role in achieving the learning goals identified for senior secondary education (EDB, 2005). *The New Senior Secondary curriculum and assessment Guide (Secondary4-6): Liberal Studies*, jointly prepared by the Curriculum Development Council (CDC) and the Hong Kong Examinations and Assessment Authority (HKEAA), highlights the alignment of teaching, learning and assessment. Below is briefly the aims, mode, content and organization of LS assessment components.

The *'Learning outcomes and assessment objectives'* (CDC/HKEAA, 2007, 2015, p. 123-4) analysis shows that the first dimension focus of learning outcomes include 7 items of attitude, 6 generic skills, and 2 knowledge assessment rubrics. Students are expected to spend more time on attitude nurturing and thinking skills. Attitudes concerning value and quality personal growth are highlighted. The objectives are equivalent to the 21st century skills framework of learning (Saavedra and Opfer, 2012; Voogt & Roblin, 2012), namely, how to live, to think and to respect each other.

Knowledge is expected to be contextualized, multi-disciplinary, also personally and socially constructed. Students are supposed to refer to a wide range of information sources such as newspapers, television programs, web-based materials, books, learning materials, or self-experiences for discussion on contemporary issues. 'Textbooks' are not necessary to students (EDB, 2010) while sample papers, practice papers and past examination papers (HKEAA, 2015b) are used to inform learning. Factual knowledge of LS is not the focus but the thinking skills are of greater concern. There is no obligatory discipline knowledge or theories. Only exemplar thematic-enquiries with guiding principles are provided.

Public examination and school-based assessment (SBA) are the two essential components of the summative assessment of LS (HKEAA, 2015a). The skills required are *"to display sound understanding of the issues, presented with data and evidences"* (HKEAA, 2015b). The public examination marks constitute 80% of the total LS marks, to be awarded to candidates who demonstrate abilities to apply appropriate thinking skills according to Bloom Taxonomy (Or, 2011) to build up knowledge from a body of relevant facts.

HKEAA has built a special monitoring mechanism to ensure validity and reliability in marking without 'model-answers'; the marking system is designed to ensure 'fairness' (Coniam, 2010; HKEAA, 2012). Credibility was confirmed (Fung & Tong, 2013). Standards-referenced reporting (SRR) is adopted for grading assessment results. Trained markers must pass a qualifying test. Discrepancy monitoring was achieved with 'Double-marking arrangement' of scanned answer scripts to be scored on screen at marking centres. That means at least eight experienced markers, each for different sections, will separately mark each candidate's examination paper. This ensures the 'reliability' and 'fairness' in marking.

The examination report provides information for university selection, for certification, and for monitoring standards to improve learning of future cohorts. While it affects students' future, it transpires to challenge accountability of teachers and schools. The Pandora box is further complicated with regular international benchmarking and struggling for global recognition, the issues of public trust and acceptability, and locally on the argumentative content of authentic current affairs used for examination papers. The influences come from various stakeholders such as media, newspapers, and independent book publishers. Political groups bring controversies and ideology conflicts to the assessment practices. Public surveillance on public examinations becomes a sensitive social and political issue. The sentiments on outcomes of assessment overpower the learning process.

Table 1.3 below summarizes LS in HKDSE curriculum system. It is different from the traditional curriculum and assessment. It seems to be a kind of outcome-based system for 21st century skills practices. *"Assessment innovations require explicitly challenging teachers' assessment conceptions. In changing towards outcome-based curricula, aligning formative to new summative assessments is a challenge"* (Gulikers, Biemans, Wesselink & Wel, 2013, p.116).

Table 1.3 The public examination in LS curriculum system

Model	• Implementation as outcome-based system • Examination→ Pedagogy / Learning process→ Aims of Curriculum
Purposes	• Learning and applying twenty-first century skills • Initial aims of Awareness of the society, Broadening perspective, Connection skills & Critical thinking (ABC)
Contents	• Thematic-based, curriculum-embedded tasks • Three areas of study, six modules, themes and key questions for enquiry • A wide range of information sources such as newspapers, television programs, web-based materials, books, learning materials, or self- experiences
Mode	• Standards-referenced; skills-based rubrics and criteria • 80% of written exam: long and short essay, written tasks etc. (Data-response questions and extended-response questions) • 20% of School-based assessment (SBA): Inquiry-oriented learning (IES)
Organization	• Local compulsory public examination • Monitoring mechanism with onscreen 'double-marking' system
Feature	• Fairness, objectivity and reliability for higher education admission • IES school-based tasks • Exam-orientated, bottom-up, decentralized, informative • Examination alignment with the curriculum • Analytical selected open-ended items and curriculum-embedded tasks that require students to analyze, apply knowledge, and communicate more extensively in theory. In practices, learning has cut corners. • Guiding principles (CDC/HKEAA, 2015, p.126-129)
Function	• For certificate and qualification, guidance, accountability, inform learning and teaching, selection, school choice, institution monitoring etc.

1.5 Problems to be addressed in this research

As a guest lecturer from 2011 to 2014 in a higher education institute in Hong Kong, I taught teaching methodologies in primary school General Studies (GS) and senior secondary school LS. I taught the module on interdisciplinary concepts and thinking skills too. I am curious how public examinations change the implementation of curriculum. I was puzzled by the nature and function of public examination in LS. How far could the aims of the core curriculum be met by quality learning practices in the cultural contexts of the exam-driven Hong Kong? The problem of examination symptoms is considered deep-rooted in society. *Assessment for learning* has been overwhelming for over a century. Academics claimed recently (Anderson, 2011; Carless, 2011; P21, 2007; Wyatt-Smith, Klenowski &

Colbert, 2014) that if external summative assessment criteria are aligned with internal formative assessment, consequential promotion towards 21st century skills practices will fulfill the curriculum aims. Breaking through the technical barriers of alignment may make the claim possible (Looney, 2011; Plake, 2011). Worldwide efforts to assess 21st century skills are still in their infancy (Rotherham & Willingham, 2010). The curiosity of how and to what extent we can enable the means of public assessment to realize the 21st century skills drove me to proceed with my research on the area.

There are three research concerns with my study. First, could public examination act as a lever to reinforce the curriculum developments for excellence? A new mode of assessment with its high-stakes criteria of assessments reshapes curriculum practices of both students and teachers. Assessment dictates the target of learning. As the views of knowledge and the assessment content changed, approaches and strategies of teaching and learning became different from before. It is interesting to see if we can enable the means of summative assessment with new technologies and reshape classroom organization to realize curriculum aims. To what extent can LS examination support and drive the education reform?

Second, the emphasis on metacognition, the fostering of creativity, the development of transferable skills in the learning process with assessment mindset and practices on tow, are still rare (Broadfoot, 2009, p.viii in Wyatt-Smith & Cumming, 2009). Will LS examination direct learning and teaching to fit into nurturing responsible independent critical thinkers?

Third, natural to educators, the tripartite sequence of planning, implementing, and evaluating (PIE), or the equivalents of setting aims, teaching and learning, and then assessing, are the procedures of the traditional input-based content-oriented curriculum. However, the reverse seems to be true despite that the guiding principle is that the outcomes of the examination should be aligned with the aims of the curriculum. How do different stakeholders interpret the relationships between assessments, pedagogy and curriculum aims? An examination-driven output-based standards-oriented curriculum is not the same as the traditional content-based norm-referenced one; does over-reliance on LS examination impede the balance of diverse purposes and practices?

21st century skills practices embrace communication and collaboration skills, thinking critically and creatively, problem solving, self-directed learning, and virtues like flexibility, respect diversity, and responsibility. The alignment of assessment with curriculum, and with teaching and learning, become the focus to achieve effective learning. Effective learning of 21st century skills requires empirical research evidences and real classroom practices instead of lip services. Finding out how teachers and students perceive the teaching and learning relationship in the new LS curriculum and pedagogy may help celebrate implementation achievement and disclose problems. To what extent did the new mode of public examinations play a role in better learning practices in line with the education reform goals? How well did teachers and students interpret assessment literacy such as the meanings of 'alignment of summative and formative assessments', 'aims of the LS curriculum' and 'components of educational assessment' ? To what extent did examination enable fitness for purposes in the LS curriculum cycle? These are the research goals. The followings are the research questions:

Main question:
Can LS examination align well with the curriculum to realize 21st century skills?

Sub research questions:
1) How do different stakeholders perceive the relationships between the LS curriculum, pedagogy and examination in Hong Kong?

2) To what extent does LS examination enable the pedagogy to realize the curriculum aims?

1.6 Summary

This chapter states my motivation and purposes of study on the public examination of LS. The changes in Hong Kong, the new insights and pitfalls of a revamped curriculum urged the need of nurturing flexible, rational, critical and independent thinker to become communicative, cooperative, informative and responsible citizens. Pooling their multi-disciplinary knowledge transfer skills to solve contemporary problems and to improve future economic and social growth are the main goals of LS curriculum.

There are several main puzzles for inquiry. This research aims to investigate the relationships or gaps between assessment, pedagogy and curriculum in LS, to what extent the new dimensions of LS public examinations are fit for purposes and whether assessment aligned with curriculum can enhance learning.

Chapter 2 will post the literature reviews on educational assessment issues and research on LS in Hong Kong. They inform me to highlight a framework of 21st century skills for the aims of LS and inspire me to formulate a structure of horizontal and vertical alignment on the assessments, teaching and learning process and curriculum for my research. Chapter 3 reports on the empirical framework of explanatory sequential mixed-methods and the design of research instruments, the process of data collection and analysis according to the research framework. Then Chapter 4 displays and explores the results of integrated quantitative and qualitative findings from the perspectives of direct manipulators and indirect manipulators. They are highlighted as "manipulators", though they are also stakeholders, because they can have access to the operation of learning or assessment processes. Espoused beliefs and theories-in-use held by insiders, group interests of outliers, and the needs of accountability imposed by different outsiders are analyzed to get the results. Chapter 5 pursues discussion around the research questions. I will discuss the extent to which LS examination has aligned with the 21st century skills targeted curriculum. A suggested structure and concept map will be recommended to close the intended aims with the implementation gaps in order to actualize 21st century skills. Chapter 6 will be the final chapter of conclusion.

Chapter 2 LITERATURE REVIEW

2.1 Introduction

LS is different from traditional subjects in high school curriculum. Curriculum reform started in the 1990s in Hong Kong, the campaign was open to input from the universities, the school sectors, and even from different interest groups. The curriculum organization is tailor-made to suit the context of Hong Kong (EDB, 2005). The open system on curriculum reform is built on a general faith in mutual respect from all stakeholders, onset of the socio-political and economic underpinning of globalization, and a belief in the power of learning for problem solving. Changes seem to fit in time with the purposes of 21st century skills learning, hence, emerged the NSS LS in Hong Kong.

The following review is divided into two parts. First, literature from around the world serve to construct understanding and quest into the educational assessment issues in global sense. It builds up why, what, how there is a need of summative assessment and quests the extent to which public examination could be aligned with pedagogy and curriculum in LS. Second, the review of research studies targeted specifically on LS of Hong Kong helps to survey the studies that have been done so as to reveal any missing links between public examination, pedagogy and the curriculum aims in LS.

2.2 Educational Assessment Issues

2.2.1 The curriculum contexts of Hong Kong

The ARG in UK recommends, *"Assessment which is explicitly designed to promote learning is the single most powerful tool we have for raising standards and empowering lifelong learners"*, (Assessment Reform Group [ARG], 1999). Confucian culture nurtures societies with strong appetite for traditional exam-driven learning, so as it is in Hong Kong. Rapidly changing digital technologies enable emphasis on reliability and validity of fair and equitable public examination. This fuels further reinforcement of trust in the significance of public assessment in Hong Kong.

On 12 June 1985, the People's Republic of China (PRC) and the United Kingdom (UK) governments registered the Sino-British Joint Declaration in 1984 at the United Nations. Upon return of sovereignty in 1997, Hong Kong enjoys high degree of autonomy in accordance with the "One country, two systems" principle. Because of the geographical location at the doorway for the world to reach mainland China (Cheung, 2007), Hong Kong could be the bridge on cultural, economic, and technological exchanges between the mainland and other countries overseas, or to the other extreme, be the frontier of conflicts between capitalistic values and communist ideology. Culture cannot be changed overnight. Unfortunately, the separate development background and deviated consequential norms over 156 years put together in a small territory leads to foreseeable conflicts and internal dilemma that could not be solved in a short period. Tensions grow. It is a goodwill that a de novo LS for all senior secondary students be created along with curriculum reform. The all-new DSE subject could inculcate logical thinking on current issues, broaden mind and inspire awareness of civic responsibility and accommodation on diversity of views. Through issue-based inquiry, we nurture civic talents and quality citizens to explore local, national and global connections. The learning process will integrate knowledge construction, culture diversity experiences and problem solving. Synergy could be released through mutual respect and wisdom to appreciate the beauty of diverse culture and contextual differences, and ultimately the tensions be eased. This is the idyllic side of the picture.

To the other side of the same picture, some educators reminded about the difficulties of the new subject. The change affects more than 3,200 teachers who teach the new subject (Yung, 2005). *"The rationale for establishing this integrated subject and the content coverage are far from convincing"* (Lam & Zhang, 2005, p.35) because of teachers' limited knowledge of content knowledge on the modules of Modern China, Energy, technology & the environment, and globalization. Teachers' preparation are not ready on the inquiry-based instruction with pedagogical content knowledge in LS, higher-order-thinking nurturing, and the integration of different subject knowledge. The daring initiation of the new curriculum of LS is based on a goodwill. *"The moral is that it is better to plan for change with a goal that fits the emerging context, rather than a tentative goal that has been chosen based on the known initial conditions alone"* (Tse, 2010a, p.197).

The unique role of LS in the context of Hong Kong attracts much effort of academic surveillance. Starting from the beginning, there are arguments and debates on pros and cons, successes and defeats. Regular reviews in the reform process through research have become crucial. Based on my previous mini study (L. Leung, 2013), exam-driven phenomena resulted in significant positive wash back effects, too good to be true; the next step is to discover pitfalls. If effort is paid on innovative design, broadened questioning modes, authentic contents and re-organization of high-stake summative assessment, could public examinations help to promote paradigm shift of pedagogy to realizing the curriculum aims? The premise of departure with my research is to believe that public examination is the key channel of leverage for change.

2.2.2 The 21st century skills movement

The focus of school education should be placed on students' learning, curriculum is to be constructed to inspire thinking and stretch students' full cognitive potential. Increased complexity of the changing world challenges acquisition of a new set of dynamic skills for life in the 21st century. The technical term *'21st century skills'* (Griffin, Care, & McGaw, 2011; National Research Council, 2011) refers to a broad set of knowledge, skills, work habits, and character traits that are believed to be critically important to succeed in this modern world. According to Giffin & Care (2015b), there is an emerging need to change the bases for hiring and firing employees depending on the change of baselines and methodologies for the assessment and on teaching of 21st century skills in the knowledge economy in a digital age (ibid, p.3). *Even so, "the term does reflect a general — if somewhat loose and shifting — consensus"* (21st Century Skill, 2016, August 25). The concept is often interpreted and applied differently in different contexts. In very brief terms, the skills include ways of thinking, ways of working, tools for working and living in the world. The organization P21 (http://www.p21.org) advocated another framework for meeting standards that address both the core academic knowledge and the complex thinking skills required for success in college, life and career (P21, n.d.). According to Voogt & Roblin's meta-analysis of eight frameworks from various countries, alignment between the 8 frameworks is essentially about what 21st century skills or competences are and why they are important (Voogt & Roblin 2012, p.299). Comparing the similarities and differences between these frameworks, a table of key competences including critical thinking, collaboration, communication, creativity and innovation, self-direction and independence, using technology etc. was constructed (ibid, p.309). The 21st century skills were suggested to be the common core goals for the evaluation and assessment of learning in many countries and regions. The characteristic of the movement is driven by a need for high-quality manpower characterized with innate commitment as independent critical thinkers and responsible citizenships. Learning has to be changed from knowledge-based to skills-based, from content-oriented to skills-oriented, from teacher-centred to student-centred, from linear to multi-dimensional, from concrete to abstract, from input-based to outcome-based endeavours. The empowerment of good citizenships demands all-compassing synthesis, resilience and fairness. Ideally,

21st century skills learning improves communication and collaboration, cherishes flexible and adaptable temperament, and hence avoid dangers of fragmentation in the current divergent Hong Kong context.

2.2.3 Shifting the learning leverage point from curriculum to assessment

Examination is contended to follow curriculum delivery but in practice, it is reversed. Ross (2002) claimed that assessment is seen as an aspect of curriculum design rather than an independent variable that causes controversy. Existence of arguments indicates that the relationship between assessment and curriculum is not clear. Newton (2007) pointed out that to discuss 'grading' or 'certification' loosely is problematic, and it is ambivalent to use assessment results if the definitions were unclear. An assessment system fit for one purpose will not necessarily be fit for the other (Newton, 2007, p.166). He stated, "*An assessment system 'designed' to support a large range of purposes might end up being fit for none*" (ibid, p.168).

Curriculum and assessment can be interpreted as two individual and interconnected systems. Employing the systems thinking (Senge, 1990), the integration of a curriculum and assessment system can be understood as a set of connected and dynamic components forming a whole. The relationships of the components are cause and effect, dependent and supporting, all held together by an imperceptible chain that binds them (Mella, 2012; Senge, 1990). '*Aims and objective, content or subject matter, methods or procedure, and evaluation or assessments*' are the four dimensions of curriculum (Scott, 2001, p. vii). Usually, content or subject matter, methods or procedure are referred to as the teaching and learning process, the pedagogy or the learning practices. Therefore, the curriculum system can be simplified into three components: aims of the curriculum (A), pedagogy of the teaching and learning process (P) and evaluation or assessment (E) as shown in Figure 2.1.

Figure 2.1 The elements of a curriculum system

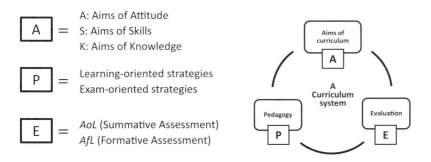

The elements of attitudes or dispositions (A), skills (S) and knowledge (K) are the particular items of the curriculum Aims. The strategies of learning and teaching in the process are dichotomized into learning-oriented and exam-oriented Pedagogies. Evaluation refers to formative assessment (Assessment for Learning *AfL*) during the learning process (Black & Wiliam, 1998a & 1998b) and summative assessment (Assessment of Learning *AoL*) at the end when learning is being summed up (Harlen & James, 1997). With the linear learning-driven curriculum, the system of examination is considered as top-down, instrumental and segregated feature from learning. Starting from the 19th century, the testing or examination form is basically content-driven and norm-referenced assessments based on relative performance of others (Anthony Leung, 2012, p.159). Anthony Leung considers it as fragmented or disconnected learning (ibid, p.152). The elements of attitude, skills and knowledge are divided and separated. The learning content, formative assessments and summative assessment are divided.

Outcome-based curriculum receives popular attentions. Early in the medieval period of Europe, vocation assessments featuring generic ways to judge skills performance were common. Assessment on competences of skills takes the form of criterion-referenced tests and were judged by adults who knew the candidate (Broadfoot, 2007, p.19) and the vocational skills. The alignment between practices and assessment was a perfect characteristic. In an essay review *'Curriculum Reform in Europe: the impact of learning outcomes',* Cort presented, *"Throughout Europe, learning outcomes are being introduced as standards for curricula at all levels of education and training* (2014)." Outcome-based curriculum was popular since. Standards-based assessment that started 1989 in the United States (Marzano, et al., 2013, p.1) is likely the manifestation of an outcome-based curriculum. Skills and capacities are the learning aims. They are defined explicitly with measurable criterion-referenced standards. Standards are therefore well-defined aims coming prior to the assessment, curriculum and instruction. The assessment design includes leverage principles, tools designed backward and evidence-centered assessment design (Huff & Melican, 2011, p.92). Spady defines it as *"starting with a clear picture of what is important for students to be able to do, then organizing the curriculum, instruction and assessment to make sure this learning ultimately happens"* (1994, p.1). The elements of attitude, skills and knowledge can either be integrated or separated depending on whether the outcomes are consistent with lesson objectives, and whether the curriculum is aligned well with the assessment instruments (Burns and Squires, 1995 cited in Anthony Leung, 2012).

To sum up, standards-based assessment is different from the traditional content-based curriculum in that it focuses more on skills and targets development. The assessment system was criticized for its limitation on specific measurable learning outcomes and its sacrifices on whole-person development. "It is instrumental and utilitarian focused" (Cort, 2014).

Standards-based assessment probably embraces a vocation screening mindset all along, and are consistent with the change on the global employment market demands. Developing capable workers with higher-order skills for the global market-economy is the first priority in many countries today. The high demand on fit for purpose on learning 21st century skills, accountability and the innovations of technology (Adamson & Darling-Hammond, 2015; Griffin, McGaw & Care, 2012: Looney, 2011) are pressing individual countries towards international integration and collaboration in the form of international assessments. *"Performance on these international assessments – TIMSS, PIRLS, PISA and others – has influenced the direction of national policy"* (Griffin & Care, 2015a, p.301). PISA results often make an impact upon government policy; international assessments like PISA provoke different policy solutions in different cultural and historical national contexts (Baird, Johnson, Hopfenbeck, Isaacs, Sprague, Stobart, & Yu, 2016).

With the backup from innovation of technology, Looney in an OECD Education Working Paper (2011) claimed that there are a number of promising developments in trying to integrate summative and formative assessments to improve learning in this decade. More coherent and coordinated assessment and evaluation frameworks are being tried. Technical barriers are broken (ibid); integration of formative and summative assessment may come true. With improvements in knowledge of learning and advances in measurement theory, strong summative assessments can shape instruction and possibly even classroom-based formative assessments (Adamson & Darling-Hammond, 2015; Looney, 2011; Plake, 2011). Nevertheless, doubt persists about the existence of any positive formative role in public written examinations. While the power of education assessment increases, we need to clarify whether we are using them suitably for improving students learning.

2.2.4 Assessment of 21st century skills

The 21st century skills projects with new skills-based learning assessment frameworks and curriculum reform are the movements to meet the needs of the century (Giffin & Care, 2015b, p.32), use of content knowledge supersedes content recall *per se*. Many academics and educators believe, *"The alignment of assessment with curriculum, teaching and learning is the linchpin of efforts to improve both learning opportunities and outcomes for all"* (Wyatt-Smith, et.al. 2014a, p.3). The issue on alignment of 'curriculum, pedagogy and assessment' (CDC/HKEAA, 2007; UNESCO, 2014b, p.42) is raised for actualizing the aims (Looney, 2011; UNESCO, 2014b; Wyatt-Smith, et al., 2014a). This shapes a new trend to advocate assessment criteria and level of standards consistent with the 21st century skills and the associated methodologies for assessment and teaching in this decade.

The belief in the power of assessment to provide a rational, efficient and publicly acceptable mechanism of judgement and control is the spirit that drives unceasing perfection attempts. The tide of assessment in education has been turning in favour of learning-oriented assessment (Broadfoot, cited in Wyatt-Smith et al. 2014a, p.v) in most parts of the world. Policy strategies provoke distribution of materials, pedagogies, classroom tools, pamphlets on guiding principles and precise standards-referencing assessments exemplars to evaluate these skills and provide incentives for those to be widely taught in class (Darling-Hammond & Adamson, 2010; Stobart, 2014).

Despite all the efforts, positive and successful exemplars of high-stakes examination are still rare in education. Educational measurement experts warn that high stakes examination may trigger "teach to the test", coach students on testing types, and re-align every focus on the content and skills most likely to appear in tests. It may lead to score inflation or grades level error (Looney, 2011). Some experts believe large-scale standards-based assessments and classroom-based formative assessments may cure the malpractice. Hence, Herde, Wüstenberg & Greiff (2016) showed a novel and dynamic problem solving process on how the developments of complex problem solving (CPS) with reliable and valid assessment is possible. Erickan & Oliveri (2016) designed an assessment construct embracing collaborative problem solving (ColPS), creativity and computer and information literacy (CIL), etc., all of which are related to ways of thinking, working, and living in the world. As the collaborative problem solving in PISA is a new trial (Organization for Economic Co-operation and Development [OECD], 2015), it takes time to prove its validity and reliability for assessing students' individual ability of problem solving from a collaborative process. Whether daily learning practices can enhance the ability of CPS through the testing mode of PISA and whether there exist unpredictable side effects and would these attempts be counterproductive or not are not yet sure.

The counter-intuitive high-stakes pen-and-paper summative examination particularly on 21st century skills are still not common, while formative assessments flourished among developed nations. According to Adamson & Darling-Hammond (2015), Australian national tests focused mainly on basic literacy and numeracy skills now. The United States has a wide range of portfolios of research, inquiry projects and collaborative problem-solving skills for international large standardized assessments but 21st century skills are not chosen for measuring basic reading and mathematics skills in accountability testing at the state level (ibid, p.303). UK and some Australian states have Project Work assessment for all pre-university students. Finnish teachers tend to focus on content-based assessments with less crosscutting skills. High-stakes testing must satisfy the demand of fairness, reliability and validity; it is cost-consuming and is highly risky to have other forms of assessment, which may influence students' opportunity choices in the world. Is fair high-stake examination on 21st century skills be only lip services or that they should only serve low-stakes international large scales assessment services?

That dilemma echo concerns in the academic world. Many scholars have pointed out that formative assessment and examination practices face fundamental dilemmas (Broadfoot, 2007; Eckstein & Noah, 1993, Ross, 2002). The relationships and differences between curriculum, formative assessment and examination are not well defined. Worldwide, recognition and support for public examination is often regarded as cynicism (Rotherham & Willingham, 2010). Scholars usually criticize and deny that the vast majority of public examinations can promote virtuous action learning. Few dare to suggest and propose an active or positive role in public examinations. *"What teachers perceive as formative, pupils may view as summative"* (Assessment reform group, 2002, cited in Carless, 2011). They notion if the attitude, skills and knowledge objectives are not aligned or integrated, there will not be summative and formative assessments coherences. Broadfoot (2003) doubted the possibility of co-existence of summative assessment and formative assessment. She asserted bluntly, *"in practice this does not happen"* (2003, p.2). Only the notion with the components of dispositions, awareness, skills, relationships, beliefs, values and attitude provides the fuel for growth and development over time (ibid). If the elements of attitudes and dispositions cannot be assessed and integrated, what will happen? Will these new trend of standard-based pretense be truly pushed towards 21st century skills practices?

Gipps (1994) cautioned that given long enough time, the negative impact of testing eventually outweighs any benefit. *"Testing distorts and corrupts the curriculum purposes or social processes."* Carless (2011) cited many scholars' notions that higher test scores do not equate to better student learning. Rapid improvement in test scores may just mimic short-term benefits but are counter-productive in the long run. Teaching to the test by direct transmission of examination tricks tends to neglect social constructivist orientation of formative assessment. It may narrow the curriculum by neglecting other social or affective elements. Students who do not adapt to the test models will be discouraged.

Moreover, the pursuit of political legitimacy and defensibility and the pursuit after consensual notions of objectivity and rigors by all stakeholders tend to change assessment into a blunt instrument that *"often misses its target and all too often cause significant damage..."* (Broadfoot, 2007, p.155). Nevertheless, the existing dominant literature is on formative assessment, which can be viewed as a continuum of possibilities for supporting summative assessment (Black, 2013; Corrigan, Gunstone & Jones, 2013) but not vice-versa. In practice, the goodwill to operate summative and formative assessment simultaneously is all theoretical priority discussions only (Newton, 2007). If the exam-driven phenomena in LS is reinforcing side effects, what will the damages be?

2.2.5 Why and how to pursue alignment of assessments?

To integrate summative and formative assessment more closely is a long-held ambition. The great challenges are on the generalizability, reliability, and validity of measurable assessment data related to student scores and reports. The barriers are on the cost and the technical impasses. Cognitive scientists made great progress in understanding the process of learning in different subject domains (Looney, 2011) in past decade. The promotion of 21st century skills projects and the standards-based education in the US seek to integrate summative and formative assessments with novel techniques and learning practices (Plake, 2011). Confucian societies cherish relative fairness and responsive examination for enhancing upward social mobility (Carless, 2011). Parents usually consider hard working, ironically even with rote learning, is a merit in conduct. Without examination, students will not pay efforts. Direct manipulators in examinations will manage their time according to their real theories-in-use rather than their espoused theories (Argyris, 1992) on what are right to be. Hui & Law (2013) criticize the cultural consequences of assessment and curriculum implementation of LS in Hong Kong as a cynical subject formation. The beliefs of examination-oriented culture are deeply influencing the learning habits of students and style of teaching (Ip, 2015). Given that examination is not avoidable, scholars tend to suggest that the alignment of summative assessment with curriculum vertically and formative assessment with summative assessment horizontally are the right things to do. The hypothetical schema is shown below.

A. Alignment of summative assessment with curriculum

According to Newton (2007), the examination design dictates the focus of both teachers and students on teaching and learning. They all trust that examination should be aligned with the learning process and the learning content. The key is on how summative assessment is organized and designed; proper deliberations can align assessment with the curriculum through some effective relevant learning process. That means pedagogy for students learning could be aligned with curriculum aims and the assessment design.

On the positive edge, testing is powerful with its very beneficial attribute if the tests truly measure the right skills learned. The big picture is evident: the goals of instruction are explicit, the targets are well defined, the standards are clear and uniform, and accountability becomes objective (Madaus, 1988). A yardstick proposal exists, namely, Gipps cites Popham's (1987, cited in Gipps, 1994) five conditions for measurement-driven instruction for improving the quality of public examination. The five conditions are: 1). criterion-referenced test, 2). measurement of non-trivial knowledge and skills, 3). measurement of a manageable number of skills or objectives, 4). targets clarity, instructional support, useful teaching materials, and 5). suggestions for how skills can be taught.

For summative assessment, the most important aspects of the construct are the development of what can be measured with a standardized procedure (Anderson, 2011, p.95). The necessary characteristics are to *"support a balance of assessments, including high-quality standardized testing along with effective classroom formative and summative assessments"* and to *"emphasize useful feedback on student performance that is embedded into everyday learning"* (P21-framework, n.d.). There are rich learning models to apply students' knowledge (P21, 2016), to evaluate evidence, to perform critical thinking and to complete analytical reasoning tasks as demonstrated in Anderson's description. However, creating assessments that can evaluate these skills and create incentives for these abilities to be widely taught as a regular part of the curriculum are big challenge overdue (Anderson, 2011, p.108). To improve nurturing 21st century skills, teaching and learning should be aligned with curriculum aims and examination paper should be aligned with teaching and learning and the explicit standard-referenced aims.

B. Alignment of formative assessments with summative assessments

Carless suggests that if formative assessment is going to flourish in test-dominated settings, we need to create productive synergies between summative and formative assessment. *"An aligned assessment, learning and curriculum triumvirate may involve a judicious balance of different assessment types and modes"* (Carless, 2011, p.207). He regards alignment of curriculum, pedagogies and assessment as a key issue in Hong Kong (he addresses mainly on Language learning) and so is in Scotland (Hayward, 2007; Hutchinson & Hayward, 2005 cited in Carless, 2011) and in Queensland (Lingard, Mills & Hayes, 2006 cited in Carless, 2011). Carless cited Biggs' claim (1988) that *"if summative assessment is criterion-referenced, incorporates the intended curriculum and is salient in the perceived assessment demands, aligned instruction is achieved, and teaching to the test is desirable because it reflects the desired curriculum"* (2011, p.37). He supported dictation in second language as a form of formative use of summative tests. Test preparation or drillings are examples used to promote performance (Lam, 2013). In test-dominated context as in Hong Kong, summative assessment is the more powerful force which comes first in the minds of key stakeholders (ibid, p.26). Formative use of summative tests (Black et al., 2003, cited in Carless, 2011, p.40), using information from tests to move student learning forward reinforces fine tune onto the focus in the curriculum. This benefit of ultimate convergence on the main focus of explicit curriculum requirements could be counter-productive towards broad skills learning as advocated with the promotion of 21st century skills. Whether summative assessment is used successfully to serve formative functions depend on: (1) accurate descriptions of test content and task types; (2) close match of test questions with instructional objectives; (3) using student performance in tests to guide teaching and learning; (4) prompt return of marked tests to enable students to identify gaps between the required performance and their current level of achievement; (5) shifting responsibility for test performance to learners such as peer-and self-assessment; (6) accompanied by discussions of student performance on tests and (7) appropriate re-teaching of misunderstood concepts identified from analysis of student performance on individual test functions (ibid, p.41).

Corrigan, Gunstone & Jones (2013) regard assessments as learning, assessments of learning, and assessments for learning should not be seen in isolation. Summative assessment for formative purposes (to provide feedback) can enhance learning. Corrigan, Buntting, Jones & Gunstone regard that *"assessment frameworks — particularly high-stakes assessments — are likely to significantly influence the curriculum implemented in the classroom and experienced by students"* (ibid, p.4). External assessment sends stronger signals that call for 'formula' to drive what is actually taught. Teachers' values and beliefs about the purposes and nature of the subject, the subject in a particular cultural setting, and the assessment determine the 'knowledge of worth' that influence teacher pedagogical decisions. Their espoused beliefs and value systems is their filter to judge what, when and how to enact the intended curriculum in the classroom. Therefore, Black concludes, *"... the quality of the day-to-day work of teachers depends on the quality of their summative assessments and on their positive link with the formative aspects of their teaching"* (ibid, p.208).

Open-ended summative assessment questions with criterion-referenced rubrics inform learner and teacher to master the key principles of learning. Through formative assessment, teachers carefully tailor learning experiences to counteract wrong concepts and malpractices when bringing controversial issues into the classroom (Mcavoy & Hess, 2013). Teacher may guide students to be critical thinkers applying discernment, reason and judgment to draw conclusion, to predict outcomes and to evaluate likelihood. They could also guide students to be creative thinkers who uncover the hidden patterns, take a step back to see the big picture, or re-conceptualize the fundaments of the current state of affairs. Teacher's values and beliefs of knowledge and learning may result in diverse design and interaction with students for better score of learning achievement. Unfortunately, research on this notion is rare. There is yet little empirical research presented with convincing evidences. It may be just an ideology if there is no supportive proved theory. It seems e-platforms, second language learning and skills application subjects are trying to realize demonstrating validity of the ideology. Low-stakes formative assessments (Black & William, 1998b) are widely used for 21st century skills practices while high-stakes assessments for the same target are still at its infancy.

C. Alignment of interactions between teacher and students

At the centre of the curriculum implementation is quality interactions between the teacher and the students (Acedo & Hughes, 2014, p.523). With standards-referenced grading on the achievement of skills, the goal is to align assessments with curriculum by increasing the level of specific skills instruction precisely. One example is to align the teaching and learning process design with level of critical thinking in assessment and instruction (Stobaugh, 2013). Another one is to align learning with learners' age according to the level of abilities in a progress scale (Acedo & Hughes, 2014, p.508). Teachers should be able to recognize a threshold stage that learning has the maximum chance of success among their students. That is where they should scaffold and facilitate students to have expert learning such as seeing patterns and 'deep structures' of a problem; to formulate strategy for quick and accurate solution, and to execute qualitative analyses to a problem (Stobart, 2014) with standards-referenced criteria.

Pedagogical quality by using the relevant progress scales as summative assessment is regarded as the vital part of educational quality. That is why teachers could exert the most important impact on students' learning (Hattie, 1999; Wiliam 2011, cited in Acedo & Hughes, 2014, p.504). Only through teaching strategies such as authentic issue-based collaborative learning, well-structured debates, good issue-based questioning, deep learning cognitive process of attaining problem-solving skills, and with appropriate content scaffolding (Tse, 2013) that teaching and learning could be aligned with the public assessment design, matched with the assessment indicators, and hence fulfilled the curriculum aims. It will be more effective to help students clarify their learning intentions, the success criteria and standards, and exemplars of good work so as to construct on their own strategies to bridge the gap at appropriate level (Stobart, 2014). Students may then be really learning to live, to think and to respect and be groomed as self-directed and life-long learners. Teachers adopting an ecological and organic approach to task design and engagement help students to find the hidden values of test taking in developing assessment criteria (Yu, 2005). Moreover, Aristotelian 'Phronesis' sees teaching as a profession based on practical knowledge and the ways of being that are context-related; teaching has to be learnt through practice and the study of practice, rather than a profession based on *implementing theory'* (Gidron et al., in Trahar, 2011, p.56). Dewey's theory of experience (1938) showed that 'reality' and 'truth' are not 'out there' waiting to be found, but are *'socially constructed'* (Clandinin and Connelly, 2000). Human interpersonal relationships, life experience, the process of learning and reflection can be regarded as pointers for display of knowledge or skills appropriate for criterion-referenced rubrics. Therefore, direct-manipulators such as teachers and students, executives from HKEAA and indirect-manipulators such as policy-makers and experts have the consensus that the alignment of summative and formative assessments throughout the LS curriculum implementation are very crucial. There is a need to find evidence on the perceptions of teachers and students about the relationships of the curriculum components, and to investigate how teachers and students join together for better learning practices, and for better outcomes on assessments.

This paradigm shift of teachers to the new outcome-based summative assessment system is essential (Gulikers, et al., 2013). The new indicators for quality learning and teaching are visualized as daily effective pedagogy such as scaffolding students learning with clear and precise formative/summative assessment tasks, rubrics or descriptors. Good teachers provide well-developed and useful teaching materials along with concrete instructions, organize students' self and peer assessments practices promptly, demonstrate good use of constructive teaching strategies, such as questioning, grouping, scaffolding learning activities, re-teaching of misunderstood concepts identified in summative assessments, encouraging students motivation, confidence, sense of ownership and control, and so on. There are certain conditions for teachers and exam-paper designers to follow, vide., feasible and concise criterion-referenced test, measurement of non-trivial knowledge and skills, measurement of a manageable number of skills or objectives with supportive exemplars, and clear targets (Gipps, 1994), consistency of the assessment criteria-referenced scales for learning, of learning, and as learning. Teachers provide professional support for learners to learn. Their quality interaction through formative and summative assessments provide effective feedback of the learning outcomes and achievement for enhancing further learning.

Research questions crystallized. Is there any assessment policy in LS? What experiences the alignment of assessment with curriculum have LS got after several years of implementation in Hong Kong? Is there any research on LS in Hong Kong evaluating some parts of the curriculum and assessments? What are the missing gaps? The following research reviews on LS in Hong Kong provide more information and insights.

2.3 Research on LS in Hong Kong

As a new unique curriculum, if the aims met quality-learning practices with examination standards, public examination might act as a lever to reinforce curriculum developments. To what extent does LS examination serve student's learning achievement? Is the research on LS in Hong Kong focus on the relationship between assessment, pedagogy and curriculum? What have we enquired in the field of research? I made use of the library engine from local and one of the UK library, to find out the main studies on LS in Hong Kong from 2005 to 2016. Findings are shown in Table 2.1.

Table 2.1 The theme of research on LS in Hong Kong

The main theme of the research	No.	Remarks	Year
LS reform in HK	6	1. Quest an illusive vision in LS 2. The implementation and challenges of LS 3. A survey on the opinion of secondary school teacher on the implementation of LS 4. The policies of reintroducing LS 5. A case study on LS (Representation of youth) 6. Colonial system, cynical subject	2005 2005 2007 2010 2012 2013
LS curriculum	7	7. The implementation of LS & the strategies 8. The formation of a school subject and the nature (Focus on content knowledge) 9. The Planning of Modules in LS 10. Curriculum Integration for LS (Leaders' insights) 11. Teachers' Decision-Making in Lesson Planning 12. The present and the future development of LS 13. Social Class and School Curriculum	2007 2009 2009 2009 2011 2013 2014
Professional development	12	14. A Hermeneutical Learning Community Approach 15. Teacher professional development 16. A reflective-participative approach to professional development 17. Teachers: Are you ready? 18. Pre-service LS teachers' decision making in lesson planning 19. Teaching and learning theory and practice in LS 20. Making sense of LS from teacher perspective 21. A study of curriculum leadership strategies 22. Teachers' attitudes towards human rights 23. LS Teachers preparation (through self-reflections) 24. A Narrative Research on Teacher Identity Construction in LS (Student-teachers) 25. Narrating the role identity of LS teachers	2007 2007 2007 2010 2011 2011 2011 2011 2012 2012 2013 2013
Pedagogy of curriculum content	3	26. Project learning in the eyes of students 27. Textbook of Religion in LS 28. Integrating media education into LS	2008 2009 2009
Pedagogy of teaching strategies	12	29. Using problem-based learning 30. Web-Quest project learning 31. Using Web 2.0 technology to support learning, teaching and assessment 32. Foster students'multidimensional and critical thinking 33. Training of critical thinking ability 34. Critical thinking through group work 35. Multiple perspectives and independent enquiry study 36. Issue-enquiry approach 37. Inculcate questioning skills 38. Group work and critical thinking 39. The constructivist classroom learning environment and critical thinking 40. A study of the teaching and learning practices of critical thinking	2007 2008 2009 2010 2012 2012 2012 2013 2013 2014 2014 2015
Summative assessment	7	41. An analysis of AS LS examination reports (1994-2005) 42. Markers' Perceptions regarding the Onscreen Marking 43. Double marking of LS exam system 44. The Comparability of Marking on Screen and on Paper 45. Markers' attitude towards onscreen Marking 46. Marking and grading procedures for 2012 47. Relationship between higher-order thinking nurturing and LS public assessment	2007 2010 2011 2011 2011 2013 2013
Formative assessment	0	/	
Outcomes/Impacts of curriculum Implementation	4	48. Marketized private tutoring 49. Expectations versus reality 50. The influence of LS on students: a case of the Umbrella Movement 51. Internationalising teacher education for LS	2014 2015 2016 2016

The list of research shows that there is relatively few research on LS in this period. As a new subject, at the early beginning, there are more curriculum and teacher professional development research. In the implementation period, there are mainly focus on the pedagogy studies. Critical thinking is the top priority. Other thinking skills are less concerned. The methodology is mainly qualitative research with some case studies. There are a few empirical studies on pedagogy. The research in the field of assessment only addresses on the functions of the new technical system.

Research prompts that there are great discrepancies between the intended aims and the implemented aims of the curriculum. Refer to Fung's study (2015) and my understanding, with a unique socio-political underpinning, the core aims of LS is nurturing independent critical thinkers with diverse perspectives (Learn to think), with awareness of social and political events (Learn to live), and respect others' opinions (Learn to respect). Fung felt disappointed that students could only master fragmented knowledge within specific module boundaries. He was discontent that teachers had low confidence in inquiry-based pedagogy. He commented, *"a certain degree of disappointment was expressed after the new curriculum came into effect"* (ibid, p.624). One of the reasons of the discrepancies between the intended aims and the implemented aims he concluded is the confusion of assessment criteria for students. Teachers have not mastered teaching interdisciplinary subject, not equipped to guide students' analytical and critical thinking. He accused that the nature of the curriculum was too broad and too ambitious. Early in 2005, Lam and Zhang (2005) predicted that the curriculum of LS is an elusive vision because teachers do not have enough knowledge on LS.

The weak content knowledge in LS has been stressed in Deng's study (2009). Deng condemns regression of the curriculum content down to a set of outcomes for standards measurement. He asserts that overlooking the meaning of curriculum content would render curriculum discourse and practice problematic and indefensible. He does not accept justifying the curriculum discourse based on standards and accountability. He points out that the meanings of content have to do with the aims and expectations of schooling in connection with culture and society. It has to do with the theory of content embedded in the school subject, which is framed subtly for social, cultural, educational, curricular, and pedagogical purposes. Moreover, a teacher's interpretation of the content should be bound by his or her understanding of the institutional expectations for teaching the subject, of learners, and of instructional strategies and resources within a particular classroom context (ibid). Deng's notion is similar to Acedo & Hughes (2014) who suggested that curriculum is not merely a written document, but a vision of how the learning will take place. What to learn and how to learn warrant a clear vision that is backed up by an account of the types of expected learning experiences (Acedo & Hughes, 2014, p.512). Deng's study points to a gap between curriculum aims and learning. He therefore suggests that empirical studies are needed to investigate the classroom realization of LS.

For learning to think, Fung & Howe's research (2012) pointed out that Hong Kong teachers and students were not familiar with critical thinking and group work. Teachers habitually deliver structured lessons to prepare for examinations. Their study proved relevance of group work in fostering critical thinking with teacher's appropriate interventions. Their further research (2014) on group work and the learning of critical thinking in LS concluded that collaborative group work was more effective than whole-class instruction, and students made better progress in 'teacher-supported' than 'student self-directed' group work in cultivating critical thinking abilities. They recommended further research on the cumulative effect of repeated practice of critical-thinking skills in LS (ibid, p.262). Ip's thesis (2015) concludes *"the implementation of critical thinking in the LS curriculum is a watered down version."* He criticizes that teaching has been formulated as a multiple-perspective thinking framework. Teaching of stereotyped views of stakeholders is skill-based but not authentic independent thinking. It is far remote from learning how to think. He finds four reasons to explain this discrepancy. The most critical one is the examination-oriented culture influencing principals, parents, teachers and students. However, the thesis does not inquire into the deeper impacts of DSE LS on thinking. In Fung & Su (2016), they investigate on how secondary student participants in Hong Kong's Umbrella Movement related their learning of LS to their choice of joining the strike in 2014; students admitted that LS offered them background knowledge necessary for understanding the movement but not the cause of their participation. Nevertheless, the authors suspect that LS curriculum has reinforced students' sense of dichotomy in judging between their local and national identities.

Questions in written examinations have in-born limitations. Tse (2013) observed, *"Questions in pen and paper written examinations are often closed loops".* Training towards expertise in answering questions is a possible short-cut for higher marks but it is inadequate for life-long learning. He pointed out that in deep learning, issue-enquiry curriculum scaffolding demands a history including far-from equilibrium disturbances, deep thinking and bifurcation to a new conceptualization paradigm process of learning, technically the "emergence" according to Chaos Theory (ibid, p.75). Quality issue-enquiry aims at guiding students for problem-questioning and problem-solving skills application in particular contexts. Well-constructed contents with suitable pedagogical content knowledge are crucial for effective teaching and learning.

In Table 2.1 displayed above, among research articles in 2005-2016, there is just a few on the relations, the implementation and the impacts of formative and summative assessment on students' learning. Most empirical researches after 2009 focus on pedagogies for better learning only. Clear-cut demarcation can be formative assessment as the feedback for students learning performances while summative assessment is the summing up of students' achievement. Research on assessment concentrated around onscreen marking system, which provide confidence of reliability and validity of the open-ended questions for the public. It seemed that in the Confucian scholastic world, there is seldom concern about the concept of formative assessment or even the high-stakes summative assessments; no matter what synergy the two functions of assessments may improve learning. Do we ever challenge the customs of overcoming high-stakes examination for better use while ignore or escape to face the influential examination system? Maybe the concept of examination is so deep-rooted in Confucian society that we dare not inquire about its strengths or pitfall.

Hui's study (2007) has a breakthrough. In his report, he claims that it is a challenge to demand teachers to ensure students getting better score and at the same time guarantee actualizing the curriculum aims. For the government (EDB, HKEAA), how to ensure fairness, reliability and validity of the public exam for selection and in the same time inculcating learning to learn are their responsibility. Under the circumstances of limited resources, selective function of high-stake examination cannot be erased; the challenge is how to use examination well to enhance learning? Hui appealed better setters for improved design of exam questions, and a review on the form of examination. To be fair, teachers can also enhance students' assessment literacy and understanding of the standards-reference rubrics. It is humorous that in these two decades, the tide of assessments is overwhelming yet we dare not to ride the tide well. There is also a significant missing link between horizontal alignments of the two well developed assessments in the western world.

In 2015, the mid-term review on LS curriculum and assessment result rated the implementation as being positive (EDB, 2015c). Teachers and students agreed with and accepted the implementation outcomes. The legitimation of the new curriculum with public examination was high as the majority of teachers agreed or strongly agreed that the assessment was aligned with learning and curriculum. *"The HKDSE is well-recognized by employers and used for selection by universities, both in Hong Kong and overseas. More than 210 tertiary institutions worldwide have indicated their acceptance of the HKDSE for indicated their admission* (ibid, p.5)". Examinations were conducted as scheduled. The assessment frameworks of LS for the 2018 HKDSE Examination remain the same as those of the 2017 HKDSE Examination.

There are three suggestions on the public assessment concerned: the format of papers remains unchanged; a greater diversity of issues, topics and concepts to be used in setting examination questions as an on-going improvement measure; the existing quality assurance mechanism of the HKDSE to be reviewed and enhanced (EDB, 2015b, p. 19).

2.4 Building a structure for research

We are living in a complex changing socio-political and economic society. Dynamical systems theory that explains unpredictability and instability in change and is the theoretical skeleton in this dissertation linking the ever-changing relationship between assessment, pedagogy and curriculum. A dynamical system is a set of inter-related input and events that change over time while dynamical systems theory maintains the gist of systems theory of input-process-output schema but extends beyond stable equilibrium to non-linear outputs predictions and explanations (Tse, 2010a, p.2). Figure 2.1 on page 24 showed the details elements of a curriculum system in a dynamic cycle. The implementation of the aims, pedagogy and assessments relationships could be interpreted clock-wise or anti clock-wise according to the priority set upon input or output of curriculum and assessment. The judgment depends on different stakeholders' filter systems in their minds according to their values and practical needs. The literature review on the educational assessment issues informed me to highlight a framework of the 21st century skills for the aims of LS and use that as the research indicators. The assessment of 21st century skills in global comparisons also provide me insight to focus on the alignment of assessments with curriculum and pedagogy horizontally and vertically. Based on Figure 2.1, this section builds a structure for research as discussed below.

2.4.1 A framework of 21st century skills for the aims of LS

The aims of LS curriculum are set in line with the learning goals of school education in Hong Kong (CDC, 2015, p.7). According to literatures and the 21st century skills movement in the world, *'Learning to learn', 'All-round development'* or *'Life-long learning'* and the aims of LS outlined in Chapter 1 are bearing the same meaning as the international goal for guiding the direction of educational reform (CDC, HKEAA & EDB, 2013a). The term '21st century skills' of LS represent a framework or a common baseline for the curriculum aims in Table 2.1. Citizenship, flexibility, adaptability, collaboration, ability in synthesizing from different information sources and so on help students 'learn how to live'. Being tolerant, self-directed and independent are the nature of 'learn how to respect'. Critical thinking, problem solving, and creativity are the higher-order thinking to nurture students 'learn how to think' and eventually to become independent thinkers in 21st century.

The core aims of LS is in nurturing students to be responsible citizens and independent critical thinkers. Teachers are supposed to align curriculum, provide learning process with suitable instruction to increase students' level of critical thinking and success of those efforts should be properly reflected in assessments. To be an independent critical thinker, students will avoid illogical and irrational thinking. They will not rely just on recalling earlier information but pay due efforts to make sense of the world by reviewing their own thinking. They use reflective decision-making, draw appropriate inferences and accommodate thinking of the others. They are encouraged to think from different perspectives; progressively they increase their adaptability and flexibility accommodating diversity and pluralistic voices. It is learning to live. Students are guided to seek the rules and the truth with evidences. They should not be the individual critical thinkers who just care for self-interest but ignore other people's feelings. They learn how to respect rules of law and the needs of other people. Therefore, the aims of LS can be recognized as nurturing students to be 21st century citizens who learn how to live, how to think, and how to respect. The learning involves a process of development of judgment, independent thinking, communication, etc., in a way of interaction and construction for enriched experiences.

Table 2.2 A framework of 21st century skills for LS

Learn how to live and respect	Learn how to think
A. Interdisciplinary skills and knowledge	Higher-order thinking and measurement skills
• Social and/or cultural skills, citizenship	• Critical thinking
• Flexibility and adaptability to core subject	• Creativity
	• Problem-solving
B. Being tolerant towards different views	• Independent thinkers
• Collaboration	
• Communication	
• Self-direction and Independence	
C. Ability in synthesizing information or evidence from different sources and perspectives	
• Information literacy	
• ICT literacy	
• Media literacy	

2.4.2 Structure of horizontal and vertical alignment

In order to achieve the aims of LS, the powerful engine of assessments should be aligned with curriculum aims and the processes of learning and instruction. Based on the previous literature review, ideas from the research on LS, my experiences of curriculum development (L. Leung, 2014) and the dynamical systems theory, I generalize a conceptual diagram on Figure 2.2.

In Figure 2.2, the gray box shows the teaching and learning processes. It is a diverse interactive opened system varying horizontally and vertically. The processes allow for the exchange or intervention from the environment. Direct manipulators such as students and teachers in the classroom carrying out learning programs and practices in order to achieve designated aims. Standard-referenced criteria, and rubrics of public examination (summative assessment) inform teachers and students how to get better scores through effective learning-strategies. Teachers adopting summative assessment level of standards to score students' individual differences for formative functions provide students with feedback on their performances for improvement of learning. During the processes, teachers make use of well-balanced learning-oriented strategies for directing students learning. Suitable exam-oriented strategies are used after students got concrete background knowledge and skills. In-direct manipulators such as policy-makers or executive and experts provide support, resources and surveillances. Outsiders such as parents, private tutorial schools, publishers, pressure groups, and mass media may intervene or participate into the processes depending on the curriculum nature and the policy.

Figure 2.2 Horizontal and vertical alignment of assessments and curriculum

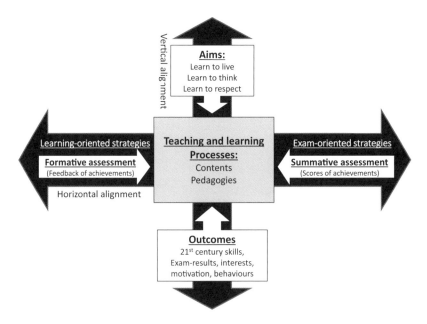

Figure 2.2 shows the ideal alignment of assessments with pedagogy and curriculum horizontally and vertically. Horizontal alignment acknowledges coherence and synergy of summative assessments (such as DSE public examination) with formative assessments. Open-ended exam questions' standards, curriculum frameworks, and assessments work together at the policy level in assessment. The authority provides internal and public guiding principles (CDC/HKEAA, 2007, with updated in 2015, p.126-129) for teachers to guide students' learning and to obtain higher achievement of curriculum aims. Teacher uses a set of summative assessment tools and content knowledge samples to provide feedback to oncoming student cohorts. The enhancement of learning is a process of formative use of summative function/tools. The alignment of formative and summative assessments is to make use of summative assessment standard-references, rubrics and criteria, and students' performances reviews to inform future formative assessment. The re-teaching of summative assessment with marking tools for the other cohort of students made it possible to align summative assessment with formative assessment during classroom practices. That accounts for success in aligning the standards for curriculum aims and system level of improvement. Vertical alignment concerns with curriculum aims, contents, classroom instruction, professional development, and student outcomes to be aligned with each other. Teacher and students' interactions during the teaching and learning process are the main challenges for success while public opinion and social demand must be awaken not to interfere the alignment.

The success or failure depends on the proper formative use of summative assessments and reciprocally that the summative assessments design and contents are based on the effective practices of formative assessments. Teaching and learning includes the ways of daily classroom experiences embedded for assessment practices. Quality formative assessment is characterized as assessment designed to provide proper and prompt feedback. Assessment providing just a final achievement score for a student is summative assessment (Marzano & Heflebower, 2012). Therefore, how to ride the tide of 21st century skills movement for better learning achievement from teachers and students' perspective is the focus of the research. Alignment of the three curriculum components, formative use of summative assessments criteria and the summative assessment effects on students are the direction of research. As the alignment of assessment with the curriculum is still a tentative suggestion by academics only (Carless, 2011; UNESCO, 2014a), urgent need for empirical study on the relationship of public examination, pedagogy and curriculum becomes crucial.

2.4.3 The gaps for enquiry

Worldview is "a basic set of beliefs that guide action" (Guba, 1990, p.17 cited in Creswell, 2014, p.6). One's worldview and value system will affect one's philosophy, epistemology and methodology (Carr, 1995; Hammersley, 2006). "*The post-positivist approach to research is based on seeking appropriate and adequate warrants for conclusion, on hewing to standards of truth and falsity that subject hypotheses to test and thus potential disconfirmation, and on being open-minded about criticism*" (Phillips & Burbules, 2000, p.86). Hold the worldview of post-positivism, I agree with Tse's dynamical systems theory on change (2010a, 2010b) for interpretation of results in the ever-changing complexity during the curriculum initiating period of LS. Dynamical systems theory is an expansion of traditional system theory (2010a, p.1). It avers that changes can occur in all dimensions in vertical and horizontal directions. Factors like time make it more complex with unpredictable non-linear development. Tse notions to adopt both traditional systems theory and dynamical systems theory to understand order and disorder. There is order behind disorder depending on how we master patterns and changing principles in the event development process with dynamic change perspective (ibid, p.103). Actually, Senge (1990) promoted Systems thinking as a strategy to see the world. With systems thinking, a body of knowledge and tools help to visualize patterns of change.

Right now, the practices of nurturing 21st century skills with assessments for learning, for accountability and certification are considered crucial to new generations. There is less agreement on how to enable power of assessment and how it should connect with accountability, with curriculum and with instruction in education systems (Looney, 2014). What the assessments of 21st century skills are and how they are operationalized and assessed in LS are seldom queried. There are not enough research evidences on the relationship between the different teaching and learning methods and the significance of assessing 21st century skills in records.

Argyris (1990, 1992 Ch.20) cautioned that what people said may not be the same as what is being practiced. The set of beliefs and values people hold to manage their life are the espoused theories of action. The actual rules they use to manage their beliefs are the theories-in-use. Very often in real world, the two are very much different. Even policy-makers or executives' espoused theories could be misleading. They may make the wrong decisions to produce what they do not intend. The paradigm of meritocracy constitutes a hidden consensus in the pursuits for preferred university places.

Premature deliberative democracy and *"changes in society's normative values, beliefs and expectations"* (Wilkins, 2002, p.14) may drift theories-in-use. It has been claimed that to rationalize and to realize aligning assessment with curriculum and learning practice is the way to enable 21st century skills practices (Acedo &Hughes, 2014; Carless, 2011; CDC/HKEAA, 2007; Looney, 2011; UNESCO,2014a). Quality criterion-referenced learning and assessment standards are constructed for performance and achievement. However, setting standards for accountability and qualification based on testing is controversial and can have unfortunate side effects (Chapman, & Snyder, 2000; Linn, 2000; West, 2010). There may also be a bitter force shortchanging for short-term performance which does not lead to mastery of material (Carless, 2011) if there are gaps of perceptions between the relationship of curriculum aims and the summative assessment, the learning practices and the curriculum aims, and also the learning practices and the summative assessment. *"...alignment research is critical for ensuring the standards-assessment-instruction cycle facilitates student learning..."* (Marione & Sireci, 2009). As there are neither local nor global research on the alignment of curriculum cycle in the interdisciplinary curriculum, how and in what way it should be implemented is unknown. Even worse, if a teacher holds a position or performs a function that answers indiscriminately to the expectations of his students, the gap between what should be done against what is really done may cause despondency and deviation. The same problem arises if a gap exists between policy-makers and practitioners.

Nevertheless, from the perspective of dynamical systems theory, unpredicted surprises need not be irrational. Surprises can be explained as consequences of multi-dimensional changes, which are the outcomes of a multiple decision points autonomous system. The immediate history of past changes and the contemporary demands for accountability, reliability, defensibility of each decision making in each unique context may change; the resultant so forth decide the success or pitfalls of competing effects. To find out the patterns or interpret the phenomena of discrepancy/gaps, only a thorough mixed-method of inquiry can help

2.5 Summary

The first part of this chapter shows that we are under the influence of global education reform agenda and assessment movement in this decade. The framework of 21st century skills globally and locally has emerged to be the targets and standards for learning and assessments. Right now, standards-based instruction and assessments are being implemented at different levels in schools. Cognitive learning and assessable materials are repeatedly divided and subdivided into measurable units. Recently, aligning assessment with curriculum and pedagogy has been the popular notion and undisputed direction both explicitly and implicitly. With new form of large scales summative assessments and new theories, some academics and educators claim that it can work. However, discovering how the alignment could be composed, and in what way may it be varied remains challenging. There are limited and scarce empirical research on the theme around the world. HKDSE LS examination is indeed a very high-stakes assessment and it should be aligned with pedagogy and educational reform aims. Despite being influential, there are limited research on these areas. In the complex post-colonial period, the city urges to nurture independent critical thinkers. Based on the vision fostering "Assessment aligns with pedagogy and curriculum to realize 21st century skills", I constructed a framework of 21st century skills for the aims of LS. I categorized the meaning of aims in 21st century into 'Learn to live', 'Learn to think' and 'Learn to respect'. Embracing a dynamic horizontal and vertical alignment of assessments and curriculum structure, I use a mixed-methods approach together with dynamical systems theory to formulate an empirical research as shown in Chapter 3.

Chapter 3

METHODOLOGY & RESEARCH DESIGN

3.1 Introduction

Following my research purposes discussion (Chapter 1) and literature review findings (Chapter 2, a structure for research), I choose to adopt a mixed-methods approach, the explanatory sequential design (Creswell & Clark, 2011) in particular, for an empirical study. The research indicators that are developed based on the 21st century skills practices are broken down into smaller items in the questionnaires as the curriculum aims and pedagogies of LS. The assessment of 21st century skills forms the metaphoric lens uncovering the extent of aligning assessments with curriculum and pedagogy both horizontally and vertically. The dynamical systems theory on complexity and chaos based on the socio-political underpinning in Hong Kong helps to inform the analysis of my research. Backed by my post-positivist personal philosophy to develop instruments at the beginning, I collected detail items of quantitative questionnaire data from one variable, the students and teachers' perceptions, in the same class based on the research questions. Then, from the constructivist vision for qualitative data (semi-structured interviews and classroom observations) explanation through dynamical systems theory (TSE, 2010a), the empirical research explores students, teachers and other stakeholders' perceptions on the relationship of LS curriculum and assessment. Both quantitative and qualitative findings are compiled, compared, correlated and triangulated to discover perceptions gaps between students and teachers. The perceptions of other stakeholders, including policy-makers, assessment practitioners and academics, are analyzed to complement understanding the whole picture of public examination implementation phenomena in Hong Kong. I analyze research results by theoretical induction. Starting with rational values in espoused theories on assessment and curriculum visions, the results are analyzed critically. I hope it will contribute to the ongoing education reform, adding concrete evidences with the case in LS.

3.2 Post-positivism & constructivism behind the explanatory design

Post-positivism beliefs, namely, doing competent, reliable, and evidence-based research, obtaining authorized conviction from competent inquiries (Phillips & Burbules, 2000, p.3) is my worldview. My faith is based on Dewey's notion that we must seek beliefs that are well warranted (Dewey, 1938 cited in ibid). As the experience of human beings, which Dewey considered subjectivist and value-mediated knowledge, is merely the perceived phenomenon, there is no absolute truth of knowledge based on such perception alone, especially with knowledge about human behaviour and actions. Knowledge, which is often imperfect and fallible, is conjectural (Phillips & Burbules, 2000). Nevertheless, *"the quest for knowledge is to a considerable extent 'self-correction'"* (ibid, p.3). The context-stripping effect can be avoided by finding a relatively stable reality that is subjectively and mentally constructed by individuals (Crossan, 2003). For instance, ripple effects of an isolated incident are elusive in the postmodern information society. However, stripping out the relationships may help to construct and reconstruct our feeling, understanding, learning and knowledge. Scientifically, human beings have discovered the DNA of life; each DNA has its pattern and arrangement order. The cells of our brain connect themselves in order to function well. The phenomena of human relationships are like the neural network, interacting with each other (L. Leung, 2003). The experiences in the field of education are both personal and social. As there are laws or theories of human experiences out there, the relationship structures can guide and conduct our learning, assessment and curriculum development and for research and criticism through constructive processes. Although we cannot find the absolute truth, it does not mean we should give up seeking truth and discovering order behind disorder through empirical research.

During the research process, I made use of Habermas' (Carr, 1995) notion of conceptualizing educational research. With the conceptual structure of horizontal and vertical alignment introduced in chapter 2, the post-positivistic research methods and inductive approach of understanding were established mainly based on the teacher and students' questionnaires. The research focuses on the missing gaps in between matching counterparts' perceptions on the relationships and impacts of the components in LS assessment and curriculum cycle. How do they perceive and to what extent do they agree public examinations can lever pedagogy to realize the curriculum aims? The results will be used to find out causal relationships. The snapshots or different kinds of isolated data will be deconstructed and reconstructed. Different data from qualitative and quantitative findings will be compiled, compared and inferred to see the patterns, structures, insights and pitfalls through the process of research construction.

3.3 Empirical framework for the study

Morris & Adamson's (2010) *"Curriculum, Schooling and Society in Hong Kong"* is my source of Stake's

Model for Curriculum Evaluation (1967). This model proposed evaluation through the comparison of the intentions and reality of a curriculum with regard to its antecedents, transactions and outcomes (Morris & Adamson 2010, p.166). I merge my structure of research with their proposal into a study framework in Table 3.1. The framework provides a structure to evaluate the differences between the intended and the implemented 21st century skills learning in the LS curriculum with regard to its aims, processes of learning and teaching, and the outcomes. It focuses mainly on the teachers and students' perceptions and practices of teaching and learning at the school level and looks into the issues of curriculum coherence (ibid). The premise avers that if summative and formative assessments are aligned with pedagogy and curriculum, it would realize the 21st century skills. Alignment means seamless connection without gaps, or just in case, all gaps been bridged effectively. The relationship between the vertical components, for instance the intended aims, should elicit implementing the intended 21st century skills learning and teaching process, and harvesting the intended outcomes (see Section 2.4). Quantitative and qualitative parallel datasets from counterparts at schools were collected to gather evidences whether there were unknown gaps in between. Semi-structured interviews, questionnaires and classroom observation analysis were conducted for triangulation. Policy-makers and other practitioners' perceptions from further interviews were explored, their views analyzed and critiqued for understanding the relationships of public examination, and curriculum aims.

Post-positivism arises out of quest, logic, reasoning, finding evidence, verification and consequences rather than antecedent conditions (Cohen, Manion, & Morrison, 2011; Phillips & Burbules, 2000). While mixed method involves both closed-ended quantitative and open-ended qualitative data, it *"can be written as QUAN + QUAL = complete understanding"* (Creswell & Clark, 2011, p.117). Therefore, it is a suitable and appropriate approach to explore students, teachers and other stakeholders' perceptions herein.

Table 3.1 The empirical framework for the study

Key Elements	Kinds of information	Sources of information	Remarks
Antecedents	Curriculum and Assessment in LS Aims of educational reform The aims and role of LS Context of LS assessment in Hong Kong Purposes, content and organization of the curriculum assessment The curriculum & assessment systems and the perspectives of crucial stakeholders	Curriculum and assessment guides and diverse resources of LS document reviews Literature reviews A framework of 21st century skills practices The LS curriculum, pedagogy and assessment cycle 6 Semi-structured interviews	1 senior policy-marker 1 Former senior LS Curriculum Development Officer 1 senior LS assessment administrator 2 LS experts from HKIEd 1 parent
Transactions	The implementation realities of the 21st century skills practices in DSE Questionnaires and semi-structured interviews for teachers and students: The assessment purposes Pedagogies for the HKDSE LS practices The impacts of HKDSE LS Lessons observation: Teachers and students teaching and learning processes	Parallel mixed methods sampling 50 classes from 42 schools in HK 50 Teachers' & 489 Students' questionnaires 6 sample schools' studies (2 from 3 banding schools) Semi-structured individual interviews: 10 LS teachers & 17 F.6 students after exam LS student teachers 10 Lesson observation	42 x1-2/per school 489 students from 42 schools 10 Teachers: 6 x 1-2/per school 17 F.6 Students: 6 x 2-3 /per school 2 LS student teachers 10 lessons (3 schools x 2 teachers x 1 or 2 lessons)
Outcomes	Discussion on the outcomes Compare and contrast different stakeholders' perceptions on the role of summative assessment Verify the extent of assessment impacts on the curriculum cycles and in different groups of students and teachers Comment and argue on the effects of DSE	Verify the research questions Compare and relate teachers' and students' questionnaires and interviews Compare and relate vertical relationship of Antecedents. Transactions and outcomes	Questionnaire data analysis Convert and interpretation of interview transcript

The explanatory sequential mixed-methods design includes a quantitative survey to teachers and students, a number of qualitative classroom observations and in depth interviews to different stakeholders. Quantitative and qualitative research studies are carried out simultaneously and data are merged during the analysis and discussion processes to resolve complicated research questions. With espoused visions juxtaposed with observed theories-in-use, I maneuver suitable theoretical induction to interpret the results. My understanding lead me to think that in a complex context open system as in Hong Kong, quantitative measurements may not effectively reflect the whole truth, qualitative interpretation with presage background knowledge and personal insight of the world may help complementing the shortcomings. As an independent unaffiliated researcher not bound by funding restrictions, the research has been carried out freely and neutrally without intended bias. The following sections outline the research methods and data collections.

3.4 Participants

3.4.1 Recruitment of students and teachers for questionnaires

I collected data from both teachers and their students in the same classes after the public examination in 2014. The participants responded to the questions without pressure. The setting is more reliable and comparable in one variable, focus only on their perceptions. In the 2013-14 school-year, there were totally 458 secondary schools in Hong Kong. In April, 2014, two sets of questionnaires (1 teacher and 10 students within the same class) together with an invitation letter, a return envelope and a return form were sent to all 458 secondary schools by mail. 50 schools totaling 62 F.6 classes returned. The response rate was about 13.5%. The final valid questionnaires were from 50 classes in 42 schools (9.2%). 1-2 classes from each school were involved. There were 50 class teachers and around 9 students from each class, totally 489 students' questionnaires were valid for analysis. The general information of participants is described in Table 3.1.

3.4.2 Participants' demographic information

All 489 students were native Chinese. They had been learning LS for 3 years. They were the third cohort of candidates who had just finished their HKDSE written examination in 2014 and waiting for the examination results. Teachers have taught the participants LS for 1-3 year (see Table 3.2). Teaching background of the teachers is shown in Table 3.3.

Table 3.2 Demographics of participants

	Student (n = 489)		Teacher (n = 50)	
	Category	N (%)	Category	N (%)
Gender	Male Female	201 (41.1) 277 (56.6) 11 (2.2)	Male Female Not answered	28 (56.0) 20 (40.0) 2 (4.0)
School Type*	Government Subsidized Direct-subsidized Not answered	97 (19.8) 298 (60.9) 85 (17.4) 9 (1.8)	Government Subsidized Direct-subsidized Not answered	6 (12.0) 35 (70.0) 7 (14.0) 2 (4.0)
Language of Instruction used in LS class*	English Cantonese Putonghua	80 (16.4) 404 (82.6) 5 (1.0)	English Cantonese Putonghua	8 (16.0) 41 (82.0) 1 (2.0)
School banding*	Band 1 Band 2 Band 3	144 (29.4) 211 (43.1) 134 (27.4)	Band 1 Band 2 Band 3	15 (30.0) 20 (40.0) 15 (30.0)

* = Adapted according to the class respondents

Table 3.3 Teaching background of teachers

Item	Category	N(%)
Experience of being HKEAA LS exam-marker	Have experience No experience Other	25(50.0) 30(40.0) 5(10.0)
Years of teaching experience	5 years or less 6 – 10 years 11 – 20 years 21 years or more Not answered	14 (28.0) 13 (26.0) 10 (20.0) 9 (18.0) 4 (8.0)
Years of experience teaching LS	2 years or less 3 years 4 years 5 years Not answered	3 (6.0) 10 (20.0) 9 (18.0) 22 (44.0) 6 (12.0)
Undergraduate degree field	Science, Engineering or Business Humanities Liberal Studies Other or not answered	11 (22.0) 26 (52.0) 3 (6.0) 10 (20.0)
Teaching subject	Science, Engineering or Business Humanities HKAL LS Other or not answered	8 (16.0) 29 (58.0) 3 (6.0) 10 (20.0)

3.5 Semi-structured interviews

3.5.1 Students and teachers

There were six sample schools' teachers willing to participate the research. Convenience sampling was applied. Two of them came from my previous research schools. Two of them were participants in the "sharing of lesson plans schools" project from Hong Kong Liberal Studies Organization[1]. The other two were schools recruited through my own connections. They came from diverse school sponsoring bodies. Participants were evenly distributed from among the three banding of schools in the total samples population. One is a Direct Subsidy School (enjoy greater curriculum choice especially in medium of instruction and student enrolment flexibility), the other five are subsidized schools. The school LS panel teachers and/or teachers willing to participate in interviews and lesson observations were invited according to a stratified purposeful criterion from January to May 2014. The stratified purpose of sampling involves deliberate pair-up by school background such as their teaching medium, school type, standard banding and students' and teachers' consent to join the interviews. Two to three students from each school, assigned by the participating teachers, were interviewed individually. In total, 10 teachers and 17 students were interviewed. Students were asked to predict their DSE LS scores of achievement (in the 2014 examination). Later, they told me the final results voluntarily. The general information of participants is described in Table 3.4.

Table 3.4 Background information of F.6 students and teachers of LS

School Code	Sch 1	Sch 2	Sch 3		Sch 4		Sch 5		Sch 6	
School Banding	1	1	2		2		3		2/3	
Language of instruction	E	E	C		C		C		C	
Teacher Code	T1	T2	T3	T4	T5	T6	T7	T8	T9	T10
LS marker with year	Y	3	Y	Y	Y	N	1	2	3	2
Years of experience teaching LS	5	5	4	3	5	3	5	5	5	5
No. of Lesson observation	/	/	2	1	2	2	/	/	1	2
Class Student Code	S1-3	S4-6	S7-9		S10-11		S12-14		S15-17	
Self-prediction of DSE LS exam result	5,5,5	5,5*,5**	4↑,3-4,4-5		3, 4		4↑,4↑,3-4		4, 2, 2	
Self-reported DSE LS exam result	5,5*,5	5,5*,5**	3, 3, 4		3, 4		3, 4, 4		4, 2, 2	

Remarks: T= teacher; S= student Sch= school C = Cantonese; E= English Y= Yes; N= No

---

[1] Hong Kong Liberal Studies Organization Limited is one of the volunteer Liberal Studies teachers organizations in Hong Kong (http://hkls.org.hk/site/)

3.5.2 Policy-makers and other practitioners:

Eight participants in Table 3.5 were interviewed before or after the distribution of DSE examination results. Purposive sampling was adopted with consideration given to their role as the curriculum or assessment in charge first; failing that then the next priority. An invitation letter, a consent form, an information sheet, research information including semi-structured questions and a research diagram (L.Leung, 2013, p.194) were sent through emails. A quarter of the first priority target persons rejected the invitation while most of the target persons accepted. The first targeted policy-maker[2] and HKEAA executive generously accepted my invitation for the semi-structured interviews.

3.6 Lesson observation

Only 3 out of 6 school panel head or teachers were willing to have lesson observations. I observed 10 lessons of 6 teachers who were invited to participate in later interviews. Five F.6 classroom observations were carried out before DSE. **Four F.5 and one F.4** classroom observations were carried out after DSE from January to May 2014 (see Table 3.4).

3.7 Instruments

There are three kinds of instruments for the mixed-methods research. They were designed according to my experiences of the previous research (L. Leung, 2013) and the research framework. The five parts of the questionnaires structure were related to the vertical and horizontal conceptual framework on Figure 2.2 while the semi-structured individual interview questions and the classroom observation checklists were related to the questionnaire survey.

3.7.1 Questionnaires

The student and teacher questionnaires were adopted from an earlier research questionnaire (ibid, p.200-207), modified base on literature reviews of 21st century skills (see section 2.4) and the structure of vertical and horizontal alignment of assessments and curriculum. The meaning of curriculum aims was elaborated into three groups of detail items. When LS curriculum aims are lined up with the

---

[2] The participant is at the apex of the Curriculum Development Institute directly under the Education Bureau, yet no single one person can strike the final bell for policy-making. Decision-making is an integrated policy in the government, and has to be consistent with what other Assistant Directors, Deputy Director and Director of Education in Hong Kong believe.

aims of 21st century skills, pedagogy including learning-oriented and exam-oriented strategies can be regarded as the processes of curriculum implementation in the middle. The outcomes of learn to live and learn to think were the indicators for assessing the impacts of public examination. The study on connections between aims of the LS curriculum and DSE involved collecting two sets of responses from students and teachers. There are Part One and Part Two in both questionnaires. The questionnaire contains five sections in Part One (see Appendix 1 and 2). Four-point Likert scale was adopted for respondents to assess to what extent do they agreed with different corresponding statements in each section. Each section contains 8-10 questions. Participants were asked to indicate the best option representing their opinion. Four choices "strongly agree" "agree" "disagree" "strongly disagree" were given in section 1, 3-5. Demographic information such as gender, school type (Government school, subsidized school, direct-subsidized school), language of instruction, school banding was recorded in Part Two. Most of the questions in both questionnaires were the same.

Section 1: The aims of the LS curriculum and the DSE.

Ten items about aims in section 1 are the same in both the students' and teachers' questionnaires. Items on aims were divided into three groups according to the 21st century skills of LS (see Table 2.2). To make the questionnaires more reader friendly to the report, I re-organized the order of all the questions a bit according to the research framework of 'Learn to live' (question item a- d), 'Learn to think' (e- g) and 'Learn to respect' (h- j) for study as in Table 3.5 (Aims). Within this section, two sets of data from teachers' understanding of the aims (1A), namely, whether they think curriculum aims can be achieved by the public examination (1B) were collected while students just did 1B.

Section 2: Different teaching methods and their effectiveness in achieving good results in DSE.

From the 21st century skills, LS curriculum and assessment guide (C & A Guide) (2007) and the Liberal Studies Curriculum and Assessment Resource Package (EDB & HKEAA. 2013, p.11), ten teaching methods were offered for responses in order to validate teachers' daily classroom practices from the perspectives of students and teachers. The re-organized question items a- e (see Figure 3.1 Pedagogy a-e) tend to use activity approach with constructive strategies which I defined as 'Learning-oriented strategies'. Item f- j are subject exam-oriented pedagogy, which I named 'Exam-oriented strategies'. Participants were asked to indicate the frequency of using/learning from different teaching methods as "often" "sometimes" "seldom" or "never".

Section 3 and 4: The impacts on how to live and how to think through DSE practices

Section 3 and some questions in section 4 focus on the impact of DSE on students. I re-organized the two sections questions order into 'Total outcomes of Learn to live' (a – h) and 'Total outcomes of Learn to think' (i – l), so that both teachers and students' questions could match for analysis (see Figure 3.1 Outcomes). For simplicity, I revised question items d, e and h from negative wordings into positive in reporting because the data were recoded positively for the convenience of statistics.

Section 5:

Students' questions are different from teachers. Students' questionnaires are comments on the impacts of DSE on their competency in LS, while teachers' questionnaire focus on recommendations for future development of LS curriculum and assessment.

Figure 3.1 The structure of questionnaires with the research framework

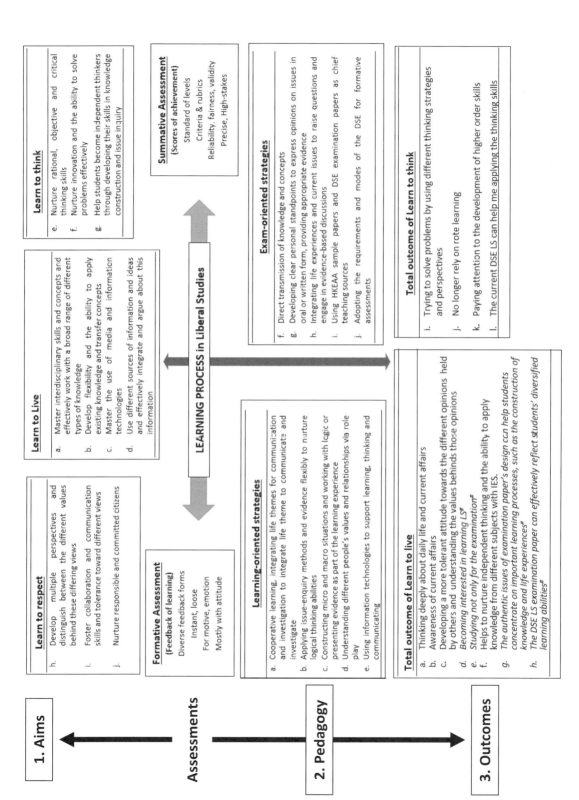

3.7.2 Semi-structured interviews

A set of questions and prompts were outlined for the in-depth interview. The types of questions and responses were outlined in Table 3.5; a figure from my previous research (L. Leung, 2013, p.194) for semi-structured interviews was provided for interviewees during the interview. The following table lists the corresponding questions directed to different groups of 35 interviewees in the research.

Table 3.5 The questions for different participants

Code of interviewee	No	Time (mins.)	Main Question types	Remarks
S= Students	17	20-40	A. What are the aims of LS? Does DSE LS help to fulfil the aims? B. How do teachers teach and how do students learn? C. What are the effects of the public examinations on teaching and learning?	B,C,D,E
T= Teachers	10	45-90	D. Do you agree that the DSE LS assessment modes, school teaching modes and learning objectives are consistent with each other?	A-D,F-G, N
R=Respondents R1= Senior policy-maker R2= Former senior officer	2	60-120	E. What standard do you predict you get in HKDSE LS examination? F. Do you agree that the design mode, content and organization of the DSE LS can help develop high quality teaching and learning by forming a reinforcing loop to achieve the aims of the curriculum? G. How do you evaluate DSE LS examination? What are your recommendations to improve? H. What are your opinions on the relationship between	H-N
R3= HKEAA executive	1	60	assessment format, school teaching style and learning practices? I. How far do you think the role and the mode of HKDSE LS examination can help candidates to acquire the curriculum aims?	H-N
R4 & R5= Experts in LS	2	60	J. Is there a conflict between learning mode and examination mode of NSS LS? K. Is LS teachers' assessment literacy rich enough to guide students to learn effectively? L. The Education Bureau emphasizes that the curriculum, pedagogy and assessment should be well aligned. How far is	A,C,F-K
R6= Parent	1	20	it true for the results of DSE LS for the three years? M. What is the pedagogical and assessment policy of educational reform in Hong Kong? N. Has a reinforcing loop framework with assessment as a lever	C,D,I
R7 & R8 = Pre-service teachers who got 5** in HKDSE examination in LS	2	40	for better learning been created? (ibid)	A-C

3.7.3 Lesson observations

With reference to the C & A Guide, the 21st century skills of LS, the research questionnaires (Appendix 1 & 2) and the researcher's experiences on LS student-teachers lesson observations, a checklist for the LS lesson observations (see Table 3.6) was created. Items under the categories of learn to live, learn to respect, learn to think and some main teaching strategies descriptors were outlined for checking the adoption frequencies of respective teaching methods during lessons.

Table 3.6 Classroom teaching methods

Learn to live
1. The introduction of the life and current events for questions, discussions, activities, or arguments
2. Building concepts through cooperative learning and showing the relationships between the concepts.
3. Transferring multi-disciplinary knowledge and concepts effectively to learning through issue-enquiry methods.
4. Integrating issues-enquiry effectively and establishing before and after class learning.
5. Constructing the opportunity of social issues involvement via role play, debate and so forth
6. Utilizing the experiences of students and the learning experiences effectively to build the learning processes
7. Integrating real life examples to discuss the cause and causation of an issue
Learn to think
1. Using the issue-enquiry framework and related concepts for problem determination and analysis.
2. Raising the questions, responding, explaining or directing the issue through vertical and horizontal perspective.
3. Teachers and students apply the art of proof: logic, rhetoric, dialectic...etc.
4. Initiating creative problem solving and innovative thinking for learning and application
5. Developing students logical thinking, namely, generalization, analogy and determination
6. Building macro or micro situation and working with logical reasoning or presenting evidences, investigating the causation of an incident as part of the learning experience.
7. Providing the opportunity for thinking and flexible application. Also, encouraging rethinking, evaluation and creativity
8. Issue-enquiry procedure, clarifying the concepts, collecting evidences and concluding evidences and determination
Learn to respect
1. Cooperative learning: group discussion of issue-enquiry and reports
2. Putting themselves into other's position and understanding stakeholders' role and importance
3. Accepting others generously and providing suitable learning environment or feedback
4. Students participate the discussion actively and stimulating freedom /in-depth thinking.
5. Teachers and students are open-minded and they think through different stakeholders' perspectives.
Main Teaching Strategies
1. Construction type: learning-oriented
2. Teach type: exam-oriented
3. Flexible: integrating knowledge and key concepts
4. Issue-enquiry based

3.8 Procedure

The four stages of research were shown in Figure 3.2, the research overview. First, design and planning: based on literature reviews and the previous mini study on cohort 2, I designed and planned my study in 2013. The second stage, data collection: the explanatory sequential mixed-methods research (Creswell & Clark, 2011) commenced in early 2014. This stage stretched from January to December 2014. Two parallel data sets: students and teachers' questionnaires, their semi-structured interviews, and classroom observations were collected with school approval from January to July. Individual consent forms were signed and research information sheets were provided. Eight other stakeholders had the semi-structured interviews from April to December. The data collection process in Table 3.7 shows the details. The third stage, data analysis, lasted the longest. Data were compared and correlated to find if gaps of missing links exist between assessments, pedagogy and curriculum aims; and to discover the impacts of DSE on students learning and practicing.

With further literature review, the announcement of EDB NAS Medium-term report, the release of more research publications on LS, and the impact of LS on students gradually revealed, I finalized my thesis in September with more nurture and evidence based interpretation backed-up by the dynamical systems theory in the final stage.

Table 3.7 The data collection process

DATE	CONTENTS	REMARKS
4-7/ 2014	Sent an invitation letter, two sets of questionnaires (1 teacher and 10 students within the same class) a return envelope and a return form to 458 secondary schools in Hong Kong by mail	To the school principals and LS panel head
1-7/ 2014	Six school studies, totally: • Ten lesson observations in 3 band 2-3 schools • Ten teachers or panel heads, 17 students participated in semi-structured interviews separately and individually	Authorization from schools or head teachers. Individual consent form
4-12/ 2014	Semi-structured interviews with 8 participants from a candidate parent, a HKEAA LS assessment executive, a former senior LS curriculum developer, an EDB policy-maker, 2 LS experts, and 2 LS student-teachers who got HKDSE LS 5** separately and individually	Individual consent form

Figure 3.2 A diagram of the research overview

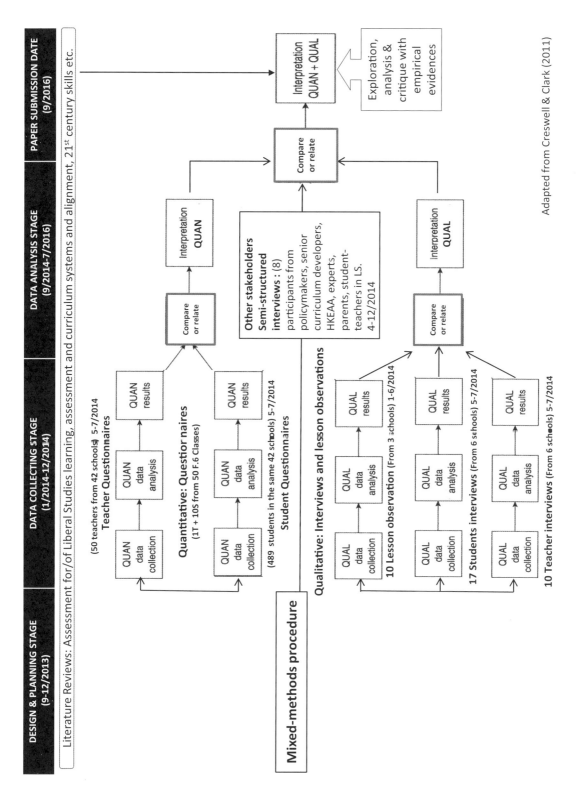

3.9 Data analysis

Questionnaires and semi-structured questions design and analysis are constructed consistent with the framework of 21st century skills for the aims of LS (see 2.4.1), and the structure of horizontal and vertical alignment (see 2.4.2). Correspondence with the aims to learn how to live, to think and to respect are used as an indicator or criteria for evaluating the strengths and weakness of LS implementation. Based on the criteria of aims, relevant teaching strategies and the impacts or effects were enquired in the questionnaires (see 3.7.1) and semi-structured questions (see 3.7.2). The direction of data analysis is on the significance of the relationship between the processes of teaching and learning and the impacts of public examinations. How and to what extent were summative and formative assessments and the three curriculum cycle components aligned with each other horizontally and vertically to improve students' learning? The variables of data analysis focused on the perceptions of subject teachers and their students on the role and impacts of public examination. Student and teachers' quantitative data sets were integrated for comparison and analysis. The processes reveal potential differences in perceptions on the vertical components or to what extent that public examinations align with the aims, pedagogies and outcomes. The perception of aims is an influential variable in the implementation process; it is relatively visible. The outcomes are the dependent products of the process. Therefore, critical examination will be concentrated on the process of teaching and learning. In-depth further analysis of the relationships between aims, pedagogy and assessments relies on the qualitative analysis of classroom observations and semi-structured interviews. As dynamical systems theory is used to explain unpredictability and instability in change (Tse, 2010a, p.5) during the data analysis, it provides flexible, non-linear, opened mindset to explore and relate the espoused-theories to theories-in-use. How different direct manipulators react to high-stakes examination and to learning for long-term goals in reality would be analyzed. More important is the awareness of the influences of vertical, horizontal and spatial complexity, such as the influences of assessment policy, the availability of teaching and learning materials, the intervention of outlying interest groups, the years of implementations and the internal and external political environment, and so on. Data interpretation embraces all dimensions of complexity. Results are further analyzed according to the pattern of changes and effects of chaos or the influences of social attractors (ibid, p.223) in the context of curriculum development in Hong Kong.

3.9.1 Quantitative data analysis

Quantitative data analysis includes descriptive and inferential statistics by using SPSS. The level of statistical significance was set at α = .05 (Cohen & Morrison, 2011). All items adopt a Likert scale of 4. They are tailored into positive sequence for statistic and comparison. The nominal value 1 represents strongly disagree while 4 being strongly agree; 2.5 is the average mean. More than 2.5 means more respondents positively agree or strongly agree with the statement and less than 2.5 is the opposite. That means higher the mean, more people agree with it and vice versa.

Most of the items were categorized into 'learn to live', 'learn to think', and 'learning-oriented strategies' and so on for statistical analysis. The process helps to verify any phenomenon of the implementation gaps within the LS curriculum cycle. Impact was considered poor with a mean lower than 2.5.

3.9.2 Qualitative data

Interview record were in Chinese; transcripts were done in Chinese first and then translated into English. The interview transcriptions were cross-checked by two assistants. Then the transcripts were read carefully to get a sense of the whole picture and then key words were grouped according to several themes. A coherent justification for the themes was made by triangulating both quantitative and qualitative data (Creswell, 2014). Accuracy validation of the transcriptions is complete during the process. Coherence and insight are obtained through a process of verification by interpreting and interrelating the meaning of the transcripts. Qualitative data are interpreted and analyzed based on the framework of five sections from quantitative findings in the questionnaires. Qualitative samples are deployed for representative or critical cases according to the development (ibid). Based on the research questions and insights from the literature, themes emerged and significant points are drawn out. Using this emergent theme analysis approach, categories emerge from the data (Weber, 1990). The representations of the themes and the range of opinions are explored. Lexical and conceptual differences on the meaning of curriculum aims, learning processes and assessment alignment, curriculum cycle, assessment literacy and so on between teachers and students are explained through qualitative data results.

As for classroom observations, I went into the classroom to observe the 10 lessons. I monitored both students and teachers' interactions and participations. With '$\checkmark$' or no '$\checkmark$' to indicate whether teachers adopted the teaching methods or not. The numbers of '$\checkmark$' in the checklist reflect the observed lesson reality. The tape records or notes of the lessons help to revise and confirm the checklist. These checklist results consolidate data on teachers' teaching methods from interviews and survey, impart insights to individual interviews and confer deep look into teachers' teaching and learning strategies. Moreover, observing five F.6 lessons before public examination and four F.5 & one F.4 lessons after examination season of that year afforded more data comparison for understanding the impacts of examination.

Applying the dynamical systems theory, complexity of change on how students link their learning strategy to the changing anticipated outcomes of curriculum aims is hinged by their transient forecast projections on public examinations. The curriculum cycle should be explained through the interpretation of both quantitative and qualitative data with evidences and suitable theories.

3.10 Ethical issues

Ethical codes and regulation for educational research were followed (Punch & Qancea, 2014): consideration of professional development, recognition of the variety of views and prioritizing respect for persons over consideration of the research. All participants voluntarily participated and were informed verbally and in writing about the study. Interviewees signed a consent form and could withdraw from the study at any time. Confidentiality was promised. All data such as questionnaires and transcripts were stored safely for an appropriate period of time. Ethic approval was sought from the University of Bristol GSoE's Ethics Committee. The highest possible level of trustworthiness was sought and considered (Creswell, 2014).

Chapter 4 RESULTS

4.1 Introduction

Including those who prepared the LS curriculum and those who teach in class, all facilitators hoped that the new DSE (Diploma of Secondary Education) LS could stand out from among all conventional examination subjects and be able to nurture acquisition of 21st century skills. The assumption is that if assessments were aligned properly with pedagogy and curriculum, LS should be able to achieve its consensual aims. If this postulation is right, we should be able to trace backward some seamless connections between public examination, pedagogy, and the aims of the curriculum. If the connections could not be proved, then discrepancy exists between what people believe, the espoused theory, and the principle they exercise in reality, the theory-in-use (Argyris, 1990, p.130) and the mismatch would be reflected as twisted pedagogy strategy. Using a mixed-methods research, this chapter reports on differences in perspectives for different stakeholders. Evidences were derived from students and teachers' discernments, supplemented with other stakeholders' perceptions.

The reality found in this research could be summarized as follows:

There exists various degree of perception and implementation gaps between aims and outcomes (public examination in particular) in the minds of different stakeholders. Issue-driven higher-order thinking skills were embedded in the curriculum. However, students do not care about the aims of LS. Teaching were exam-oriented in practice. Both teachers and students perceived that this is more effective for winning scores. Changes in HKEAA's support pattern reflected that the original ideology was compromised; the types of critical thinking learning to be assessed was reduced. Formative use of summative criteria and rubrics during class were encouraged in a pragmatic manner. Interest groups interfered the LS learning process. Exam-oriented teaching and learning ended up in argumentative procedural drilling. Students are relatively strong in Learn to think in a confined scope but weak in Learn to live and ignored Learn to respect. Their interest depleted; their learning motivation in LS were low. Forecast on issue topics likely to be asked in oncoming round of public examination is common. From there, students were asked to memorize structured answering patterns that give a flavour of argumentative procedure. This enables students to produce ostensibly sensible judgmental answers with much less critical thinking. On the positive side, LS examination's standards-referenced criteria and rubrics have informed classroom collaborative skills learning and it has great potential to lever professional change, yet it caused unpredicted counterproductive side effects. Aligning summative assessment with holistic curriculum aims through formative functions for learning will be the way ahead.

4.2 Aims of LS in teachers' mind versus students' needs

The following Table 4.1 of findings serve both sections 4.2.1 and 4.2.2. Non-parametric statistic tests such as Wilcoxon rank test, Mann-Whitney U test were used. There is a main reason of using non-parametric tests in the study. Result from Shapiro-Wilk normality test showed that most of items do not follow a normal distribution. For example, among student, the result of Shapiro-Wilk test of the item 'Learn to live' is <.001, which means the item is not statically normal. It violates the assumption in parametric statistic which the distribution of data should be normal.

4.2.1 Aims of LS – Teachers' perspective

Data prompt tentative assertion that there exists remarkable discrepancy between teachers' perceptions on the aims of LS and whether the aims can be achieved through examination. Learning to think is about critical thinking, broadening students' mind. Learning to live is about arousing social awareness of students. Teachers care and make an effort to fit them into the examination but they care less about attitude, innovation, connection and the nurture of balanced thinking. Teachers' perceptions on 'Aims of LS' do not endure throughout real examination preparations. Teachers do not put espoused aims in use if they predict those components do not stand a chance to appear in public examination papers.

Table 4.1 Comparison between teachers' and students' perceptions on aims and how DSE helps fulfill the aims

Part 1 A and B: Please indicate (1A) the extent to which you agree that each of the following statements is aim of the Liberal Studies (LS) curriculum and (1B) the extent to which the DSE helps to achieve these aims. Item	Recognition of aims T1A (n=49) Mean (SD)	How DSE helps fulfill the aims		Mann-Whitney U test T1B vs S1B Z (p)	Wilcoxon rank test T1A vs T1B Z (p)	Spearman correlation T1A vs T1B r
		T1B (n=49) Mean(SD)	S1B (n=489) Mean (SD)			
Learn to live	3.22 (.353)	2.92 (.370)	2.94 (.465)	-.691 (.490)	-4.184 (.000**)	.379**
a. Master interdisciplinary skills and concepts and effectively work with a broad range of different types of knowledge	3.16 (.468)	2.96 (.515)	2.90 (.565)	-.539 (.590)	-2.500 (.012*)	.381**
b. Develop flexibility and the ability to apply existing knowledge and transfer concepts	3.18 (.523)	2.8 (.619)	2.90 (.613)	-1.066 (.286)	-4.025 (.000*)	.547**
c. Master the use of media and information technologies	3.16 (.426)	2.85 (.595)	2.89 (.673)	-.590 (.555)	-2.982 (.003**)	.161
d. Use different sources of information and ideas and effectively integrate and argue about this information	3.38 (.53)	3.09 (.509)	3.06 (.620)	-.139 (.889)	-3.638 (.000**)	.503**
Learn to think	3.17 (.482)	2.81 (.49)	2.90 (.547)	-1.045 (2.96)	-4.191 (.000**)	.373*
e. Nurture rational, objective and critical thinking skills	3.26 (.565)	2.98 (.577)	3.01 (.655)	-.506 (.613)	-2.977 (.003**)	.402**
f. Nurture innovation and the ability to solve problems effectively	2.98 (.553)	2.57 (.62)	2.78 (.715)	-1.743 .081)	-3.648 (.000**)	.301*
g. Help students become independent thinkers through developing their skills in knowledge construction and issue inquiry	3.26 (.565)	2.89 (.64)	2.90 (.654)	-.095 (.924)	-3.391 (.001**)	.387**
Learn to respect	3.17 (.443)	2.69 (.509)	2.93 (.556)	-2.979 (.003*)	-4.563 (.000**)	.174
i. Develop multiple perspectives and distinguish between the different values behind these differing views	3.36 (.525)	3.09 (.694)	3.10 (.635)	-.168 (.866)	-2.676 (.007**)	.385**
j. Foster collaboration and communication skills and tolerance toward different views	3.08 (.566)	2.65 (.72)	2.91 (.700)	-2.243 (.025*)	-3.257 (.001**)	.392**
k. Nurture responsible and committed citizens	3.08 (.534)	2.44 (.659)	2.80 (.767)	-3.288 (.001**)	-4.272 (.000**)	.179
All items' average	3.19 (.370)	2.83 (.403)	2.91 (.458)	-1.419 (.156)	-5.029 (.000**)	.331*

*p <.05, **p<.01

Remarks: Shapiro-Wilk test for normality confirmed that the data are non-parametric. Non-parametric tests with SPSS were used for all data output in the research.

Teachers admitted identification with the official curriculum aims (Table 4.1). The average rating of all items in T1A column was 3.19 (*SD*=.370). However, teachers generally rated lower 2.83 (*SD*=.403) in T1B column for how DSE can fulfill the aims. Wilcoxon rank test, the non-parametric SPSS test, was used for statistical assay. It serves to explore differences between teachers' recognition of the aims of LS and also how they perceive that DSE could be able to fulfill the aims. There is a significant discrepancy between teachers' perception of the usefulness of public assessment and if it fits to fulfill the aims of LS.

Spearman correlation revealed that most items have a positive correlation between recognition of aims and perception on DSE. In refined detail, perception of DSE in Learning to live (*r*=.379, *p*<.001) and Learning to think (*r*=.373, *p*<.05) are both positively correlated. However, there were no correlation between the aims and the perception in mastering the use of media and information technologies, nor to nurture responsible and committed citizens. Teachers tend to think public examination do not correlate with nurturing students to become responsible and committed citizens.

Qualitative interviews provided evidences to inquire into their relationship. The semi-structured interview question, *"What are the aims of LS? Does DSE LS help to fulfill the aims?"* revealed that most teachers accept that the aim of LS is to broaden students' minds, to enhance their awareness on social hot issues, on environmental development and to cherish critical thinking. T1 complimented, *"LS allows students to explore the knowledge out of the established discipline."*

In addition, LS also aims at helping students to develop into independent thinkers. Teachers recognized that the aims of LS include nurturing students' social responsibility and values but they agreed less that DSE help nurture the aims adequately (T2, T3, and T4). Nevertheless, it is difficult to evaluate one's values through exam-oriented assessment. T3 expressed, *"Because of the examination nature, the teaching objectives crucially aim at increasing the criticial, correlative thinking and the knowledge contents. Consequently, it rarely touches on the values that may affect one's standpoint".* Teachers T2, T6, T9, and T10 regarded that it could not help to nurture innovation nor the ability to solve problems effectively. T5 sighed, *"The aim is too high. It is good to set a high goal but time is limited for learning and teaching".*

4.2.2 Aims in-use – Students' point of view

Compared to teachers, students are indifferent to the learning aims stipulated in curriculum papers. They are pragmatic; some aim only for scores while some think learning has to be interesting. Both students and teachers tend to agree that examination could help achieve the aims of learning to live and learning to think, but teachers agree less on the aims of learning to respect. Teachers concur that examination helps develop multiple perspectives, distinguishing between different values behind differing views, and using different sources of information and ideas. They have dilemma on espoused beliefs and practical needs of students. Students aim unanimously at getting better examination results. They crave for minimum effort but maximum scores. They seem not having conceived any of the different aims of learn to live, learn to think and learn to respect. They are firmly instrumental and pragmatic for scores.

Since it was assumed that students do not know enough about the LS curriculum aims, student's questionnaire was simplified to just one part. Results show that students generally agree well with how public examination can help fulfill the aims of LS (Table 4.1). The average rating of all items in S1B column was 2.91 (*SD*=.458). Mann-Whitney U test explores the difference between how teachers (T1B) and students (S1B) perceive on the usefulness of public examination in fulfilling the aims of LS. In the domain learn to respect, it was found that students have a significantly higher score (*M* =2.93, *SD* =0.556) than teachers (*M* =2.69, *SD* =0.509), (*z*=2.979, *p*<.03). Teachers significantly trust less than student that examination can help to fulfil learning *how to respect.*

During the interviews, all students except S2 and S4 paid attention to the effectiveness of learning techniques on how to get high marks. They were also concerned about hot issues and if the learning processes were interesting (S4 & S15). Some have preferred modules and invested greater attention on those, such as Today Hong Kong. Nevertheless, they seldom care about the curriculum aims.

Most of the teachers consider students' examination goals should contribute to demonstrate the ability of critical thinking, individual thinking on controversial issues and hence fulfilling the LS aim learn to think. To other curriculum aims, they hold diverse beliefs. T2 was concerned about students' values. He expressed that LS required students to conduct a general analysis with multiple perspectives, inductive reasoning, critical thinking, *"at last, to sort out their own opinion. However, some of the opinions are ... in conflict with positive values"*. T6 aimed at helping students to get good marks: *"If I teach a lot which widen students' horizon but, finally, they cannot get good marks...I think it is my failure".*

4.2.3 Environmental influences on Aims in-use

Demographic differences reflect contextual influences on students' recognition and perception of aims and examination. There was no gender difference among item *a* to *j* using Mann-Whitney Test.

Mann-Whitney Test confirmed that there were significant differences between Cantonese and English groups in 7 out of 10 items *(p< 0.05)* (Table 4.2 Demographic comparison of students' perceptions on how DSE helps fulfill the aims). The overall scores that include all items show significant difference between the two language groups *(p< 0.01)*. For all of the aims above, students receiving Cantonese instruction had significant higher score than English group. Students doing LS in English as the medium of instruction were likely to see LS as instrumental to public examination instead of Learning to live or Learning to think. Innovation and developing into responsible and committed citizens were traded off when learning is done in a second language.

Many of them considered DSE had numerous inadequacies. S1 from a Band 1 school said, *"When we were preparing for this LS examination, there was no single session that made us feel being responsible to the society or we belonged to this society".* Band 2 and 3 students (S7-17) were more positive; they believe reading newspapers help them get better marks in exams. It seems that Band 1 school students and government school students using English as the medium of instruction fail to agree with the positive relationship between DSE and achieving the aims.

Moreover, students from families of better socioeconomic status background trust their private tutorials and school-based strategies for accomplishing educational aims. Government schools follow the directions of respective school boards assigned by the Bureau. S6, who got 5**, expressed his viewpoint, *"I didn't like having LS class because the learning style was just filling in the blanks... First of all, for utilitarian purpose, everything I learnt is for public examinations. ... I think the tutorial school can provide these answers to me."* This is a pedagogical defeat; students remain in faith that there must be a correct answer to every question, even with debatable social issues inquired in LS. Most likely, students tend to agree less with a belief that DSE help them experience nurturing innovation and reach the ability to solve problems effectively, nor nurture responsible and committed citizens.

Students embrace an aim in-use for better score. They crave paying less effort to obtain maximum scores through any personal tutor or private school.

The LS curriculum implementation expands the school ecological setting beyond the campus. As aims of educational reform concerns the entire society, LS being the key newborn integrated interdisciplinary curriculum to achieve those aims, that triggers much concerns from among springing interest groups, external agents (such as the newspapers, professional bodies and teacher unions), and many local and global research institutes. These outlier groups interact loosely but reinforce each other through the media when an issue arises to their benefits, say, for benefit of publicity and exposure in the media, hence, distort bias-free independent thinking in class. Media, teachers' union and pressure groups meddle in argumentative current hot-issues; news clippings become learning contents for LS. The window is open for co-evolution of value judgment from the standpoint of the interest of various intervening agencies through mass media but these agencies not professional with education sidetracked the aims of LS.

4.2.4 Aims Acumens – Perspective of other stakeholders

A. Parents:

A parent of a F.6 student (R6) from a government school, herself being a primary school teacher, initially thought that LS combined the features of Art, Sciences and Commerce but eventually admitted that her knowledge about the aims of LS is inadequate. At the end, her son sought extra classes from tutorial schools after school in order to get better score. Most likely, parents let schools or students decide on what to do and they sponsor unconditionally.

Table 4.2 Demographic comparison of students' perceptions on how DSE helps fulfill the aims

Please indicate the extent to which the DSE examination helps to achieve those aims.	Language of Instruction			Types of School				School Banding			
	Cantonese (n = 404)	English (n = 80)	Mann Whitney test (Z)	Gov. (n = 97)	Subsidized (n = 298)	Direct-Subsidy (n = 85)	Kruskal-Wallis test (χ2)	1 (n = 144)	2 (n = 211)	3 (n = 134)	Kruskal-Wallis test (χ2)
a. Master interdisciplinary skills and concepts and effectively work with a broad range of different types of knowledge	2.93(.56)	2.76(.53)	-2.370*	2.80(.59)	2.91(.58)	2.98(.51)	3.998	2.83(.53)	2.90(.64)	2.98(.46)	4.932
b. Develop flexibility and the ability to apply existing knowledge and transfer concepts	2.94(.59)	2.71(.68)	-2.608**	2.79(.63)	2.91(.62)	2.99(.59)	4.457	2.78(.59)	2.92(.66)	2.99(.54)	7.269*
c. Master the use of media and information technologies	2.91(.67)	2.82(.68)	-1.040	2.80(.72)	2.90(.68)	2.96(.65)	2.800	2.90(.70)	2.91(.69)	2.87(.62)	.403
d. Use different sources of information and ideas and effectively integrate and argue about this information	3.06(.63)	3.04(.58)	-.340	2.93(.62)	3.09(.61)	3.11(.66)	5.521	3.02(.57)	3.07(.70)	3.08(.54)	1.227
e. Nurture rational, objective and critical thinking skills	3.04(.65)	2.88(.68)	-2.153*	2.91(.69)	3.05(.65)	3.00(.64)	2.897	2.93(.64)	3.03(.69)	3.08(.61)	4.301
f. Nurture innovation and the ability to solve problems effectively	2.84(.69)	2.45(.75)	-4.497**	2.61(.80)	2.81(.70)	2.86(.68)	6.407*	2.57(.73)	2.81(.73)	2.96(.63)	20.295**
g. Help students become independent thinkers through developing their skills in knowledge construction and issue inquiry	2.94(.66)	2.72(.60)	-2.652**	2.77(.65)	2.94(.65)	2.92(.68)	4.257	2.79(.60)	2.93(.71)	2.99(.60)	7.204*
h. Develop multiple perspectives and distinguish between the different values behind these differing views	3.12(.64)	2.99(.56)	-1.907	2.97(.64)	3.13(.64)	3.14(.62)	4.827	3.05(.57)	3.11(.69)	3.13(.59)	1.533
i. Foster collaboration and communication skills and tolerance toward different views	2.94(.69)	2.75(.70)	-2.170*	2.74(.74)	2.96(.67)	2.89(.71)	7.185*	2.85(.69)	2.91(.72)	2.96(.67)	1.337
j. Nurture responsible and committed citizens	2.83(.76)	2.63(.79)	-2.219*	2.74(.77)	2.83(.76)	2.75(.80)	1.682	2.64(.76)	2.81(.78)	2.96(.72)	13.297**
All items' average	2.94(.45)	2.75(.44)	-3.174**	2.79(.47)	2.93(.46)	2.95(.45)	6.492*	2.82(.42)	2.92(.50)	2.98(.40)	7.902*

* $p < .05$; **$p < .01$. a - d = Learn to live; e- g = Learn to think; h – j = Learn to respect

Remarks: Shapiro-Wilk test for normality confirmed that the data are non-parametric. Non-parametric tests with SPSS were used for all data output.

B. Policy-makers & curriculum developers:

A policy-maker (R1), and a former senior curriculum developer (R2) of EDB were both concerned about the curriculum aims of interdisciplinary learning and learning to learn. R1 claimed that, *"The implementation of 'Learning conceptions of including Art in Science and Science in Art 文中有理，理中有文' will become feasible through the senior secondary LS subject".* R2 addressed that LS allows students to understand more about the society by turning them aware of current affairs and their concerns for society increase. Education reform aims are: learning to learn, learning to live, and whole-person development; those are espoused theory that they wish would also be the theory in-use. Policy-makers and curriculum developers focused more on the ideal theoretical aims and wished to accomplish that through formative assessments of IES. R1 said, *"Our main goal on foundation education is to focus on the primary subject matter of Education System Reform – 'learning to learn'."* and *"Teaching and learning are the prime purpose, teachers should put it their first priority. Consequently, assessment is for cooperating teaching and learning to realize the aims".* Yet, R2 worried, *"If there are too much involvement by people from society when setting up the curriculum, that curriculum will not be professional."*

In reality, they emphasized less about the connections between the aims and the public examination. In different teacher training events, they strived to balance the diverse aims in actual practice. Curriculum developers tend to neglect students' short-term needs. By design, Government schools and volunteer Collaborative Research and Development ("Seed") Projects schools (Seed-schools) were designated to highlight the goodwill of curriculum developers.

C. HKEAA executives:

The examination authority HKEAA is responsible for public examinations. In line with the backdrop of a major system change (undergraduate degree programs change from three to four years since 2012/13), a senior executive from HKEAA being interviewed (R3) asserted that the practical aim of launching LS in the DSE examination was to level LS to be equivalent to a University admission examination subject. Students do not have time to study too many subjects in one year less than before; the requirements for the University admission examination were higher than the previous HKCEE standard. In order to match up to the admission standards of local and global high schools (which used to be the Advanced Level examination two years after the HKCEE), HKEAA have to consider the fairness, feasibility, validity and reliability of constructing a compulsory new subject. He claimed *"Both students and teachers cherish public examination; it is therefore normal to place assessment before the teaching and studying".* He expected that, *"In general, what should be learned are what being examined".*

To facilitate the transformations, HKEAA conducts executives' seminars and dispenses examination reports. Samples and guidelines for next cohort were dispatched to schools and any people interested. These information and instructions attract great concerns from teachers.

Consequent after rounds and rounds of hard dialogues dealing with a deep general concern about the trustworthiness of examined results, a relatively narrow range of assessment tasks were agreed; risk-taking grey areas would not be an option. The examination authority must focus more on fairness, validity, reliability, accountability and at least satisficing implementation of curriculum aims. High-risk aims that might stir up much grading controversies, such as creativity, problem solving and values testing are to be dropped. Teachers take these examination constraints as their beacons; any aims with which achievements could not be measured through public examination become non-essential.

D. LS experts:

An expert in LS (R4) nailed the aims of LS as *"to understand the rationale of the matter, in other words, what makes you hold different points of view from others!"* R4 contended that LS is a bridge for student growth. Attitudes, generic skills and knowledge have to be integrated and be mutually supportive. Knowledge and facts have to be well-knitted, scaffolding strong evidence to support sound reasoning. *"The examination and assessment ought to be aligned with teaching and studying."* She embraces the curriculum aims of integration and she believes it is the rationale for the assessment and curriculum alignment. Another expert (R5) also pointed out that curriculum developers hoped students knew how to think and eventually think critically through more practices with LS topics. That is her vision of less rote learning but more thinking; and greater concern on social affair and national education in the new curriculum.

Experts emphasized deep-learning through knowledge construction; this would enable integration of key concepts, skills and values. They were inspired to promote deep-learning theory faithfully in curriculum documents. They pursued to bridge the gaps between ideal and practice, to enhance teachers' ability and to influence teachers' beliefs and values to close the gaps. Some experienced teachers such as R1 also held similar values and beliefs.

4.2.5 Section Summary

This section concluded that different stakeholders agreed with the curriculum aims of learn to live, learn to think and learn to respect but each clipped to some parts of the spectrum of aims only. In practice, they filtered out unmeasurable soft skills that should work at least in theory and formulate their hidden aims-in-use selectively. There exists a perception and implementation gap between aims and public examination in the minds of different stakeholders. Teachers' perceptions are different from students especially on the aims of learning to respect.

4.3 Assessment for learning and Assessment of learning strategies

4.3.1 On Pedagogy and Formative assessment

Pedagogy is *'The method and practice* of teaching, *especially as an* academic *subject or* theoretical concept ("Pedagogy," 2016). In this research, the concern is about strategy in the process of teaching and learning to boost 21st century skills; and how formative assessments relate to the public summative assessment. Formative assessments provide quick 'feedbacks for learning' to students while summative assessments yield final standard scores of achievements. Effective teaching and learning strategies combined with concrete suitable timely feedback (formative assessment) may support the students' desire to maximize the public examination (summative assessment) scores with minimal effort. Educators know that students put better examination performance their short-term goals higher in priority than the 21st century skills that should be their long-term goals of achievement. How to help students acquire the soft 21st century skills while getting good better achievements are the espoused visions of combining formative and summative assessment. The delivery of knowledge, nurture of values and beliefs are parts and parcel of accountability in preparing pupils for public examination. Teachers are in control to filter, to choose and to decide on suitable efficient strategies for teaching and learning. Simultaneously, teachers have to entertain students' wish, to meet the accountability expectations, and to improve teaching and learning as their immediate goals. Thinking skills are the key 21st century human resources development aims but detectable achievements could be remote. In theory, the scores in LS examination represent the abilities of skills. Assessment criterion with rubrics show the level of standards. Could formative feedbacks using summative assessment criterion and standards be effective or not depends on teachers' skill on alignment; and it is important to make students understand the relationships. That is why some teaching strategies need to be persisted and more recursive feedback needed.

To simplify the scenario, discussion here sorted stakeholders into two groups, the direct manipulators and the indirect manipulators to the pedagogical process. The direct manipulators are students, teachers and HKEAA assessment experts; they tilt towards adopting pragmatic strategies down the road preparing for LS examinations. Teachers and students believe that using exam-oriented strategies more often than the learning-oriented strategies is the right thing to do. Teachers adopt accommodative strategies to focus on the types of critical thinking that narrow assessment styles could afford according to the curriculum aims of *ABC* (*Awareness of the society, Broadening perspective, Connection skills & Critical thinking*. See chapter 1). They adopt formative use of summative criteria and rubrics in class. HKEAA directly inform teachers how to make use of examination strategies to achieve better scores that could successfully reflect relevant learning. Other indirect stakeholders uphold the espoused theories to support or intervene the teaching and learning processes intentionally or unintentionally.

Table 4.3 Comparison of responses among teachers' and students' perceptions on pedagogies

Please indicate 2A the frequency with which you use the following teaching methods and 2B how effective you think these methods are in achieving good results in the DSE.	2A: Frequency		2B: Effectiveness	Mann-Whitney U test	Wilcoxon rank test	Spearman correlation
	S2A	T2A	T2B	S2A & T2A	T2A & T2B	T2A & T2B
	Mean (SD)	Mean(SD)	Mean (SD)	Z (p)	Z (p)	r
Learning-oriented strategies	3.19 (.499)	3.17 (.356)	3.07 (.396)	-.645 (.519)	-1.676 (.094)	.545**
a. Cooperative learning, integrating life themes for communication and investigation to integrate life theme to communicate and investigate	3.24 (.713)	3.14 (.645)	2.83 (.601)	-1.165 (.244)	-3.138 (.002**)	.418**
b. Applying issue-enquiry methods and evidence flexibly to nurture logical thinking abilities	3.27 (.659)	3.39 (.571)	3.34 (.522)	-1.081 (.280)	-.655 (.513)	.248
c. Constructing micro and macro situations and working with logic or presenting evidence as part of the learning experience	3.12 (.723)	3.06 (.633)	3.17 (.486)	-7.95 (.426)	-1.279 (.201)	.279
d. Understanding different people's values and relationships via role-play	3.11 (.754)	3.08 (.862)	3.17 (.670)	-.074 (.941)	-.726 (.468)	.467**
e. Using information technologies to support learning, thinking and communicating	3.20 (.719)	3.16 (.657)	2.87 (.575)	-5.80 (.562)	-2.884 (.004**)	.345*
Exam-oriented strategies	3.29 (.478)	3.57 (.341)	3.38 (.394)	-4.028 (.000**)	-3.162 (.002**)	.373*
f. Direct transmission of knowledge and concepts	3.44 (.611)	3.54 (.613)	3.02 (.668)	-1.263 (.206)	-4.642 (.000**)	.522**
g. Developing clear personal standpoints to express opinions on issues in oral or written form, providing appropriate evidence	3.30 (.643)	3.61 (.492)	3.43 (.542)	-3.278 (.001**)	-2.183 (.029*)	.374**
h. Integrating life experiences and current issues to raise questions and engage in evidence-based discussions	3.37 (.653)	3.69 (.508)	3.43 (.580)	-3.44 (.001**)	-2.982 (.003**)	.363*
i. Using HKEAA sample papers and DSE examination papers as chief teaching sources	3.10 (.796)	3.41 (.643)	3.50 (.548)	-2.571 (.010*)	-.894 (.371)	.433**
j. Adopting the requirements and modes of the DSE for formative assessments	3.26 (.734)	3.60 (.610)	3.48 (.623)	-3.249 (.001**)	-1.732 (.083)	.629**
All items' average	3.24 (.440)	3.37 (.264)	3.23 (.345)	-2.056 (.040*)	-2.891 (.004**)	.488**

*p <.05, **p<.01

4.3.2　Pedagogy in-theory and its variations in-use – teachers' perspective

Table 4.3 listed ten commonly used teaching methods in LS. By comparing their perceived frequencies of use, teachers preferred learning-oriented strategies at least in theory but in practice, they use exam-oriented strategies more often to entertain students' short-term needs for better examination scores.

Classroom observations data verified use of summative assessment types of questions in class, with rubrics and prompts on level of standards, used formatively in the instruction process. Examination plays key role as a lever to drive and guide teachers' teaching methods. The design of lessons seemed to have simulated the process of scaffolding to foster writing argumentative essays in the public examination.

A. Pedagogy in-theory and its variations in-use

Teachers' knowledge and beliefs on the teaching strategies determined their frequency of using the strategies. Wilcoxon signed ranks test showed that teachers tend to agree that 'exam-oriented strategies' (M=3.38, SD=.394) are more effective than 'learning-oriented strategies' (M=3.07, SD=.396) in helping students achieve good results in DSE (T2B), (z=4.00, p<.001).

Teachers tend to use 'exam-oriented strategies' (M= 3.57, SD=.341) more often than 'learning-oriented strategies' (M=3.17, SD=.356). Wilcoxon signed ranks test showed that the difference between them (z=4.51, p<.001) was statistically significant.

From semi-structured interviews data, many teachers agreed that current DSE helped them change their teaching styles, specifically, becoming more student-oriented. Seven out of ten among them often use a constructivist approach in lessons. Cooperative learning such as group discussions, debates, issue-inquiry based role-plays, mind-maps drafting and *'concept notebook"* are regularly used.

> T4 shared his experiences, *"we will do 'concept notebook' which establishes the structure where concepts generalize the knowledge…our homework is cooperating with the question technique and issue-enquiry that students learn".*

T9 commented, *"The analysis should be simple and systematic... to view both sides of the coin. Effectiveness should also be taken into account. The effectiveness of that standpoint or opinion depends on the proof procedure."*

The other three teachers used direct transmission of knowledge and concepts more often. They believed that is a more suitable strategy for their students. The aims were clear-- to guide students answering questions in the examinations.

T2 said, *"I will talk about examination questions.... mention the news... I will tell what is relevant to the concept, what is relevant to the module..."*

T5 commented that, *"Cooperative learning is a good thing ... but I think that there is no big difference between what they have done and what I have given to them (direct transmission of knowledge and concepts)".*

T6 said *" Usually I won't divide students into groups and cooperative learning is not an option ... in a limited period of time. I will clarify directly if deemed neceessary."*

Contradictory to teachers' general belief, Spearman correlations revealed that eight out of the 10 common LS teaching method items bear positive correlation between the teaching methods and their effectiveness for better DSE. Positive correlation means that when the frequency of the teaching methods increases, the DSE scores will be better. Wilcoxon rank test showed that teachers had a significantly higher rating in using exam-oriented strategies (M=3.57, SD=.341) (T2A) than their recognition of the effectiveness on better DSE (M= 3.38, SD=.394) (z=-3.162, p<.01) (T2B). Except *f, direct transmission of knowledge,* all four exam-oriented strategies means were higher than the learning-oriented strategies means. Teachers adopt exam-oriented strategies more frequently because they believe these methods were more effective though not data-driven.

T10 expressed, *"Our teaching is basically placing more importance on ability training ... if there are examinations, there must be examination technique. As a result, it strangles creativity. Our problem is a case of mass production ... it's like we use the mould to make the moon cake."*

Results show that teachers use evidence-based discussions, the various recommended modes of

DSE for formative assessments, and developing clear personal standpoints, yet more often direct transmission of concepts for teaching because they believe these strategies are more effective in achieving good results in the examination. Teachers also commonly use HKEAA sample papers and DSE examination papers as chief teaching sources during the process.

B. Pedagogy in-use — classroom observation

Classroom observation results were used as another source of data for trianguation (Table 4.4). The results from 10 LS lesson obervation classes in the check-list indicated use of 5 out of 7 items of 'Learn to live' pedagogic strategies, 5 out of 8 items of 'Learn to think', and 2 out of 5 items of 'Learn to respect' strategies. The numbers of ' √ ' were more than half. Learn to live has more counts than learn to think, and Learn to think has more counts than Learn to respect. Six lessons were rated to have more than half of ' √ '. It is pleasing to see that teachers used a variety of both learning and exam-oriented methods in class. Duirng these observations, all LS instruction lessons were issue-enquiry oriented. The assessment formats employed simulate the high-stake public examination. Students practised using issues analysis for handling open-ended questions. The practice routine conveyed messages that there exist established evaluation criteria, which represent the demand of assessment. Repeated use of different procedures for critical thinking has been reinforced. Procedural knowledge applied to key concept knowledge leading to presentations of the intended answers are the real content to learn in class.

L4 and L5 were special big classes, happened to be combined lessons from three classes after mock examinations. Those were lessons (see Table 4.5) organized by the form teachers. Divison of labour among LS teachers were that each one would be responsible for drafting and grading one or two exam-paper questions, grading for a particular question is to be performed by one corresponding teacher for the whole form of students taking that question. The respective teachers gave feedback to the whole form and taught the entire cohort specific answering techniques using that question as example. Teachers used both merits and weak samples to demonstrate how markers rated the grade according to the criterion-referenced standards. Comments and feedback to students were provided for all. After that, students' mock exam-papers were given back.

able 4.4 Lesson observation checklist

The extent to adopt the following teaching methods / Learn to live	Total no.	L1 T3	L2 T3	L3 T4	L4 T5	L5 T6	L6 T5	L7 T6	L8 T9	L9 T10	L10 T10
1. The introduction of the life and current events for questions, discussions, activities, or arguments	7	√	√	√				√	√	√	√
2. Building concepts through cooperative learning and showing the relationships between the concepts.	4	√	√	√							√
3. Transferring multi-disciplinary knowledge and concepts effectively to learning through issue-enquiry methods.	10	√	√	√	√	√	√	√	√	√	√
4. Integrating issues-enquiry effectively and establishing before and after class learning.	10	√	√	√	√	√	√	√	√	√	√
5. Constructing the opportunity of social issues involvement via role-play, debate and so forth	5	√	√	√				√			√
6. Utilizing the experiences of students and the learning experiences effectively to build the learning processes	8	√	√	√	√	√		√		√	√
7. Integrating real life examples to discuss the cause and causation of an issue	7	√	√	√				√	√	√	√
Learn to think											
1. Using the issue-enquiry framework and related concepts for problem determination and analysis.	10	√	√	√	√	√	√	√	√	√	√
2. Raising the questions, responding, explaining or directing the issue through vertical and horizontal perspective.	8		√	√	√	√	√	√	√		√
3. Teachers and students apply the art of proof: logic, rhetoric, dialectic...etc.	3	√		√							√
4. Initiating creative problem solving and innovative thinking for learning and application	1		√								
5. Developing students logical thinking, namely, generalization, analogy and determination	10	√	√	√	√	√	√	√	√	√	√
6. Building macro or micro situation and working with logical reasoning or presenting evidences, investigating the causation of an incident as part of the learning experience.	3			√					√		√
7. Providing the opportunity for thinking and flexible application. Also, encouraging rethinking, evaluation and creativity	7	√	√	√	√	√	√				√
8. Issue-enquiry procedure, clarifying the concepts, collecting evidences and concluding evidences and determination	9	√	√	√	√	√		√	√	√	√
Learn to respect											
1. Cooperative learning: group discussion of issue-enquiry and reports	5	√	√	√						√	√
2. Putting themselves into other's position and understanding stakeholders' role and importance	5	√	√	√					√		√
3. Accepting others generously and providing suitable learning environment or feedback	6	√	√	√				√		√	√
4. Students participate the discussion actively and stimulating freedom /in-depth thinking.	4	√	√	√							√
5. Teachers and students are open-minded and they think through different stakeholders' perspectives.	8	√	√	√	√	√		√		√	√
Total	/	17	17	20	9	9	6	12	10	11	19
Main Teaching Strategies											
1. Construction type: learning-oriented	5	√	√	√						√	√
2. Teach type: exam-oriented	6				√	√	√	√	√	√	
3. Flexible: integrating knowledge and key concepts	9	√	√	√	√	√		√	√	√	√
4. Issue-enquiry based	10	√	√	√	√	√	√	√	√	√	√
Remarks: School Banding: A=Band1. B=Band2. C=Band3;		A6	A5	A5	A6	A6	A5	A4	B6	B6	B5
Class: 4=F4, 5=F5, 6=F6; Period: I= Before Exam; II=After Exam		I	II	II	I	I	II	I	I	I	II

The lead teacher told researcher that early in the year-term beginning, they had conducted analysis and prediction of the themes and the modes for public examination. They used that as the themes of contents and types of the exam-questions for mock-exam. They shared the workload to prepare teaching materials and to draft the exam-papers, which followed their predictions on the public examination.

Table 4.5 Topics spotted during the classroom observation

Topic before DSE	Topic after DSE
L1: Globalization—The iPhone impact on society	L2: Energy efficiency technologies
L4: Cultural preservation, Social conflicts in Hong Kong (Mock-exam paper feedback)	L3: How to resolve the conflict between the international community
L5: Economic globalization - The pros and cons, Issues of human right in Mainland China (Mock-exam paper feedback)	L6: Analysis of past-exam papers and the use of strategies
L8: Analysis of 2013 exam-papers	L7: Health care-- Plastic surgery
L9: The relationship between social participation and the learning of LS	L10: The role of government in the prevention of infectious diseases

Upon rush time immediately before DSE, focus of lessons was directed mainly to exam-oriented strategies, tightly coupled with standards-referenced reports samples dispatched by HKEAA. Exam-questions were used to serve formative functions. During the class, an issue as a theme was raised for discussion with the whole class. This collective learning process provided students an experience to answer an exam-question in written form. Time being inadequate within one lesson, it was common to command a follow-up homework, to write a short essay about the issue with the learning concepts and materials in the lesson. Constant feedback from teachers were recorded for the purpose of this classroom observation process. In L5 and L9, teachers provided feedback for students during the class. T6 chose a student's homework essay for essay writing demonstration. T10 took a photo of a student's note after group discussion and then displayed on screen at once for whole class discussion.

Lessons after DSE were more group-work and a variety of self-directed activities with some hints of examination. For instance, L2 incorporated one of the exam-questions from 2014 paper, "'The costs of wind power outweigh the benefits.' … Do Sources A, B and C support this view? Explain your answer" into his lesson construction for group-work. The lesson guided students to argue about the pros and cons in an issue of legislation for environmental protection in F.4. Teachers like to use sample papers and exam papers as chief teaching sources.

We observed that teachers developed patterns and mental models to guide answering argumentative exam questions. Students were drilled to assess whether they can use valid reasons and relevant evidence to demonstrate in-depth inferences and applications. Original outcomes of writing can demonstrate understanding of key concepts, ability to make conceptual observation, aptitude to apply relevant knowledge, capacity to draw critically conclusion or to discern views, according to the HKEAA DSE LS examination objectives (HKEAA, 2016). Most likely, the procedure flow in sequence are: (1) Introduce a precise claim (Standpoint), (2) Develop 3 claims and 1 counterclaim with evidences fairly, and (3) Provide a concluding statement to support the claim. An alternative flow could look like: (1) Reiterate the question, (2) Pros, (3) Cons, (4) Make your choice, (5) State reasons for your choice. Nevertheless, common logical errors (Marzano & Heflebower, 2012, p.44) are seldom alerted or taught. Contradiction, false cause, arguing from ignorance, seeing a part as the whole or seeing the whole as a part (composition and division) errors were found in group discussions without specific feedback in groups.

To sum up, most teachers applied summative assessment examples to direct the formative learning process. They applied charts, images, examples to verify a wide and deep analysis feedback to issues. They modeled how to express opinion or standpoint with clear evidences, using verbal or graphic descriptions, and in formal presentation wording, which are common exemplars in sample papers and exam-papers. The teaching style was mostly exam-oriented while different learning strategies were integrated into the lessons. Sometimes, students had peer-assessments on their work and chose the best for sharing. L5 and L6 teachers even copied the highest score answers for all students. Overall, teachers adopted exam-oriented teaching strategies more often than learning-oriented strategies. Teachers' real beliefs, values and knowledge of worth exposed in real practice, they tend to give up espoused ideal pedagogy but to give in to enforce strategies that both teachers and students believe could enhance scores when high-stake examination was coming close.

4.3.3 Pedagogy used – Students' point of view

Students perceived that teachers used exam-oriented strategies more often than learning strategies during lessons, but not yet to saturation. Students expect teachers to use sample papers and examination papers even more than it is. Their pragmatic focus on scores are explicit. They do not care about learning strategies and curriculum goals that are likely to benefit them in the long run.

To recap from Table 4.3, Students rated on the frequency of different teaching methods their teachers used.

Please indicate 2A the frequency with which you use the following teaching methods and 2B how effective you think these methods are in achieving good results in the DSE.	2A: Frequency		2B: Effectiveness	Mann-Whitney U test	Wilcoxon rank test	Spearman correlation
	S2A	T2A	T2B	S2A & T2A	T2A & T2B	T2A & T2B
	Mean (SD)	Mean (SD)	Mean (SD)	z (p)	z(p)	r
Learning-oriented strategies	3.19 (.499)	3.17 (.356)	3.07 (.396)	-.645 (.519)	-1.676 (.094)	.545**
Exam-oriented strategies	3.29 (.478)	3.57 (.341)	3.38 (.394)	-4.028 (.000**)	-3.162 (.002**)	.373*

Mann-Whitney U test showed that students think teachers use less 'exam-oriented strategies' than teachers themselves think. (M_S = 3.29, SD= .478: M_T = 3.57, SD= .341) (z=-4.028, p<.001). Teachers' pedagogy in-use was the same as students' preferences.

> S1 said, *"When it comes to Form Six* (equivalent to K12)*, we have to face the DSE examination, we spent more time practising past papers"*. S6 expressed,*"I feel that the teacher does not tell us clearly how to answer the LS examination questions … I think the tutorial school can provide these answers to me."* Students seemed reconizing what teaching strategies were better for examination. They preferred teachers to focus more on effective examination techniques.

A minority of the students (5 out of 17) interviewed disagreed that the DSE assessment modes, school teaching modes and learning objectives were consistent with each other, while the majority (12 out of 17) of them agreed. The qualitative findings contradicted the quantitative. Nevertheless, sample schools tend to be positive and students just regard all the learning processes are for preparing examination, indifferent to variations in teaching strategies. S1, S2, S5, S6 and S11 thought that the assessment modes are different from the teaching and learning.

Most of the students considered the techniques and the issue-based contents of teaching and learning were consistent with examinations during the process of learning. *"Teachers instructed us to choose a news article from newspaper every day and then to paste it in our notebook"* (S4). *"Normally, teachers' teaching style is the same as the examinations"* (S7). *"Form Six teachers taught us based on the past examination questions so that I think the learning is consistent with examinations"* (S8). *"The teacher also aimed to let us get good marks by telling us how to improve our answer"* (S15)

To sum up, students care only the public examination scores. They would like to learn the shortcut to examination skills-based techniques and effective procedural knowledge from sample papers and past exam-papers. They focus on theme-based controversial hot issues. They do not care about the learning process like collaboration, problem solving or other soft skills. Rote learning of key concepts, repeated use of complex issues procedures, express points with evidences clearly, and take precise standpoints were the rules for better scores. As for results, they demand more practices on examination papers with no regard to any espoused beliefs, such as 21st century skills practices.

4.3.4 Pedagogy in reality – Contextual influence

LS is a new interdisciplinary curriculum with standards-referenced assessment system. The social environment exerted great influences to the process of teaching and learning. Internally in schools, the culture of exam-oriented competition and rote learning tradition influence the process of teaching and learning. Externally, the legitimacy of admissions to educational institutions around the world and global competition on comparable standards demand reliability and validity of every subject in DSE. Locally, learning materials such as controversial hot issues are constructed through school-based collaboration, occasional publishers, interest groups, tutorial schools, or even political parties; quite often items captured from mass media. Nevertheless, the most important influences are in the classroom. Naturally, demographic difference among students affect students learning style and teachers teaching.

With regard to teaching methods perceived by students from different demographic background (Table 4.6), school banding made no significant difference on all items concerning the frequency on use of different teaching methods. Mann-Whitney Test confirmed that there were no significant perception differences of students irrespective of different languages of instruction in all items except c. *"Constructing micro and macro situations and working with logic or presenting evidence as part of the learning experience".* Cantonese as medium of instruction (*M*=3.17, *SD*=.70) have significantly higher score than English group (*M*=2.89, *SD*=.795) (*z*=-2.93, *p*< 0.001). Language is the main obstacle for instruction and communication in logical thinking and presentation of evidences.

Kruskal-Wallis test showed that among students in different types of school, there was significant difference on the item *i. "using HKEAA sample papers and DSE examination papers as chief teaching source"* (*X²* = 35.096, *p*<.001) and *j. "adopting the requirements and modes of the DSE for formative assessments"* (X^2 = 8.625, *p*<.05). Teachers from government schools tend to believe examination is the endpoint to evaluate students' learning abilities. Yet, the learning process should focus on knowledge constructions with long-term skills. They do not prefer investing time on examination or drilling on examination papers but they did in order to please students. Else, students find others ways to fulfil their own needs for better scores.

Table 4.6 Demographic comparison of students' concepts on the frequency of teachers' teaching methods

Please indicate the frequency with which your teacher use the following teaching methods.	Language of Instruction			Types of School				School Banding			
	Cantonese (n = 404)	English (n = 80)	Mann Whitney test (Z)	Gov. (n = 97)	Subsidized (n = 298)	Direct-Subsidy (n = 85)	Kruskal-Wallis test (χ2)	1 (n = 144)	2 (n = 211)	3 (n = 134)	Kruskal-Wallis test (χ2)
a. Cooperative learning, integrating life themes for communication and investigation to integrate life theme to communicate and investigate	3.24 (.694)	3.26 (.791)	-.582	3.15 (.741)	3.29 (.714)	3.19 (.681)	3.798	3.30 (.739)	3.21 (.708)	3.23 (.693)	1.835
b. Applying issue-enquiry methods and evidence flexibly to nurture logical thinking abilities	3.28 (.634)	3.20 (.770)	-.620	3.22 (.680)	3.29 (.676)	3.25 (.596)	1.423	3.28 (.694)	3.28 (.658)	3.23 (.624)	.867
c. Constructing micro and macro situations and working with logic or presenting evidence as part of the learning experience	3.17 (.700)	2.89 (.795)	-2.93**	3.06 (.761)	3.13 (.731)	3.16 (.670)	.958	3.08 (.771)	3.13 (.702)	3.16 (.707)	.637
d. Understanding different people's values and relationships via role-play	3.11 (.760)	3.05 (.727)	-.711	3.05 (.782)	3.12 (.756)	3.12 (.747)	.714	3.15 (.683)	3.06 (.820)	3.14 (.717)	1.244
e. Using information technologies to support learning, thinking and communicating	3.19 (.710)	3.26 (.742)	-.913	3.06 (.801)	3.26 (.700)	3.18 (.693)	4.945	3.31 (.712)	3.14 (.716)	3.20 (.723)	4.942
f. Direct transmission of knowledge and concepts	3.42 (.610)	3.53 (.616)	-.161	3.55 (.578)	3.42 (.610)	3.36 (.652)	4.390	3.53 (.578)	3.41 (.621)	3.37 (.621)	5.660
g. Developing clear personal standpoints to express opinions on issues in oral or written form, providing appropriate evidence	3.32 (.652)	3.19 (.597)	-1.835	3.23 (.715)	3.31 (.619)	3.29 (.651)	.702	3.29 (.619)	3.27 (.683)	3.34 (.612)	.538
h. Integrating life experiences and current issues to raise questions and engage in evidence-based discussions	3.38 (.641)	3.30 (.701)	-.902	3.25 (.722)	3.39 (.639)	3.41 (.623)	3.176	3.37 (.657)	3.34 (.651)	3.41 (.653)	1.359
i. Using HKEAA sample papers and DSE examination papers as chief teaching sources	3.13 (.766)	2.95 (.926)	-1.522	2.62 (.929)	3.19 (.726)	3.28 (.683)	35.096**	3.08 (.881)	3.06 (.791)	3.18 (.703)	1.640
j. Adopting the requirements and modes of the DSE for formative assessments	3.27 (.739)	3.21 (.724)	-.834	3.07 (.767)	3.30 (.731)	3.35 (.685)	8.625*	3.32 (.706)	3.20 (.742)	3.31 (.748)	3.134
All items' average	3.25 (.446)	3.18 (.409)	-.893	3.13 (.429)	3.27 (.446)	3.26 (.421)	8.384*	3.27 (.423)	3.21 (.445)	3.26 (.448)	2.542

*p < .05,   **p < .01   Learning-oriented strategies: item a-e; Test-oriented strategies: item f-j

4.3.5 Pedagogy Acumens – Perspective of other stakeholders

A. Direct manipulators

Direct manipulators are people who can affect the successful teaching and learning in class; they are the teachers, students and HKEAA executives. R3 the senior executive from HKEAA addressed the difficulties of initiating an interdisciplinary curriculum, *"the learning style and the content of curriculum of LS are different from other curriculums ... teachers have to shift paradigm of traditional subject teaching to facilitate a weakly structured curriculum or non-content-based structure curriculum. It is challenging to adapt to such drastic change."* He contended that, *"... if we cannot draw out the knowledge in our teaching process, or if we fail to convey the ideas or to apply them, students can never deal with the examinations... our understanding to the curriculum [as curriculum specialists] should not be different from that of the teachers."*

The executives from HKEAA played active roles to inform teachers the requirements of LS through dispatching sample papers, seminars, post-exam feedbacks, examination reports, marking scheme moderation meeting and training on other requirements. HKEAA administrators hold the belief that summative assessments could play a role as *assessment for learning* for teachers but not for students. Teachers might learn from the HKEAA feedback system and could improve according to their students' outcomes. HKEAA administrators have to oversee how teachers and students practice teaching and learning in reality to make sure the public examinations live up to local and global standards with trusted reliability and validity.

B. Indirect manipulators

Indirect manipulators of LS teaching and learning are policy-makers, curriculum developers, university LS experts and the like; they influence classroom teachings indirectly. Policy-maker R1 appreciated the collaborative constructive process to learn and considered examination as an instrument to assess the relevant knowledge. She reminded us not to emphasize too much on the role of examination papers and idealized expectation of question design.

> *"Those examination questions are the tools for understanding to what extent a student has learnt from the curriculum or how a student has performed."*

She pointed out

> *"We use standards-referenced reporting and it implies assessment of learning. … (The examination authority) need to distinguish students' levels. However, we hope that the assessment can facilitate students' learning."*

She stressed, *"IES plays a role in the assessment because LS does not merely look at paper, written form."* She emphasized that teachers should not be misled by misconceptions inferred based on the consistency in formats and question types of LS in the first three years. Teachers should not only limit teaching according to the examination designs and demands. R2 the former senior curriculum developer emphasized the basics, *"The assessment for learning is a formative evaluation procedure. It is a procedure to let students know how to master the fundamental knowledge, but it is not a procedure to let them copy and paste that fundamental knowledge."*

Both R1 and R2 believe that teachers should structure learning process constructively for their students. For R1, assessment was supposed to make teaching and learning their top priority to work both in harmony. The aims, pedagogy and assessment were to be aligned to achieve the fundamental education goal of 'learning to learn'. In pursuits of assessment for learning and assessment of learning, the use of standards-referenced reporting (SRR) system are instrumental to facilitate student learning. The reality of examination-driven curriculum cycle was not to be denied; deviance should only be tolerated for a very short initial period while implementing a new curriculum. Both R1 and R2 stress on the teaching and learning process. Summative assessment mirrors outcomes of the learning process. They see examination-oriented proclivity to teaching and learning as negative and it should only be a transient phenomenon. Through teacher training, examination-driven pedagogy would be mitigated. It seems that there exists no assessment policy to lever examination to improve students learning. They interpreted that formative assessments should be different from summative assessment. teaching and learning should focus on the enrichment of teaching and learning and must not let assessment get overwhelming. They uphold espoused theory as ideal and try every effort to comfort teachers' worries on the development of LS.

R4 the LS expert considered that the motivation, the respect for fair judgments and the belief on facts-driven support are the foundations buttressing attitudes and rationales for inquiry, application, argument and proof, while evidences are knowledge for the process of application. That means attitude, skills and knowledge are not to be separated and there were coherence and synergy.

> *"LS is a progressive ladder. It starts from the elementary school, secondary school and then to university. ... We call this the stages of cognitive development. In that stage, these three [knowledge, skills & values] can be applied simultaneously".* R4 added, *"In new senior secondary school, students are required to construct their own standpoints and opinions. Unfortunately, this (students have their own standpoint) might not be achieved. Sometimes, when a teacher expresses his/her standpoint, students think the idea is good and subsequently they use the idea of the teacher without thinking of any possible alternative standpoint independently."*

R5 reminded of pragmatic need of teaching and learning , *"Hong Kong has this important public examination, students continue to study hard and they cannot give up this 'learnt by rote' tradition... I won't deny that evaluation is an important tool that can boost thinking and creativity. Maybe, we need to examine the evaluation system; there could be lots of constraints. The system cannot be changed as one wants to."* She furthered, *"Assessment can lead to change but it only steers the feasible change".* In her viewpoint, public examination has its practical role; existing running pattern cannot be changed overnight.

For better learning, R4 considered LS as a bridge for students' cognitive, attitude and mental development in different stages. She believed professional development, concrete teaching materials provided, experiences shared, teacher collaboration and experts support could enhance teachers' pedagogy and expert assessment abilities. She regarded summative and formative assessments can and should be integrated for better learning. R5 admonished that the culture, existing environmental factors and the pattern of rules in examination systems should not be violated.

4.3.6 Section Summary

On pedagogy, teaching strategies of teachers in practice are exam-oriented. As direct manipulator, both teachers and students perceive exam-oriented strategies as being more effective for winning scores. Issue-driven higher-order thinking skills are built in but of secondary importance. Teachers adopt compromised strategies through HKEAA's support to narrow down the focus on the types of critical thinking learning and assessments. Formative use of summative criteria and rubrics during class are encouraged in pragmatic manner. All walks of life in the city have involved in the learning process in LS.

4.4 Effect of summative assessment learning outcomes

Explanations on the data listed in the following table expanse throughout section 4.4.

Table 4.7 A comparison of responses between teachers and students' perception on students' learning outcomes

The effect of LS examinations	Mann-Whitney U test		
	Students Mean (SD)	Teachers Mean (SD)	S vs T z (p)
Total outcome of Learn to live	2.69 (.424)	2.77 (.431)	-3.443 (.001**)
a. Thinking deeply about daily life and current affairs	2.98 (.646)	3.00 (.612)	-.233 (.815)
b. Awareness of current affairs	3.00 (.800)	3.00 (.639)	-.169 (.866)
c. Developing a more tolerant attitude towards the different opinions held by others and understanding the values behinds those opinions	2.95 (.658)	2.76 (.657)	-2.115 (.034*)
d. Becoming interested in learning LS#	2.48 (.842)	2.50 (.614)	-.117 (.907)
e. Studying not only for the examination#	2.30 (.838)	2.34 (.658)	-.405 (.685)
f. Help to nurture independent thinking and the ability to apply knowledge from different subjects with IES.	2.75 (.771)	2.71 (.764)	-.458 (.647)
g. The authentic issues of examination paper's design can help me concentrate on important learning processes, such as the construction of knowledge and life experiences#	2.85 (.713)	2.67 (.747)	-1.550 (.121)
h. The DSE LS examination paper effectively reflect student diversified learning abilities#	2.18 (.743)	2.43 (.736)	-2.026 (.043*)
Total outcome of Learn to think	2.83 (.560)	2.91 (.469)	-.947 (.344)
i. Trying to solve problems by using different thinking strategies and perspectives	2.99 (.657)	3.10 (.544)	-1.008 (.314)
j. No longer rely on rote learning	2.65 (.842)	2.70 (.647)	-.372 (.710)
k. Paying attention to the development of higher order skills	2.80 (.727)	2.88 (.659)	-.628 (.530)
l. The current DSE LS can help student applying the thinking skills	2.87 (.638)	2.94 (.592)	-.752 (.452)

*p <.05, ** p <.01   d, e, g, h Italics remarks: # = recoded item from negative statement to positive statement

Good mastery of examination techniques is believed to correlate with better scores students might get. Past LS exam-question pattern always involves controversial hot-issues worthy of argumentative writing. This new pattern of LS exam focuses on skills of thinking, invigorating certain kind of answering models or procedure patterns. The reference standards and examination models of LS become very crucial. High reliability and validity of LS examination were established on critical thinking but not with multiple intelligences. Nevertheless, results in Table 4.7 showed that students are weak in learning to think and worse in learning to live. Learn to respect is almost neglected. HKEAA is responsible for the examination results internally and externally. Teachers were often made accountable for the results, by school, by parents and students, while administrators and other social stakeholders were responsible for the outcomes of LS implementation. 'Argument made only for dispute' as the vehicle of training on critical thinking hijacked good intentions of LS skills transfer and turned LS into exam-oriented learning.

4.4.1 The Success, Constraints and Inadequacies of LS learning outcomes

Compulsory LS examination succeeded in enhancing students' awareness to current social affairs, yet the mode of operation at present has the following difficulties:

A. Distorted development of independent critical thinking

B. Narrow validity on broad LS curriculum aims

C. Feeble support to Learning to live

D. Lost interest in learning LS

Both quantitative and qualitative results in this section reflect teachers and students' insight about the examination of LS and their perceptions on the impact of the new form of public examination.

A. Distorted development of independent critical thinking shown

Statistical comparisons have been made, Mann-Whitney U test showed that both teachers and students bear high recognition on the statement *"If I / student can handle more of the referenced standards and examination models, it will help me / them to get better results"* (N_S = 483, M_S = 2.90, SD =.723: N_T = 49, M_I = 3.20, SD = .577). Students agree less, and strong statistical significance (z=-2.762, p<.006) holds. Chi-square test showed that there is significant difference in the distribution of agreement between teachers and students: X^2 (2, N = 532) = 8.04, p <.05. This is consistent with the convergent attention on marking standards.

Mastery of the referenced standards and examination models is essential because the examination patterns and issues are predictable (T5, T7, R5). Experienced teachers grow to surmount the patterns and models behind public examination. They found that if they become adept with the referenced standards and examination models, their students could get better results. T7 summarized his experiences, *"… inquiry issues relating to polarization become regular…it is easy to guess/predict the questions … there is 90 percent of chance for me to guess a question (in examination) right".* For the first examination year, he guessed 1 question right and 2 out of 6 questions correctly in subsequent years. T2 also stated that, *"Every day we have extra tutorial classes for practising examination papers because we have to practise all types of questions."* Same question types would be repeated, such as "To what extent do you agree...?" (T5) in sample papers and examination designed in the first three-years (HKEAA, 2016).

Students made similar discovery on patterns of examination in LS. S1 reflected, *"What I meant is not about the contents, it is the format that is formal. They usually ask you certain type of questions ...".* S14 had the impression that, *"After learning the examination techniques and practising the questions a while, I think it's quite easy and it can also train my critical thinking."* S15 said, *"The teacher also aimed to let us get good marks by telling us how to improve our answer and the ways to deal with the questions to get certain marks."* S3 critiques *"... during the examination, I think the issue cases used in setting the questions has sometimes been simplified. There are very superficial facts, which constitute an argument. I do not think it fits... as it may make things either black or white".*

R7 was a pre-service teacher-training student; he got HKDSE 5** in 2014 examination in LS. He shared his personal examination and teaching practices experiences, *"I think students answer the LS questions on the basis of media reports and the development of the incident (Umbrella Movement). If the students answer the question in a narrow perspective, or from a minority perspective, ... if the answer does not follow what the majority think, the examiners may not agree with the opinion at all".*

Goodwill for acquiring 21st century skills gives way to practical examination strategies in-use. The results substantiated that examination questions were narrowed down to exclusively assessable and measurable cognitive skills and knowledge (Amadio et al., 2015; Broadfoot, 2007; Gipps, 1994). Sample papers and examination questions in the past three years boiled down to certain patterns and models mainly based on Bloom's taxonomy (Or, 2011). It is a shame that public examinations can only align with a narrow scope of the initial official aims but not the holistic aims of curriculum. The wish for whole-person development is distant despite better endorsement on goals related to Learning to think.

Take an optimistic look, LS teachers trained to master examination rubrics is itself quite a success. The criteria-standards assessment mode coupled with central onscreen marking system is an innovation. Many teachers are markers; they join the professional moderation process. Through these in-service preparations, both external written examination and school-based assessment designs could be matched against a set of performance standards. A group of randomly assigned teachers could successfully make consensual and explicit measure based on the implicit standards of the rubrics. If there is a way to assess on the other 21st century skills goals, the annual training events may help teacher realign their teaching towards the ideal long-term goals.

B. Narrow validity compared with broad LS curriculum aims

Result revealed that both students and teachers have a negative rating on the item *'DSE paper could effectively reflect students' diverse learning abilities* (item *h* in Table 4.7, M_S =2.18, *SD*=.743: M_T=2.43, *SD*=.736), (*z*=-2.026, *p*<.043); students gave a significantly lower rating than teachers.

Students knew that many factors other than their learning habits or examination disposition influence their DSE performances. The writing speed, written presentation skills, good memorizations, the ability to predict exam questions and drilling for the exam issues, teaching and learning strategies and so on influenced their examination results.

S6 (Later he got 5** grade in DSE LS exam) identified, *"Classmates asked me the reasons why I got such good grade ... because I memorized those 'papers' and fill in the right words for composing the answers. In that [examination] situation, there is nothing we can do but to use those keywords."*

Teachers reflected the inadequacies of written examination in LS, *"It was holistic marking but subsequently evolved to become mechanical marking... As we want the result to be more reliable, we have to sacrifice the validity"* (T2).

Both students and teachers discounted the validity of written LS examination to manifest students' diverse abilities. Nevertheless, 11 out of 17 students were able to estimate their examination result ranking accurately. 2 out of 17 got higher ranking than their estimated grades while 4 out of 17 got lower. That means students formative assessments such as teacher's feedback in the classroom, feedback of homework, self-assessments or mock exam results succeeded in predicting the public examination results. If both formative and summative assessments were both exam-oriented with certain critical thinking patterns drilling, and the latter was judged to have narrow validity, how could LS effectively reflect diversified learning abilities of students' ability? Multiple-intelligences are neglected. Learning to live and learning to respect are even less bothered. Only narrow academic thinking skills are taught and progressively become procedural knowledge; scaffolding fragmented hot-issues without consideration of contextualized environment constitutes the norm.

C. Feeble support to spend teaching time on Learning to live

To recap from Table 4.7 comparing outcomes (Students vs. Teachers)

The effect of LS examinations	Mann-Whitney U test		
	Students Mean (SD)	Teachers Mean (SD)	S vs T z (p)
Total outcome of Learn to live	2.69 (.424)	2.77 (.431)	-3.443 (.001**)
c. Developing a more tolerant attitude towards the different opinions held by others and understanding the values behinds those opinions	2.95 (.658)	2.76 (.657)	-2.115 (.034*)
Total outcome of Learn to think	2.83 (.560)	2.91 (.469)	-.947 (.344)

It showed that teachers had significantly lower score on the impact of LS examination on item *c, the developing of a more tolerant attitude.* Nevertheless, more teachers gave higher positive scores than that of students on the total outcome of learning to live. There are significant discrepancy of value or view between teachers and students on the impact of DSE about learning to live.

T3 found that, *"it is hard to assess the values through examinations…the course places more importance on values, maybe it would be nice to remove the examinations so that it can become more flexible."* Teachers may not have enough training on value teaching. *"We were used to being spoon-fed. Suddenly we are forced to become learners taking initiative to search for inquiry issues from 'one way spoon-fed' learning. When studying in universities, it may be hard to handle the issue. For political and related controversies … values nurturing? … I think I have to be more cautious"* (T9).

A more tolerant attitude towards different opinions did not advance the will for truth seeking, value nurturing nor expression of self. S5 said, *"When I answered the questions, my answers are not either agree or disagree … truly I did not disclose my usual standpoint but to answer something I did not agree with because I want to get high marks in the examination."*

Both teachers and students regarded that learning outcome of LS on thinking has a better prospect of success than on living. Despite that observation, teachers and students found that learning might get side tracked by fads and trends of the current social context.

T8 asserted, *"If higher order thinking skill relates to the training of the way of thinking, I think it is achievable. In terms of students' attitudes, aesthetic standard, ability to determine right or wrong, it depends on the background. Some students are sensitive to social and political issue such as Occupying Central".*

Talking about students' attitudes during argumentative issue discussions, T4 criticised, *"because they would use certain extreme expressions in an agitated way, for example, by saying "go, go! (To take actions) … It seems like they cannot grasp the concepts of the issue-enquiry but thinking something else".*

In reality, memorization distorted and corrupted the 'learning to learn' processes towards thorough thinking. Thorough thinking could even become a manifestation of 'brain-wash'.

S11: *"The requirements of LS are quite easy and obvious. … It is because one newspaper covers different stakeholders' opinions so I did not need to read other newspapers"*

T6: *"You have to memorize some basic concepts for sure…if you want to have good marks, you need to memorize the examples…to practise continuously and work on one question a number of times. You can only answer the question after you are completely brain-washed."*

Although T2 observed, *"Students' critical thinking can be achieved by acquiring more knowledge and arousing awareness to our society", both* quantitative and qualitative evidences showed that special model memorization could hijack learning of critical thinking. They might answer in a way they do not agree with but trust that is the way to earn higher marks. The fake deep learning outcome is just 'shallow learning' (Gowda, Baker, Corbett & Rossi, 2013; Chapman and Snyder, 2000). The acquisition of principles, from a teacher or other instructor, without commitment or deep consideration is shallow learning. Students can manipulate complex formulae and work through relevant exercises while not understand the fundamental principles. Misconceptions and misunderstandings about an issue (Yu, 2013) would show up like jumping to conclusions without examining the logic of the argument or relating evidence to conclusions. Bias without self-reflection may cause new conflicts and new problems. It is going the opposite direction intended in the original purposes of the curriculum.

D. Lost interest in learning LS

To recap from Table 4.9, for Learning to live

The effect of LS assessments	Mann-Whitney U test		
	Students Mean (SD)	Teachers Mean (SD)	Students vs Teachers z(p)
d. *Becoming interested in learning LS*[#]	2.48 (.842)	2.50 (.614)	-.117 (.907)
e. *Studying not only for the examination*[#]	2.30 (.838)	2.34 (.658)	-.405 (.685)

 # = recorded item from negative statement to positive statement

Both students and teachers ranked these two items below or equal 2.5 on average. That means students' learning motivations on LS were below public expectations. The hope for LS to serve achieving the aims for 21st century skills learning gets dim. The world trend towards 21st century is to encourage pupils to become self-directed life-long learners; however, many students and teachers recognized that students are learning by rote memorization (S6, S10, S11, S13, T2, T5, T6). S11 argued that, *"In these days, everyone aims for a high mark but not for learning. I think this curriculum (LS) should not have existed … Original objective of LS will fail…it is meaningless to memorize all the materials for examination."*

S1 commented, *"… they (the exam-paper drafters) rarely raised special questions. They can find out students who are doing not too bad in the examinations but not those talented students if they rely on this examination paper."* It seemed that the combined judgments of different assessors still could not solve the constraints of high-stake examination. The measurable narrowed pattern of examination fulfilled the demand of reliability and validity for vigorous standard, and gave way to pragmatic practicable and achievable forms of assessments within the current context.

It was a pity that Independent Enquiry Study (IES) was not appreciated as a way to cultivate learning to live. T1 sighed, *"I do not feel enjoyment … I think if there is no IES, everything can be better".* IES in LS was a crucial element integrated into the learning process for self-directed learning, and mark is king. T5 asserted, *"The mark appropriated for IES is too low… it only weights 20%".* For students and teachers, if there are examination, the effort they pay will be weighed according to the chance to get high scores.

Fortunately, there were positive effect for some students. S17 who got Level 2 in exam said, *"LS gradually lets you understand more about independent thinking, ... not merely rely on teachers".* S16 recalled their self-directed studies, *"My friends in class would have a group discussion in relation to an issue-enquiries".* S3 pointed out the charasterestic of exam in LS, *"(You) have to understand how to express yourself to make others understand and also the logic has to be improved."*

LS tends to test the skills of thinking using contents from authentic hot-issues. The examination challenges candidates to present vague ideas and standpoints. The standards rubrics and markers' collective judgment provide the learning directions. Students' interest come primarily from the process of knowledge construction based on themes. Without rich and concrete background knowledge, students could only memorize dead fact knowledge, drill to follow procedural practices. Learning motivation was low and students became uninterested in learning LS.

4.4.2   Environmental interferences

Language of instruction, types of schools and school bandings make a difference in the student responses on the effects of LS examinations.

There was difference between students who use different language of instruction. Mann-Whitney Test (Table 4.8) disclosed that overall, students using Cantonese for learning tend to rate more positive in their learning than students using English. For instance, students using Cantonese instruction (M=2.71, SD=.812) had significantly higher score than English group (M=2.33, SD=.916) (z=-3.635, p< 0.001) in *j,* *"No longer rely on rote learning".*

Kruskal-Wallis test showed that among students, there are significant difference on three items *c, j,* and *k* (Table 4.8) in different types of schools. Students from government school were least identifying themselves with nurturing tolerant attitude and values compared with subsidized and Direct Subsidy School. They relied more on rote learning and played less attention to the development of higher order skills than the other two. Overall (X^2=5.203, p>.05), there were no significantly different impacts of school type.

The shrinking number of students in the secondary schools' sector, compared notes between schools, participation of tutorial schools, new neo-liberalism, marketization of education and so on are all drastic influences on the examination implementation in the vibrant environment. The new form of on screen public examination open-end question marking central monitoring system provides a technical breakthrough. The system comprises multiple subjectivities, which involve judgments from several different markers at different times independently, intended to be objective by design (Broadfoot, 2007). Reliability, validity and fairness were proven (Fung & Tong, 2013). As a result, open-ended essays by candidates provide evidence to be judged according to standards-referenced assessments. The exam-papers can be designed according to non-trivial issues and skills, a manageable number of objectives and any kinds of learnt elements. However, as public examinations are high-stakes, the examination papers have to be designed conservatively with well-developed marking criteria.

Table 4.8 Demographic comparison of students' perceptions on the outcomes of DSE

To what extent do you agree with the following statements?	Language of Instruction			Types of School				School Banding			
	Cantonese (n = 400)	English (n = 80)	Mann Whitney test	Gov. (n = 97)	Subsidized (n = 292)	Direct-Subsidy (n = 85)	Kruskal-Wallis test	1 (n = 143)	2 (n = 211)	3 (n = 131)	Kruskal-Wallis test
a. Thinking deeply about daily life and current affairs	2.97 (.631)	2.99(.720)	-.230	2.83 (.691)	-3.02 (.617)	2.96 (.680)	5.324	3.04(.659)	2.90 (.684)	3.02(.555)	4.550
b. Awareness of current affairs	2.99 .768	3.05(.855)	-.910	2.92 (.842)	3.04 (.773)	2.95 (.849)	1.568	3.15(.781)	2.85 (.849)	3.06(.702)	13.241**
c. Developing a more tolerant attitude towards the different opinions held by others and understanding the values behinds those opinions	2.97 (.646)	2.79(.688)	-2.559*	2.76 (.677)	2.98 (.647)	3.01 (.645)	9.637**	2.92 (.698)	2.93 (.649)	2.99(.631)	.956
d. *Becoming interested in learning LS#*	2.46 (.858)	2.56(.744)	-.985	2.44 (.896)	2.47 (.841)	2.55 (.794)	.564	2.60 (.843)	2.41 (.853)	2.46(.819)	4.564
e. *Studying not only for the examination#*	2.26 (.850)	2.47(.748)	-2.399*	2.29 (.944)	2.30 (.792)	2.31 (.887)	.035	2.46 (.824)	2.25 (.864)	2.20(.793)	10.037**
f. LS helps to nurture independent thinking and the ability to apply knowledge from different subjects with IES.	2.79 (.753)	2.51(.815)	-3.145**	2.66 (.844)	2.78(.732)	2.72 (.811)	1.326	2.60(.845)	2.77 (.745)	2.89 (.701)	10.011**
g. The authentic issues of examination paper's design can help me concentrate on important learning processes, such as the construction of knowledge and life experiences.	2.88 (.712)	2.67(.639)	-2.549*	2.69 (.813)	2.88(.629)	2.89 (.836)	5.483	2.72(.710)	2.90 (.739)	2.90 (.659)	7.361*
h. *The DSE LS examination paper effectively reflect my diversified learning abilities.#*	2.20 (.746)	2.06(.700)	-1.505	2.17 (.777)	2.16 (.729)	2.29 (.753)	2.001	2.18(.759)	2.19 (.738)	2.17 (.740)	.071
i. Trying to solve problems by using different thinking strategies and perspectives	2.99 (.658)	2.96(.645)	-.383	2.89 (.738)	3.03 (.622)	2.93 (.669)	3.108	3.04(.659)	2.93 (.666)	3.03 (.636)	2.882
j. No longer rely on rote learning	2.71 (.812)	2.33(.916)	-3.635**	2.48 (.870)	2.65 (.837)	2.81 (.794)	7.249*	2.51(.931)	2.62 (.802)	2.85(.771)	12.035**
k. Paying attention to the development of higher order skills	2.80 (.734)	2.80(.701)	-.051	2.64 (.783)	2.85 (.689)	2.80 (.768)	6.325*	2.85(.737)	2.70 (.715)	2.91(.720)	8.429*
l. The current DSE LS can help me applying the thinking skills.	2.88 (.640)	2.81(.618)	-.733	2.77 (.657)	2.89(.631)	2.91 (.648)	3.169	2.89(.597)	2.82 (.661)	2.93(.645)	2.233

*p < .05, **p < .01   d, e, h Italics remarks: # = recoded item from negative statement to positive statement.

4.4.3 Exam misfit -Perspectives of other stakeholders

A. Administrators:

R1, who played a role as an administrator, observed, *"Many university lecturers express that students nowadays know how to think when they are in university; at least, it is not like that they know nothing at all."* Because of LS, students could not recite direct answers. R2 regretted that *"In examination, if the questions we asked are personal, it will be difficult to mark the answers. In any case, we do not handle personalized answers."*

Administrators support the espoused visions and beliefs on the curriculum implementation. It seems that administrators uphold ideal visions without pragmatic concerns and effective strategies. Executive curriculum developers bear in mind the dilemma during the developing processes and difficulties pushing forward to schools. There is no firm and precise assessment policy supported by empirical evidences to direct how to align assessment with pedagogy and curriculum aims. They perceive exam-driven impact as negative but accept that as normal within the short time-frame of LS implementation.

B. HKEAA:

R3 retorted, *"I found many students memorizing some frameworks as if model answer exists. This doesn't work and the outcome is not good."* He suggested teachers and students to understand that *"HKEAA sets the questions on the basis of the course content and assessment directives, including LS course guideline and target directed assessment work. Students' answer will be analyzed in detail and inferences will be returned to teachers and stakeholders so that during the next round of assessment, teaching and learning can be improved. … Every stakeholder can obtain the relevant information from the assessment report to improve learning."* HKEAA defines summative assessment as formative opportunities for teachers. That means for student candidates, the LS examination is a single point-in-time judgment on their performance potentials while the use of information from the results enables teachers to identify in general students' areas of strength and weakness as insight to improve teaching and learning for the next cohort. The information are open public property on the HKEAA website.

According to the examination report and question papers (with marking schemes) (HKEAA, 2012; 2014), the suggested marking guidelines demand candidates to present their stances precisely and consistently. The rules of examination game seem to encourage students to hold the utmost ideal positions for argument.

C. Others

LS experts: R4 and R5 sighed that teachers often extracted only shallow and superficial learning for students to get a pass. R4 expressed, *"... It is also questionable whether the teacher can help redirect students to make objective judgment."* She worried that, *"... thirty percent of LS questions are related to politics... anything about livelihood will be mis-directed to politics... our society is politicalized, that have an influence on students and also on our teachers. ... there are so many disputes every day but these are not what curriculum and examination questions aim to have."* She reminded most teachers do not have strong and relevant pieces of content knowledge and procedural knowledge relating to higher-order skills. They chase after issues as if those were content-based learning. She had a passionate outcry that everything would become mechanized if proper links between aims, skills and knowledge were broken. R5 insisted IES should be the learning process that meets the curriculum aims.

R5 described the practical circumstances, *"For parents, students and teachers' mind-set, if hard working students failed to get better scores, it is their teacher's fault..."*. Nevertheless, R4 found positive effects on whole-school pedagogy expansion. R5 found students *"write more than before and really think"* and she pointed out an implementation reality between different stakeholders, *"... the most progressive ... experts from HKEAA ... explained often how and why they drafted question in such a way... the HKEAA, EDB, the curriculum development institute always yield to grumbles from teachers. Examinations could exert excessive stress to the teachers, negative eddies emerge, they have to give in"*. Experts hold different espoused beliefs and they actualize them according to the progress of professional development.

Social and political stakeholders: As most of the examination contents were drafted on authentic disputed topics and most likely the argumentative issues, 'text-books' publishers, mass media or political parties who are not education professional often intervened in the learning process. Refer to the exam-papers (ibid), many text-resources came from public media. Editorial, special topic videos, issue analysis from the mass media or political parties have their stances by providing large amount of teaching materials and comments on social issues. There is no suggested textbooks or rich concrete learning content knowledge (R3, R4). The learning medium is most likely the emergence of issues and certain procedural knowledge; those are so claimed pros and cons evidences, key concepts without systemic historical, cultural, or situational based knowledge.

4.4.4 Section summary

On assessment, exam-oriented teaching and learning ended up in argumentative procedural drilling. Conative soft skills and other skills knowledge were limited. Students ignore Learning to respect and they focus on Learning to think and are weak in Learning to live. Students learning motivation in LS were low. They learn for examination and their interest are depleted. Rote learning is common but seem to have greater improvement in learning if they are instructed in Cantonese. Special model memorization hijacked learning of critical thinking. The predictable and well-structured answering patterns with argumentative learning procedure may enable students to shunt critical thinking but make sensible judgment on issues asked. Nevertheless, thinking skills instead of knowledge learning criteria in public-exam drive collaborative learning. Certain sample schools in this study have professional cooperation to adopt exam-oriented strategies for formative use in constructive learning. LS examinations seems to have great power to lever change but it cause unpredictable impacts or even being counter productive. The first five years served narrowed aims of ABC, realized the narrow thinking skills. The successful initiation of *learning to think* shows the potential of summative assessment alignment with formative function to lever collaborative learning in the classroom.

The following chapter will further analyze the successes and pitfalls from a broader view to answer the research questions. Aligning summative assessment with curriculum aims for 21st century skills learning may be the way ahead for further LS development.

Chapter 5 DISCUSSIONS

5.1 Introduction

"We cannot always build the future for our youth, but we can build our youth for the future."

— Franklin D. Roosevelt (September 20, 1940)

How can we build our youth for the future effectively with limited resources in the ever competitive changing 21st Century? We educate them through schools where good quality teaching and learning are expected. We motivate them to reach certain academic level through various ways of assessment on stipulated curriculum. Alignment of assessment with pedagogy and curriculum is claimed to be able to enhance and promote students' acquisition of 21st century skills, comprising critical thinking and elements for better living with our neighbours together as a community.

The word 'alignment' often appears in government documents. The claims for 'alignment' in LS trio of curriculum, pedagogy and assessment make a guiding principle to enable summative assessment to serve assessment for learning implicitly, then assessment can lever pedagogy to realize the reform aims. However, such alignment has not yet been clearly defined. On the planning board, the vision, mission and philosophy on which LS curriculum is founded anticipated that the new compulsory subject for all DSE candidates to be an interdisciplinary curriculum. 'Science in art and art in science' is an ideal to initiate balanced curriculum learning for all senior secondary students. Through issue-enquiry and the crucial key concepts transfer practised in class, with repeated application to explore a wide range of knowledge scenarios, it is presumed that the process can help liberate students' open minds. As Hong Kong is situated in the crossroad of Asian political entities and is itself a complex open system, learning to think objectively, learning to live with reflectively and independently, and learning to respect with open-mindedness are all essential for building a constructive optimistic new generation. Only an efficient basic education system can effectively enable the nurturing of informed talents, reasonable and responsible citizens; they shoulder transferable acumen and adept adaptability of 21st Century attitudes, skills and knowledge (Binkley, Erstad, Herman, Raizen, Ripley, Miller-Ricci & Rumble, 2012; Griffin, 2015). Modern schooling aims at helping students to succeed through life-long learning, learning to learn, and whole-person development. The research processes and the results in this current project provide lots of insights and thinking. Enabling summative assessment with professional thinking can be a powerful way for better learning. The opposite could ruin a new generation contaminated with unintended wrong ways of thinking habits in future.

5.2   Research question 1: Stakeholders perceptions on the LS curriculum cycle

How do different stakeholders perceive the relationships between the LS curriculum, pedagogy and examination in Hong Kong?

Qualitative data from semi-structured interviews and lesson observation are consistent with quantitative findings. Both students and teachers regarded the aims of LS as mainly nurturing thinking skills while values, attitudes or disposition were seldom considered. Critical thinking with clear standpoints is the basic strategy for answering argumentative type of questions. Key concepts but not knowledge of facts is the learning elements through issue-enquiry. Examination-driven teaching and learning is a common phenomenon and most of the respondents accept it as normal. Teach to the test and learning for the examination is the norm. More than two third of students and teachers agreed it to be ideal if the DSE LS assessment modes were aligned with the school teaching modes and learning objectives. The three components of curriculum (aims, pedagogy and assessment) are consistent with each other.

Exam-orientation predominated curriculum delivery and hence pedagogy made a significant sector for 'the quality agenda', this substantiate demand for monitoring and accountability (Broadfoot, 2007). The mixed-methods results in Chapter 4 reported that students in Form 6 focused their minds to get high scores with fewer efforts as their short term goal. Students do not care much about the curriculum aims. They seek for help in schools or through tutorial schools outside for better achievement. Teachers highly identify themselves with the aims of LS, yet in reality, they endorse that public examination could only help to fulfill the aims of learn to think and learn to live but not in nurturing values and attitudes. Teachers' espoused visions of learning through life and whole-person development gave way to theory-in-used for maximizing learning effectiveness through procedural knowledge drilling (Argyris & Schon, 1974). They choose models to drill their students based on their prediction on exam-question types and question content of issues. Examinations driven pedagogy for obtaining better scores was the norm.

HKEAA, as a direct manipulator of examination and the executive representing the authority, actively inform and support teachers to ensure the new subject is implemented with a high scholastic standard, and also with reliability, fairness and validity acceptable to the global comparative examinations community. HKEAA believes summative assessment could be used for formative functions to improve teaching and learning for teachers. Teachers run deep-reflections with authority's feedback on the performed examination outcomes and use the exam-papers subsequently in class to guide next cohort of students to learn accordingly.

Administrators from EDB and experts from tertiary institutions sustain their espoused beliefs to guide teachers' professional improvement. These optimists uphold formative assessment as to serve learning (assessment for learning) while summative assessment is put lightly to their concern (assessment of learning). They advocate their espoused visions but at the same time accommodate concerns on teachers' difficulties. They address some phenomena, pitfalls and constraints from different perspectives.

Other stakeholders such as publishers, mass media, teachers' associations and interest groups trample into the implementation processes too. They would not consider the relationships of curriculum aims, pedagogy and examination in the same manner as the education professionals. Anyway, exam-driven phenomena overwhelm the curriculum aims in an early version of parents' handbook with the title *'Aware of the society. Broadening minds and have critical thinking learning processes' (ABC)* (see Chapter 1). The enlightening change from conventional monologue of class instruction is that diverse teaching and learning strategies are used in LS. Whether public examination aligned successfully with pedagogy and curriculum aims is another level of professional concern. Different stakeholders take on board various different pattern of perceptions on the assessment, pedagogy and curriculum cycle, based on their different positions, self-interests, beliefs and practical needs. The direct manipulators on classroom teaching and learning, and examinations, such as students, teachers and executives of HKEAA tend to agree that the three components are consistent with each other. They have concrete strategies to follow and have less internal conflicts in their minds. They played down contradictory worth that confronted their perceptions of aims, and then continued with selected spectrum of learning and evaluating.

Both quantitative and qualitative findings verified that all different stakeholders perceived LS as being different from any other traditional subjects. Most of them noticed the new mode in the relationship of LS curriculum, pedagogy and public examination, new contents and new organization of exam-driven teaching and learning and they were positive with the unique change. They agreed that public examination has successfully assessed thinking skills instead of knowledge, but has ignored attitudes. Pedagogy changed from direct transmission into diverse interactive strategies. Although most stakeholders agreed examination has aligned with pedagogy and curriculum, there were diverse interpretations of the relationships between these three components to fit in with their implicit agenda, some emphasized political conversion, some simply for high marks.

5.3 Research question 2: Examination vs. pedagogy & aims

To what extent does LS examination enable the pedagogy to realize the curriculum aims?

Quantitative results show the average mean of using learning-oriented strategies is 3.17 in a Likert scale of 4 whereas it is 3.57 for exam-oriented strategies, a very high rating. Both students and teachers perceived that teachers adopted the requirements and modes of the DSE assessments for formative purposes (mean 3.26). It shows that public examination assessment monitoring, standards-referenced criteria, question types and issue-based contents were commonly used in the classroom teaching and learning processes. Nevertheless, following public examination protocol does not preclude full coverage of the primary aims of LS curriculum by design. Less than half of the students and teachers expressed that LS examination could reflect their diversified learning abilities. In the report on the *New Academic Structure (NAS) Medium-term Review and Beyond* (CDC, HKEAA & EDB, 2015), the education authority admitted that public examination could not reflect students' variety of learning outcome too. It states, *"SBA* [School-based Assessment] *is an integral part of the curriculum, pedagogy and assessment cycle. The primary principle is to enhance the validity of the overall assessment and extend it to include a variety of learning outcomes that cannot be readily assessed through public examination"* (ibid, p.38). The joint review by the three direct trio authorities downplayed the significance of IES (Independent Enquiry Study, the only school-based assessment included as 20% in the final public examination grade). They admitted that certain learning outcomes could not be readily assessed through the pen and paper written public examination; unfortunately, they overlooked possible potentials of reinforcing IES as the vehicle to strengthen nurturing learning to live and learning to respect.

LS examination is a kind of high-stakes summative assessment. It serves certification for school-leaving qualification at the end of the senior secondary school. Students and parents treasure the pen-and-paper examination because it is accounted for 80 out of 100 percent scores. Schools, teachers and various other stakeholders were involved one way or another in the implementation processes. If the examination fails to evaluate students' abilities reliably from this compulsory and highly concerned public examination, the validity of such summative assessment for selection to university admissions can never be honoured. The problems or strengths flourished in public exam merit regular continual reviews. LS as a new subject, its valuable public examination implementation experiences should be well analyzed to discover the strengths and pitfalls. It is a pity to overlook or neglect it.

It is ideal to be able to align formative assessment instruments such as criteria descriptors in class for better examination preparation. Chapter 4 verified that to a certain extent LS public examination enables the pedagogy to realize learning to think. Learning to respect was excluded while attention to learning to live was relatively weak. Students ignored the former totally and the impact of the latter was barely remembered. Teachers adopted exam-oriented strategies most of the time. The level of thinking skills-based, standards-referenced criteria and rubrics were observed while organizing their teaching lessons. Patterns and mental models were used, simulating the exam-question types. To save time for wider exposure, answering in class were oral drill instead of writing. Constant feedbacks with standard criteria were used precisely to inform students their level of standards so that they may learn to get better scores. Pedagogies change towards being student-centred in this sense. Teaching and learning processes were narrowed down to help boost students' abilities of thinking for answering argumentative issues questions with evidences. Did they really acquire flexible transferrable thinking skills (Barnett & Ceci, 2005) to be applied in other de novo situations? Drilling on past papers should not be enough.

Teachers thought that they have had a paradigm shift in response to changes in the perceived examination mode. As past examination results, matched against new summative assessment aims, contents, forms and organizations were being recognized and put in use practically for guiding students, they considered they have constructed a new instruction style unique for LS. Both learning-oriented strategies such as using diverse sources of social issues for integration and argument while conducting group discussions and examination-oriented strategies were used in instructions. My findings coincide with that the authority described. According to the Report on the New Academic Structure Medium-term Review and Beyond *"Observations from school visits revealed that in*

Liberal Studies a wide variety of assessment tasks facilitated the development of students' skills and knowledge. These aligned with the curriculum aims and learning and teaching objectives of promoting higher-order thinking. Students worked in groups and participated in discussions, debates or presentations as part of continuous assessment." (2015, p.37). It proved LS examination enable the pedagogy to achieve learning to think.

The examination authority stressed on *"Aligning assessment to teaching and learning"* and *"what to assess should reflect the teaching content"* (ibid). With reference to the set criteria, both teachers and students can diagnose their learning situation, standards of assessment and probable level of grades reachable. Clarity created both positive and negative wash-back effects. The impact of success and pitfalls on the curriculum and teaching would be inevitable. (Gipps, 1994, p.34) *'Teachers pay particular attention to the form of the questions on a high-stakes test and adjust their instruction accordingly'* (Madaus, 1988, p.95 cited by Gipps, 1994, p.36). Nevertheless, Dixon, Frank & Worrell highlight that formative and summative assessment are complementary. The differences between them are just the way these assessments are used (2016, p.157). After five years of employing the standards-referenced reporting system based on the initial aims of ABC especially target on critical thinking, teachers were reasonably familiar with the assessment system. This research sees the possibility for aligning examination with pedagogy to achieve aims. Could the strengths outweigh the pitfalls? That is the question in the following critical evaluation.

5.3.1 Strengths

A. Use of formative assessments in preparation for the ultimate summative examination:

During the learning process, teachers used the assessment criteria with precise descriptors and sample papers unanimously for scaffolding students learning. Teachers from sample school 4 (see section 4.3.2) built a team for the whole year curriculum planning and implementation. T5 as a LS head-teacher shared workloads of LS with other teachers such as T6. They built consensus on division of labour on streamlining contents of issue-based materials effectively for supporting their students. Each teacher was an expert on some special areas. They prepared learning materials and scaffolded teaching and learning process to meet the main goals. For mock examination, they tested what students learned from the teachers' feedback. The contents of issues and the types of questions drilled repeatedly were those that teachers predicted to have a high probability of appearance in public examination that corresponding year. The predicted issues were well prepared for learning through construction or drilling. They have become samples simulating deep learning. Students were trained to transfer the answering techniques in whatever the questions might be in different module of themes. They drilled some basic key concepts in planned target-issues into different kinds of question forms, so that students could answer all forms of related questions accordingly.

Team building is just the organic side of strategic management of specific LS examination in Sample school 5. Teachers there analyzed and determined examination prong hot-issues and short-listed feasible questions forms at the beginning of the academic year (Thong, 2013). From there they fixed the issues, contents and question modes, and live their forecasts as assembled collaborative learning process. Whole class debate followed by whole form debate was their favourite learning strategies. Through amusing and attractive activity design, students were absorbed into series of learning processes but still the output is an argumentative writing. Students sketched concept-maps and were requested to write some key points during the process. Analysis and prediction for hot issues were crucial. It seems that students' originality and abilities in responding to the exam questions were molded; the answers are often very much predictable. Tests are readily coached. Continuous virtuous feedback loops tune students' learning performances in preparation for questions anticipated to appear in the very last summative assessment.

B. Use summative assessments formatively

Quantitative results show the average mean of teachers using HKEAA sample papers and DSE examination papers as chief teaching sources is 3.41 in a Likert scale of 4 whereas developing clear personal standpoints to express opinions is 3.69, a very high rating. In lesson L2 observed, T3 adopted the 2014 exam-paper-question 2 on wind energy dilemma for part of that lesson. He used question types requiring pros & cons contra T-table for group discussion. As usual, he constructed the lesson with standards-referenced criteria for learning feedback. All the lessons (see Table 4.4) were issue-enquiry based and the exam-oriented summative assessment application styles were the rule, even if it is intended to be learning-oriented. As a result, learning to think was accomplished and it is happening every day in the classroom. R4 was excited with the shift of paradigm expressed as a new teaching style that he described as "almost flipped the classroom". Teachers affirmed possible use of public examination (summative assessment) experiences to fulfill formative functions during the learning processes (Kennedy, Chan, Yu, and Fok, 2006; Brown, Kennedy, Fok, Chan, and Yu, 2009; Carless & Lam, 2014); in this way, subject aims could be attained.

C. Integrate values into issue enquiry

Although T3 accused that examinations rarely touch on values, and S1 did not think it help to nurture value, some observations in this project found that it could. Some teachers constructed alternative scenarios for class discussion and provided feedback for nurturing values learning. In class observation L3, teacher assigned two students to conduct a simulation role-play in conflict. Then they had a whole class discussion on a spectrum of scenarios ranging from local to international cases of conflicts, reinforced with visual power-points to guide students to think. They discussed in small groups on how to resolve conflicts between countries. Communication, bargaining, concessions, values like respect diversity etc. were highlighted. In L10, teacher assigned different roles to selected students on the stage; each student took consideration for a different government department to take action on preventing flu. Students on the floor asked and challenged peers on the stage in the position as citizens, on "what could they do to prevent flu?" Therefore, through the design of scenarios manifesting possible cases to be included in exam-questions, it may be possible to lever value enquiry.

D. Fuel professional dialogues

Traditionally, only few teachers participate in the marking process in days when one teacher covers all questions on the same answer script. LS employed a double-marking system (Coniam, 2011) to take place exclusively onscreen in the marking centre. Tight monitoring mechanism becomes technical feasible to ensure fairness and uniformity of marking reliability. This demands lots of teachers to get involved in the labour intensive marking process within a tight schedule. *"Policy is both text and action, words and deeds; it is what is enacted as well as what is intended"* (Ball, 1994, p.10). Individual practitioners execute power of control during the marking examination processes. Assessment reform as a policy in the context of influence, the context of policy text production and the context of practice all influence the curriculum implementation results (Broadfoot, 2013). The design of the test papers demands candidates to demonstrate various higher-order skills. There will not be any "model answers" in LS, a sound understanding of the issues with data and evidences are required. Hence, teacher markers are trained and everyone have to pass a qualifying test. Through markers' meeting, consensus has to be reached on the marking criteria and tedious standards for each question. There are also systematic check-marking system, markers' work will be supervised by the Chief and Assistant Examiners (Fung & Tong, 2013). As a result, school subject panels become eager to organize school teachers to attend markers meeting, to participate and to observe how consensus on the marking criteria were reached and they mimic the process seriously in their own school examinations. The multiple subjectivists' combined judgments by a number of different assessors may be the best basis for fair judgment (Broadfoot, 2007, p.159). The use of assessment as a rational device for rare opportunities initiate students towards self-assessment to maximize learning (Stiggins, 2004).

5.3.2 Pitfalls

Section 4.4.1 discovered inadequate results of LS learning outcomes; that is significant. To expand further, I highlight the following three points.

First, examination of LS is not really an "innovative" or "authentic assessment" as wished. The answers are quite predictable, and by close coaching, probable outcome of the test could be achieved through drilling. Synthesis by induction is a necessary skill, hence, seeking for patterns and formats is good. Stereotyping patterns and formats and jumping to conclusion are bad, and they contradict nurturing 21st Century skills. Use of examination and sample papers formatively for students learning in some case-schools is a good demonstration, but use of the same resources mechanical drilling and for better scores (Chan & Bray, 2014) only (from students S6, S11) is bad. Practise handling broader stretch of examination models by students is good, even if the goal is to get better results; widening horizon reduces time available for drilling on any particular model. Unfortunately, classroom observation confirmed behavioural patterns of drilling from among sample schools. Teacher could only spend a few lessons or even as little as two lessons for one issue. They squashed time to provide more learning materials on complex issues in dispute (see Table 4.5). Flood of reading materials replaced quality lesson delivery as if it would insure students from surprise topics covered in examination papers. R8 (a pre-service teacher who got 5** in 2013 HKDSE examination in LS) showed his exemplar exam-paper to the researcher. His exam-answers demonstrated mature application of procedural patterns (see 4.3.2) in answering argumentative questions. He described in wordings like *"In conclusion, ... prove with evidences, sincerely with no bluffing. (總括而言 ... 證之論據，誠非虛言)"* exactly four times in different sections of the answers in the same exam-paper. This is good for exam but not good for broad learning purposes. As R5 observed, teachers tend to cover all the modules or forecast issues for students. Otherwise, they might feel guilty for not yet fulfill their responsibility in full. Yet, flexibility and adaptability are the aims of nurturing 21ˢᵗ century skills. The gap in lack of confidence with their students (and with their own teaching) distorts the pedagogy alignment. As a result, they fell in the vicious whirls of delivering predominantly procedural knowledge application by over-drilling different kinds of issues without nurturing independent critical thinking.

Secondly, to what extent could the present form of examination questions measure or assess students' critical thinking and the extent of originality in response to a new topic? Students considered marker's standpoints and they did not really express their own. If students recall from memory and fill in ready-made standpoints, how can it be independent critical thinking? This contradicts frequent reminder to students, urging them to present his/her stance clearly and consistently as rubric of marking. Limiting the scope of learning to familiar issue-based learning packages degrades ostensibly systematic arguments with consistent stance to become superficial critical thinking. The teaching materials studied in this project tend to oversimplify the issue premise without giving relevant and rich historical and contextual background knowledge. Repeatedly forcing students to have clear stances for argument may trap students inside the cage others set up in early stance. There may be skewed bias based on packaged standpoints from unprofessional sources or social contention. Interestingly, the meaning of 'critical thinking' in English term is perceived as negative criticisms or only for the sake of being critical in Chinese (EDB, December 3, 2014). Therefore, the term is redefined in Chinese. However, will it just be the problem of translation? R4, the expert in LS (R4), had her consideration on mastery of content knowledge and quality learning. *"Because we have little experiences and knowledge to understand or respond to complicated, sometimes contradictory, issues in Hong Kong, we, not just students, even teachers, do not really know how to inquire into issues through a deep learning process. As a result, the exam-questions did not assess of learning but assess whether students could apply the procedure knowledge of reactions well."* Students were not demanded for or did not need to master a process of learning inquiry.

Thirdly. Over-simplification of some concepts without prompting connections: The difference between learning-oriented strategies and the exam-oriented strategies depends on the process and the learning purposes. Role-play can be learning-oriented if for self-reflection, or feeling about experiences of real life for another party, or consideration of other people's values, or respecting each other and growing concern with other's difficulties during the learning process. In the opposite, role-play can also be exam-oriented for drilling dead-fact knowledge of certain roles; simplified roles crumpled into stereotypes in the society as 'yellow or blue ribbon', 'black or white' with colored lens without consideration of the contextual circumstances are all bad examples. For both teachers and students, they may not have disciplined themselves with any deep thinking about the differences between these two kinds of teaching strategies. If learning is honoured as the first priority, the process will be designed primarily for students' involvement and participation. Through the scaffolding process, students apply knowledge and thinking skills to illustrate underlining values. They seek evidences and for relatively acceptable reasons to respond to the inquired question. Conversely, the inferior learning processes mentioned above could only nurture individual thinking. By focusing on marks and beating rivalry, a learner will just consider himself/herself without caring for others. Unfortunately, think individually this way only feed explicit selfish untrustworthy liars, consuming community resources just for self interest. Think independently makes oneself free from persuasion, lobbying or discouragement from surrounding interest parties and noise. In the context of LS curriculum discussions, independent critical thinking is the destination, not musing individually. The process has to be backed up by infusion of a sense of being accountable and responsible for one's own choice of actions and decisions. That is 'learn to live'. Be responsible to others, that is 'learn to respect'. Some youth attacked police in 2016 Lunar New Year night and fought for 'Hong Kong independence' without premise logic and knowledge. Does LS produce numerous individual thinkers but not independent critical thinkers unintentionally and unpridictably?

To very limited extent, LS examination enables the pedagogy to realize the curriculum aims. Based on the qualitative and quantitative results, the HKDSE LS examination has limited leverage on individual critical thinking, and awareness of the society (Fung & Su, 2016). The future is to broaden practices to realize the curriculum initial aims.

5.4 Research question 3: Alignment of assessment and curriculum

Can LS examination align well with the curriculum to realize 21st century skills?

Before answering this research questions, we need greater clarity on the purpose of curriculum of LS for realizing 21st century skills. Does examination ensure the 'fitness for purpose' (Broadfoot, 2007, p.158)? It has been the established blueprint of educational reform (Education Commission, 2000); we need to nurture good citizens and talents through basic education in Hong Kong. Learning to learn, whole-person development and life-long learning, which have already been summarized in the research agenda as 21st century skills, could only be realized through the practices of 'Learn to live', 'Learn to think' and 'Learn to respect' in daily classroom activities. 21st century skills have become the learning and assessing indicators, which serve for both the learning construction targets and also the precise assessment criteria and rubrics.

Anyway, LS as an integrated curriculum for supporting the New Academic System (NAS) (Fok & Wong, 2011). the goal is to mature a student to become a highly adaptable, responsible, independent thinking, critical, creative and communicative citizen or talent who can own the ever-changing 21st century skills practices. According to a recent school survey, *"over 90% of the teacher respondents were of the view that students could achieve the curriculum aims of Liberal Studies after completing secondary education* (EDB, 2015a, June 8: 8)" and *"Students were able to demonstrate critical thinking skills and the ability to think from multiple perspectives"* (ibid). The public release of the EDB NAS Medium-term review result in LS also shows that 87% of teachers agreed or strongly agreed with the alignment of assessment, pedagogy and curriculum (EDB, 2015a). Consistent with my findings and the EDB report (CDC/HKEAA/HKEDB, 2013b; CDC, 2015), teachers and the public highly accept LS in this curriculum cycle, before launching a revision. It is easy to jump to conclusion that existing public examination aligned well with the curriculum as if it realized 21st century skills. However, based on the aims of LS, referring to the findings of the mixed-methods research and wisdom of scholars and researchers, the answer is not likely to be so simple. In the following, I would like to analyze and answer the question referring to the three components of the curriculum cycle.

5.4.1 Precise stance in exam shaping a trend towards dichotomy

First, conceptually, critical thinking on controversial social issues is often characterized by an argumentative stance, without necessarily much regard to the quality or appropriateness of participation (Ryan & Louie, 2007). Students were asked to express precise stance in many examination questions. It tends to shape a trend towards dichotomy. Student S3 was unhappy that the controversial questions make things either black or white. R4 the expert discontented with the society being politicized. Anything about livelihood was misdirected to politics. LS is criticized as publicizing political inclinations. There were 30% exam-papers about politics from 2012-2014 (Chan, 2014). Questions were about the *'developing impact of stronger political parties on governance'* (2012), *'whether filibustering by Legislative Councilors is counterproductive to the welfare of the public'* (2013) and *'Do demonstrations and marches contribute to the betterment of life?'* (2014). However, there were no suggested content knowledge demand. Students or even common people in Hong Kong have limited knowledge about Basic Law or the transitional knowledge of 'One country, two systems' but only information from mass media and different kinds of interest groups, quite often with biases. The questions did not really assess the outcome from students' authentic processes of learning but mainly the abilities of applying procedural knowledge of argumentative issues. Instead, they could be reinforcing the numerous polarized binaries between self and the other, between natives and non-natives (Kostogriz & Doecke, 2006, p. 2, cited in Ryan & Louie, 2007, p. 414), between 'Yellow and Blue ribbon' as it was in colour revolution, and between pro-establishment and pan-democratic camps. In premise, critical thinking makes sense in light of the paradoxical dichotomy if properly and fully discussed and guided by teacher mentors. If not, it will become sidetracked or fuzzy and confused. Skeptically, it might not be wise to learn critical thinking with political contents in a post-colonial context without concrete background knowledge and teachers' close guidance for senior secondary school students. Students trained to think habitually into a dichotomized polarity are running the opposite direction that 21st century skills purports.

5.4.2 Exam-oriented critical thinking hijacked good intentions of LS

Second, the stereotyping of specific group of stakeholders or ethnic minority, or new immigrants from mainland China, is equally problematic. Stereotyping can only result in sowing in the wind and reaping in the whirlwind. By doing so, educators were lifting a rock only to drop on their own feet. Critical thinking is to sharpen thinking skills, challenging assumptions, having multiple perspectives (Mishra & Kotech, 2015). Vigorous assessment criteria about politics among immature minds of young students? It is inviting a lot of problems.

It seems that teachers T6 & T7 and students (S5, S6, S11, S14) prefer learning materials which have precise and significant stance for learning references. T7 encouraged students unintentionally by watching certain precise standpoint channel of video daily for class activities. It seems self-hypnotizing that if they hold certain premises seeing through color lens, they can more or less show an ability of individual thinking. R4 the expert explained that learning process should be, *"from the interpretation to differentiate genuine knowledge, learners know how to choose a suitable argument, the argument inferences lead into a certain position"*. Nevertheless, the consistent patterns, mental models and question forms that have been asked enable students to bypass critical thinking, produce seemingly sensible judgment on issues asked in exam without considering fundamental reasoning under question. R4 doubted that, *"it is not only a problem of premature argument, but also the argument is not substantial"*. 'Arguments presented only for dispute' seemed hijacking good intentions of LS and turned it into exam-oriented learning. Negligence to pursue long-term learning to live is counter-productive to acquisition of 21st century learning skills.

5.4.3 External and internal filters narrowed down intended aims

Although the designs and jurisdiction of examination questions were determined by HKEAA, many of the source excerpts come from the media. Sample papers for the first three years tended to have formulaic-type responses (T5, T8, R5, and R8). 'Teaching to the formula' or providing a set of pre-specified decontextualized notions were possible (S1, S2, S3, S5, S6, S9, S11, T5, R5). Actually, in the initial stage of curriculum execution, argumentative examination questions using valid reasoning and evidence to support claims in an analysis text were the main type (HKEAA, 2015a; Marzano et al., 2013).

LS examination could be aligned with the curriculum to realize some items of 21st century skills if the espoused theory was to be put into routine practices. Filtering out the unmeasurable learn to live and learn to respect elements out could only focus learn to think restrictively on individual but not on independent critical thinking. That is not favourable for nurturing whole person with 21st century learning skills.

5.5 Insights from the research

5.5.1 Executive insights:

A. My research proved that what the majority believe may not be the whole truth. It may be true in a particular part but not the truth in the whole picture. For instance, majority teachers and students believed public examination in LS is aligned with pedagogy and curriculum aims; however, the research finds that, it is only true because the public examination focused mainly on the initial aims. Next, I explore and discover that we are weak in assessment literacy. We have been borrowing and referencing other countries' theories (Forestier, Adamson, Han & Morris, 2016) on assessment and curriculum development with less concern about the local context and we do not understand the theories thoroughly. There are many implementation gaps between the alignment of summative assessment, pedagogy and curriculum in LS.

B. With dynamical systems theory, what the direct manipulators perceive were not sure the truth exactly what they had implemented because of their need for getting higher score (Students and teachers) or paying attention on reliability, validity, fairness and feasibility practically (HKEAA executives). They had great concern about their accountability and defensibility. What the indirect manipulators claimed, suggested and conveyed to teachers might not have been used by direct-manipulators in practices. The indirect manipulators believed theories they espoused, yet paid lip services only because they did not really understand or provided appropriate supports to the direct-manipulators. Moreover, there are the intervening environmental factors, the outsiders might side-track the original aims and cause unpredictable side-effects.

C. The collective subjectivity for outcome based open-ended exam-questions marking system has caused unpredictable counterproductive compromises with argumentative political hot-issues under the circumstances of socio-political underpinning inconveniences such as the essential one country, two systems in Hong Kong. As the learning processes were interfered by outsiders such as the mass media, interest groups, political parties or private tutorial school teachers, EDB, HKEAA, educational institutions and schools could not assure full professional control.

D. Establishing the assessment criterion and level of standards based on the 21st century skills and methodologies for public examination and teaching, is an excessive ambition in the case of LS in Hong Kong. Even many developed countries do not tap *21st century skills* in high-stake accountability testing at the state level. Aligning assessment with curriculum aims and teaching and learning can reach certain goals yet overall it is still in the infancy stage only.

5.5.2 Fit for purposes?

Learn to live: A mile wide and inch deep of learning, awareness of social life, broadening mind, more collaborative learning, communication, use of digital technology in the learning process are visions for the future. At present, LS learning is weak in multi-intelligent nurturing, neglect learning interest, emotion and motivation, not enough consideration of situation, historical and cultural factors; these have to be reinforced

Learn to think: Individualized critical thinking only but not independent critical thinking; weak in other soft skills; fragmented issue-based mindsets instead of holistic interdisciplinary minds nurturing. High-stakes examination may drive our new generations into dark alleys and blind bends of dichotomous mind-sets and stereotypes

Learn to respect: Effective scenario construction, wider scope of role simulation may help respect each other and respect diversity of values. Worry is there that instead of having responsible citizens, the contrary is blooming; a young generation being very weak in respecting rules, not abiding to established principles, not genuine in seeking truth, and not exercise sincere respect to each other

5.5.3 Learning characteristic in practice:

A.   Achieved shallow official aims of awareness of the society, broadening their minds and connection skills and critical thinking (ABC) in a five-year initial period but not the original broader aims of the curriculum

B.   Shifting learning focus from knowledge-based to skills-based; input to output; top-down to bottom-up; norm-referenced standards to criteria-referenced standards

C.   Students have more thinking exposures and more application of cognitive knowledge instance of multiple intelligences nurturing

D.   More constructive learning such as group discussions, role-plays, presentations and self-directed learning

E.   Learning focused on fragmented social issues with less concrete disciplinary knowledge and theories. See the tree but not the forest. Touch only parts but not the whole; inferring based on part of truth but not the whole truth; unpredictable choice based on binaries mind-set; education being unintentionally hijacked by interest groups

5.5.4 Assessment for learning?

In theory:

- Put learning first
- Recognize the powerful positive potential of assessment as a means of supporting learning. Seamless alignment of both formative and summative assessment with curriculum aims help learning achievement or it will just be an illusion
- Recognize that life-long learning is about feelings, emotions, interest and motivation while formative assessment means constant feedback to facilitate prescribed learning outcomes
- Recognize the benefits of ensuring quality and standards through summative assessment while being caution that there may emerge undesirable side effects and unpredictable damages

In practices:

Exam-driven pedagogy may cause the following impacts if misused. Some of them are counter-productive. It needs a call to arms towards a responsible assessment culture:

- Distorted development of independent critical thinking
- Over learning or drilling narrowly on the measurable, predictable, feasible, high probability disputed hot-issues with patterns and mental models for exam-question types if focus on learning for scores
  - o Jump to conclusion prematurely in a short period of time
  - o Teach to the test, learning fo r better scores
  - o Special model memorization hijacked learning of critical thinking
  - o Some question types tend to nurture undesirable dichotomy on some socio-political issues
- Narrow validity on broad LS curriculum aims
- Feeble support to Learning to live and Learning to respect
- Lost interest in learning
- Learning shallow facts without contextual consideration, nor background knowledge and awareness of dynamic systems changing
- Examination has become a pointer or a roadmap for over learning or drilling
- Formative use of summative assessment (exam) criteria, rubrics, procedures and forms without suitable assessment literacy training:

Overuse of exam-paper for formative functions such as mechanical procedural skills drilling, key concepts and keywords memory. The past papers were designed for summative assessment. Teachers may not have ability to point out students' learning weakness in the past paper. Nevertheless, majority of teachers tend to use them

- Summative assessment is at the prime which nevertheless test mainly the measurable skills without consideration of the holistic aims of the curriculum:

  o The examination questions did not come from the learning materials or the learning processes of experiences but derived mainly from totally different source, the authentic argumentative social hot-issues.

  o The demand for precise positioning of the exam-paper marking criteria encourage students to take stance at the beginning of answering. Follow one stance from exaggerated and enlarged mass media with no query on the premises save time and energy. It is more attractive and easy going for minimizing efforts to maximizing scores.

5.5.5 Limitation

Examinations have been around all years with people of my generation, based on norm-referenced scaling culminating attainments by counting only the right answers. We became accustomed to assume absolute right or wrong as being measurable on pen and paper examinations. That is our learned bias. LS is different. However, there are limited empirical research on both high-stakes summative assessment of interdisciplinary curriculum globally and LS locally in the context of Hong Kong. Pioneer work like this probably had not escape the curse of cognitive bias. I adopt single-loop system to carry out this research but not double-loop systems for deeper inquiry. It may not provide deep structure of the systems in values or mind-sets as evidences to understand the phenomenon. If resource for support and team-works are available, we could conduct further double-loop systems research such as case studies, self-reflections from different stakeholders or narrative inquiries. Professional dialogue on the field of summative assessments could be carried out and how it can be genuinely aligned with pedagogy is valuable for further research.

On the other hand, it is a pity that many brilliant ideas from the interviewees could not be expressed in the research thoroughly. The experts, policy maker, former senior officer, and HKEAA executive responses especially related to the research abstract or philosophical visions and opinions on assessment and curriculum were very rich. They have provided diverse suggestions and contributions for the research topic. Nevertheless, as the focus of my dissertation has to be narrowed and limited, their opinions could not be expressed in this research.

Lastly, the participants might tend to support and is eager to concern about the development of LS. There might be bias. The findings might not be the whole picture. The reality might be even worse than the research findings.

5.5.6   Summing up

The diagram below (Figure 5.1) provides the overall research finding outcomes of the first five-years of LS examination implementation. Three main suggestions are outlined and discussed below. Would the damages override the benefits? What are the way forward to serve from education reform aims? Let us bear responsible assessment in mind for professional diagnoses in the near future.

Figure 5.1 Overview: the outcome of vertical and horizontal alignment

Aims:

Phenomenon: Learn to think > Learn to live > Learn to respect
Basically reach the initially objectives of ABC:
Aware of the society. Broadening minds and have critical thinking
Weakness: Fragmentation of Attitude, Skills and Knowledge,
Fragmentation of Learn to live, Learn to think and Learn to respect

Horizontal alignment between summative and formative assessments for learning did not exit

Phenomenon: Exam-driven, short-term summative assessment override long-term formative assessment concrete feedback
Suggestions: Summative assessment for formative functions to enhance diverse learning. Alignment of Exam with pedagogy & aims

Recommendations:

1. Widen the targets/aims in exam. Fitness for purposes of the learning how to live, how to think and how to respect processes are 'health check'.
2. An ecological and organic approach to task design and student & teacher assessment criteria development
3. The assessment standard-criteria are stuck to the learning process for obtaining aims
4. Quality involvement of internal and public guiding principles for formative and summative assessments
5. Provide in-depth case studies issue samples with precise exam-criterions and sample of concrete feedback. School-based + central professional teaching materials. They are created and constructed with formative guidelines.
6. Students are really learning to be the self-directed and life-long learners with suitable social collaborative scaffolding.
7. Pedagogy for students learning is aligned with curriculum aims and the assessment design
8. Quality T&S interaction, feedback and support.
9. Professional development to move student learning forward
10. To be responsible assessment: Recognized the pitfalls of narrowly focused exam with multiple subjectivities.
11. The skills are well chosen; the goals of instruction are explicit; the targets are well-defined; the standards are clear and uniform; re-teaching of misunderstood concepts

Weak vertical alignment between public examination, pedagogy and aims:

Aims: Serve for ABC (Awareness of the society, Broadening minds, Critical thinking) Separation of ASK (Attitude, Skills and Knowledge)

Pedagogy: Exam-oriented strategies > Learning-oriented strategies
(Process) Predictable authentic issue-based contents knowledge + argumentative skills
Procedural knowledge of argumentative writing with patterns and forms
Make use of self-assessment & peer-assessment, constant feedbacks
Criteria and rubrics with level standards in Exam-papers for learning in class
Issue-enquiry procedures in exam-papers, mock paper & classroom learning
Encourage clear personal standpoints expression with evidence
Limited to critical thinking strategies with less multi-intelligences learning
Individual critical thinking rather than independent critical thinking
Politicization of argumentative issues with weak foundations

Outcomes:
Positive: Awareness of current affairs, broadening minds, trying to apply critical thinking. LS is highly accepted by local and international colleges, formatively use summative tools, teacher-centre to student-centre, content-based to skills-based, norm-referenced to standards-referenced assessments, teacher professional development...

Negative: Exam-paper cannot reflect students' diversified learning abilities, studying only for the exam, low interested in learning LS, weak in learning to live and neglect learning to respect. Touch only part but not the whole; part of truth but not the whole truth; unpredictable towards binaries mind-set, unintentionally hijacked by interest group, exam-oriented critical thinking hijacking the goodwill of LS.

Figure 5.2 Framework of aligning assessment with pedagogy and curriculum aims in LS

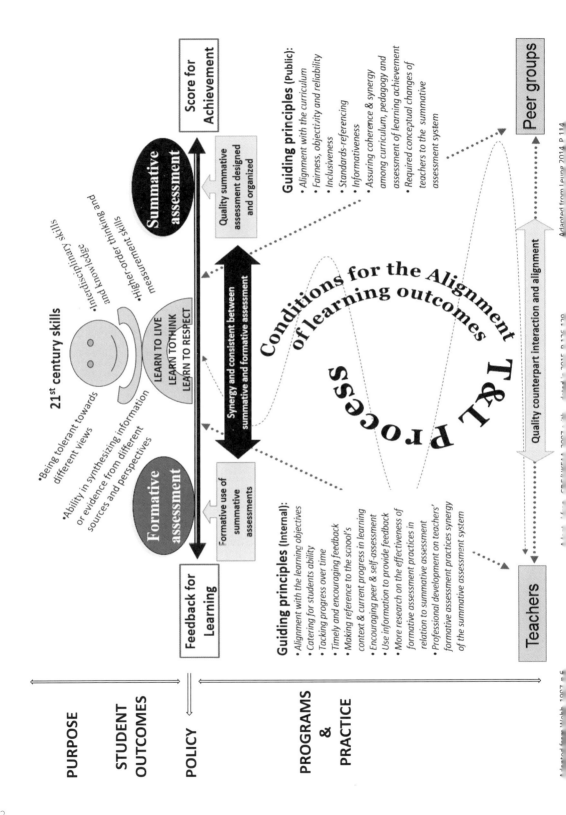

5.6 Recommendation

The concept of 'assessment' is developing and is therefore changing (Fullan, 1999; 2009). Its nature, both systems structure and procedures may facilitate or inhibit transfer of learning (OECD, 2013; UNESCO, 2015) in different contexts. Assessment is the practice of collecting evidence of student learning for allocating achievement scores (summative assessment) and it is also the feedback for improving learning (formative assessment). They are the continuum of quality of standards and an instrument empowering the efficiency of encouragement. Assessment should embrace the rubrics, descriptors, levels of standards of curriculum aims. Through interactions between teachers and students in the teaching and learning process, students are motivated and inspired to be effective, active and eager learner. To levy the best out of the value chain of aims, pedagogy and assessment, assessment should be properly aligned with pedagogy and curriculum aims (OECD, 2013; Webb, 1997 & 2007; Wheeler, 2007). The assessment policy should highlight how to make use of both formative and summative assessment for organizing the learning procedure and process (Wyatt-Smith & Gunn, 2009; Wyatt-Smith, Klenowski & Colbert, 2014c). Guiding principles should be well published and be widely recognized, used and evaluated. The quality of assessment literacy among teachers should be enhanced for the functions of both summative and formative assessments. Students' outcomes of learning should be comprehensively reflected and matched with the curriculum aims. Framework of aligning assessment with pedagogy and curriculum aims in LS are shown in Figure 5.2 with the following recommendations.

5.6.1 Balance summative assessment in the curriculum cycle with opened-mindedness

Living in this Chinese city, the Confucian culture treasures fairness of public examinations. With an open rigorous monitoring mechanism in marking, empowering learning and judgment, together with the legitimacy of the alignment of public assessment in curriculum cycle, large-scale testing has wide potential for promoting quality learning. We are to be the master of the assessment fire. If we can understand the nature and potentials of this fire well, including its pitfalls and damages, we can conduct and control it to be our servant to serve for students' learning. Due respect has been paid on public assessment; compliance to its nature and rules were dutifully observed. 21st century skills nurturing could be furthered through incorporating assessment into teaching and learning as the processes of knowledge building and construction advance. Micro skills and macro skills are empowering the new professionals if applied with creativity (V. Cheng, 2011) and positive attitudes.

With new goals, new forms, new contents and new organization, soft skills and opened-questions will be used reliability and validly in daily practices. Summative assessment forms used in formative processes will nurture multiple intelligences (Gardner, 1998) for 21st century skills learning.

5.6.2 Uphold assessment for learning

As a new curriculum, the subject content knowledge gathered in daily life, the transferrable concepts structure and knowledge on pedagogy should be ripened by shaping theories-in-use to coincide with the espoused theories. Past-papers should be used properly with rigorous criteria accompanying concreted basic knowledge. Usually, the appearing of social issues are the phenomena of the conflicts in the social system structure, in diverse thinking modes or premature inferences and prediction made at different stages of change. Experts from different areas can help analyze the issues and find out the fundamentals of respective problems from different systems perspectives. They may provide basic historical, cultural or political knowledge for teachers and students to follow. What is worth learning is the basic and fundamental questions to ask. Teachers should grasp the questions types first (Tse, 2013). Some kinds of questions may not be useful for senior secondary school students. They may be too broad for inquiry in short period of time. Background knowledge may not be proven or too limited to warrant life-long retention. The expert teams should help to provide basic concepts based on cases, help teachers to build up confidence to guide students analyze argumentative issues. Appropriate feedback during the processes of learning should be expected from teachers. Common habitual contemplations like these should become routines: *vide*

   o What are the common errors of argumentation?

   o Are the premise of information or claims proved?

   o Are students answering questions by self-fulfilling prophecy strategy, without seeking truth?

Only through daily learning process in class with feedback would students understand how to respond to argumentative questions with independent critical thinking. In order to promote transferrable 21st Century skills learning, diversity of testing types should be constructed systematically through the learning process. The testing types with feasible rigorous rubrics are used constructively only through abundant teachers' practices. Continual effort should be made to audit public assessments on what students have learned. The contents can be changed but the learning and assessment modes and the key concepts are the elements to learn. Professional development on pedagogy, with feasible, structural and diverse empirical researches, should be promoted (Fung, Fok, Laitsch, Wong, & Yin, 2012).

5.6.3 Smart use of Exam-driven learning strategies

Knowing that written examination will remain the most cost effective, reliable, and controllable assessment mode today despite lots of evidences on its limitation and damages. This research visited the pros and cons effects of DSE LS examination as it was during the first few years of implementation. As Popham suggests, non-trivial knowledge and skills are the more appropriate measures for the quality of public education improvement. If possible, experiment should be done on the wider scope of constructive learning processes being aligned with examination types. Widening targets/aims in exam could be possible. As technology has the power to help, oral presentations, group discussion or debate can eventually be assessed, graded and being accepted in the long run even for grading individual contributions in group project work. Diverse forms of public assessments will be more effective to promote multiple intelligences.

With accomplishment of technology, greater proportion of marks could be attributed for IES in public examination; collective subjectivity may one day ensure the reliability and validity. Based on the reality today, we can try a variety of examination paper forms by providing concrete exemplars. STEM education on Science, Technology, Engineering and Mathematics, careers planning educations are needed for coming cohorts of students. That kind of well-developed learning materials could also be adopted as content materials for LS. Standards-referenced criteria of different examination forms would spring to replace the problematic predisposition towards political and social issues as it was.

5.6.4 Nurture independent but not individual critical thinking

We should put nurturing students learning to be responsible and reasonable independent thinker at the centre in LS. Independent critical thinking is not equivalent to being individual critical thinker. Think individually is just musing alone, could be selfish, as one not counting others in, no element of altruism. Think independently makes oneself free from persuasion, lobbying, discouragement etc. Learning how to live, how to think and how to respect should be balanced and well planned in deliberative learning process. It helps nurturing responsible independent thinker. Otherwise, students will only concern oneself without consideration of others. The independent thinker will be responsible citizens. Not only critical thinking, but also creativity, problem solving, crucial concept connections are all needed with non-trivial knowledge. This could be accomplished by scenario construction that nurtures independent thinkers in parallel in the same lesson. Assessment policy should be put in practices based on caring for students' needs. Internal and public guiding principles should be reminded and focused in the teaching and learning processes. Summative assessment question setters, markers, and monitoring executers should have consensus based on the guiding principles to align the three components of the curriculum cycle. Enhanced assessment literacy could facilitate all stakeholders to become masters of assessments. It will help everybody to avoid being sidetracked, shortsighted or trapped in one's own pitfalls. Student-centred pedagogy should be carried out precisely and rigorously as shown in Figure 5.2 above.

5.6.5 Dynamic systems thinking for further development

A new interdisciplinary curriculum should have the potential of identifying certain unique content knowledge and patterns of skills. The application of procedural knowledge, the prediction of examination hot issues are the teachers' wisdoms to guide students' learning. However, to what extent the learning processes are just fit and not over-drilled or overdone depend on our professional judgment. Quality assessment literacy becomes very crucial pending to be mastered. Building consensus on summative assessment criteria, rubrics and descriptors with action research or daily experiences will be related to pooled experiences on formative assessment. Suitable theories, pattern of strategies, new minds for the construction of suitable assessment and curriculum in the complex conflicting world have become a new direction for professional development. In order to achieve curriculum aims with accountable assessments, the guiding principles for teaching and learning processes should be well deliberated and established by the use of dynamical systems theory. Only with due respect to natural rules and thorough understanding on human and social changing patterns that we can become more objective to interpret the complex changing world (Zokaei, Seddon & O'Donovan, 2010). Only through sustaining the espoused beliefs to learn how to respect, how to live, and how to think could we build up consensus flexibly for objective long-lasting evaluations. How can innovations of LS stand out in line with sustainable development? There are new elements of skills, pedagogical content knowledge and foundation of subject content knowledge in the unique context. Summative assessment as a precise and rigorous instrument for guiding learning in the new interdisciplinary curriculum, we should better master that with complexity theories, systems thinking, Chaos Theory or other thinking patterns or thinking modes under the big umbrella of dynamical systems theory for substantial changes.

5.6.6 The future practice of LS in Hong Kong

Although the original aims of LS were ideally fit for the development of 21st century, the implementation of LS in the first five years has narrowed the aims. It is found that we have not well mastered the alignment of summative and formative assessments for better learning. We did not scaffold the teaching and learning process for students to master holistic interdisciplinary concepts and knowledge. The revamped NSS LS did not follow ASL LS that provided well evaluation on concrete content knowledge and teaching materials. The Individual Enquiry Study (IES) also did not relate to the lessons of teaching and learning. As LS is a special 21st century curriculum for the unique context in Hong Kong, we should need more research and practices for inquiry. It is great that we have realized the initial aims of ABC. We have well mastered the pattern, the procedural knowledge of teaching and learning on individual critical thinking. The reliability and truthfulness of the examination on LS was established. We have good foundation for further development and exploration on the other skills of learning. It is on the precedent experiences, the successes and pitfalls, that we can grow.

Professional resources with new minds and time for changes are the keys for success. Think out of the box with new minds may guide our way out in the near future. The following chapter will be the research conclusion. Before that, I suggest three main points according to their priority for the future practices in LS:

Firstly, establish a team of curriculum and assessment experts to conduct further research enquiry. They should help to find out the deep insights for building up the theoretical suggestions for LS and surveil how to prevent the counterproductive in LS. They are supposed to provide concrete suggestions for the interdisciplinary curriculum and assessment development and surveillance in the near future.

Secondly, the policy of alignment of curriculum and assessment through effective teaching and learning processes should be highlighted and be executed on the existing curriculum and assessment systems. EDB should establish a team of professional teachers to collect and deliver concrete quality teaching and learning materials including assessment samples and guidelines for the key concepts and foundation knowledge of perennial issues. HKEAA should follow the guidelines based on the aims of learn to live, learn to think and learn to respect to design summative assessment questions. The concrete materials will be provided for schools as samples for learning transfer. Summative assessment should be aligned with the teaching materials and the formative assessment samples and guidelines will be provided to follow.

Lastly, teachers training should be reconstructed and more to be provided. Assessment literacy enhancements, how to integrate attitude, skills and knowledge in different scenarios, professional dialogues on different kinds of 21st century skills practices through concrete learning material design and classroom observation, paper-and-pen assessments inquiry, formative assessments and so on will be carried out. Concrete and diverse public examination questions design with integrated teaching and learning contents knowledge will be very useful for teachers' training.

Chapter 6 CONCLUSION

Hong Kong is an international city facing keen global competitions and a new unrealistic demand for self-administration beyond 'one country, two systems' policy. She needs quality citizens and talents for sustenance of successes and further development of the city. Complement with the education reform blueprint targeting 21st century responsible citizens is the NSS LS, a new compulsory curriculum with a final public examination for all DSE students. It is designated one of the four main core subjects.

After seven years of curriculum implementation and five-years of DSE public examinations, the summative assessment design is expected to have aligned with curriculum aims and learning processes of the subject concerned. With a single stage convergent mixed-methods approach and an explanatory sequential design, this research asserted the powerful effects of exam-driven tradition steering the new interdisciplinary curriculum implementation.

In principle, LS examination with its standards-referenced, onscreen marking monitoring mechanism can accomplish putting the primary objectives of learning to think into practices. Professional dialogue in pedagogy and assessment moderation has become routine in promotion of formative use of summative assessments in the process of learning and teaching. The public examination (DSE) has successfully enhanced critical thinking practices, broadened students' mind and aroused students' social awareness. The new curriculum is well accepted. This research finds that positive effect of DSE examination stopped short at achieving initial narrow aims of inculcating critical thinking at a price of unpredictable side effects. The control over the curriculum content and interpretation of current issues drowned under loud voices of diverse stakeholders, often contaminated with biases related to benefits of particular interest groups or political parties. Behind the superficial success, fitness for purposes with the broader curriculum aims was not asserted.

The original aim of building a generation of responsible young citizens for the future seems not very effective through LS. They were expected to be communicative, flexible and be effective thinkers who solve problems independently; yet, almost half of the students were not interested in LS. They learned only for the mandatory examination scores. They conceived that results of LS examination do not reflect their diverse abilities. To a limited sense, high-stakes summative assessment motivate students' learning to think while it could not effectively motivate learning to live. Negative exam-driven phenomenon is reinforcing fragmentation in arguments, yet yielding deep thinking about the premise and genuine problem solving.

Examination shaped students' mind precisely towards a habit of dichotomized logic structuring. Polarized political stances, like binaries between yellow or blue, black or white, pro-establishment or pan-democratic, independent localized disputes, etc. happened in Hong Kong lately; picking these confusing issues into LS deliberation agenda distant students away from the aims of learn to live and learn to respect. Utilitarianism drove both students and teachers to jump to conclusion promptly in a short period of time. Exam-oriented critical thinking hijacked the goodwill of LS. Students answer questions according to opportunity of getting better scores. Overwhelming use of examination-driven drills bred rote practices on key wordings and concepts. Over-learning of procedural patterns on argumentative writing, shadowed with pre-specified viewpoints and decontextualized notions on social hot-issues were common. Disputed hot-issue contents with relevant procedural techniques is the target of drilling towards what guessed be the exam-questions. Right now, the most challenging counter-productive part for curriculum development in LS is likely to be the politicization of assessment.

It is true that argumentative questions are challenging. A good answer requires deep thinking and a great amount of basic knowledge. Even teachers themselves may not have enough basic knowledge about the 'two systems', the 'Basic Law', and the history of China and Hong Kong. Being in the transitional period from colonial rulings to post-colonial partial autonomy, disputes and disagreements are inevitable. However, to be responsible assessors in public examinations, we should test what students have learnt in the classroom based on a broad base of classroom experiences but not the fragmented knowledge of procedures or answering strategies. It would not be reasonable to expect candidates to be able to accomplish comprehension on a given over-complicated current issues that they barely understand and proceed to explain their stances on written examination paper. Most political agenda fall in this murky category, Themes reaffirming a humanistic and holistic approach to education would be more constructive in LS examination papers.

In connection with Learn to respect, humanitarian education to develop individual stance against violence, intolerance, discrimination and exclusion is the core value (UNESCO, 2015, p.10) to be inculcated. Making bipolar grouping a routine thinking habit on social issues could be damaging to young minds. Preventing extreme politicizing social issues and precluding their penetration into high-stake assessment is our responsibility. Narrow utilitarianism and elusive political ideology should not be encouraged. Professional rethinking on future development of the subject is urgent. We need further professional collaboration of various stakeholders engaged in research and inquiry. Clarify the essence of learning aims, avoid undesirable side effects of political argument and focus more on the crucial transferable concepts may help.

There are rooms for further study on the alignment of attitude, skills, and knowledge (ASK) on themes relevant to LS curriculum, and on the alignment of examination, pedagogy and curriculum aims in the arena of this unique non-content-based compulsory subject. On the recognized exceptional foundations of effective standards-referenced reporting on open-ended examination questions, timely use of contemporary theme-based issues in examination question setting, onscreen marking and double-marking arrangement, validity and reliability were asserted. On such favourable basis, there stand good prospect for the implementation of exam-driven pedagogy and curriculum cycle being balanced by the standards-based instruction. Hence, it is still optimistic to look forward to great possibilities despite challenges for using public assessment formatively as accessible practices in new ways in the 21st Century.

Further from this research, there are a few possible directions for further study. One of them is to enhance our understanding and knowledge by a new mind of dynamic systems thinking to make assessment our servant for consolidating students learning. Assessment today evolved like a conglomerate enterprise where different stakeholders share a bite. With their self-interests and political biases, some of them may not help realize basic educational goals, nor would they support professional development in the socio-political context. However, the potential of assessment is so powerful and influential that we as educators and researchers need to take a responsible stance to right the wrongs that distorted justifiable assessments. The curriculum experts, assessment professionals and policy-makers should also make deep reflections and evaluation on assessment policies.

Another direction is to build productive synergy between formative and summative assessments. Current reality is that summative assessment dominates the learning focus and the pedagogy process. Educationally, constructing thematic based learning activities side-by-side with formative assessment need not be tunneled towards preparing for summative assessment alone. If we over-emphasize that formative assessment has a key role in preparing students for summative assessment (Carless, 2011), we are stressing on the burden of selection function to examination by formative assessment. Efforts to return students' whole-person development and life-long learning into curriculum implementation perspective are overdue.

Existing dominant literature on formative assessment, which can be considered as a continuum of numerous possibilities for supporting summative assessment (Corrigan et al., 2013; Black, 2013), reflected that alignment of summative examination with formative assessment is merely a theoretical discussions priority (Newton, 2007). It is time to explore further. As direct manipulators, students are free to choose what to prepare for public examinations. Naturally, they focus only on exam-oriented learning but neglect the less measurable soft skills. In this pragmatic perspective, the curse of summative assessment has not been resolved.

On the bright side, summative assessment has the rich potential for driving change. Rigorous standards guiding assessment of measurable tasks are valuable. The examination questions with precise standards-referenced criteria and descriptors provide students and teachers with both skills and knowledge learning, echoing curriculum goals and prompting feedback. Teachers learned to adopt summative assessment tools and logistics into their daily formative assessment enjoy enriched pedagogical practices. The process of formative assessment feedback aligned with summative assessment demands matches students' expectations towards public assessment goals. The mediation of formative assessments in the classroom modelling summative assessments with group discussions or various other activities motivate students to participate actively in the learning process. Standards-referenced descriptors are used for self, peer or teachers' feedback but daily drills turned these tools for display of knowledge and skills demonstration in text-form on paper metamorphosed into a transfigured monster of rote learning. As professionals and direct manipulator of public examination successes, it is our way forward to have more research based on practices promoting each item of 21st century skills in the normal class learning context. Only with vast body of shared practical experiences and empirical experiments can we master the new form of examination, with the strengths and pitfalls identified to avoid damages.

Right now, because of the constraints due to limited experiences and research, examination can only be used to leverage narrow measurable knowledge and skills. This empirical mixed-methods research proves that LS has served narrow precise aims. These successes could be transferred to apply on new contents and new organization of assessment system. Examination with 'multiple subjectivities' may cause undesirable side effects. Towards responsible assessment, we had better to elevate fitness for 21st century skills for 'health check' (Broadfoot, 2007).

Traditionally, we do not measure learning. It might be wrong to measure every aspect of learning. It is equally wrong to believe that quality learning will not exist without appropriate measurement (exam is a precise measurement). We are concern that the more we focus on assessment, the more likely we may lose the more important learning focus. However, if assessment is a well-developed weapon or tool that we could not afford to neglect but fail to master, we will lose the time to harvest its benefit yet suffer from all its backfire. Maybe, assessment for learning is so far just an espoused theory; we need to turn it into theory-in-use through daily classroom practices.

Teaching and learning should be the first priority of concern in the entire process of curriculum implementation, and the process of daily routine practice in class. There could be a rich source of successful experiences and thinking models towards pedagogical improvements. However, harvesting such data is immensely costly. Teachers and educators should focus on professional dialogue and research for better learning with the precise standards of feedback appropriately. Aligning summative assessment with curriculum aims is our way ahead for professional growth in really building our students towards learning to live, learning to think and learning to respect.

All in all, the initiating LS in the context of Hong Kong is a goodwill for nurturing new generation. After seven-years of implementation, to some extent, we have changed our pedagogy from teacher-centred to student-centred, from content-based to skills-based, and from norm-referenced to standards-referenced assessments. Teacher professional development is flourishing. It is a pity if that bold breakthrough has gone into the '*dark alleys and blind bends*' (Broadfoot, 2005). We have to take action bravely to stop it from happening and have a lesson to avoid this possibility. Vertically and horizontally aligning summative assessment with curriculum aims with constant concrete and inspiring feedback in LS is the way towards improvement. It is our responsibility to inquire espoused theories and put them in use. We should ride the tide of assessment for better learning so that we can practically and confidently flourishing the 21st century skills at schools.

KEY REFERENCE

21st century skills (2016, August 25). In The glossary of education reform. Retrieved from http://edglossary.org/21st-century-skills/

Acedo, A., & Hughes, C. (2014). Principles for learning and competencies in the 21st-century curriculum. UNESCO IBE. *Prospects*, 44(4), 503–525. doi:10.1007/s11125-014-9330-1

Adamson, F., & Darling-Hammond, L. (2015). Policy pathways for twenty-first century skills. In P. Griffin & E. Care (Eds.), *Assessment and teaching of 21st century skills:* Methods and approach, 293–310. Dordrecht: Springer.

Amadio, M., Opertti, R., & Tedesco, J. C. (2015). *The curriculum in debates and in educational reforms to 2030: For a curriculum agenda of the twenty-first century.* Geneva, Switzerland, UNESCO International Bureau of Education. Retrieved from http://unesdoc.unesco.org/images/0023/002342/234220e.pdf

Anderson, K. J. (2011). *Assessing 21st Century Skills: Summary of a Workshop.* Washington, US: National Academies Press. Retrieved from http://site.ebrary.com/lib/cityu/reader.action?docID=10506510&ppg=105

Argyris, C. (1990). *Overcoming organizational defenses: facilitating organizational learning.* Wellesley, Mass.: Allyn and Bacon.

Argyris, C.(1992). *On Organizational Learning. Blackwell.*

Argyris, C., & Schon, D. (1974). *Theory in practice: increasing professional effectiveness.* San Francisco: Jossey-Bass.

Assessment Reform Group. (ARG). (1999). *Assessment for learning: beyond the black box.* Cambridge: University of Cambridge School of Education. Retrieved from http:www.assessment-reform-group.org.uk

Assessment Reform Group. (ARG). (2002). *Assessment for learning: Ten principles.* London: Nuffield Foundation.

Baird, J. A.; Johnson, S.; Hopfenbeck, T. N.; Isaacs, T.; Sprague, T.; Stobart, G. & Yu, G. (2016). On the supranational spell of PISA in policy, *Educational Research*, 58(2), 121-138, doi: 10.1080/00131881.2016.1165410

Ball, S. J. (1994). *Education reform. A critical and post-structural approach.* Philadelphia, PA: Open University Press.

Ball, S. J. (1990). *Politics and Policymaking in Education*, London, Routledge.

Ball, S. J. (1998). Big Policies/Small World: an introduction to international perspectives in education policy. *Comparative Education,* 34(2),119-130.

Ball, S. J. (2008). New philanthropy, new networks and new governance in education. *Political Studies*, 56, 747-765.

Barnett, S. M. & Ceci, S. J. (2005). Reframing the evaluation of education, assessing whether learning transfers beyond the classroom. *Transfer of Learning from a Modern Multidisciplinary perspective*, 295-312, Information Age Publishing.

Berry, R. (2008). *Assessment for Learning,* Hong Kong University Press.

Berry, R. (2011). Assessment trends in Hong Kong: Seeking to establish formative assessment in an examination culture. *Assessment in Education: Principles, Policy & Practice.* 18(2), 199-211.

Biggs, J. (1998). Assessment and Classroom Learning: a role for summative assessment? *Assessment in Education: Principles, Policy & Practice*, 5(1), 103-110. Taylor & Francis.

Binkley, M., Erstad, O., Herman, J., Raizen, S., Ripley, M., Miller-Ricci, M., & Rumble, M. (2012). Defining twenty-first century skills. In P. Griffin, B. McGaw, & E. Care (Eds.), *Assessment and teaching of 21st Century skills*, 17-66. Dordrecht: Springer.

Black, P. J. [et al.]. (2003). *Assessment for learning putting it into practice*. Maidenhead: Open University Press.

Black, P. & Wiliam, D. (1998a). Assessment and Classroom Learning. *Assessment in Education: Principles, Policy & Practices*, 5(1), 7-74. UK: Routledge.

Black, P., & Wiliam, D. (1998b). Inside the black box: raising standards through classroom assessment [electronic version]. *Phi Delta Kappan*, 80, 139–418.

Black, P. (2013). Pedagogy in theory and in practice: formative and summative assessments in classrooms and in systems in D. Corrigan et al. (eds.). *Valuing assessment in science education: pedagogy, curriculum, policy*. Doi:10.1007/978-94-007-6668-6_11. Springer Dordrecht Heidelberg New York London.

Bloom, B. S., Engelhart, N. D., Furst, E. J., and Krathwohl, D. R. (1956). *Taxonomy of educational objectives: the classification of educational goals*. Handbook 1: Cognitive domain. New York: David McKay Co.

Bray M., & Koo R. (2005). *Education and society in Hong Kong and Macao: Comparative perspectives on continuity and change*. Springer, Dordrecht

Broadfoot, P. (2003). Thinking about feeling: transforming learning through assessment. *At the Challenges and issues in educational evaluation conference*.

Broadfoot, P. (2005). Dark alleys and blind bends: testing the language of learning, *Language Testing*. 22(2), 123-141.

Broadfoot, P. (2007). *An introduction to assessment*. London: Continuum.

Broadfoot, P. (2009). Foreword in Wyatt-Smith, C. & Cumming, J.J., (ed.) *Educational assessment in 21st century, connecting theory and practice*, viii. Springer.

Broadfoot, P. (2013). Preface in Wyatt-Smith, C. et al. (eds.) (2014), *Designing assessment for quality learning, the enabling power of assessment 1*, © Springer Science+Business. Media Dordrecht.

Brown, G. T. L., Kennedy, K. J., Fok, P. K., Chan, J. K.S. and Yu, W. M. (2009). Assessment for student improvement: understanding Hong Kong teachers' conceptions and practices of assessment. *Assessment in education: principles, policy & practice*, 16(3), 347-363.

Burns, R., and Squires, D. (1995). Curriculum organization in outcome-based education. In C. B. Smith, E. Macfarlane, and C. Essex (eds.), *Outcome-based education: Defining the language arts curriculum*. Bloomington, IN: ERIC Clearinghouse on Reading, English and Communication.

Carless, D. & Lam, R. (2014). Developing assessment for productive learning in Confucian-influenced settings, potentials and challenges in Wyatt-Smith, D. et al. (eds.). (2014). *Designing assessment for quality learning. The enabling power of assessment 1*, © Springer Science+Business Media Dordrecht.

Carless, D. (2011). *From testing to productive student learning: Implementing formative assessment in Confucian-heritage settings*. Abingdon: Routledge.

Carr, W. (1995). Philosophy, values and educational science. Chapter 6 from, *For education: towards critical educational inquiry.* Buckingham: Open University Press.

Cerny, P. (1990) *The Changing Architecture of Politics: structure, agency and the future of the state*, London, Sage.

Chan, C. & Bray, M. (2014). Marketized private tutoring as a supplement to regular schooling: Liberal Studies and the shadow sector in Hong Kong secondary education. *Journal of curriculum studies,* 46(3), 361-388. 28p. 3 Charts. doi: 10.1080/00220272.2014.883553.

Chan, G. (2014.09.25). *Liberal protests are learning outcomes? - Discussion on"Liberal Studies emphasis on politics" of the underlying causes.* Ming Po. (In Chinese only)

Chapman, D. W. and Snyder, C. W. (2000). Can high stakes national testing improve instruction: re-examining conventional wisdom. *International Journal of Educational Development,* 20 (6), 457-474.

Cheng V. M. Y. (2011). Infusing creativity into Eastern classrooms: evaluations from student perspectives. *Thinking skills and creativity,* 6(1).

Cheng, Y. C. (2013). *The true meaning of education, its development and effectiveness: four models,* in Conference on "Curriculum Development and Teaching" on March 23, 2013.

Cheng, Y.C. (2009). Hong Kong educational reforms in the last decade: reform syndrome and new developments, *International Journal of Educational Management,* 23(1), 65 – 86.

Cheung. B. L. (2007). *The Basic Law and Hong Kong SAR's political development: a living constitution or straitjacket?* "Hong Kong' s Basic Law: The First Ten Years and Its Future"—Hong Kong SAR Tenth Anniversary International Conference.

Chou, B. K. P. (2012). The paradox of educational quality and education policy in Hong Kong and Macau. *Chinese Education & Society,* 45(2), 96-110. 15p.

Clandinin, D.J. & Connelly, F.M. (2000). *Narrative inquiry: experience and story in qualitative research.* San Francisco, Ca: Jossey-Bass.

Cohen, L., Manion, L., & Morrison, K. (2011). *Research methods in education, 7th edition. Oxfordshire. Routledge.*

Collins, J W. & O'Brien, N. P. (2011). *The Greenwood dictionary of education,* 2nd Edition, Retrieved from http://lib. myilibrary.com/Open.aspx?id=315945

Coniam, D. (2010). Markers' perceptions regarding the onscreen marking of Liberal Studies in the Hong Kong public examination system. *Asia Pacific Journal of Education*, 30(3), 249-271.

Coniam, D. (2011). The double marking of Liberal Studies in the Hong Kong public examination system. *New Horizons in Education,* 59(2).

Corrigan, D., Gunstone, R. & Jones, A. (2013). *Valuing assessment in science education: pedagogy, curriculum, policy.* Springer Dordrecht Heidelberg New York London. doi:10.1007/978-94-007-6668-6.

Cort, P. (2014). Europeanisation of curricula in Europe: policy and practice. *European Educational Research Journal,* 13(5), 595-600.

Creswell, J.W. (2014). *Research Design Qualitative, Quantitative, and Mixed Methods Approaches.* 4th Edition, London: Sage.

Creswell, J.W. and Clark, V.L.P. (2011). *Designing and conducting mixed methods research.* 2nd Edition, London: Sage.

Crossan, E. (2003). Research philosophy: towards an understanding. *Nurse Research*, 11 (1), 46-55.

Curren, R. R. (2007). *Philosophy of education: An anthology.* Wiley-Blackwell, New York.

Curriculum Development Council and Hong Kong Examinations and Assessment Authority. (CDC/HKEAA). (2007, with updates in November 2015). *New senior secondary curriculum and assessment Guide (Secondary4-6): Liberal Studies.* Hong Kong: Education and Manpower Bureau. Retrieved from http://334.edb.hkedcity.net/doc/chi/curriculum2015/LS_CAGuide_e_2015.pdf

Curriculum Development Council, Hong Kong Examinations and Assessment Authority and Hong Kong: Education Bureau. (CDC/HKEAA/EDB). (2013a). *The new senior secondary learning journey – moving forward to excel (Extended version).* Retrieved from http://334.edb.hkedcity.net/doc/eng/ReviewProgress/Report_Extended_e.pdf

Curriculum Development Council, Hong Kong Examinations and Assessment Authority, Hong Kong: Education Bureau. (CDC/HKEAA/EDB). (2013b). *Progress report on the new academic structure review, the new senior secondary learning journey –moving forward to excel.* EXECUTIVE SUMMARY. Retrieved from http://334.edb.hkedcity.net/doc/eng/ExecutiveSummary.pdf

Curriculum Development Council, Hong Kong Examinations and Assessment Authority, Hong Kong: Education Bureau. (CDC/HKEAA/EDB). (2015). *Report on the New Academic Structure Medium-term Review and Beyond.* Retrieved from http://334.edb.hkedcity.net/doc/eng/MTR_Report_e.pdf

Curriculum Development Council. (CDC). (2001). *Learning to learn: The way forward in curriculum development.* Hong Kong: The Government Printer.

Curriculum Development Council. (CDC). (2015). *Ongoing renewal of the school curriculum of the school curriculum -- focusing, deepening and sustaining an overview.* Retrieved from http://www.edb.gov.hk/attachment/en/curriculum-development/renewal/Overview_e_2015Dec.pdf

Dale, R. (1997). The state and the governance of education: An analysis of the restructuring of the state-education relation. In A. Halsey, P. Brown, H. Lauder, and A. Stuart Wells (eds). *Education, culture, economy and society.* Oxford: Oxford University Press.

Darling-Hammond, L., & Adamson, F. (2010). *Beyond basic skills: The role of performance assessment in achieving 21st century standards of learning* (Technical report). Stanford, CA: Stanford Center for opportunity policy in education, Stanford University.

Deng, Z. (2009). The formation of a school subject and the nature of curriculum content: an analysis of Liberal Studies in Hong Kong. *Journal of Curriculum Studies*, 41(5), 585-604.

Dewey, J. (1938). *Experience and Education.* New York: Macmillan.

Dixson, D. D., Frank C. & Worrell, F. C. (2016). Formative and summative assessment in the classroom. *Theory into practice.* 55(2), 153-159. doi:10.1080/00405841.2016.1148989.

Eckstein, M. A. & Noah, H. J. (1993). *Secondary school examinations: international perspectives on policies and practice.* (New Haven, Yale University Press).

Education and Manpower Bureau (EMB). (2005). *The new academic structure for senior secondary education and higher education - Action plan for investing in the future of Hong Kong.* Hong Kong: Education and Manpower Bureau.

Education Commission, (2000). *Learning for life, learning through life, reform proposals for the education system in Hong Kong*. Retrieved from http://www.e-c.edu.hk/eng/reform/annex/Edu-reform-eng.pdf

Ercikan, K. & Oliveri, M. E. (2016). In search of validity evidence in support of the interpretation and use of assessments of complex constructs: Discussion of research on assessing 21st century skills. *Applied Measurement in Education*. doi:10.1080/08957347.2016.1209210.

Fischer, C., Bol, L.& Pribesh, S. (2011). An Investigation of Higher-Order Thinking Skills in Smaller Learning Community Social Studies Classrooms. *American Secondary Education*,39(2), 5-26.

Fok, P. K. & Wong, H. W. (2011). The decision making of Liberal Studies in Hong Kong new secondary school curriculum: Process and nature. *Journal of curriculum studies*, 6(2), 31-61.

Forestier. K., Adamson, B. Han, C & Morris, P. (2016). Referencing and borrowing from other systems: the Hong Kong education reforms, *Educational Research*, 58(2), 149-165, doi: 10.1080/00131881.2016.1165411

Fullan, M. (1999). *Change forces: The sequel*. London: Falmer Press.

Fullan, M. (2009). *The challenge of change: Start school improvement now!* Corwin Press.

Fung, D. C. L & Yip, W. Y. (2010). The policies of reintroducing Liberal Studies into Hong Kong secondary schools. *Educational research for policy & practice*, 9(1), 17-40.

Fung, D. C. L. & Su, A. (2016). The influence of Liberal Studies on students' participation in socio-political activities: The case of the Umbrella Movement in Hong Kong, *Oxford review of education*, 42(1), 89-107, DOI: 10.1080/03054985.2016.1140635.

Fung, D. C. L. & Howe, C. (2012). Liberal Studies in Hong Kong: A new perspective on critical thinking through group work. *Thinking skills and creativity*, 7(2), 101-111.

Fung, D. C. L. & Howe, C. (2014). Group work and the learning of critical thinking in the Hong Kong secondary Liberal Studies curriculum. *Cambridge Journal of Education*, 44 (2), 245-270.

Fung, D. C. L. (2015). Expectations versus reality: The case of Liberal Studies in Hong Kong's new senior secondary reforms. *Compare: A journal of comparative and international education*, 46(4), 624-644, doi: 0.1080/03057925.2014.970009.

Fung, D. C. L. (2014). Promoting critical thinking through effective group work: A teaching intervention for Hong Kong primary school students. *International Journal of Education Research*, 66, 45-62.

Fung, T. H. & Tong, C. S. (2013). Marking and grading procedures for 2012 HKDSE Liberal Studies examination. *Hong Kong Teachers' Centre Journal*, 12. Retrieved from http://edb.org.hk/HKTC/download/journal/j12/HKTCJv12_05-A01.pdf

Fung, Y. (2012). A study of curriculum leadership strategies in different curriculum implementation stages: Liberal Studies of new senior secondary curriculum in Hong Kong. *ProQuest Dissertations and Theses*.

Gardner, H. (1998). A multiplicity of intelligences. *Scientific American presents: Exploring Intelligence (A special issue of Scientific American)*, 19–23.

Gipps, C. V. (1994). *Beyond testing: Towards a theory of educational assessment*. London; Washington, D.C.: Falmer Press.

Gowda, S M., Baker, R. S., Corbett, A. T. & Rossi, L. M. (2013). Towards automatically detecting whether student learning is shallow. *International Journal of Artificial Intelligence in Education*,.23 (1-4), 50-70 [Peer Reviewed Journal].

Griffin, P., Care, E. & McGaw (2011). The changing role of education and schools. In P. Griffin, B. McGaw, & E. Care (Eds.). *Assessment and teaching 21st century skills*. Heidelberg: Springer.

Griffin, P., McGaw, B., & Care, E. (Eds.) (2012). *Assessment and teaching of 21st century skills*. Dordrecht: Springer.

Griffin, P. & Care, E. (Eds.) (2015a). *Assessment and teaching of 21st century skills: Methods and approach*, 293–33. Dordrecht: Springer.

Griffin, P. & Care, E. (2015b). The ATC21S Method. In P. Griffin & E. Care (Eds.). *Assessment and teaching of 21st century skills: Methods and approach* (pp. 3–33). Dordrecht: Springer.

Griffin, P. (2015). Preface. In P. Griffin & E. Care (Eds.). *Assessment and teaching of 21st century skills: Methods and approach* (pp. v–x). Dordrecht: Springer.

Guba, E. G. (1990). The alternative paradigm dialog. In E. G. Guba (Ed.). *The paradigm dialog* (pp. 17-30). Newbury Park, CA: Sage.

Gulikers, J. T. M., Biemans, H. J.A., Wesselink, R., & Wel, M. (2013). Aligning formative and summative assessments: A collaborative action research challenging teacher conceptions. *Studies in educational evaluation* 39, 116-124.

Hammersley, M. (2006). Philosophy's contribution to social science research on education. *Journal of Philosophy of Education*, 40(4).

Hargreaves, A., & Shirley, D. (2009). *The fourth way: The inspiring future for educational change*. Thousand Oaks, CA: Corwin.

Harlen, W. & Deakin-Crick, R. (2003). Testing and motivation for learning. *Assessment in education: Principles, policy & practice,* 10 (2), 169-207.

Harlen, W. & James, M. (1997). Assessment and learning: differences and relationships between formative and summative assessment. *Assessment in education: Principles, policy & practice,* 4 (3), 365-379.

Hattie, J., (1999). *Influences on student learning*. Inaugural lecture: Professor of education. University of Auckland, Auckland.

Hayward, E. L. (2007). Curriculum, pedagogies and assessment in Scotland: the quest for social justice. 'Ah kent yir faither' *Assessment in education: Principles, policy & practice,* 14 (2), 251-268 [Peer Reviewed Journal] Routledge.

Herde, C. N., Wüstenberg, S., & Greiff, S. (2016). Assessment of complex problem solving: what we know and what we don't know, *Applied Measurement in Education,* DOI: 10.1080/08957347.2016.1209208

Hong Kong Education Bureau (EDB). (2015a, June 8) Panel on education discussion on *"The Liberal Studies subject under the new senior secondary curriculum"*. LC paper No. CB (4)1098/14-15(01) Retrieved from http://www.legco.gov.hk/yr14-15/english/panels/ed/papers/ed20150608cb4-1098-1-e.pdf

Hong Kong Education Bureau (EDB). (2015b, June 8) Panel on education discussion on *"Background brief on issues related to the Liberal Studies subject under the New Senior Secondary curriculum"*. LC Paper No. CB (4)1098/14-15(02). Retrieved from http://www.gov.hk/en/about/abouthk/facts.htm

Hong Kong Examinations and Assessment Authority. (HKEAA). (2012). *2012 HKDSE Liberal Studies examination report and question papers (With marking schemes)*. HKEAA.

Hong Kong Examinations and Assessment Authority. (HKEAA). (2014). *HKDSE: Liberal Studies 2014 examination report and question papers (with marking schemes and with listening test CD)*. HKEAA.

Hong Kong Examinations and Assessment Authority. (HKEAA). (2015a). Assessment information. Retrieved from http://www.hkeaa.edu.hk/en/hkdse/assessment/

Hong Kong Examinations and Assessment Authority. (HKEAA). (2015b). Sample questions. Retrieved from http://www.hkeaa.edu.hk/en/HKDSE/assessment/subject_information/category_a_subjects/hkdse_subj.html?A1&1&3_15

Hong Kong Examinations and Assessment Authority. (HKEAA). (2015c). Liberal Studies - Other resources. Retrieved from http://www.hkeaa.edu.hk/en/hkdse/hkdse_subj.html?A1&1&3_5

Hong Kong: Education Bureau and the Hong Kong Examinations and Assessment Authority. (2013). *Liberal Studies curriculum and assessment resource package interpreting the curriculum and understanding the assessment*. Retrieved from http://ls.edb.hkedcity.net/LSCms/file/ENG_CARP.pdf

Hong Kong: Education Bureau. (EDB). (2010). *The new senior secondary curriculum Liberal Studies parents' handbook*. Retrieved from http://334.edb.hkedcity.net/doc/eng/ls_parent_handbook_eng.pdf.

Hong Kong: Education Bureau. (EDB). (2015a). *SSE & Higher education new academic structure web bulletin*. Retrieved from http://334.edb.hkedcity.net/EN/334_review.php

Hong Kong: Education Bureau. (EDB). (2015b). Press release: *Education Bureau concludes new academic structure medium-term review*. Retrieved from http://www.info.gov.hk/gia/general/201506/29/P201506290567.htm

Hong Kong: Education Bureau. (EDB). (2015c). *Implementation of the new academic structure for senior secondary education and higher education (2015/16 school year): Holistic update on the new academic structure review (EDB CM No.106/2015)*. Retrieved from http://334.edb.hkedcity.net/EN/EDBCM15106E_NAS%20implementation_2015.pdf

Huff, K. & Melican, G. J. (2011). Revising a large-scale college placement examination program: Innovation within constraints. In, J. A. Bovaird, K. F. Geisinger, & C. W. Buckendahl (Eds.). *High-stakes testing in education: Science and practice in K 12 settings,87-100*. American Psychological Association.

Hui, P. K. & Law, Y. F. (2013). Colonial system, cynical subject: The case of Hong Kong new secondary school Liberal Studies subject. *Hong Kong journal of Social Sciences,* 44,39-59.

Hui, P. K. (2007). Learning experience in public-exam-oriented "Liberal Studies" – an analysis of AS Liberal Studies examination reports (1994-2005). *Hong Kong Teachers' Centre Journal*, 6, 29-40. Retrieved from http://edb.org.hk/HKTC/download/journal/j6/p030_040.pdf

Hutchinson, C. & Hayward, L. (2005). The Journey So Far: Assessment for Learning in Scotland, *Curriculum Journal,* 16(2), 225-248.

Ip, W. H. (2015). *The implementation of Liberal Studies in Hong Kong - A study of the teaching and learning practices of critical thinking at school level*. Chinese University of Hong Kong. Graduate School. Division of Education.

Kennedy, K.J. (2011). Transformational issues in curriculum reform: perspectives from Hong Kong. *Journal of Textbook Research,* 4(1),.87-113.

Kennedy, K., Chan, J.K.S., Yu, W.M., and Fok, P.K. (2006). *Assessment for productive learning: Forms of assessment and their potential for enhancing learning.* Paper presented at the 32nd Annual Conference of the International Association for Educational Assessment, May 21–26, in Singapore.

Kostogriz, A. & Doecke, B. (2006). Encounters with 'Strangers': Towards dialogical ethics in English education. Paper presented at *'The Natives are Restless' : Shifting boundaries of language and identity' Conference,* Monash University, Clayton, Australia.

Krathwohl, D. R. (2002). A revision of bloom's taxonomy: An overview. *Theory into Practice,* 41(4), 212–218.

Lam, C. C. & Zhang, S. (2005). Liberal Studies: An illusive vision? *Hong Kong Teachers' Centre Journal.* Vol. 4. The Hong Kong Teachers' Centre 2005.

Lam, R. (2013). Formative use of summative tests: using test preparation to promote performance and self-regulation. *The Asia-Pacific Education Researcher,* 2013 – Springer.

Lau, C. S. (2011). Challenges to teaching citizenship education in Hong Kong after the handover. *JEP: e-Journal of Education Policy.* Fall 2011, p1-1, 1p.

Leung, L. (2003). The wonderful use of Structural Imaginative Mind Image. In M. Y. V. Cheng (Ed.), *Development of Creativity in Teaching*. 271-278. Hong Kong: Ming Pao Publication Ltd. (in Chinese).

Leung, L. (2013). An inquiry of teachers' perception on the relationship between higher-order thinking nurturing and LS public assessment in Hong Kong. *Hong Kong Teachers' Centre Journal*, 12, 183-215. Retrieved from http://edb.org.hk/HKTC/download/journal/j12/HKTCJv12_14-C01.pdf

Leung, L. (2014). A case study of educational change and leadership in Hong Kong primary schools. *Hong Kong Teachers' Centre Journal*, 13, 97-123. Retrieved from http://edb.org.hk/HKTC/download/journal/j13/C01.pdf.

Leung, W. L. A. (2012). Change in Models and Practice of Curriculum Organization. In Shirley S.Y. Yeung, et al., (2012). *Curriculum change and innovation.* Hong Kong: Hong Kong University Press; London: Eurospan, 149-170.

Lin, Q. (2002). Beyond standardization: Testing and assessment in standards-based reform. *Action in teacher education,* 23(4), 43-49, DOI:10.1080/01626620.2002.10463087

Lingard, B., Mills, M., & Hayes, D. (2006). Enabling and aligning assessment for learning: some research and policy lessons from Queensland. *International Studies in Sociology of Education,* 16(2), 83-103 [Peer Reviewed Journal].

Linn, R.L. (2000). Assessments and Accountability. *Educational Researcher,* 29 (2), 4-16.

Lo, M. W. K. (2010). To what extent educational planning and policy decision ought to be guided by economic considerations - a case study on recent educational developments of Hong Kong. *International Education Studies.* 3(4), 107-120.

Looney, A. (2014). Assessment and the reform of education systems from good news to policy technology. In Wyatt-Smith, C. et al. (eds.). (2014). *Designing Assessment for Quality Learning.* The Enabling Power of Assessment 1, DOI 10.1007/978-94-007-5902-2_15, © Springer Science + Business Media Dordrecht.

Looney, J. W. (2011). Integrating formative and summative assessment: Progress toward a seamless system? *OECD Education Working Paper No. 58*.

Madaus, G. (1988). The distortion of teaching and testing: High - stakes testing and instruction. *Peabody Journal of Education,* 65(3), 29-46.

Marzano, R. J. & Heflebower, T. (2012). *Teaching & assessing 21st century skills,* Bloomington, IN: Marzano Research Laboratory, c2012.

Marzano, R. J., Yanoski, D. C., Hoegh, J. K. & Simms, J. A. (2013). *Using common core standards to enhance classroom instruction & assessment.* Bloomington, in: Marzano Research Laboratory.

Martone. A. & Sireci, G. S. (2009). Evaluating alignment between curriculum, assessment, and instruction. *Review of Educational Research*, 79(4), 1332-1361.American Educational Research Association.

McAvoy, V. & Hess, D. (2013). Classroom deliberation in an era of political polarization, *Curriculum Inquiry,* 43(1), 14-47, DOI: 10.1111/curi.12000.

Mella, P. (2012). *Systems thinking, perspectives in business culture.* doi 10.1007/978-88-470-2565-3_2, © Springer-Verlag Italia 2012. Retrieved from http://link.springer.com/book/10.1007%2F978-88-470-2565-3

Mishra, R & Kotecha, K. (2015). *Thinkers in my classrooms: Teaching critical thinking deductively.* 2015 5th Nirma University International Conference on Engineering, 1-4.

Morris, P. & Adamson, B. (2010). *Curriculum, schooling and society in Hong Kong.* Hong Kong University Press. Retrieved from http://lib.myilibrary.com/Open.aspx?id=275032

National Research Council. (2011). *Assessing 21st century skills.* Washington, DC: National Academies Press.

Newton, P.E. (2007). Clarifying the purposes of educational assessment. *Assessment in Education: Principles, Policy & Practice*,14 (2), 149-170.

OECD (2013). *"Trends in evaluation and assessment", in Synergies for Better Learning: An International Perspective on Evaluation and Assessment,* OECD Publishing. Retrieved from http://dx.doi.org/10.1787/9789264190658-5-en.

Or, S. C. (2011, September 22). Examination paper design. *Ming Po*. Reproduced original from HKEAA (Chinese only).

Organization for Economic Co-operation and Development. (OECD).(2013). *Synergies for better learning: An international perspective on evaluation and assessment.* Final synthesis report from the review. Retrieved from http://www.oecd. org/education/school/oecdreviewonevaluationandassessmentframeworksforimprovingschooloutcomes.htm.

Organization for Economic Co-operation and Development. (OECD). (2015). *PISA 2015 Draft Frameworks*. Retrieved from http://www.oecd.org/pisa/pisaproducts/pisa2015draftframeworks.htm

P21. Framework for 21st Century Learning (n.d.). Retrieved from http://www.p21.org/about-us/p21-framework

Pedagogy (2016). In Oxford dictionaries language matters. Retrieved from http://www.oxforddictionaries.com/definition/english/pedagogy

Phillips, D. C. & Burbules, N. C. (2000). *Postpositivism and educational research.* Rowman $ Littlefield Publishers, INC.

Plake, B. S. (2011). Current state of high-stakes testing in education. In, J. A. Bovaird, K. F. Geisinger, & C. W. Buckendahl (Eds.). *High-stakes testing in education: Science and practice in K–12 settings*, 11-26. American Psychological Association.

Popham, J. (1987). The merits of measurement-driven instruction. *Phi Delta Kappa*, May, 679-82.

Punch, K. F. & Qancea, A. (2014). *Introduction to research methods in education*, (2nd ed.). SAGE

Robertson, S. (2012). The state as a policy actor, EDUCD0068 In-class power point.

Roosevelt, F. D. (September 20, 1940). Address at University of Pennsylvania. Online by G. Peters and J. T. Woolley. *The American presidency project.* Retrieved from http://www.presidency.ucsb.edu/ws/?pid=15860

Ross, G.M. (2002). External pressures on teaching external pressures on teaching. *PRS-LTSN Journal*, 1(2), 98-103.

Rotherham, A. J. & Willingham, D.T. (2010). "21st-Century" Skills: Not New, but a Worthy Challenge, *American Educator,* 34(1), 17-20.

Ryan, J. & Louie, K. (2007). False dichotomy? 'Western' and 'Confucian' concepts of scholarship and learning, *Educational Philosophy and Theory*, 39(4), 404-417, DOI: 10.1111/j.1469-5812.2007.00347. Retrieved from http://www.tandfonline.com/doi/pdf/10.1111/j.1469-5812.2007.00347.x?needAccess=true

Saavedra, A. R. & Opfer, V. D. (2012). Learning 21st-century skills requires 21st-century teaching. *The Phi Delta Kappan.* 94(2), 8-13.

Scott, D. (Eds.) (2001). *Curriculum and assessment.* International perspectives on curriculum studies, volume 1. London. Ablex publishing.

Senge, P. M. (1990). *The Fifth Discipline: The Art and Practice of the Learning Organization.* Century Business: London.

Spady, W. G. (1994). Choosing outcomes of significance. *Educational Leadership,* 51(6), 18-22.

Stake, R. (1967). The countenance of education. *Teachers' College Record.* 68, 523-540.

Stiggins, R. (2004). New Assessment Beliefs for a New School Mission. *Phi Delta Kappan*, 22-7.

Stobart, G. (2014). *The expert learner: challenging the myth of ability.* Maidenhead: Open University Press/McGraw Hill Education.

Stobaugh, R. (2013). Assessing critical thinking in middle and high schools: meeting the common core [1-59667-233-1; 1-138-14853-9].

Tang, S. (2011). Teachers' professional identity, educational change and neo-liberal pressures on education in Hong Kong. *Teacher Development: An international journal of teachers' professional development.* 15(3): 363-380.

Thong, Y.Y. (2013). Teachers' perceptions of issue-enquiry approach of liberal studies in Hong Kong. *Cypriot Journal of Educational Sciences.* 8(4), 391-402.

Trahar, S. (2011). *Learning and teaching narrative inquiry: Travelling in the Borderlands.* MyiLibrary; Amsterdam; Philadelphia: John Benjamins Pub. Co.

TSE, P.H.I. (2010a). *Order behind disorder in school change: Dynamical systems theory and process structures.* 354 pages. Germany: Lambert Academic Publishing. April. ISBN (978-3-8383-3395-3).

TSE, P.H.I. (2010b). Which curriculum design on sustainable development education may last? An easy demonstration on case application of dynamical systems theory. *New Horizon in Education*, 58(1), 141-147. Hong Kong Teachers' Association.

TSE, P.H.I. (2013). Inculcate questioning skills and Incubate personal knowledge networking for self-directed and life-long learning. *New Horizon in Education* 61(1): 73-90. Hong Kong Teachers' Association.

United Nations Educational, Scientific and Cultural Organization (UNESCO). (2014a). *UNESCO Education Strategy 2014–2021.* France. Printed by UNESCO Retrieved from http://unesdoc.unesco.org/images/0023/002312/231288e.pdf

United Nations Educational, Scientific and Cultural Organization (UNESCO). (2014b). *Learning to live together Education policies and realities in the Asia-Pacific.* UNESCO Bangkok Office. Retrieved from http://unesdoc.unesco.org/images/0022/002272/227208e.pdf

United Nations Educational, Scientific and Cultural Organization (UNESCO). (2015). *Rethinking Education Towards a global common good.* 75352 Paris 07 SP, France.

Usher, R. (1996). A critique of the neglected epistemological assumptions of educational research in Scott, D. and Usher, R. *Understanding Educational Research,* London, Routledge.

Voogt, J. & Roblin, N. P. (2010). *21st century skills discussion paper.* Report prepared for Kennisnet. Enschede, University of Twente iov Kennisnet.

Voogt, J. & Roblin, N. P. (2012). A comparative analysis of international frameworks for 21st Century competences: Implications for national curriculum policies. *Journal of Curriculum Studies,* 44(3), 299-321.

Weber, R. (1990). *Basic content analysis.* Newbury Park. London: Sage, 2nd ed.

Webb, N.L. (1997). *Criteria for alignment of expectations and assessments in mathematics and science education* (Research monograph no. 6) National Institute for Science Education, University of Wisconsin-Madison, Madison, WI (1997)

Webb, N.L. (2007). Issues related to judging alignment of curriculum standards and assessments. *Applied Measurement in Education,* 20(1), 7–25.

West, A. (2010). High stakes testing, accountability, incentives and consequences in English schools. *Policy And Politics,* 38(1), 23-39.

Wheeler, D. (2007). *Using a summative assessment alignment model and the revised Bloom's Taxonomy to improve curriculum development, instruction and Evaluation*

Wiliam, D. (2011). Embedded formative assessment. Bloomington, IN: Solution Tree.

Wilkins, A. S. (2002). *The evolution of developmental pathways.* Sunderland, Mass: Sinauer.

Wyatt-Smith, C. W. & Cumming, J. J. (Ed.). *Educational assessment in the 21st century, connecting theory and practice.* Springer Dordrecht Heidelberg London New York, 83-101.

Wyatt-Smith, C. W. & Gunn, S. (2009). Towards theorizing assessment as critical inquiry. In C. W. Wyatt-Smith, and J. J. Cumming, (Ed.). *Educational assessment in the 21st century, connecting theory and practice.* Springer Dordrecht Heidelberg London New York, 83-101.

Wyatt-Smith, C. W., Klenowski, V., & Colbert, P. (eds.) (2014a). *Designing assessment for quality learning,* © Springer Science+Business Media. Dordrecht ISBN: 978-94-007-5901-5 (Print) 978-94-007-5902-2 (Online)

Wyatt-Smith, C. W., et al. (eds.) (2014b). The enabling power of assessment 1. *Designing assessment for quality learning.* doi 10.1007/978-94-007-5902-2_1. © Springer Science+Business Media Dordrecht.

Wyatt-Smith, C. W., Klenowski, V., & Colbert, P. (eds.) (2014c). Assessment understood as enabling a time to rebalance improvement and accountability goals. In C. Wyatt-Smith et al. (eds.), *Designing assessment for quality learning*. The enabling power of assessment, 1, 1–20. Dordrecht: Springer.

Yeung, S. Y. S. (2012). Critical problems of contemporary society and their influence on the curriculum. In S. Y. Yeung, John T. S. Lam, Anthony W. L. Leung & Y. C. Lo, *Curriculum change and innovation*. Hong Kong University Press.

Yeung, S.Y., Lam, T.S., Leung, W.L.A. & Lo, Y.C. (2012). *Curriculum change and innovation*. Hong Kong: Hong Kong University Press; London: Eurospan.

Yu, G. (2005). *Towards a model of using summarization tasks as a measure of reading comprehension*. Doctoral Thesis, Graduate School of Education, University of Bristol.

Yu, G. (2013). The use of summarization tasks: some lexical and conceptual analyses. *Language Assessment Quarterly*, 10, 96-109.

Yung, M. C. (2005). The implementation and challenges of Liberal Studies in education reform in Hong Kong. *Hong Kong Teachers' Centre Journal, 4, 43-53,* Retrieved from *https://www.edb.org.hk/HKTC/download/journal/j4/P043-053.PDF*

Zokaei, A. K, Seddon, J. & O' Donovan, B. (2011). *Systems thinking: From heresy to practice: Public and private sector studies*. Palgrave Macmillan.

A chart for the original contribution of the study

Item	Description
Figure 2.1 The elements of a curriculum system	The research outlines the key elements of a curriculum system with a diagram on p.24. It shows the aims of Attitude, Skills and Knowledge (ASK) should be integrated and the aims of ASK should be the first priority for 21st century curriculum. The teaching and learning can be divided into learning-oriented strategies and exam-oriented strategies. The assessment is integrated by the summative assessment and formative assessment. The relationship between the aims, pedagogy and assessment should be enquired and analyzed thoroughly so that we can understand the phenomena correctly and rationally.
Figure 2.2 Horizontal and vertical alignment of assessments and curriculum	The diagram on p.49 shows a framework of the horizontal and vertical alignment of assessments and curriculum for 21st century skills practices. The aims of 'Learn to live', 'Learn to think' and 'Learn to respect' are highlighted with detail descriptors for the 21st century interdisciplinary curriculum. 2.4.2 introduces the structure of the diagram.
Figure 3.1 & Figure 5.2 The structure of questionnaires and an elaborative framework	Based on the framework on p.66, the structure of questionnaires and an elaborative framework of aligning assessment with pedagogy and curriculum aims for the vision, mission and implementation of LS on p.139 Figure 5.2 are designed and established.
Section 3.3.1 Setting of questionnaire data collections	Successfully focus on one variable to collect questionnaire data from the setting for both teacher and students in the same class after the public examination. The method is quite original and effective. As there is relatively little research on the impacts of both teachers and students' perceptions on public examinations, the relationship among curriculum and assessments, learning and teaching practices and the realization of aims, this study has filled these gaps. How teachers and students consider the role of examinations on the learning process of cognitive, affective and skills achievemewnt is analyzed and focused upon.
The main findings of the horizontal and vertical assessments and curriculum alignment framework	The research makes use of dynamical system theory to bridge the gaps between the causes and the effects in the horizontal and vertical assessments and curriculum alignment framework. It helps rationally and firmly to reveal the phenomena of high-stakes public examinations with outcome-based curriculum of LS which has had the following main findings:

	• The research verified the powerful effects of summative assessments on teaching and learning in the context of Hong Kong. • Paradigm shift in the mind for teachers to some extent: from teacher-centred to student-centred, from knowledge-based to skills-based, from norm-referenced to standard-referenced, from content-based to issue-based, from rote-learning to constructive-learning, from the intended linear and top-down curriculum to a non-linear bottom-up school-based curriculum • implementation, etc. The empowerment of assessment judgements to teachers and students: the central monitoring mechanism assert the reliability and validity of open-ended exam-papers with 'multiple subjectivities' judgement by makers. The empowerment demands for professional dialogues and central support for direct manipulators, such as raising quality • assessment literacy. In opposite, it may cause damages and pitfalls. The majority believe may not be the whole truth. It may be true in a particular part but not the truth in the whole picture. It is because we tend to have fragmented issue- • based mindsets in stance of holistic interdisciplinary minds for understandings. As a result, the research findings are difference from the others results. The learning processes have nurtured individual critical thinkers but not independence critical thinkers. The demand • for precise stances in answering public examination questions encourages shallow learning and self-fulling prophecy without strong historical and cultural background knowledge. The direct manipulators tend to adopt theories-in-use for pragmatic short-term goals of minimum effort but maximum scores while indirect manipulators cherish espoused theories but pay lip services of 21st century skills practices only. The mode of authentic argumentative social hot-issues especially political issues for examination design provides chances for outsiders to intervene the teaching and learning progress.
Section 5.6 Recommendations	Five main directions and three future practices of LS in Hong Kong are recommended.

APPENDIX 1 Teacher questionnaire

《通識教育科文憑試、學與教及目標達成關係的研究》

Investigating the relationship between HKDSE Liberal Studies, teaching pedagogy and the aims of the LS curriculum

A questionnaire for teachers 教師意見調查

第一部份：你對通識教育科考評與教學關係的意見 Part one: Your opinions about Liberal Studies and the DSE	通識科目標 The aims of LS				DSE 有助目標達成程度 To what extent the DSE helps to achieve these aims			
1. 就你個人的理解，LS 學習的目的是什麼？公開文憑試 (DSE) 是否有助目標的達成？ Please indicate the extent to which you agree that each of the following statements is aim of the Liberal Studies (LS) curriculum and the extent to which the DSE helps to achieve these aims.	非常同意 Strongly agree	同意 Agree	不同意 Dis-agree	非常不同意 Strongly disagree	非常同意 Strongly agree	同意 Agree	不同意 Dis-agree	非常不同意 Strongly disagree
a. 掌握跨學科技能與概念，有效運用廣博的知識 Master interdisciplinary skills and concepts and effectively work with a broad range of different types of knowledge	○	○	○	○	○	○	○	○
b. 靈活變通及轉移運用已有知識概念的能力 Develop flexibility and the ability to apply existing knowledge and transfer concepts	○	○	○	○	○	○	○	○
c. 培養具理性、客觀的批判思考能力 Nurture rational, objective and critical thinking skills	○	○	○	○	○	○	○	○
d. 培養具創新與有效解決問題的能力 Nurture innovation and the ability to solve problems effectively	○	○	○	○	○	○	○	○
e. 從建構知識與議題探究中，成為獨立思考者 Help students become independent thinkers through developing their skills in knowledge construction and issue inquiry	○	○	○	○	○	○	○	○
f. 掌握與運用傳媒與資訊媒體學習的能力 Master the use of media and information technologies	○	○	○	○	○	○	○	○
g. 善用不同訊息來源與觀點，有效綜合與論證 Use different sources of information and ideas and effectively integrate and argue about this information	○	○	○	○	○	○	○	○
h. 懂得從多角度思考，分辨不同意見背後的價值觀 Develop multiple perspectives and distinguish between the different values behind these differing views	○	○	○	○	○	○	○	○
i. 培養協作與溝通能力，寬容對待不同意見 Foster collaboration and communication skills and tolerance toward different views	○	○	○	○	○	○	○	○
j. 培養對社會有責任與承擔的公民 Nurture responsible and committed citizens	○	○	○	○	○	○	○	○

	頻率 Frequency				有助於文憑試中獲取佳績 Effective to achieve good results in the DSE			
2. 你個人採用下列教學方法的頻率為何？ 就 DSE 的要求，下列教學方法的採用，是否有助學生獲取較佳成績？ Please indicate the frequency with which you use the following teaching methods and how effective you think these methods are in achieving good results in the DSE.	經常 Often	間中 Some-times	甚少 Sel-dom	從不 Nev-er	非常 同意 Strongly agree	同意 Agree	不 同意 Dis-agree	非常 不同意 Strongly disagree
a. 直接講解傳授基礎知識及概念 Direct transmission of knowledge and concepts	○	○	○	○	○	○	○	○
b. 提供合作學習，結合生活議題作交流與探究 Cooperative learning, integrating life themes for communication and investigation to integrate life theme to communicate and investigate	○	○	○	○	○	○	○	○
c. 運用議題探究靈活論證與訓練邏輯思考能力 Applying issue-enquiry methods and evidence flexibly to nurture logical thinking abilities	○	○	○	○	○	○	○	○
d. 建構宏觀或微觀、推理或舉證的學習歷程 Constructing micro and macro situations and working with logic or presenting evidence as part of the learning experience	○	○	○	○	○	○	○	○
e. 透過角色代入，瞭解各持分者的價值觀與相互聯繫 Understanding different people's values and relationships via role play	○	○	○	○	○	○	○	○
f. 運用資訊科技協助學習、思考與交流 Using information technologies to support learning, thinking and communicating	○	○	○	○	○	○	○	○
g. 導引清晰表達立場，表達或書寫對議題具理據的意見 Developing clear personal standpoints to express opinions on issues in oral or written form, providing appropriate evidence	○	○	○	○	○	○	○	○
h. 引入生活與時事作提問、討論或論證 Integrating life experiences and current issues to raise questions and engage in evidence-based discussions	○	○	○	○	○	○	○	○
i. 運用考評局練習卷及 DSE 試題作教學藍本 Using HKEAA sample papers and DSE examination papers as chief teaching sources	○	○	○	○	○	○	○	○
j. 採用與 DSE 要求及模式一致的形成性評估 Adopting the requirements and modes of the DSE for formative assessments	○	○	○	○	○	○	○	○

3. 你是否認同現行 LS 考評對學生構成下列的影響？ To what extent do you agree with the following statements about the effects of LS assessments on students?	非常 同意 Strongly agree	同意 Agree	不同意 Dis-agree	非常 不同意 Strongly disagree
a. 對身邊事物作更深入的思考 Thinking deeply about daily life and current affairs	○	○	○	○
b. 嘗試用不同的思維策略、角度，來解決問題 Trying to solve problems by using different thinking strategies and perspectives	○	○	○	○
c. 經常關注時事 Awareness of current affairs	○	○	○	○
d. 改變死記硬背的學習方式 No longer rely on rote learning	○	○	○	○
e. 注重高階能力的掌握 Paying attention to the development of higher order skills	○	○	○	○
f. 關注不同意見背後的價值觀，並能寬容對待 Developing a more tolerant attitude towards the different opinions held by others and understanding the values behinds those opinions	○	○	○	○
g. 對 LS 學習不感興趣 Becoming uninterested in learning LS	○	○	○	○
h. 只為考試的需要而讀書 Studying only for the examination	○	○	○	○

4. LS 考評與本科學習目標的關係有何觀感與意見？ To what extent do you agree with the following statements about the relationship between the LS assessment and its learning objectives?	非常 同意 Strongly agree	同意 Agree	不同意 Dis-agree	非常 不同意 Strongly disagree
a. 現行 DSE LS 有助 學生改變學習的範式，例如思維運用 The current DSE LS can help students change their learning styles, e.g., how they apply their thinking skills.	○	○	○	○
b. 現行 DSE LS 有助 教師改變教學的範式，例如以學生為本 The current DSE LS can help teachers change their teaching styles, e.g., becoming more student oriented.	○	○	○	○
c. 學生愈能掌握 LS 標準參照及考核模式，愈有助獲取佳績 If students can handle more of the referenced standards and examination models, it will help them to get better results.	○	○	○	○
d. 個人獨立專題探究有助培養獨立思考及運用各科知識與能力 Help to nurture independent thinking and the ability to apply knowledge from different subjects with IES.	○	○	○	○
e. DSE LS 的設計模式、內容與組織能夠促進優質學與教的實施及達至課程目標的良性環迴效果 The design mode, content and organization of the DSE LS can help develop high quality teaching and learning by forming a reinforcing loop to achieve the aims of the curriculum.	○	○	○	○
f. 現行 DSE LS 主要考核時事議題，無助全局縱觀思考 The current DSE LS mainly assesses current affairs and does not help students to develop an aerial view and thorough thinking.	○	○	○	○
g. 筆試的重點在評估考生的知識概念和思維運用，記憶與背誦無助 提升考試成績 The written examination can assess students' concepts and thinking abilities well and memorization does not help to achieve better examination results.	○	○	○	○
h. 真實情境的考卷設計無助師生重視學習過程，包括建構知識及多作生活體驗 The authentic issues of the examination paper's design cannot help teachers and students concentrate on important teaching and learning processes, such as the construction of knowledge and life experiences.	○	○	○	○
i 應試策略與學習策略有很大分別，不能相容 Examination-oriented and learning-oriented strategies are not compatible with each other.	○	○	○	○
j DSE LS 考卷設計未能有效反映學生的多元學習能力 The DSE LS examination paper cannot effectively reflect students' diversified learning abilities.	○	○	○	○

5. 2015 年教育局將為 LS 的課程作中期檢討修訂，你是否認同下列對課程與考評的建議？ The Education Bureau (EDB) will have a medium-term LS curriculum and assessment evaluation and modification period in 2015. To what extent do you agree with the following recommendations for consideration as part of this evaluation?	非常同意 Strongly agree	同意 Agree	不同意 Dis-agree	非常不同意 Strongly disagree
a. 加強師生對現行評估模式的理解與掌握 Strengthen teachers' and students' abilities to understanding and handle the nature of the assessment	○	○	○	○
b. 加強多元模式的議題考評變化，避免死記硬背或固有的模式出題 Strengthen the diversification of assessment modes to avoid rote learning and the use of standard examination questions	○	○	○	○
c. 改善現行 DSE LS 試題內容，增加創意解難與創造力元素 Improve the present DSE LS examination content to increase the emphasis on creative and problem solving skills	○	○	○	○
d. 以評估促進跨學科概念的掌握及轉移有關概念運用的能力 Assess and increase the ability of students to handle integrated knowledge and to transfer concepts	○	○	○	○
e. 加強切身生活事例的考評，促進文化脈絡理解與掌握 Increase the assessment of life issues to promote cultural understanding and grasp context	○	○	○	○
f. 維持目前 DSE LS 考核模式與評估原則 Maintain the current HKDSE LS examination model and assessment principles	○	○	○	○
g. 加強培育以寬容與尊重的態度面對多元的文化與價值觀 Strengthen the emphasis on and respect for the pluralism of cultures and values	○	○	○	○
h. 加強小學、初中至高中 LS 獨立專題探究的系統研究及銜接 Strengthen the LS IES connection and systematic studies across primary, junior, secondary and senior secondary levels	○	○	○	○
i. 以跨學科的 LS 獨立專題探究取代其他文理選修科的校本評核 Replace other art and/or science subjects' school based assessments (SBA) with the LS IES	○	○	○	○
j. 加強掌握評估本科多元學習能力的目標以平衡 DSE LS 與教學 Strengthen the grasp of and assessment of multiple learning objectives to balance teaching and learning in the HKDSE LS	○	○	○	○

第二部份：個人資料
Part Two: Personal information

性別 Sex：	○ 男 Male	○ 女 Female		
學校類別 School Type：	○ 官立 Government school	○ 津貼 Subsidized school	○ 直資 Directly subsidy school	○ 私立 Private school
曾任考評局 LS 評卷員： HKEAA LS marker	○ 1 年 1 year	○ 2 年 2 years	○ 3 年 3 years	○ 沒有 None
教學年資： Years of teaching experience	○ 5 年或以下 5 years or less	○ 6-10 年 6 to 10 years	○ 11-20 年 11 to 20 years	○ 21 年或以上 21 years or more
任教 LS 年數： Years of experience teaching LS	○ 2 年或以下 2 years or less	○ 3 年 3 years	○ 4 年 4 years	○ 5 年 5 years
課堂教學語言： Language of instruction	○ 廣東話 Cantonese	○ 英語 English	○ 普通話 Putonghua	○ 其他 Other
大學本科： Undergraduate degree field	○ 理、工、商科 Science, engineering or business	○ 人文學科 Humanities	○ 通識教育科 LS	○ 其他 Other
曾任教學科： Teaching subject	○ 理、工、商科 Science, engineering or business	○ 人文學科 Humanities	○ 高補通識科 HKAL LS	○ 其他 Other
本校收生的主要組別是： School band	○ 第一組別 Band 1	○ 第二組別 Band 2	○ 第三組別 Band 3	

APPENDIX 2 Student questionnaire

《通識教育科文憑試、學與教及目標達成關係的研究》學生意見調查

Investigating the relationship between HKDSE Liberal Studies, teaching pedagogy and the aims of the LS curriculum. A questionnaire for students

第一部份：你對通識教育科考評與教學關係的意見

Part one: Your opinions about Liberal Studies and the DSE

1. 是否同意公開文憑試（DSE）有助以下 LS 學習目標的達成？ Please indicate the extent to which the DSE examination helps to achieve these aims.	非常同意 Strongly agree	同意 Agree	不同意 Dis-agree	非常不同意 Strongly disagree
a. 掌握跨學科技能與概念，有效運用廣博的知識 Master interdisciplinary skills and concepts and effectively work with a broad range of different types of knowledge	○	○	○	○
b. 靈活變通及轉移運用已有知識概念的能力 Develop flexibility and the ability to apply existing knowledge and	○	○	○	○
c. 培養具理性、客觀的批判思考能力 Nurture rational, objective and critical thinking skills	○	○	○	○
d. 培養具創新與有效解決問題的能力 Nurture innovation and the ability to solve problems effectively	○	○	○	○
e. 從建構知識與議題探究中，成為獨立思考者 Help students become independent thinkers through developing their skills in knowledge construction and issue inquiry	○	○	○	○
f. 掌握與運用傳媒與資訊媒體學習的能力 Master the use of media and information technologies	○	○	○	○
g. 善用不同訊息來源與觀點，有效綜合與論證 Use different sources of information and ideas and effectively integrate and argue about this information	○	○	○	○
h. 懂得從多角度思考，分辨不同意見背後的價值觀 Develop multiple perspectives and distinguish between the different values behind these differing views	○	○	○	○
i. 培養協作與溝通能力，寬容對待不同意見 Foster collaboration and communication skills and tolerance toward different views	○	○	○	○
j. 培養對社會有責任與承擔的公民 Nurture responsible and committed citizens	○	○	○	○

2. 你的 LS 科任教師採用下列教學方法的頻率為何？ Please indicate the frequency with which your teacher use the following teaching methods.	經常 Often	間中 Some-times	甚少 Seldom	從不 Never
a. 直接講解傳授基礎知識及概念 Direct transmission of knowledge and concepts	○	○	○	○
b. 提供合作學習，結合生活議題作交流與探究 Cooperative learning, integrating life themes for communication and investigation to integrate life theme to communicate and investigate	○	○	○	○
c. 運用議題探究靈活論證與訓練邏輯思考能力 Applying issue-enquiry methods and evidence flexibly to nurture logical thinking abilities	○	○	○	○
d. 建構宏觀或微觀、推理或舉證的學習歷程 Constructing micro and macro situations and working with logic or presenting evidence as part of the learning experience	○	○	○	○
e. 透過角色代入，瞭解各持分者的價值觀與相互聯系 Understanding different people's values and relationships via role play	○	○	○	○
f. 運用資訊科技協助學習、思考與交流 Using information technologies to support learning, thinking and communicating	○	○	○	○
g. 導引清晰表達立場，表達或書寫對議題具理據的意見 Developing clear personal standpoints to express opinions on issues in oral or written form, providing appropriate evidence	○	○	○	○
h. 引入生活與時事作提問、討論或論證 Integrating life experiences and current issues to raise questions and engage in evidence-based discussions	○	○	○	○
i. 運用考評局練習卷及 DSE 試題作教學藍本 Using HKEAA sample papers and DSE examination papers as chief teaching sources	○	○	○	○
j. 採用與 DSE 要求及模式一致的形成性評估 Adopting the requirements and modes of the DSE for formative assessments	○	○	○	○

3. 你是否認同現行 LS 考評對你構成下列的影響？ To what extent do you agree with the following statements about the effects of LS assessments on you?	非常同意 Strongly agree	同意 Agree	不同意 Dis-agree	非常不同意 Strongly disagree
a. 對身邊事物作更深入的思考 Thinking deeply about daily life and current affairs	○	○	○	○
b. 嘗試用不同的思維策略、角度，來解決問題 Trying to solve problems by using different thinking strategies and perspectives	○	○	○	○
c. 經常關注時事 Awareness of current affairs	○	○	○	○
d. 經常評論時事 More frequently commenting on current affairs topics	○	○	○	○
e. 改變死記硬背的學習方式 No longer rely on rote learning	○	○	○	○
f. 注重高階能力的掌握 Paying attention to the development of higher order skills	○	○	○	○
g. 關注不同意見背後的價值觀，並能寬容對待 Developing a more tolerant attitude towards the different opinions held by others and understanding the values behinds those opinions	○	○	○	○
h. 對 LS 學習不感興趣 Becoming uninterested in learning LS	○	○	○	○
i. 只為考試的需要而讀書 Studying only for the examination	○	○	○	○

4. 你對 LS 考評與本科學習目標的關係有何觀感與意見？ To what extent do you agree with the following statements about the relationship between the LS assessment and its learning objectives?	非常 同意 Strongly agree	同意 Agree	不同意 Dis-agree	非常 不同意 Strongly disagree
a. 現行 DSE LS 有助 我的思維運用 The current DSE LS can help me applying the thinking skills.	○	○	○	○
b. 愈能掌握 LS 標準參照及考核模式，愈有助我獲取佳績 If I can handle more of the referenced standards and examination models, it will help me to get better results.	○	○	○	○
c. 個人獨立專題探究有助培養獨立思考及運用各科知識與能力 Help to nurture independent thinking and the ability to apply knowledge from different subjects with IES.	○	○	○	○
d. 真實情境的考卷設計有助我重視學習過程，包括建構知識及多作生活體驗 The authentic issues of examination paper's design can help me concentrate on important learning processes, such as the construction of knowledge and life experiences.	○	○	○	○
e. DSE LS 考核模式、學校教學模式與學習目標相互一致 The DSE LS assessment modes, school teaching modes and learning objectives are consistent with each other.	○	○	○	○
f. 現行 DSE LS 主要考核時事議題，無助全局縱觀思考 The current DSE LS mainly assesses current affairs and does not help students to develop an aerial view and thorough thinking.	○	○	○	○
g. 筆試的重點在評估考生的知識概念和思維運用，記憶與背誦無助提升考試成績 The written examination can assess students' concepts and thinking abilities well and memorization does not help to achieve better examination results.	○	○	○	○
h. 應試策略與學習策略有很大分別，不能相容 Examination-oriented and learning-oriented strategies are not compatible with each other.	○	○	○	○
i. DSE LS 考卷設計未能有效反映我的多元學習能力 The DSE LS examination paper cannot effectively reflect my diversified learning abilities.	○	○	○	○

5. 你對學習 LS 有何自評？ To what extent do you agree with the following assessment of your competency in LS?	非常 同意 Strongly agree	同意 Agree	不同意 Dis-agree	非常 不同意 Strongly disagree
a. 對 LS 學習有自信 I am confident in my LS learning.	○	○	○	○
b. 已掌握 LS 的基本學習方法 I have mastered the basic learning concepts of LS.	○	○	○	○
c. 已掌握 LS 考評的基本知識基礎 I have developed a basic knowledge of the LS assessment.	○	○	○	○
d. 已能掌握 DSE LS 的水平參照評分標準 I have grasped the referenced DSE LS standards.	○	○	○	○
e. 已能掌握和瞭解個人 DSE LS 的水平 I have been able to grasp and understand my personal level in the DSE LS.	○	○	○	○
f. 養成閱讀訊息或報刊的習慣 I have developed a habit of reading information and news.	○	○	○	○
g. 養成對爭議性議題作思考的習慣 I have developed a habit of thinking critically about controversial issues.	○	○	○	○

第二部份：個人資料

Part Two: Personal information

性別 Sex：　　　　　　○ 男 Male　　　　○ 女 Female

學校類別
School Type：

○ 官立
Government school

○ 津貼
Subsidized school

○ 直資
Directly subsidy school

○ 私立
Private school

課堂教學語言：
Language of instruction

○ 廣東話
Cantonese

○ 英語
English

○ 普通話
Putonghua

○ 其他
Other

本校收生的主要組別是：
School band

○ 第一組別
Band 1

○ 第二組別
Band 2

○ 第三組別
Band 3

作者簡介

梁麗嬋（Simy Leung），教育博士。學友社智庫召集人、學友社現任理事會理事、創意教師協會（CTA）主席。曾任前教育學院客席講師數年、學友社課程及教育發展主任五年、小學教師二十三年，期間任課程發展主任（PSMCD）四年。梁老師對教育充滿熱情，曾為學校申請優質教育基金，組織教師進行北京奧運教學研發，並將有關實踐製作成中小學教材，推廣至全港各校。近年放下教鞭，專注於跨學科課程、學與教及評估的教育專業研究，對當前本港及國際教育的實踐與追求進行具學理的反思與探求。先後完成多篇論文投稿於香港教師中心學報等，並將研究與實踐心得整理，於報刊發表。梁老師為社會動態變化尋求更有效人才培育的理據，過程身體力行，終身學習。先後於羅富國教育學院完成教育文憑、香港公開大學完成社會科學學士（成績優異，獲頒獎學金）、香港大學理學碩士和英國布里斯托大學教育博士。梁老師扎根於跨學科課程設計、評估與教學實踐，以及青年學生培育工作，宏觀動態地探求社會、科技與教育變化對學生個性與思維成長的影響，尋求當中的規律，並將之應用到教育專業和學生培育工作，以更好地面對未來。

《香港高中通識教育科實證研究與啟示》

作者：梁麗嬋博士
鳴謝：（排名按英文姓氏序）馮俊樂副教授、林建教授、蘇詠梅教授、謝伯開博士、黃玉山教授、Dr. Guoxing Yu

策劃：學友社
香港九龍深水埗長沙灣道 141 號長利商業大廈13樓
電話：2397 6116
網址：www.hyc.org.hk

學友社學生輔導中心
香港九龍長沙灣麗閣邨麗荷樓地下 129 號
電話：2728 7999
一站式學生資訊網站：www.student.hk

出版：陸續出版有限公司
香港九龍長沙灣道 760 號香港紗廠第 5 期 4 樓 C 室
電話：3111-2033 傳真：3175-3903
網址：www.underproductionhk.com

設計及排版：陸續出版有限公司
印刷：彩印有限公司
發行：聯合書刊物流有限公司
出版日期：2019 年 4 月第一版
ISBN：978-988-77785-1-6